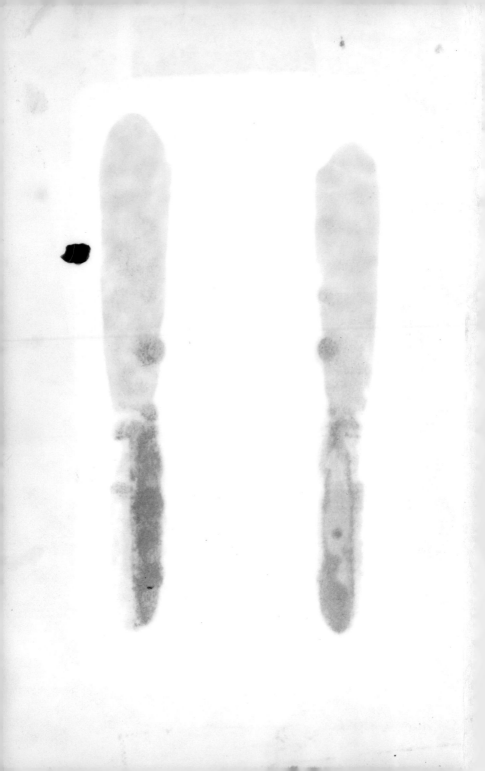

Match
for a Murderer

Match
for a Murderer

Dorothy Dunnett

MIDNIGHT
NOVEL OF
SUSPENSE

Houghton Mifflin Company Boston

1971

International Standard Book Number: 0-395-12343-7
Library of Congress Catalog Card Number: 74-144078
Printed in the United States of America

The lines from "God's Garden" by Dorothy Frances
Gurney quoted on page 154 originally appeared in
God's Garden and Other Verses, published by Burns &
Oates, London.

With affection for
Doctor Jennifer (Hardy) Robertson,
who can outclass Beltanno MacRannoch
in every field except maybe
playing the bagpipes

Author's Note

The author's thanks are due to the developers of Great Harbour Cay, Bahamas, for suffering her to locate on their beautiful island an outbreak of violence and an exhibition of Celtic nostalgia which have no possible place in that well-ordered and elegant community.

Match
for a Murderer

Chapter 1

I SHALL CALL IT, with levity, the bifocals syndrome. And yet, I am deeply disturbed. Why should my professional life be cast into chaos by a simple case of presbyopia, adequately safeguarded? I might by now have finished my paper on Frederickson's Hyperbetalipoproteinaemia; I might be a rheumatism research fellow at Leeds Public Dispensary; I might at least be part-time medical officer at Holloway Prison.

Why instead am I lying under this palm tree, watching a banana bird?

Because of a killing, you might correctly reply. A killing, and an individual with the classification (creeping, aquatic) of Johnson Johnson.

That was a joke. As a medical student at Edinburgh University I considered such lapses beneath me. I did not attend Union dances or Christmas balls. I noticed that those who did so were the same as those who vanished for coffee during whole-body dissection, leaving me to do the work of three on each side of a male Blumer's shelf. They were the same who turned over in their sleep when the bell rang from the delivery room, where I alone walked barefoot through the tunnel and stood in my pajamas, rapt and shivering, while the consultant discoursed on the unhurried arrival of triplets.

None of this, I must truthfully say, sprang from any feeling whatever of service to ailing humanity. I did not become B. Douglas MacRannoch, M.B., from any love of my fellow men, all of whom I held in well-founded disdain. I achieved it as a means to a research fellowship which would enable me to get shot of my father.

My mother died at my birth, a woman of limited impact, leaving me the only offspring and heir of a madman.

That to others this man appeared sane was not the least of my undeserved burdens. Christened James Ulric MacRannoch, he is known simply as the MacRannoch, a title indicating that in the eyes of the Lord Lyon King of Arms, he is forty-fifth Chief of Clan Rannoch and Keeper of Rannoch Castle, Argyll, Scotland.

In youth short and dark, like myself, the MacRannoch is now white haired, volatile, and subject to nasal polyps and asthma in winter, during the Perth bull sales, and when the stock market wavers. Until recently, he has assuaged his martyrdom happily by going abroad every autumn and letting the castle to foreigners.

The day came, however, when I received a cable at the British Research Council, Cambridge, where, fully qualified, I was peacefully investigating the habits of a Coxsackie-B virus. My father's condition had become strikingly poorer. A Scottish summer was out of the question. He must leave the country. He must remove, perhaps for good, to a warm, even climate, such as the British West Indies.

Neither he nor his specialist quacks would be shaken. I gave up my job with the B.R.C., packed my cases and those of my father, and in a short space of time was installed, irrespective of my personal feelings, as medical officer in the United Commonwealth Hospital, Nassau, in the self-governing British island group off the Florida coast called the Bahamas.

As a literate member of society you are not, I take it, familiar with skin diving, rum punches, calypso nightclubs, surfing, dancing, gambling, and lying oiled in the sun. That some people do so indulge, many of them failed medical students, is fortunate for the Bahamians who have no taxes, a warm climate, and small scope or aptitude for intensive cultivation and industry. Sunshine, palm trees, and hibiscus flowers naturally improve the exterior appearance of any hospital, and made soothing the drive to my work, in the 1961 Ford Anglia I purchased for £20 from an outgoing houseman. To a trained mind, however, a hospital is a hospital wherever it may be; the work was routine; my C.M.O. and fellow doctors were not unduly conversational, and I was able to play an excellent game of golf almost every day. My father's health improved, and he began to talk about bridges.

My father's paranoia, to which I have made slight reference before, takes the form of an absolute and unreasoning obsession to do with the building of bridges. Its focal point is the family seat, a small but finely preserved twelfth-century castle on a sea rock off the west coast of Scotland. My father's object in life, apart from corresponding with and dispensing hospitality to the world population of exiled MacRannochs, has been to form a permanent bridge from the castle across to the shore.

It is not only that he is a martyr to an abysmal and incurable seasickness. There is a family legend that the thirteenth MacRannoch of MacRannoch, on building the castle did indeed achieve such a bridge, with the help of the fairies. And what the thirteenth MacRannoch could do, the forty-fifth is determined to surpass.

It has brought him nothing but trouble. The seabed is deep; the currents strong and irregular. Every bridge my father has built so far has been a failure; and indeed his personal involvement on the day the fifth bridge fell down resulted in tragedy. Two days later, the melancholy news was broken to my father in hospital that I, then a child at school, was and must remain forever the sole heir of the MacRannochs.

His asthma dates from that day.

I was giving some thought to his condition as I stood on the up escalator in Kennedy Airport, after some months' residence in Nassau with my father. Visits to New York from the United Commonwealth Hospital are not frequent, but an interesting renal case due for specialist care had clashed with a diver flown in with the bends. One of my fellow doctors, working extremely hard, managed to clear his own schedule in order to fly with the diver to Miami, while I was asked to take the renal by air to New York. It was winter.

After a sufficient meal of creamed chipped beef on corn bread, two dollars, I had walked through the city, jostled by Chinese, Germans, South Americans, Swedes, and ladies in Fortissimo garterless panty girdles with blue wigs. The Tishman Building had red stars blinking in and out all the way up its multiple stories, and Korvette's still had a four-story Christmas tree in green lights. The Plaza fountain was outlined in white stars, and there was a line of expensive, lit fir trees down Park. The Steuben display was three stories high, of spinning snow crystals three feet in diameter. In the window they had a crystal cheese wedge with a gold mouse, 18 carat, price: $600. In Lord and Taylor's a snow leopard lay in a gilt cage with a diamond bracelet clasped around its white neck. I will not mention Tiffany's.

All the way to Kennedy Airport, I had thought of my father, who has squandered the MacRannoch fortune all his life on St. Jean Cap Ferrat and bridges. I was still thinking of him with, no doubt, a severe cast of expression when the door of the BOAC Monarch Lounge at the head of the escalator was flung crashing open. A distraught woman in blue darted out, stopped dead with her eyes on the small medical grip in my hand, and said, "Oh,

4

Nurse. Could you come quickly? Something terrible's happened."

I am a person of well-balanced psyche, with a large spectrum of complete psychological control. I need it all when I am summoned as Nurse. I said, "My name is Doctor MacRannoch. I am prepared to help. You have, however, an exceedingly capable medical staff of your own. I suggest you summon them."

My tone braced her sufficiently. "I have," she said. "They're coming. But he's collapsed in there. He may be dying . . ."

"Show me," I said.

The patient was in the men's lavatory: a well-nourished large-featured man in his fifties with longish, waving gray hair, a mohair suit of good cut and an English Guards tie. His face was vaguely familiar, although I could not at once place it and he was in no state to communicate with me, at the moment being engaged in getting rid of the entire contents of his stomach in no uncertain fashion.

There was a strong smell of brandy, which seemed to remove some of the urgency from the situation. Kneeling beside the unlucky man, I caught the stewardess's attention and lifted my eyebrows.

A younger man, an American, who had been supporting the patient by the head said, "He isn't drunk. He tried to tell me. He thinks it's crab sandwiches."

"Oh," I said. A different matter. Gastro-intestinal infection is a tricky thing, and no good doctor would treat it lightly. I said, "When did this happen?" His pulse was quick and irregular and his fingers were cold; he resisted any efforts to lay hands on his abdomen, which puzzled me slightly.

"He had a brandy out there," said a cockney voice, surprisingly, behind me. "And a cup of tea. Then he said he felt faint and I brought him in here. He was complaining of this hellish pain in his stomach."

5

"And the crab sandwiches," I said rather sharply. "Did he have these in the Monarch Lounge too?"

My patient raised his head from the washbasin and looked at me with unfocused eyes. "Denise made them. My wife," he said. "I ate one and put the rest down the loo." He stared at me and said, "My stomach hurts. Over here."

I did what I could until the doctor and then the ambulance came, helped by the senior stewardess, who was more competent than I had feared. She was worried, naturally. "He only helped himself to a brandy," she kept saying. "And a cup of tea with a biscuit. He couldn't have got anything wrong out of that. I mean, other passengers have been eating and drinking all day."

I said, "He believes it was one of his own sandwiches. It might even have been something wrong with his breakfast. In any case, he's now out of danger, I fancy. Although it was a nasty attack and the sooner the hospital has him, the better."

The American said, "It wasn't his breakfast. We had that together, and I ate everything he ate. At the Bull and Bear, as a matter of fact."

He was a tall, underweight man in his early thirties, Wallace Brady by name. I could feel the stewardess's surprise as I bent over my patient. She said, "Do you know him? I thought you and Sergeant Trotter had come in together."

The cockney voice (first class—cockney?) said, "No, I was just sitting near when the old chap began to act dizzy."

"I knew him," said the American, Brady. "He's a neighbor of mine. We met this morning by chance. We were going back on the same plane to Nassau—he was only here for twenty-four hours. And there wasn't a thing wrong this morning." He looked at the television screen by the door and added: "Damn. We've lost the last plane."

I only half heard him because the airport doctor had arrived

6

with two nurses and I was busy. We got the man on the stretcher and watched him being carried away. The doctor, effusive in his thanks, shook his head at last and said, "Why the hell should he eat a crab sandwich?" and the American, who was still standing beside us, said, "His wife made them and he forgot to have them last night. He didn't want to disappoint Lady Edgecombe."

Edgecombe. I began dimly to remember. A former minor ambassador, I rather fancied. Retired and living on one of the Bahamian Out Islands. Living on a generous pension, perhaps, and devoted to gracious living, Lady Edgecombe, and crab.

It was nothing to do with me, and I was pleased that it wasn't my case. On the other hand, public health is a doctor's concern, and the man would be returning to Nassau. I laid in my bag, before I left, a small specimen bottle marked *Edgecombe, Kennedy Airport*, and the date. It was a minor precaution. I saw no reason to mention the fact. I was more concerned, as I remember, with the nuisance of having lost the last plane back to Nassau that day.

It did not occur to me, as I left the airport and made my way to the hotel in which the BOAC, with its customary propriety, were paying my expenses overnight, that I had just taken the most significant step of my life.

*   *

Since I am not what a patient of mine once seriously referred to as a night person, and had no desire to see a homosexual play, a rave musical, or a small intimate nitery, I watched the news summary on television, and retired at 9:30.

At 10:15 P.M. the airport doctor rang, a courtesy call, to inform me that Sir Bartholomew Edgecombe had received the necessary treatment, was quite out of danger, and was now resting comfortably in the hospital. I thanked him, and went back to sleep.

7

At 11 P.M. the telephone rang again, and an unknown American voice said, "Is this Doctor MacRannoch?"

"It is," I said. Night interruptions are part of a doctor's life, which is why I go to bed early. "Who is speaking?"

"Doctor Douglas MacRannoch?" The voice was muted and overfamiliar in manner, reminding me of a chocolate commercial to which I am not at all partial.

"Speaking. Who is calling?"

"Doctor MacRannoch," the voice said again lovingly. I can use no other word. "Today you saved a man's life. Just don't do it again, will you? Just don't do it again." And there was a tap followed by the pneumatic drill noise of a broken connection. I quickly put the phone down.

At that moment, someone banged on my door.

I sat still. The Trueman is a respectable business hotel just off Times Square with perhaps twenty-five stories of bedrooms, mostly occupied by travelers who mind their own business and seldom stay more than one night. The staff are adequate but quite uninvolved, their main concern being to make the beds if possible by 8 A.M. each morning. At night the guests may do each as he pleases.

One of the guests, it seemed, was pleased to knock on my door in a city where I knew no one. On the other hand, the telephone was by my side, and I had put the chain on the door, receiving my customary electric shock as I did so. Since both the ringing of my telephone and my voice had undoubtedly also been heard, I filled my lungs and said, "Yes? Who is it?" just as the knock was repeated. At the same time I lifted and opened my medical bag, which stood on the chair by my bed, and began to locate and fill a standard plastic syringe with 10 cc. of a seven-percent solution of Pentothal sodium.

The knocking stopped. "Doctor MacRannoch? I beg your

pardon," said another American voice through the door — a voice I had recently heard. "I do beg your pardon if you were asleep, but this is Wallace Brady, remember? I've just been to the hospital and seen Sir Bartholomew Edgecombe. I've got something to tell you."

"I know." I said. I finished filling the syringe, wiped it, repacked my bag and reached across for my dressing gown. "I've just had a call from Doctor Radinski. I hear he has made a good recovery. Thank you for coming to tell me."

"He has, but it isn't that. Doctor MacRannoch — " It was an educated voice, in so far as such a thing may be said of a transatlantic inflection, and socially confident. "—Doctor MacRannoch, I know it's late and our acquaintanceship is of very short standing, but I have a message for you from Sir Bartholomew which I promised to give you tonight. I'll tell you through the door if you wish, or I'll telephone you, but I'd appreciate it if you felt able to see me."

"Just now?" I said. I tied the dressing gown, put the syringe in one pocket, and rang the bell for room service.

"Two minutes?" he said, instilling appeal into his voice. All the same, it was not quite sufficiently flexible, I judged, to be the murmuring voice on the telephone.

"Very well," I said, and unhooking the chain, drew open the door. "I've just rung for some coffee. Perhaps you will join me."

Mr. Wallace Brady entered, fully dressed I was happy to see, crossed the room, and sat in a distant armchair. He made no attempt whatever to molest me. In fact he seemed, if anything, to find the situation amusing. I put my hands in my dressing-gown pockets and remained standing. "Yes?"

"Do sit down," he said. "You must be tired, and I've interrupted your sleep. And the coffee's on me. Unless you'd prefer something stronger?"

9

"The refreshment, so far as I know," I said, "is on the British Overseas Airways; but please order whatever you wish. I do not take alcohol."

"Now that," he said regretfully, "I should have guessed."

"And the message?" I said. The floor waiter appeared at the open door; I gave him the order and he disappeared.

"It's an appeal, really, from patient to doctor," Wallace Brady said. He had light brown hair and the type of thick skin which browns without burning; his eyes were light gray, almost white, the lids well opened. He was in my view too thin, but not otherwise ill-formed. When I refrained from speaking, his hand moved for the first time to his jacket pocket and then he removed it. "You don't like smoke in your bedroom, I guess."

"The air conditioning will remove it," I said, "if you cannot endure a conversation without it."

He looked at me thoughtfully, then smiling, leaned to one side and took a cigarette case from his pocket. "You're a woman who knows her own mind," he said. "Bart Edgecombe was right."

I waited.

"The problem is," said Brady, "that Bart wants to get back to Nassau. His wife's there, Denise. I gather he doesn't like to leave her for long. But the hospital isn't keen."

"I should think not," I said. I could see what was coming. I said, "I thought he lived in one of the Out Islands."

"He does. Great Harbour Cay. I'm working there myself at the moment — that's how I know him. He came to New York for a couple of days and Denise took off for some shopping in Nassau and expected him back there tonight. The point is, he wants to get the eleven-thirty flight tomorrow morning, and if he does, would you look after him? He'll go straight into the United Commonwealth, if need be, the moment he arrives."

The coffee came. I allowed Mr. Brady to tip the waiter, since his presence was entirely his responsibility, and poured. As I had

10

hopes of being allowed to sleep at least part of the night, I made my own mostly hot milk. I said, "The hospital is perfectly right in not wishing Sir Bartholomew to travel. My advice would be to send for Lady Edgecombe instead."

The man Brady sipped his coffee and then sat and looked into it. "She's highly strung," he said. "He's dead set on getting back with no fuss, and he has a great opinion of your abilities. When he heard what you did at the airport — " He broke off. "He's met you, you know. Don't you remember?"

"I have no clear recollection," I said.

"He came to the hospital in connection with the New Year parade, and you dealt with him then most efficiently, he says. That's why he thought you might help him. Of course," Mr. Brady said quickly, "I shall be on the plane, and Sergeant Trotter, who lent us a hand. But it would really set his mind at rest to have you, I can see that. And . . . I hope it won't embarrass you, but I have to say that of course he will make up any difference between your fare and his own. I don't suppose the hospital lets you travel in luxury."

They don't. I only travel in luxury when I am traveling with my father, who used this method among many to promote me into a wealthy and suitable marriage. Since I broke the news to him that I do not intend to marry at all, he has traveled in luxury still more frequently, in an insane ambition to spend all the family wealth before it falls into the hands of his successor, the forty-sixth titular chieftain, one T. K. MacRannoch, a native of Tokyo.

I felt that my broken night's sleep entitled me at least to a first-class flight to the Bahamas. "Very well," I said. "If you will kindly arrange to transfer my ticket. Tell Sir Bartholomew I shall call at the hospital at ten-fifteen A.M. The airport should be warned that he is a sick man, and they must waive all formalities."

"I'll do that," said Mr. Brady. He looked a trifle unsettled.

11

"I should say," he said, "that I don't know Bart Edgecombe all that well myself. You know, we play golf occasionally. But I didn't even know he was in New York until we ran into each other this morning."

The world is full of people who regard medicine as a public charity. "Oh," I said. "And is Sergeant Trotter a friend?"

Instead of looking irritated, his expression became merely rueful. "Sergeant Trotter," he said, "is everyone's friend, as you will find out. He's regular army and going to Nassau on business, that's all I know. But he was the only other man to jump to it when Bart conked out and fell, and he stayed with me till you came. In fact, he's in the next room to mine now, waiting to hear what you say. Just one of nature's samaritans."

I know that type too. I almost changed my mind; but it was a two-hour flight, that was all, and a first-class passenger lunch would save me buying a supper. I stood up and said, "Since we have an early start, perhaps we should have some sleep then. Good night, Mr. Brady."

He put down his coffee cup and got up. For a moment I thought he was going to reduce the conversation to personalities; then he shut his mouth and held out his hand. "Good night, Doctor," he said.

I put the chain back on the lock and emptied the syringe before getting into bed. It was 11:40 P.M.

*   *

There is nothing to sap the moral fiber quite like a first-class flight on a Super VC–10, from the nuts and taped music to the champagne and hot cologne-scented towels which quickly succeed them.

The journey to the airport with Sir Bartholomew, who was quite sensible although unsteady on his feet, had passed without incident, and after installing him in comfort on a double seat on the other side of the gangway, I was able to put my walking shoes on the scarlet plush footrest and receive the menu with pleasure. Hot prawns in butter were passed around. "Looks a bit better than he did yesterday, doesn't he?" said a London voice in my ear, and I perceived that I was sitting next to Mr. Brady's helper of the airport lounge, and that Mr. Brady himself was nodding good morning from the seat just behind. "Rodney Trotter," the cockney voice further volunteered, with accents of boundless good will. "Sergeant Trotter of the Royal Scots. Your part of the world, eh, Miss MacRannoch?"

I smiled slightly, without, I trust, showing my irritation. Behind, Brady's voice said, "*Doctor* MacRannoch, Trotter. Name, rank, and number, you know?"

The sergeant was a small muscular man, aged perhaps forty-seven, with the lined face of one much given to bawling commands. His voice was rich and unexpectedly carrying. He took Brady's intervention in good humor. "I thought she was traveling in civvies like myself," he said. "Don't want all the world to know you're a doctor, eh, Doctor? The arguments I've got into about the army, so soon as I mention me rank. Besides, a girl wants to be chatted up as a girl, not a bloody meat butcher, don't she?"

I am aware that I lose color when angry, but I am perfectly capable of keeping my temper under provocation. "If you address me as Doctor," I said, "I shall be perfectly satisfied."

His eyes became round, and for a moment I thought he was going to add to his impertinence. However, he merely said, after a moment, "Well, my name's Rodney, and you can call me that any time you like, Doctor. You did a great job on that chap, anyway. You can quote me for reference." Then the drinks trolley came around, followed by lunch, and he was snoring before the brandy was finished.

I had caviar, clear turtle soup with sherry, lamb noisettes with truffles, cherry-meringue gâteau with coffee, and two petits fours. Sir Bartholomew, to whom I had given a mild sedative, slumbered peacefully through lunch, and had a little warm milk on awakening. Shortly after this, he expressed a wish to retire, and since both Brady and Trotter were slumbering, he was aided to do so by the steward, assisted by a Turkish youth sitting behind him. I thought when he returned he looked pallid; his pulse rate had risen and his breathing had become rapid and more shallow. He showed no wish to speak. I moved over beside him and had just fastened his seat belt for the descent when he became rigid, and I saw that another attack was imminent, on at least the same scale as the one he had suffered the previous day. I pressed the button for the steward and opened my bag with one hand, supporting him with the other.

The details of what followed are not particularly attractive or even clinically abnormal, given the proper diagnosis, and I shall not dwell on them. Enough to say that the worst was over by the time the ambulance got us from the New Providence airport through Nassau and up the incline to the United Commonwealth Hospital, and that by the time he was settled in the private ward — with the entire staff hanging about chattering, Bahamian style outside his open door — he was conscious and weakly recovering. Indeed he smiled up at me as I bent over him, changed into my white coat. "What was it?" he said.

"Something you ate. Sir Bartholomew, did you have anything to eat or drink on the plane, apart from the warm milk?"

"You know I didn't," he said. He had a slow, mannered voice: a remnant perhaps of official days in Britain. I would guess at public school and Cambridge, perhaps. His face changed. "At least — I had an aspirin in the lavatory, from the pack in my pocket. Had a crashing headache."

"In water?"

14

"Steward gave me a glass."

"Do you mind, Sir Bartholomew," I said, "if I remove the aspirin and subject them to some tests? If food poisoning is at the root of your trouble, we must for everyone's sake discover the source of bacteria. Contaminated tablets for example might have caused both attacks. There is another thing I wish to ask you. Sir Bartholomew, do you know of anyone in New York with a personal grudge against you?" And I informed him of the telephone call I had received at the Trueman.

"A joke, perhaps," I said. "On the other hand, there was a degree of menace in the words. They implied, quite clearly, that the caller did not wish your life to be saved."

He laughed. It was a laugh I had heard many times before when questioning patients. It is important to show no disbelief. He said, "When you said *joke,* I got it. It's all right. I haven't got an enemy, but I have a very funny brother-in-law called George. His idea of humor. I'm sorry, Doctor. Did it keep you awake?"

"Not at all," I said. "I was hardly to know a second occasion would involve me so quickly. Your wife has been sent for. I shall be in to see you again, but I suggest you allow at least two days in bed before you attempt to go home to Great Harbour Cay. Is there anything further you wish done for you?"

"No, thank you," he said slowly. "At least — "

"Yes?" I had a round of the wards to do in five minutes.

"I have another favor to ask you," he said. "I'd ask my wife, but she's . . . well, she gets easily upset. I'd rather Denise thought it was a bad case of air sickness . . . something small, something like that. If I'm going to get bills from New York, and maybe inquiries and correspondence, I'd rather a family friend looked after it all. I still have some small business interests, and — "

"You won't feel like business for a day or two," I said. "You want me to telephone a friend? Where can I reach him?" I opened my notebook.

He lay scanning my face, and I concealed my impatience. This meant, presumably, a mistress in another part of the island. However, no patient will recover unless his mind is at rest. I waited.

"I want you to take a letter," he said. "To Coral Harbour. That's where he is. Or so the papers all said three days ago. He's Johnson Johnson, the portrait painter, maybe you know the name? And you'll find him on his yacht, a biggish ketch called the *Dolly*."

I said I would think about it, and left him to write his letter while I did a tour of my cases. My two stomachs were doing quite well, the perforation having dispensed with his Levine already. We had lost the cervical spine dislocation. An amoebic abscess had come in, and two new tubercular cases; I read the notes on my desk. After a thorough afternoon's work I walked through the private wing and across the path into the laboratory. There I found a room to myself, and set to analyzing the four samples I had taken from my bag in the hospital. One was of warm milk and the other of aspirin. The remaining two were from the contents of Sir Bartholomew Edgecombe's stomach after each of his attacks.

The warm milk was innocent, and so was the aspirin. But both the samples from Edgecombe confirmed my own clinical diagnosis. Neither attack had been caused by *B. botulinus,* or *B. enteritidis*, or anything resembling an infected crab sandwich.

Sir Bartholomew Edgecombe had been poisoned by arsenic.

Chapter 2

James Ulric MacRannoch was at home when I called in, on my way to the Coral Harbour marina.

My father, in his efforts to deny to Japanese hands the substance of the MacRannochs, had rented for his sojourn in Nassau a delightful and expensive villa with a white-pillared porch and a swimming pool. Hummingbirds, species Calliphlox evelynale, lurked in the butterfly flowers, and the coconut palms were placed as nicely as sutures.

Inside, he had pink bamboo furniture on pink mohair carpeting, offsetting the large native staff who stood about smiling because of the amount he was paying them. This had all been settled by his friend the Begum long before we arrived, and I took nothing to do with it. I stayed with my father because he needed to be under medical supervision, but I was financially independent of him and intended to remain so, although the cost of living in the Bahamas was reducing my bank account to eunuchoidism.

However, since I had finally made a clean incision in the chain of worthy and well-connected young suitors prepared by my father, I felt that this unfilial action should at least discharge the MacRannoch from the duty of paying for me as a daughter. What he chose to do with his money was therefore his affair, although he made it, such was his excitable nature, all the world's.

There was in fact a crowd of people on the terrace when I made my way through the house. They had not changed for dinner and from their costume I guessed that there had been a tennis party on our excellent hard court. One couple, from Government House, I recognized, and there was a titled lady from the retired British colony, a banking family, and one or two of the younger moneyed set from Lyford Cay. There was also a tall, hair-sprayed blond lady in a bikini a little too smart for her, for whom my father, in flowered Bermuda shorts and green shirt, was pouring a large Bloody Mary. I noticed that it was more blood than Mary, and after a second hard glance at the lady, diagnosed why. Then he turned around.

"Beltanno! Did you kill 'em off early? Come and get a nice strong tomato juice under the whalebone. You know my daughter Beltanno, Denise, everyone?"

I call myself, as I have said, Dr. B. Douglas MacRannoch, Douglas being my middle name and the surname of my mother. It is unimportant, but perhaps simpler to explain now that I was christened Beltanno, which was the name of Cairbre's wife, the daughter-in-law of Cormac. Since it conveys nothing but a sense of ridicule to members of an Anglo-Germanic culture, I never use it and dislike hearing it used, as my father well knows. The woman called Denise smiled graciously, and someone said, "Good evening"; then they all returned to their drinks. The MacRannoch said, "Denise here has been deserted by her dear husband. The hotel wouldn't let her hang on to her room. I've said she can stay here till he comes."

Denise. The white population of Nassau is not all that enormous. I said, "Is his name by any chance Edgecombe?" and received half my tomato juice down my Bri-nylon two-piece as the woman jolted my arm. "He's in hospital? Bart! Is he hurt?" she said, her voice sliding upward.

18

Conversation stopped. There was no point in doing anything about the tomato juice. It is in any case possible to put the whole garment into a washing machine. I said briskly, "He is perfectly well: only getting over a fairly sharp stomach upset. The hospital has been trying to reach you, Lady Edgecombe, all afternoon."

She stared at me, frowning. Her voice was attractively husky: her accent less native, I felt, than the result of an excellent tutor. She said, "Oh, Bart! I had to leave my hotel. He was a day late . . ." She pressed my wrist again. "You work there! Is he all right? He's not badly ill? Oh, dear!" She broke off to stare at me as a new danger occurred to her. "I hope he has a good doctor!"

"Does he have a good doctor, Beltanno?" asked my father, his hair a quiff of white above that ridiculous gnome's face, and the orange and green flowered shorts.

Spasmodic childishness is a feature of my father's condition. I addressed Lady Edgecombe. "I am his doctor. I am sure my father will arrange for you to go straight to the hospital and find another hotel in Nassau for a day or two. Perhaps your brother George could assist."

"Who?" said Lady Edgecombe. Her hair, I now saw, was not naturally blond, although it had been skillfully treated, and she wore false eyelashes, though no other make-up. A certain development of the leg muscles, added to the undoubted grace of her carriage, made me think that she had belonged at one time to some branch of the dancing profession. "I haven't got a brother George," said Denise Edgecombe.

"Of course," I said. "It was another patient. I do beg your pardon. Father — "

But Sadic, Father's big Bahamian driver from Eleuthera, was already waiting to take Lady Edgecombe to see her husband. It was not until after he had gone that I discovered he had used my car. "But you're not on call?" my father said. "I forgot to tell you they were mending the Chevrolet." He stood, vodka bottle in hand, and surveyed my juice smeared two-piece. The remaining guests, finishing their drinks, lay about chatting. My father said, reasonably, "I wasn't to know you had a date to hear Bang Bang Lulu at the Bamboo Conch Club."

The years have made him, as you can see, inexorably frivolous. I said, "I have an appointment at the Coral Harbour marina." There was a slight pause, then one of the Lyford Cay group said, "I'll drive you." His martini was still three quarters up and the offer was hardly enthusiastic. I accepted, however, politely. After retiring briefly to change my two-piece for a pleated cotton dress I have found comfortable for many years, I returned to the drive where a car was drawn up waiting. My father was nowhere in sight, so I got in. The driver started the engine.

We were halfway to the gates before I realized that the man sitting beside me at the wheel was not the socialite from Lyford Cay. I saw an older man of dark coloring and insignificant features, wearing neither a Bermuda beach outfit nor the briefer assembly of, I understand, St. Tropez. I observed well-worn slacks and a still older shirt made of thick terry toweling. There was a bulge in his left trouser pocket. It could have been caused by a pipe. It was quite possibly due, I considered, to a small firearm of the automatic variety.

I had no syringe with me this time. As we swung onto the road, I gripped my bag hard with one hand and I let my other fall idly close to the door handle just as the driver said, agreeably enough, "I swopped with Booby Swanston. I hope you don't mind. Who is George?"

"I should like you to stop this car," I said evenly.

Behind us was a truck piled with bananas and a small horse-drawn surrey full of tourists with *This horse is called Elvis* scrawled on the front board.

"What — *now?*" said my driver. The spectacles he wore covered his eyes, but his tone was justifiably surprised.

"When you have an opportunity."

The glasses flashed in my direction, and I saw then that he had adjusted presbyopia: his spectacles were bifocal. Why did nothing forewarn me? Why did I think my only danger was physical? He said, "I thought you had a date in Coral Harbour?"

"I have," I said, "a message to take to a person named Johnson Johnson."

He put his hand out of the window and waved; the banana truck passed by, and the surrey, and Smiley and the Boys' Bus Service and a bicycle advertising the Nassau Conference of the Seventh Day Adventists. He slowed, drew into the side, and came to a stop.

Then his arm came around, and I stiffened. But he merely reached to the back of the car, hauled toward him an old corduroy jacket, and emptying the pockets quickly and neatly, laid on the seat between us a driver's license, a passport, a number of envelopes, and a folder advertising a one-man exhibition of paintings in the Fontainebleau Hotel, Miami. "Indeed you do?" he said. "Then you can deliver it. I'm Johnson Johnson."

I read the documents. While I did so, he drew the object from his pocket, which was indeed a blackened briar pipe, filled it, and struck a match, his eyes all the while watching me, as I was aware. He said, "Does the thought of my bronchial carcinoma upset you?" And as I looked up with impatience, he smiled slightly and applying the match, lit his pipe. "You're very patient with all us frail humans," he said. "If I had your message, I might know what's frightening you."

"Frightening?" I said.

"Well," he said, puffing. We had stopped beside the life-sized white horse outside Hobby Horse Hall, between the golf course and the lacto calamine pink of the Emerald Beach Hotel. "How many other times have you jumped into a car and then immediately demanded to get out?"

"Three," I said shortly. "Once with a depressive case turned hypomanic, once with an intoxicated ambulance driver, and once to escape carbon-monoxide poisoning from a faulty exhaust pipe. The emergency situation is perhaps more frequent in medicine than in portrait painting."

"You'd be surprised," said the man Johnson gently. He received back his documents and taking the sealed letter from Bartholomew Edgecombe which I handed over in silence, he read and then pocketed it.

"I understand," he said. A bus full of tourists passed by. The sun, low in the palm trees, was losing some of its heat. You could smell the sea on the other side of the road. I waited.

After a moment he said, "Bart Edgecombe is an old friend of mine. You did your duty, I know, but I want to thank you nonetheless for dealing with a rather nasty chain of events." He paused. "Doctor MacRannoch . . . There are some things I'd rather like to ask you, and perhaps there are some you want to find out from me. Would it scare you to come with me now and share a meal and a talk aboard *Dolly*? I'd run you back afterward. You could phone home from the club if you wanted."

Johnson Johnson, the Miami folder had said. *One of the World's Foremost Portrait Artists Displays His Paintings in Florida. Forty of Society's Most Prominent Luminaries.* I could see no sign of schizophrenia. It seemed unlikely that a sane man would perpetrate any public illegality before his exhibition. I am not in the least easy to scare. I agreed to dine with Johnson on his yacht *Dolly*.

Coral Harbour is a private development in one of the moneyed quarters of New Providence Island, and about twenty minutes from Nassau. To get to it you have to drive over the hill, where the Bahamians live in huts and houses of clapboard and peeling

22

stucco with dingy netted windows, or with no windows at all, shacks perched up high in the dirt with the crumbling doorstep a gap of three feet away from the threshold. Men were pouring out of the work yards and children were wavering up and down the narrow streets on high-handled American bicycles. I noted a child I had treated the previous week for a cranial lesion; her mother had been told to keep the child indoors and quiet.

Then we passed through Oakesville, by the supermarket and Sir Harry's monument, and were in a green and white well-kept road network again, ending in the Lyford Cay–Nassau roundabout beyond which were the cone-topped pharos guarding the entrance gate to Coral Harbour's 2500 acres of golf course, beaches, villas, and waterways. And the yacht club with *Dolly*.

". . . This fashionable community; a wonderland of spacious home sites and silken beaches in the heart of a tax-free, sun-blessed economy. Are you a radical doctor, Doctor?" asked Johnson.

We were driving along a broad avenue lined with bush-cut pines spaced like green wigs on wig stands. A nursery on the right displayed a drilled squad of short potted palms, destined for landscape designing. We passed the golf course. ". . . Or," Johnson added, "do your fellow men hold no charm for you, anyway?"

"Very little," I said calmly. "I prefer to pit my wits against science. My relaxation, for instance, is golf."

"And bridge? No, not bridge," Johnson answered himself as it happened, quite accurately. "To depend for success on a partner would be highly unethical. But I'll take you on at golf sometime, Doctor MacRannoch."

I felt no need to say anything. We came to the double road, with its spine of hibiscus and palms, and the water-based villas with their polyethylene cars and cruising boats tied up on the patios. A palm roundel with flags stood in front of the club, which was low and modern with a lot of plate glass and crazed stone facing and a white wrought-iron balcony. Johnson parked the car and we went in.

I waited on the fur rug. The scarlet-lit water grotto under the open-tread staircase glowed in the deepening dusk; someone lit a cigarette in one of the group of armchairs. A voice, bodiless above my head, said: *"Don't do it again, will you? Just don't do it again."*

My epidermal hair follicles sprang upright, but I do not give way easily to emotion. I set my foot on the stairs, just as Johnson, arriving suddenly with some letters in his hand said, "What's the matter?" and a couple, laughing, began to come down the steps over my head. The young woman, in a white-lace trouser suit, said in an American voice, "Sure I'll do it again, and you'll stand by and like it. It's a free world, darling David."

I stepped back, my hand prodding Johnson, to allow them to pass. Darling David was quite unremarkable, in long shorts and a sweater and graying brown hair. I had never seen him before. Then he said, "Well, come along. Bar's open," and the voice was quite different, too, from that caressing voice in the Trueman. Johnson said, "It's a lovely evening for a sail. You don't mind, do you, having dinner on board? Spry is quite a good cook."

"If I might make that phone call first," I said, and I saw him smile.

"Of course, Doctor. Go ahead. I'll wait just outside."

There is no point in being foolishly trusting.

After I had called my father, who displayed a mild interest that Johnson Johnson should have sought my company and no interest whatever in my immediate and future plans, I joined my host outside and we walked along the well-manicured edge of the marina where the cruising yachts lay under the palm trees like bedpans, I thought, in a sterilizer. Johnson said, "Here is *Dolly*," and led the way up on deck.

24

If you know about boats she is a gaff-rigged auxiliary ketch, of about fifty-odd tons, which implies a great deal of money. She had a curious detachable shell fitted over the cockpit, which Johnson slid back without explanation. For the rest she was quietly and expensively fitted, not only with awnings and Nieman Marcus soft furnishings, but with a depth finder and RDF unit. I noticed a big-scale radar set, which I'd heard one of the lab technicians daydreaming about over a sputum swab. They cost ten thousand dollars.

I cut the tour short in the pricey salon and led the way back to the cockpit. The big diesel engine was rumbling. A small middle-age man in white overalls and yachting cap stepped aboard, the mooring rope in his hand. He coiled it and came forward toward us, expressing inquiry.

"Never mind," said Johnson. "There's not enough air. I'll take her."

He had a hand on the wheel as he spoke. He moved a lever and *Dolly* began to nose out into the waterway. "Get us some drinks, Spry, will you? We'll get up the coast a bit and find some quiet water for dinner . . . Spry does all the work here, Doctor MacRannoch. What will you drink? We've all kinds of fruit juice. Or something carbonated, if you'd rather."

I settled for fresh lemon and soda, and sat carefully in the deep cockpit cushions, the wind stirring but not untidying my hair, which I like to keep short. The palm trees moved past, and the other boats, their lights drawing the eye in the gathering dark. I wondered, acidly, if Johnson also had a Japanese heir. The slight savor I had begun to feel in the occasion had vanished. Johnson said, "What do you spend on your golf?"

I said, "I beg your pardon?" Moneyed persons often do this. In Nassau there are only two topics of conversation: business and sex.

He increased his speed slightly, but the engine was still very soft. He said, hardly raising his voice, "Greens fees, eight dollars; power cart, ten dollars; balls, eighteen dollars fifty, the dozen. And a complete set of clubs and bag, if you have them. What? Four hundred dollars?"

"Ten pounds," I said. "Second-hand, five years ago."

"Relative to an M.O.'s salary," he said, "it still adds up. *Dolly* is *my* battle with nature."

He grinned, and I expect my expression relaxed. Then Spry arrived with the drinks and Johnson, giving him the wheel, stepped up and perched on the side deck, his feet malelike on the cushions, the wind flipping his hair. He said, "About George."

It felt, suddenly, rather like an operating day: nine till two, three days a week. You press the electric eye with your elbow and the double doors slide silently open and you are first. The room on the left is empty, where later you will sit waiting while your fellow doctors talk fast cars and fishing and swop stained, sexy paperbacks. Around the corner you can hear the chink as the nurses work at the instrument trolley, and the black rubber masks hang like burst tires in a long drooping row on the wall. Then the doors slide noiselessly open again behind you and Barber, your surgical consultant, strides in and says, "Well, McGonagall?"

I said sharply, "Suppose you tell me first what was in Sir Bartholomew's letter?"

"That he had been poisoned," Johnson said. "He was quite convinced, and I believe him." He paused, and then said, "You suspected that?"

"I knew it," I said. "I took samples. It was arsenic."

We had moved out to the open sea. Trees on the shore were dense green, the palms still, like fringes on thinly bent wire; while on the horizon the paling sky was banded with cloud banks like meths-tinted wadding. The sun, hesitating, lingered rose pink on Spry's overalls. Johnson said, "And you had a threatening phone call. Yet you didn't go to the police?"

"I didn't perform the tests until this afternoon," I said.

"And the phone call?"

"Sir Bartholomew said it was a joke by his brother-in-law, George." I paused, and then said, "In the clubhouse just now, the man who came downstairs spoke the identical words."

"I wondered why you were staring at him," said Johnson. "So I made some inquiries while you were phoning. He is well known and accepted, although the girl was not his wife. He has not left the island for three weeks at least . . . So now you know that Bart Edgecombe was attacked by a prisoner, and that his wife has no brother named George. It was, incidentally, a stupid story to tell you."

"Not wholly," I said. I kept my voice calm. "It told me that Sir Bartholomew also knew what had happened, and didn't want police interference. I should imagine he is expecting you to explain why. At a guess, it concerns his wife, Lady Edgecombe."

"Poor Denise," said Johnson unexpectedly. "No. It only concerns Lady Edgcombe in that she is the neglected spectator in a scene of continuous short-fall pandemonium. Bartholomew Edgecombe was a highly paid servant of the Crown and is now the chief British Intelligence agent in the Bahamas."

I am aware that I have a first-class brain. It is always a pleasure to meet with another. I said, "You are his superior?"

Johnson smiled, wryly, in the gathering dark. "I am his nursemaid," he said. "And you, for your sins, are his doctor."

*   *

We had grouper for dinner — a good, solid fish with a sauce — followed by a first-rate orange soufflé. It was a change from hotel Franco-American catering: *Jumbo Frog Legs Provençale.*

27

It was also a change from Minnie Pearl's Chicken. I enjoyed my meal, during which Johnson would not talk at all about the Bart Edgecombe business; and even after it, in the coolness of the cockpit with the engine shut off, when he talked a great deal.

There are four main rocket tracking stations in the Bahamas, with an American staff drawn from the Air Force, Pan American World Airways, and the Radio Corporation of America, as well as one or two smaller two-person affairs on the minor islands. The tracking of moonshots and other missiles from the American rocket range is done by the electronic brains in these stations, a submarine cable transmitting their findings to Cape Kennedy, which is only forty miles north of Miami across a narrow stretch of Atlantic.

Permission may be obtained without difficulty to see these tracking stations, which have about them nothing either glamorous or peculiarly interesting, and whose staff tend to be jocular in the extreme. It had never struck me therefore that there could be any purpose in espionage in this part of the world. Which was, I suppose, precisely what the public was intended to think.

"Bart's a good man," Johnson said. "Hardworking. Thorough. The last person to run into trouble." The sun had gone down on a copper band into the sea, and it was now perfectly dark, with the *quock* of a night heron coming occasionally over the water. *Dolly* moved slackly, with the waves and the steam from our coffee coiled white in the warm air, lit from below, where Spry was clearing the meal.

"So why now?" I asked. "Why should someone try to kill him now? And do you know who it is?"

"The answer to that is: I don't know, in triplicate," Johnson said.

I was not sure whether I believed him. I said, "Has it happened before?"

28

"Not to my knowledge. If it had, he would have reported it. In fact, it's the sheerest chance that I'm here now. I only arrived three days ago for this thing in Miami. He must have seen a report in the papers." He finished lighting his pipe, sent the match flaring into the darkness, and said, "Incidentally, there was nothing wrong, he says, with the crab sandwich. He mentioned it to stop any public health fussing, but he's sure the crab was all right. If it was. . . . How do you think the two doses of arsenic were administered? If there were two doses?"

"I think there were two quite distinct episodes," I said. "Arsenic works quite quickly, and the only food Sir Bartholomew had had before coming to the airport had been shared by Mr. Brady. Even if Mr. Brady had poisoned that meal, it would have worked, I think, before four-thirty. There remains the staff of the Monarch Lounge and Sir Bartholomew's fellow travelers. The fact that no one else turned ill means, I think, that the poison was put specifically into something Sir Bartholomew ingested, and was not dropped into the open bottles, or introduced into the tea or the sugar. It argues, I think, action by someone sitting beside him. His drink is the likeliest thing. And he served himself, I was told, to that."

"Who told you?" asked Johnson.

"The stewardess. But it was corroborated by Trotter."

"Brady and Trotter. The two men who sat nearest to Edgecombe and therefore were able to help when he collapsed. In fact, Brady had already met him by chance in New York. Trotter, I gather, had no idea who he was, but merely assisted out of good will . . . And both men were on the plane the next morning."

"Yes. Well, they both missed the last plane as I did, through helping," I said.

"And the second attack? You were with Bart all the time except when he went to the lavatory?"

29

"Apart from the water and aspirin, he had nothing to eat which I cannot vouch for," I said. "Again, anything he had before I met him that morning would have shown its effects before then. On the other hand, no one was to know that he would leave his seat in the plane. If anything happened to him in the lavatory, it was sheer opportunism, I fancy."

"The steward I can find out about. What about the other young man who helped him? Could you describe him?"

"He was Turkish," I said. "At least he carried a Turkish passport through Immigration Controls. Aged about twenty-four, medium height, dark complexion, of extremely sinewy build. His face was Mongoloid with high cheekbones and long hair. He was clean and well groomed, but unconventionally dressed in a Mogul silk tunic suit with a mandarin collar. He spoke hardly at all, but his English had a slight American accent."

"A good piece of observation," Johnson said. "I wish there were more like you. Do you know where he was going?"

"No. But he was met at the airport by a green Rolls-Royce Silver Cloud. He had a great deal of luggage." I recalled something. "There was a press photographer waiting for him. He certainly looked like a celebrity."

"He was," said Johnson, "if your description is accurate, and I am sure that it is. Does the name Krishtof Bey mean anything to you? Or do you not frequent the world of the dance?"

He did not, I suppose, refer to ballroom dancing, but to the equally tedious business of jumping about in white tights. "He is a ballet dancer, I take it?" I said. "I know nothing of the subject, I am afraid."

"No," said Johnson thoughtfully. "I can't sic you onto Krishtof Bey, I'm afraid. But if one of the others reappeared in your life, what do you think your reaction would be?"

I employed my intelligence. "The only person likely to be

dangerous to me is the would-be murderer, should he suspect that I have diagnosed Sir Bartholomew's illness as poisoning. I must therefore reassure him that I have not, upon which I trust he will lose all interest in me."

"Could you do that?" said Johnson. "Remember, we don't know who it is. And if they do try to pump you, they'll go about it in an oblique and unexpected way." He paused, and said, "Well, at least they should make sure you are well out of the way before the next attempt on poor Bart is made."

Espionage has always seemed to me a childish game, and this aspect of it the most tiresome. "You don't intend," I said, "to report this and give him adequate police protection? Surely these things can be done quite discreetly? After all, a man's life is in question."

For a while, irritatingly, Johnson did not speak. Then he said, "He took that risk when he joined us. No. Until I know more about it, I can't call in the police."

"I would remind you," I said, without hiding my feelings, "that through no fault of my own I have some personal stake in the matter."

"Quite," said Johnson; and rising, he put his hand on the wheel and with a touch started the soft buzz of the engine. "But as you so recently pointed out, the emergency situation is perhaps more frequent in medicine than in portrait painting. And if ever I met a person who can take care of herself, it is Doctor B. Douglas MacRannoch."

It was 10:30 P.M. when I got home, and my father, as he often does when bored, had gone off to bed. There was a note by the telephone in his writing. It read: *Beltanno. Some American creep telephoned at the start of "The Fugitive" to invite you to golf at 7 A.M. tomorrow morning. I offered him $75,000 to marry you, but he says he just wants to play golf. Please keep your love* *life out of my "Fugitive."* It was unsigned, but he had written beneath, as an afterthought, *Name of Broody.*

I had promised Johnson two things: one, to tell no one what I had learned from him that evening, and second, to report any overture whatever from one of our suspects. I therefore telephoned the Coral Harbour Yacht Club and had Johnson brought to the instrument.

"Brady has telephoned," I said. "He wants to golf with me tomorrow. On Paradise Island. At seven in the morning."

"How energetic of him," said Johnson's voice regretfully. "Could you go?"

"I have to be at the United Commonwealth later. I could manage nine holes," I replied.

"Will you?" he asked.

My father has an impression of himself as a wit. It was unlikely that he had actually spoken to Wallace Brady of marriage.

"Yes. I'll meet him," I said, and listened to Johnson's voice, distantly congratulating me.

Whatever it was, it had started.

Chapter 3

Two DOLLARS to my mind is a high price for the half-moon toll
bridge which connects Nassau to Paradise Island. Since I have
no interest in the Casino and the golf course has only recently
been restored, I seldom trouble to cross it. At that hour in the
morning the gamblers, the tennis players, the water-skiers and
sun-bathers were asleep, the helicopters and the yachts not yet in
motion. Only a few other cars besides the Ford Anglia crossed
the bridge with me: contractors for the development company,
early morning golfers like myself. It is warm for golf by mid-
morning in the Bahamas, and some people still have work to
attend to.

Wallace Brady awaited me at the golf course, which is on the
right, or eastern end of the island. Although several luxury hotels
and duplex villas have been created, and the excellent beach is
fully equipped, some of Paradise Island is still largely jungle,
and the straight avenues of pines dissolve into unmade roads
edged with scrub, partly cleared here and there for new sites.

Bought originally by Mr. Huntington Hartford, it bore the
name Hog Island, I understand. The new packaging, I have no
doubt, will match the new brand name chosen for it. Hog Island,
to my mind, is the more honest appellation: both simple and
etymologically sound.

However, my views on such subjects are not generally the

popular ones. I drew up outside the low, canopied entrance of the golf club, greeted Wallace Brady without undue fuss, and brought my clubs around the corner, where he had already hired an electric golf cart, a sorry sight. We entered, and he put his foot down and drove off.

I should here mention, I think, that golf, a game played in Scotland largely by the unemployed, is regarded in America and those countries adjacent to her coasts as a highly esoteric pursuit, followed largely by the middle-aged and the elderly and requiring real wealth and leisure. The equipment and facilities, as Johnson had noted, are all accordingly priced for this market, in addition, naturally, to the obvious cost of maintaining in prime order many acres of grass which in Scotland would be watered, free, by the elements. For all these reasons I have noticed that if an American can afford to play golf at all, he can usually afford to do it better than anyone else.

Mr. Wallace Brady, self-styled acquaintance of Bartholomew Edgecombe and working on Great Harbour Cay, was an American. The first hole was over three hundred yards long, a dog-leg to the north: par for both, 4. I took out a No. 1 wood, flexed my knees, dug in my unlined Gullanes with white aprons and replaceable spikes, and swung.

There was a whicker and a click, and my ridiculous American ball flew, straight as a rule, well over two hundred yards down the fairway. Wallace Brady said, "I knew it. I've asked to play ball with a tiger."

"Not a tiger, Mr. Brady," I said. "Just an average player from Scotland."

There is no virtue in exaggeration, after all.

To describe the round would be tedious. Paradise Island golf course is scenically attractive, with coconut palms, flowering bushes, and a small lake stocked by coots, whose wooden bridge

34

we crossed in the golf cart. An advantage perhaps in the long American fairways, these are still to my mind no substitute for a caddy. However I am, I know, a reactionary.

I played well that morning, and the two balls I shot into the rough I recovered, although on the fourth I had to play a tricky chip shot from the sand. The fourth, fifth, and sixth at Paradise all run by the sea, and I have known couples to break off their game to sit on the rock-strewn white sand and foster their sun-induced cutaneous cancer.

But then, on an American course one can hardly tell golfers from sun-bathers. Brady was moderately dressed in thin stone-colored trousers and a knitted white shirt with short sleeves. But three of a foursome behind us, I noted, sported all the atrocities of bright shirts and long colored Bermudas: one over-weight person in a straw hat was playing in his bare feet. For golf, I have always worn an Orkney tweed skirt with a low inverted pleat at the back, and oversocks with good shoes. If one wishes to play properly, one must be properly dressed.

I won that hole, and Brady the next, which reduced my slight lead, but not enough to concern me: I was clearly the better player of the two. As we turned from the sea I noticed, a little way out in the channel, the long white lines of a gaff-rigged ketch tacking idly in the light wind; her power boat was quite clearly missing. Someone on *Dolly* had risen early this morning. I wondered who was ashore, Spry or Johnson, and where. The thought gave me confidence, and at the next hole I got a birdie which Brady, unlike many of his sex, took in good part. After the doubtful start at the Trueman Hotel, I was finding him mildly congenial.

He kept his good temper even at the end when we finished our nine holes, he one over and I one under par. There was time for coffee, but he would not consider help-yourself instant on the terrace and asked me instead to wait and accompany him up to the hotel. Thus it was that I entered the pro's shop to look around while he paid for the cart.

As usual, the golf bags looked like elephant howdahs, and there was a display of crossed irons which would have done credit to the Great Hall at Inveraray itself. The guest book was open on the counter, where he had written our names, and below it were the names of the players behind us, presumably including the ill-attired foursome who were now playing the ninth. Most of the golfers behind us gave Nassau addresses; but one quartet player gave no address at all, not even Scotland.

But the name was MacRannoch. T. K. MacRannoch. The name of James Ulric's despised heir.

It was the merest coincidence, but I always prefer to make certain. I walked out of the pro's shop, almost bowling over Wallace Brady, who was coming to find me. I had no time for Brady just then. I was looking at the fourth, sober member of the gaily dressed foursome, who was occupied, head bent, in holing an extremely difficult putt. He looked up, smiling, and I saw that my native sixth sense had not failed me. The player was Japanese.

"What's the pitch?" said Wallace Brady eventually, after we had driven in silence to the hotel complex, walked through the darkened casino with its covered tables and clicking, glimmering rows of one-armed bandits and up through the simulated leopard skin to a lounge where we could sit and have coffee. "You don't like playing golf with poor performers? I thought gilt-edged was weakening there for a bit."

He had, after all, paid for the round. "I beg your pardon," I said. "I enjoyed the game very much. I dare say I have more practice than you do. I play whenever I can."

"Outside Mickey Wright, I don't know who you'd have trouble

beating," said Brady. "Did you ever think of becoming professional?"

I have, of course. There is a great deal of money in golf. But one needs money, or backing, to start with. I said, "Someday, perhaps. My father has multiple allergic sensitivity, and it will be difficult to leave Nassau until he improves."

He had an extremely deep suntan, in which his eyes were quite pale, but the eyeballs unveined and apparently healthy. It was hard to guess his profession. "You miss your home, Doctor MacRannoch?" he said.

Across the lounge I had just spotted the back of Johnson's head. The question reminded me of my anger. "Unfortunately," I said, "I have little chance to do so. My father is head of a Scottish clan, Mr. Brady, and is prone to bring his surroundings with him, wherever he goes."

"His drapes, you mean?" He looked slightly bewildered.

"His clansmen, I mean," I said, no doubt with some grimness. "Even here. It was there on the register. T. K. MacRannoch."

"You don't say?" He looked duly astonished. Then he said, "Well, I wouldn't bawl out the old man too quickly. There are an awful lot of Scots in the Bahamas."

"There may be, but they are not all MacRannochs. The word gets around. Even among the unwanted, like T. K. MacRannoch, the word travels like typhoid," I said. "I knew it. Father is planning a MacRannoch clan Gathering."

"Here?"

I wasn't thinking of Brady. I was thinking of James Ulric's bronchial spasms.

"Here, or at the Begum's house," I said, on reflection.

"But," he said, "I thought the Begum spent the winter at your castle in Scotland."

37

I stared at Wallace Brady with surprise, and then with increasing suspicion.

I hadn't told him that. I had no desire to talk about the Begum, who is the decayed English widow of an extremely rich Indian prince, and who annually rents Castle Rannoch as a shooting lodge from James Ulric MacRannoch.

While he disports himself in the sunshine, the Begum Akbar from the time of my senior school days has moved into the castle with her clothes, her butler and maid, and using our gillies, our cook, and our housestaff, has killed deer and fished salmon and shot our grouse with her friends. I had never met her. I would never go home when she was there, and I had avoided her house here on Crab Island by Nassau. It was she who had found our present villa and rented it in advance for my father. It was because of the Begum, I was sure, that James Ulric had come to Nassau at all. They were welcome. I do not care for life on the edge of a Barclaycard.

But I had said nothing of all that to Brady. I said, "How do you know that? You knew about Father before I mentioned him to you?" Then an unlikely thought struck me. "Mr. Brady. What do you do for a living? On Great Harbour Cay?"

To do him credit, he looked me in the eyes as he answered. "My firm has a project there," he said. "A big constructional project. I'm a civil engineer, Doctor MacRannoch."

There was a deadly and sundering silence, fully understood by both parties.

"You build bridges," I said. I opened my handbag, selected my car keys, snapped it shut, and stood up. "I'm sorry I can't introduce you to my father," I said. "He has built five bridges, Mr. Brady. And those were five bridges too many. Thank you for the golf and the coffee. Good-bye."

He didn't say anything, but halfway to the door a thought

38

struck me, and I went back to give him the benefit of it. "You might go back to the golf course and try Mr. T. K. MacRannoch," I suggested.

*   *

The hospital was busy when I drove in under the blue arch: there had been a triple crash in Bay street and a British frigate had called on her way south for combined exercises, which meant sixty pints for the blood bank and a long robust queue of A.B.'s calling four-letter words to the nurses while poor Currie, the lab technician, sat inside draining them off in batches of four. It was necessary to keep our blood stock replenished. But I sometimes wondered if the naval platelets storming through the Bahamian vascular system were not the source of the strange tribal love-rock appeal of New Providence Island.

However, it was cool as yet, which cuts down the casualties, and too early for the rum and fuel drinkers. So we got through the work unimpeded, and by midafternoon I was able to look in on Sir Bartholomew Edgecombe, about whom I had already taken advice. Although there was no cause for anxiety, renal function after the second attack had undoubtedly been more seriously impaired than the previous day, and was not responding to treatment as well as it should. Dialysis was indicated, and after this had been settled, I walked through the private wing to inform Sir Bartholomew.

The United Commonwealth is an informal hospital: peanut sellers and news vendors have free access to the front door and it is the habit of the staff to take matters at comfortable speed and with many sociable exchanges in the passages. While white patients and even white doctors require to be reassured about this, there is no doubt that the Bahamian cases thrive in such an atmosphere. I was surprised, therefore, amid the hum of conversation and laughter coming from the short private wing, to distinguish the complaint of a woman coming from Sir Bartholomew Edgecombe's room. I walked in briskly, closed the door, and folded back the short screen.

It was Denise, Lady Edgecombe, seated on a chair with her head on her husband's sheeted lap, sniveling. I can use no other word. I have no patience with this sort of thing. I said, "Well, this is hardly the way to cheer up your husband, Lady Edgecombe"; and she sat up looking tearful and sulky, and attempted patently to recover her lost dignity.

My patient, throwing me a wretched look, patted the woman's hand and said, "She's just upset. We both thought I'd be out of here by now, you see. It's our wedding anniversary."

I have never been able to fathom why the elapse of the arbitrary number of 365 days or its multiple from any significant event should be a matter for either celebration or mourning. I have known a Trendelenburg sink into a condition of acute postoperative shock, because she had forgotten to mark her dog's birthday. It is as well that in this world we are not all alike.

I said, "It's a pity, but perhaps she'll enjoy a day or two in Miami instead. I'm sending you over to the Jackson Memorial Hospital in the morning, Sir Bartholomew. Their equipment is just a little more sophisticated than ours, and the right treatment now could cut your recovery time by quite a few days. I imagine you know Miami well?"

That had roused Lady Edgecombe. She sat erect of a sudden, her blond hair stuck to her cheeks and her mascara running, and said in an excited voice: "What's wrong with him? What will they do to him there?"

One has to simplify. I explained that they would clear the remains of what he had eaten out of his system and enlarged on this until she was satisfied; I had no time to deal with hysteria.

40

No sooner had I done this, however, than she felt able to return to her first complaint. Addressing her husband in a shaken voice, she observed that it would be the first anniversary since their wedding they had not spent together.

Over her head, I met Sir Bartholomew's eye. I knew, without being told, that it would do no good to suggest that she might, with the greatest of ease, draw up a chair and spend the whole evening in the hospital with her husband if she so wished. It was the celebration she had been counting on, not Bartholomew Edgecombe's company.

He knew it, too. He squeezed her hand and said, "Denise. Wallace Brady would take you out like a shot. Why not phone him?"

"I'm tired of Wallace," she said. I could imagine it. Wallace Brady was interested in bridges, not in café society.

"Well, Johnson then?" he said. "He squired you about all day yesterday. Charm him into painting your picture for nothing."

She gave a watery smile, and I gave her husband top marks for diplomacy. I said, "Would you like to use the hospital telephone, Lady Edgecombe? I think you could get Mr. Johnson at Coral Harbour." I added, civilly, "He would give you a splendid evening out, I am sure."

"I don't much like yachts," said Denise; but she was clearly thinking.

"Café Martinique? Junkanoo Club? Charley Charley's? Tell him I'll spring the cash," said Edgecombe, smiling. He had had, I judged, just about enough, and I wished the woman would make up her mind before I had to do it for her. He added, "Or the Bamboo Conch, Denise. The nurse said they're putting on a special show there for Krishtof Bey."

I should think Lady Edgecombe and I stiffened at the identical moment. Her nylon lashes fell wide apart and she exclaimed,

41

"Not Krishtof Bey? Bart, is he going to be there?" But I was quite silent because I was using my brain.

I said, "You should meet him, Lady Edgecombe. He was on the plane yesterday morning, but perhaps Sir Bartholomew doesn't remember? The young Turk who helped out the steward?"

His lips parted, and a little color came into his face. He had been, and was still, a man of striking appearance, and until lately, I judged, in perfect condition. I understood why Denise had married him, and thought too that he probably had all the qualifications for a secret agent in this part of the world: socially acceptable, noncompetitive, and a handy man, I supposed, in a fight.

He said, "Was he the ballet dancer? I didn't even look at him properly. It was damned embarrassing as it was." He grinned at me over his wife's head. "A firsthand unique encounter with one of the world's greatest dancers, and I can't even describe it in company."

"How kind you are, Doctor," said Lady Edgecombe. "Did you say there was a telephone?"

I had her husband medicated and settled for the night by the time she came back. Her walk down the corridor was slow, and at first I assumed that Johnson had turned her down flat.

But it wasn't that at all. She came in, leaving the door open, and said to me, "He would like *you* to go with us."

I make it a matter of practice to show no surprise. In any case, I could think of one or two possible reasons why Johnson Johnson might want my presence at a nightclub attended by both Bart Edgecombe's wife and one of our suspects, although Denise clearly could think of none. I said, "Well, I'm free, as it happens. But I am sure you would prefer a tête-à-tête."

"No. I expect he's right," said Denise, and bending, ranged

42

her husband's two slippers firmly under the bed with brittle efficiency. She straightened. "In these colonies people do talk."

I took her with me out of the room.

I went back once, to check on Edgecombe before I left. He was alone this time and not yet asleep. He looked up vaguely and smiled. "I hope you don't find it too dreary. Johnson tells me you know what we're up to."

"Yes."

He said, "I've got one worry. They might try to get at me through Denise."

"I expect Mr. Johnson is thinking of that," I said. "We'll take good care of her."

"She used to be in the theater," he said. "She'd set her heart on ballet, and once she wants to do something, she's really determined, you know. She would have done very well. But when she grew too tall, there was only show business. She missed the stage when we were young. And now, of course, she rather misses the embassy life."

"You didn't have any family?" I said.

He was far too sophisticated to show any emotion. He said, "Denise wasn't too keen. And in my kind of job it isn't wise. Look at the worry we might be having now if we had youngsters to think of as well."

Look at the worry you are having now with Denise instead, I nearly remarked. But I didn't. Recommending children as one form of therapy can be a dangerous business.

*   *

The Bamboo Conch Club is contained in the basement of a large Nassau hotel called the Ascot. I met Lady Edgecombe and Johnson there in the foyer, and he led us into the hotel Hibiscus Room restaurant, where the three of us were first to have dinner.

Lady Edgecombe was gracious, and in the faintest degree nervous of Johnson. I wore a navy blue, tailored, silk dress I had bought five years before for a wedding. Denise, her hair perfectly set, had put on a knitted silver dress which bared the fatty pads at the tops of her arms.

On the other hand, Johnson looked to my mind perfectly harmless. The terry shirt he had naturally changed, his black hair was brushed down and glossy, and his burnished bifocals glimmered in the fashionable dark of the foyer. He wore a wide shot-silk tie in crimson and a pale shantung jacket a shade too large for his shoulders.

He was quick to notice my glance, ushering us into the floral delights of the Hibiscus Room. "It's a double-blind controlled trial for Hung on You," he said. "My underprivileged wardrobe has got itself burgled, and Lady Edgecombe has lent me the wherewithal to be a turned-on type for the evening. Denise, what will you do if my trousers fall down?"

Denise smiled, with dignity. "Time your reflexes," I said. Someone had to say something.

It was one of those dining rooms with hibiscus blossoms lying all over the table and a bottle-top dance floor. Upon this, obese tourists of both sexes in pant suits revolved to the tunes of their courtship, watched with distaste by their offspring, attired in bow ties and a flourish of bacterial acne.

I do not dance. Johnson, maintaining a gay conversation of determined vacuity, managed to withstand until after the clam chowder the wistful gleam in Lady Edgecombe's fringed eyes. After that, with an apology to me, he stood up and asked her to dance.

He had picked an unfortunate moment. The small, native orchestra, which up till then had contented itself with fox trots, waltzes, and cha-cha-chas of genteel moderation, suddenly broke with relief, for all I know, into a request number for jiving. Or it may have been rock and roll. At any rate, the rhythm became syncopated and ragged, the percussion appeared suddenly to have a major epileptic convulsion, and the elderly matrons melted away, to be replaced with three or four younger couples, and some who were obviously not couples at all in the traditional marital sense. These Johnson and Lady Edgecombe found themselves joining. They halted.

"Who's got your bet?" said the voice of Wallace Brady unexpectedly from just above me. "I think I'd back Denise to pull him through, but it's going to be a near thing."

He stopped. Dressed in white tuxedo and tie, he looked both distinguished and nervous, I was not surprised to observe. He said, "Look, I hate misunderstandings, and I'd like to clear this one up. D'you think I could sit down? While they dance?"

I didn't answer. I was watching the floor. "Christ," said Wallace Brady with reverence, and sat down unasked. I couldn't have stopped him.

Dragooned occasionally by fellow students into the Bring-and-Buy Sale for the King George V Fund for Sailors, I have known this stiff-arm, roll-and-unroll form of jig to break out, with a stack on the stereo, after the last fruitcake was bartered. But I have never seen it done with such impassive expertise as Johnson lent to it now.

Her eyes wide open, Denise found herself gripped, twirled, and launched into disciplined motion which lost never a beat, an opportunity, or a new angle for torso or limb. Johnson's face, which wore a kind smile, altered not at all from the moment he flung her from him into the lip of the trumpet and sucked her with the next beat from the path of the advancing trombone. Lady Edgecombe's, ranging quickly from amazed horror to dawning respect, settled for open-mouthed concentration.

In twelve bars she progressed from being an aging self-centered woman to one with the firm confidence of an expert performer, and Johnson helped it to happen. Then he released her to dance face to face. They improvised; they came together dead on the beat. They circled. They danced back to back, her long, well-shaped legs flashing, his hair bouncing above the gaudy swish of his tie, the shantung rippling like sheeted snakes down his arms.

"Christ," said Wallace Brady again. "Will you look at that? Now, isn't that just a breeze?"

It was a gale, and it wasn't hard to look at them either: no one else on the platform was dancing. The diners made a ring around the two of them, applauding and laughing, and at length fell into a regular clap. The musicians dropped out. The drums carried on, coming to a rattling crescendo. Johnson hadn't slowed up, but you could see the sweat as bright as the tinsel under Denise's mesh.

I saw Johnson assessing her. He put her into a quick spin, which he braked almost immediately. Then with a brisk heave he swung Lady Edgecombe up to his shoulder, where she posed, arms outspread, while he walked off the floor. He let her down, the band stopped, and a great deal of alcoholic cheering broke loose, with some stamping and clapping.

A bottle of champagne, ordered by Wallace Brady, had appeared at our table. As the performers freed themselves and presently approached, Denise bright eyed and laughing, Johnson mopping his brow, Brady held out two brimming glasses. "Sir, we haven't met, but I hope you'll accept this in heartfelt tribute. Denise, I want to buy shares."

"Wallace Brady," I said to Johnson, to make everything clear. I added, "You have our congratulations, for as long as your diastolic pressure will allow you to enjoy it."

He grinned and sat down beside me, accepting the alcohol.

46

"Look: no blood," he observed in reply. And for the next five minutes, blandly, he parried Lady Edgecombe's intensive if lilting inquiries, while I waited for the music to strike up so that I could make my diminished cordiality to Wallace Brady perfectly clear.

My plan misfired completely. As the band returned, settled, and emitted the first notes of a tango, a brilliant figure arrived at our table, smiled at me, and addressed itself to Lady Edgecombe. "Doctor MacRannoch will tell you I had the honor of meeting your husband on his flight yesterday from New York to Nassau. I come to inquire if he finds himself better?"

He wore a silver rope bracelet and a tunic suit in plain violet silk. Krishtof Bey, the Turkish dancer, come to induce Denise Edgecombe to dance.

She did. She had already performed longer that evening than I personally would have suggested. I doubt however if the sure foreknowledge of a major cardiovascular event would have stopped her. She did well, and her partner's muscular processes, I admit, were an exceptional treat. They were wildly applauded.

Wallace Brady watched their encore in a trance, his champagne dripping unnoticed onto his shirt cuff. Johnson, catching my eye, made a brief face indicative of deeply sympathetic emotion and excused himself to dry off in the washroom.

Brady came to, mopped up his cuff, and said to me, "I want to explain."

I have no time for tedious repetitions. I said, "Do you build bridges?"

"Yes."

"Then there is nothing to explain," I said. There was no point in thanking him for the champagne, since I was drinking fruit squash.

"Yes, there is," he said. He sounded quite firm, which surprised me. "I do make bridges, Doctor MacRannoch, and tunnels, and other major constructions which people are fortunately quite pleased to pay for. I have no need to tout for my business, even such important business as the MacRannoch of MacRannoch could give me. In point of fact, as I would have told you if you hadn't rushed off in such a hurry, I know the Begum Akbar not through your father, but because I happen to be doing a job for her on Crab Island. I regard her as a great and elegant lady. I admire a professional in whatever field it may be, and I felt an equal admiration, Doctor MacRannoch, for the way you dealt with Bart Edgecombe at that airport, which was why I asked you to golf with me. Not to mention the hypodermic syringe."

"What syringe?" I said. I was unable to prevent myself from flushing.

"It was sticking out of your dressing-gown pocket. Would it have put me to sleep?" he said. "That might have been awkward. The Trueman always makes the beds first thing in the morning."

"It would have kept you quiet until the police took you away," I said coldly. I do not enjoy being provoked.

"Incidentally, what did the police do about Bart?" Brady asked.

"What do you mean?" I said. The next course had come: sliced coconut and orange in sherry. I eyed it without appetite.

"Well, food poisoning's dangerous, isn't it?" said Brady. "Don't they have to track down the bacillus by law in case other people get poisoned? Or did they fix the blame on Lady Edgecombe's crab sandwich?"

"Luckily, New York seems to have escaped," I said. "The doctor in charge, I imagine, found the crab was the culprit and took no further action. Certainly there were no police involved that I know of."

I had got it in before Johnson came back. I saw him as I spoke, threading his way between tables. The music ended at the same time and Pavlova and her partner began to return.

"Poor Bart," said Brady and grinned. "He had it public enough as it was, without the cops interfering. Listen, don't you dance?"

"No. The place of science," I said, "is to observe."

*   *

In the end we were a party of eight for the cabaret, for Krishtof Bey and his three friends insisted on our joining them, and Brady stayed stuck like surgical tape to Lady Edgecombe, Johnson, and myself. We walked together out of the light of the restaurant, across the hall, and down the dim-lit stairs to the Conch Club. I was not feeling cheerful, and the general inebriated levity of the large crowd accompanying us into almost pitch darkness did nothing to make my mood less gloomy. It came to me that I was probably the only entirely sober person in the room. Then Johnson's hand gripped my arm lightly, and I realized that I was not. We found a large round table with a red mat, and sat at it.

The cabaret at the Bamboo Conch Club, although paid for by the Ascot, is chosen and run entirely by the chief drummer, Leviticus, whose solo turn on the congo drums is the subject of most of their publicity. Inside the architect has tried to give the impression of a native hut, with a wickerwork lining dimly lit by fake torches burning luridly red on the walls. The roof, as I pointed out to Johnson, was low, dodecahedral, and wooden, thus increasing both the noise and the fire risk. Round tables like our own pressed against each other without order between the low stage and the doors and an ultraviolet light, placed strategically overhead, made Wallace Brady's teeth glitter and turned Lady Edgecombe's tall gin and tonic into a sugar-frosted tumbler of

49

silver. I ordered a jug of fruit squash, and Johnson, surprisingly, a magnum of champagne. Krishtof Bey had whiskey and water.

I was listening to him attempting to explain to a waiter, against the uproar of conversation and the near tinkling of a small piano, that he wished an admixture of water, not carbonated liquid or ice, when someone slammed me on the back and said, "Blimey, it's Doctor MacRannoch! Hullo, Doctor! How are you, Doctor? I didn't expect to run across you in these parts, I must say. How's the chop and rummage trade?"

It was Sergeant Trotter: Sergeant Rodney Trotter, who had been in the Monarch Lounge when Edgecombe took ill. He was lightly intoxicated, with a blood-alcohol level, I estimated, of 120 milligrams to the hundred or so.

I said, "Sergeant Trotter. Let me introduce Johnson Johnson, the portrait painter. And this is Lady Edgecombe, whose husband was taken ill in New York. Lady Edgecombe, the sergeant here was most helpful both in the airport and on the flight the following morning."

Denise Edgecombe gave the sergeant her hand with strictly moderate warmth, but Johnson edged one-handed a free chair beside him and lifted his bottle out of the ice bucket. "A glass of champagne, Sergeant?"

It was not my place to point out the effect of this upon an unknown quantity of iced beer. He accepted and sat down, grinning, next to Brady as all the lights except the ultraviolet one went out.

There is no nobler sound, to my mind, than a march of massed pipes and drums, playing *Tail Toddle*. I learned to pipe as a girl, back in Scotland. Trained on this, the aural senses could withstand, as they were now called upon to do, a full percussion group of drums and marimba, trumpets, saxophone, piano, and electric organ. The resulting cacophony, in quick tempo, made speech quite impossible and even, as I saw glancing around me, acted as a mild anaesthetic. Under the assault, the faces of Lady Edgecombe, Trotter, and Krishtof Bey's companions displayed a type of ultraviolet-lit stupor. Krishtof Bey himself merely showed pleasure, and Johnson, a glass in one hand, was drumming on the table with the other in time with the beat. Wallace Brady was watching me. I looked away.

The singer came on, in frilled peach-colored satin slit to the knee. The songs in these quarters are predictable: *Yellow Bird, I'll never Fall in Love Again, Island in the Sun,* proceeding purposefully through a brief range of calypsos and finishing with *Back to Back and Belly to Belly* about the third serving of alcohol.

With enthusiasm the other members of my party ran this predictable gamut. All the verses of *Shame and Scandal in the Family* were sung without stint by Johnson. Denise, following his lead slightly out of tune, was becoming faintly confused. The singer left, and Leviticus walked up to his drums. "Leviticus' number," said Johnson, and signaled the red-waistcoated waiter for another bottle of champagne.

Leviticus was of typically African appearance: the face strongly prognathous, the nasal bridge flattened, the two rows of teeth approximately parallel and in excellent condition. He wore black trousers and a black and white striped shirt unbuttoned to the waist, with a large gold locket glittering on his chest. Due to the drumming, the muscular development of neck and shoulders was almost sufficient to dwarf the profile of jawbone and chin; to shake his hand, as I had once done, was like gripping a flat plank of wood.

He came forward and sat facing us, between his two tall oval drums. The electric organ began, followed by the saxophone and trumpets, and as they gained tempo, Leviticus joined in, the thudding beat mingling agreeably with the strident instruments in a strong rhythm which visibly excited his audience. Then the other instruments reached their fortissimo and broke off, leaving Leviticus to continue his drumming alone.

The effect on a healthy adult of insistent rhythmic experience these days is a common subject for study. At the Bamboo Conch Club that night I watched with interest four hundred people receive the maternal 72-pm heartbeat with ecstasy. The drummer showed great skill in his evocations. From an exercise in varying resonance he insensibly improved on the speed until he reached a single-toned patter of sound, so quick that the notes blurred one into the other and the bleached palms, flat and flickering, moved too fast for the eye. Behind the barrier of sound a broken rhythm made itself felt, deeper in tone, syncopated and stealthy; it stopped; then the drumming stopped, and Leviticus began slowly to slap the parchment of each drum with his hands.

It seemed to me that I could feel the resonance of it in my soft palate, interspersed with bony clatter from my tympanic plates, as tempo, tone, and timbre changed from second to second. Leviticus played with incision, his head flung up and down with the rhythm, the speed and color of the rattling beats stirring the motionless audience, his hands raking curves in the air from one drum to the other.

A ball overhead began to revolve, light from coinlike apertures spinning over the musician's face, chest, throat, and hands in a long wheeling spatter. The drumming rose to a frenzy. Leviticus' head turned from side to side, his eyes rolling, his upper lip long and underfolded, his nostrils distended. His body glittered with sweat. I wondered what I would do if he had a frank hemorrhage into the ponto-midbrain junction, as seemed very likely. The noise stopped.

The intoxicated applause continued for a long time, and was

greeted most civilly by Leviticus, who finally signaled for silence. He then leaned forward, and placing his left elbow carefully on the light skin of the drum, he began with his right hand to pat out a tune on the parchment.

Performed on a single drum surface, the range of notes available to him was not of course large. However, by adjusting the strain on the skin, he produced a simple tune, very soon recognizable. The audience, with shouts of joy, began to break into song with the words, and he acknowledged with smiles their acuity. He played several in fact, and they roared them all in cheerful oblivion. *Jingle Bells*, I remember, was one; *Merrily We Go Along*, I suspect, was another. English student songs were never my forte, even when among students in England.

Silence fell. The patting fingers began the last childish tune. From behind me, quite clearly, a sexless whisper came to my ears: *"Don't do it again,"* said the murmur, into the silence. *"Do you hear, Doctor? Just don't do it again."*

Chapter 4

BEFORE THE FIRST PHRASE was half spoken, Johnson had swung around in his seat, and I was not far behind him. I remained outwardly calm even while I scanned the dim ranks of intent faces, all watching the drummer. No one looked at us. No one moved. Stare as one might into the darkness from which the whisper was coming, it was impossible to distinguish the speaker. And so close were the tables that to rise and struggle toward it would do nothing but make us conspicuous. Johnson said in a murmur, "It's no good. Was that the same voice?"

"I don't know," I said. Our companions had broken into fresh song, and I could see the trumpets lifting again. No one else seemed to have heard. "You can't identify whispers."

"Why are they trying to frighten you?" They had switched on all the lights, but with his back to the stage, Johnson's glasses were black.

I didn't answer, but I thought about it as the solo finished in a spasm of activity and the band, wildly applauded, gave way to the limbo dancer, a handsome Indian in tight floral trousers, who retired face upward under a low cotton wool bar, a flaming Coke bottle upright on his brow and one in each hand. Since he had been trained to it from childhood, he cleared the bar easily with a flick of the pelvis, the flame from the bottles setting fire to the bar as he did so, with spectacular results. Denise, who had clearly viewed it all too often, had allowed her attention to wander, but I saw that Krishtof Bey was quite rapt, and Sergeant Trotter was in a state of near-hypnotic trauma. Wallace Brady grinned, and I looked away quickly.

They were all there, my suspects, and had been there since it started. Who, then, had whispered?

"Look at that!" said Sergeant Trotter in a reverent whisper.

They had lowered the bar to lie across the necks of two bottles. The spiked flames ran like bunting along the lumpy cotton wool swathing, glazed and sodden like coconut fondant. To get under this time, the performer had to fold his knees under him, the sides of his feet wide apart, his hands off the ground. I began to work out the areas of grossest muscular strain. He lit a cigarette from the bar as his head went under.

The fire dancer came on. "Perhaps they don't realize," said Johnson, topping up the champagne in Trotter's half-empty glass, "what an excellent autonomic nervous system you possess."

The fire dancer was a young Negress in a sequinned brassiere and a minimal triangle to which an ostrich feather tail had been sewn. In this exposed condition she danced over and around two shallow bowls filled with flaming cotton wool, one of which she later placed on her head. Presently, at the climax of her dance around the other, she jumped forward and tramped out the flame with bare feet.

I have treated blisters on these performers often enough to know that the risks they run for applause and financial reward are quite genuine. A skilled fire dancer, however, knows to the thousandth part of a second when it is vital to demit. I had no apprehension for the girl, although some for her audience, as the flames from the bowl on her head swept the low rafters. Then

55

she laid this down, and lighting from it two bud-headed spools, she proceeded to dance to Leviticus' drumming, a stick of flame in each hand.

The lights had gone out again. Beside me, amid the prevalent wheezings of alcoholic excitement, I was aware of Johnson's still glasses, and of the fact that for the last few minutes he had been watching not the stage but the audience. The girl came down the steps from the stage and, leaning forward, thrust her torch into the face of the nearest man. He recoiled, his womenfolk shrieking with scorn and excitement, and a bearded young fellow opposite, catching the girl's eye, turned toward her and opened his mouth. He allowed her to place the flame inside his lips, his mouth straining open, and kept it open until she removed it. I could see some blackened crumbs of cotton wool, still glowing red, lying behind the base of his teeth. He grinned, his jaws rigid, in the ensuing laughter and applause, but hesitated for some time, I noticed, to close his mouth in the customary way, or even to swallow. The dancer moved on.

It is, I suppose, a test of crude valor, which the Bahamian in his new freedom finds some amusement in applying to his white fellow mortals. At any rate, it was instructive to see which guests flinched and turned aside, which pressed forward eagerly to display their courage, and which, with resignation, opened their mouths and allowed the girl, swaying to the rattle and play of the drums, to thrust the flaming mass into their throats.

Sergeant Trotter was one of the fervent adherents. As the girl approached closer and closer, he half rose from his seat, his eyeballs red in the flame, his whole attention fixed on attracting her. Hence he had his back to the red-waistcoated waiter bringing, at last, the jug of water for Krishtof Bey's whiskey.

The girl moved, the waiter leaned forward, and Sergeant Trotter jumped to his feet at one and the same moment. And the jug of water, tilting, missed its target completely and emptied itself with a gush over Johnson's jacket and shirt.

The waiter exclaimed. Krishtof Bey got up quickly, and Lady Edgecombe, pushing her chair back, anxiously patted the damp crochet work of her dress. Johnson himself, his expression rueful, had just gripped the cloth of his jacket to shake off the water when the fire dancer swerved around his shoulders and stood rotating her pelvis, holding high the two torches.

Wallace Brady grinned at her, and nodded at Johnson. "Try him: he's wet enough," he remarked.

The girl looked at Johnson. Krishtof Bey smiled. Trotter, still standing, lifted his hand, and then swallowing his disappointment, sat down. The girl smiled. She swayed forward and whirled the flame of the torch closer and closer, the red and blue light flashing in Johnson's bifocals. The waiter picked up the jug and moved off. Krishtof Bey and the others sat down.

I was looking at the splashes on the red tablecloth. As I looked, they vanished.

I think Johnson saw it, too. As the fire dancer, undulating, brought the torch lower, close to his face, he suddenly moved. There was a cackle of laughter. The dancer, her expression derisive, made the movement again. This time he not only dodged, he collided with Lady Edgecombe, and sent her chair flying. She gasped. Krishtof Bey grinned. The laughter became widespread and raucous. The girl, smiling, bent and he shrank back; the torch, teasing, darted after him.

The tip of the flame, held like a pencil, toyed with one soaked edge of his jacket. With a tearing hiss the sodden cloth burst into fire.

My jug of fruit squash hit him in a tenth of a second, and with my other hand I already had a grip of the ice bucket. It stopped the fire reaching his hair, although it was still licking the

57

skirts of the jacket when the first squeals started up. Johnson himself had it half peeled off by then, beating out the lower flames with a napkin; but the tablecloth flared and I knew the roof would catch next.

At any rate, I have seen too many first-degree thigh burns to hesitate. I got up, jerked Johnson's chair back, and said, "Tip it!" just as I did the same for Lady Edgecombe. Someone obliged, and the whole table with its contents fell toward us with a crash, putting out the fire like a lid.

Johnson's jacket was off, and he had the blazing cloth almost smothered already. It was not before time. His shirt was netted with odd blackened holes, and there was a strong smell of singed flesh and material.

The band, unequipped with Victorian fortitude, had allowed the instruments to sag from their faces; Johnson paused for the first time in an extremely rapid series of actions and called, tentatively, " 'Nearer my God to Thee'?" The surging movement of alarmed clients slackened shamefacedly, and Lady Edgecombe showed signs of projecting a hysterical outburst. The Turkish dancer went to her side just as Wallace Brady, crunching around the ruins of glassware to Johnson, said, "My God. Are you all right?"

Johnson was already edging out of the limelight, his bifocals glinting emptily over the room. "Thanks to Doctor MacRannoch," he said.

"The jug," someone said. Sergeant Trotter, I saw.

"Yes," said Johnson, looking at him.

"The waiter," said Trotter.

"I wondered," said Johnson.

"I'm sure," said Trotter. "He went that way." And, with a wriggle, he began to back out through the crowd.

Lady Edgecombe let out a sob. I gave a quick look at her, and

58

deduced that there was nothing there that a sharp slap from a layman wouldn't cure. I let Johnson thrust past me and followed.

*   *

The door to one side of the bar led out straight into the street. It took us several minutes to reach it through an assault course of chairs, tables, fellow Englishmen, claustrophobics, and drunks. The waiter, fortunately, had also been slowed. At least, when Trotter, Johnson, and I emerged into the neon-lit darkness, we could still hear, quite plainly, the sharp distant crack of feet running quickly. They were running, I was interested to discover, along past Government House, and in the general direction of the hospital.

"That's him," said Trotter, breathing lightly. He was wearing, I saw in the lurid gloom, a smartly cut gray suit with a bright orange cummerbund. "I saw him make for the exit . . . Mr. Johnson, the lady oughtn't to be here."

The glasses flashed briefly at me. "What do you say? You know Nassau."

I set off running without wasting time or breath on an answer. I knew Nassau. The waiter had to be caught. The liquid in that water jug had been high-proof alcohol. It is men who turn a simple exercise in the science of reasoning into an Offenbach operetta.

We ran well, as it appeared: Sergeant Trotter on the balls of his feet like the P.T. instructor he most likely was, Johnson with the unexpected bounds of a gun dog. Since golf keeps me in good muscular trim, I found little hardship in following. In this way we had gained a little before long on the fugitive: he did not appear to have the sense to find a hiding place and simply keep quiet. Or perhaps he had one particular refuge in mind. The distant footsteps, laboring, turned a corner and began to run up the steep hill which passes the Out Patients' and Casualty Entrance to the United Commonwealth Hospital.

We ran past it. We ran past the pension offices and up the incline, our breathing no longer so silent; and then Trotter suddenly said: "There he is!"

The steep road we were climbing runs into a cutting of gray pitted rock, rising higher and higher to right and to left of the path, which at night is perfectly dark. It was not, however, dark over our heads. Between the lips of the gorge a blaze of stars could be seen, and another light — a large unseen beam, like that of a lighthouse, which swept the sky at ten-second intervals. It came from the Fort Fincastle Water Tower which was up there, perched out of sight beyond the right-hand cliff. To reach the water tower and the old fort which lay beside it, one traveled between the high walls to the end of the gorge, which was blocked by a steep range of steps known as the Queen's Staircase. Anciently built, it is said, by slave labor, these sixty-six steps provide a formidable climb and are a popular subject for amateur Kodaks in daytime. In further pursuit of the picturesque, the margin between the staircase and the left-hand canyon wall has been filled with a many-staged waterfall, which accompanies the steps from bottom to top in a series of platforms and jets. A wall divides the steps from the cascade.

We were looking at that, when the reflected beam from the water tower, sweeping around, caught a movement inside that dark gorge. And as we saw it and hurried to follow, the figure vanished, and in a moment even the sound of his footsteps had stopped.

We ran into the shadows and halted. Ahead, black against the dark blue sky, reared the staircase, with the water slope dry and silent beside it: night-shift waterfalls are uneconomic. On either side, the cliffs rose, soft and scratched, broken by roots and cacti and feathery plants, with here and there a shelf of debris, I remembered, left by some fall. Not a hard task for an agile man to scramble up, although no one was attempting it now: the smallest sound would have been audible, there where we stood.

He was waiting, therefore. For what? For us to begin noisily searching, there in the dark? For us to tire and walk off, leaving him to climb those steps unhindered? For the steps must be what he was making for. And he had had no time to climb them — of that I was quite sure.

"Oh, well," said Johnson, and put his hand in his pocket. "Here's to my rust-proof drip-dry titanium vest, and all who sail in her." And the beam of a pocket flashlight sprang out and swept the cliffside.

There was a bang, rocketing about between the cliff walls, and a tinkle of glass. The light went out, smashed by a bullet. "It's all right," said Johnson's voice peacefully from another direction. "I wasn't holding it. But now we know where our fellow is . . ."

"On the waterfall slope," Trotter said. Johnson, who was running already toward the place of the gun flash, didn't answer, and we both took to our heels in his wake. The gun fired again, and we could hear the howl of the shot, and the clatter of chippings from the rock face. Johnson said curtly, "Get behind those bushes, and down."

I saw him walk slowly forward. Ahead, the rising slopes of the dry waterfall gave nothing away. Even the sweeping light from the tower barely touched its dark corners and ledges, masked with ferns and boulders. Nothing moved. Johnson said, raising his voice, "We know you are here, and we have guns too. There is nothing at all to prevent one of us going back for the police while the others stay and keep you cornered till they come. Throw your gun down and climb out with your hands up. You know what you're in for if you damage us with that thing."

The reply was a shot, aimed accurately at where Johnson had been standing; answered before the echoes had stopped by a thunderous shot from the gun in Johnson's hand. I saw Trotter's head turn toward me, his eyes glinting, and remembered the bulge in Johnson Johnson's pocket when I first met him in the Buick outside my father's that day. But I had assumed his threat just now to be bluff. Then Johnson fired again and I saw something move this time: a plant dimly shook and a figure, moving in and out of the dark, began quickly to scramble up the waterfall bed. "On the left," I said suddenly to Johnson. "Can you pick a lock?"

"My darling doctor," said Johnson distractedly. "It's a palmetto western." But he'd got the point. He ran like a hound to the door in the cliff where I'd pointed, and in a trice had it open. In a moment more, he'd turned on the water.

The man fell, I should think, about twelve feet when the sheet of spray hit him: the jets sprang from above and below, and interleaved in front of the gathering fall of straight water. From a fussing hiss, the falling gush began to set up a rumble. The man scrambled to his feet and turning, began to climb on all fours.

Stumbling, sliding, his clothes glossed like PVC with the water, he scrambled across the smothering jets. The wall was high. We saw him drop back once; then he was over, and onto the Staircase. He began to race up the dark steps.

Johnson raised his gun steadily and took aim, and Trotter knocked it out of his hand. "If you murder without evidence, sir, you're asking for trouble. He can't fire his own gun. We can easily catch him."

It sounded simple. I saw the icy flash of bifocals, then Johnson without speaking flung himself at the steps, and we followed.

Where his gun had rolled in the darkness was not immediately obvious, but I took my time and found it before I followed, now far behind. Shadowed by the sheer wall of the gorge, the stairs were in complete blackness. It was only when I got to the top, not unpleased by the ease of my breathing, that I found Johnson and Trotter casting about helplessly in the roadway.

The waiter had vanished.

"He went that way," said Johnson. "Toward the fort, I think. Or what about that bloody great tower?" For this tall white shaft with the cotton-reel top was now just beside us, its white and green light still sweeping the town. Behind it lights showed from a row of low houses. On the other side of the road was the squat triangular shape of the old fort, its door closed. No one moved on its walls: the bare grass around the tower was empty of people. On the path in front of the tower lay a few spots of water.

We stood and listened. There was no sound. "I wonder," said Johnson. "What sort of people live in those houses?"

"Dahlia lives there," I said. "Dahlia is the little girl who works the lift in the water tower." A thin child with two fuzzy pigtails and a penchant for popcorn, who had already been through Out Patients' twice for the same thing. "She likes seamen and waiters," I said. "But she has eleven brothers and sisters."

Johnson swerved from the houses and turned. "So she wouldn't take him home. But she might hide him."

The beam swept around again and I nodded. "The water tower is closed to the public at four-thirty," I said. "But she'd have a key. Shall I go and find her?"

I had imagined he might want to question her. Instead, he took my remark as a further incentive to burglary.

"No need," said Johnson. "I always carry a hairpin. It keeps

63

my hairnet out of my eyes." And watched by Trotter and myself, he fiddled for a moment with the water-tower door. There was a click, and it swung slowly open.

I think we all hesitated. Sergeant Trotter said, "It isn't right, you know. We should call the police."

"We'll call them when we find him," Johnson said. "As you pointed out, after the wet, his gun can't likely be working. And hell, he did shoot at us. What's more, he's got my wallet, I think."

Trotter stared at him. "You mean he went to all that trouble to steal . . ."

"It had two thousand dollars in it," said Johnson simply. "So if you don't mind, I mean to go in." And pushing the door wider, he entered the blackness within.

The beam swept around as he did it, and a glow of reflected light lay on the paving just inside the door. The stone was spotted and blotched with dripped water, and the trail led around the turnstiles, past the elevator door, and up the twisting stone steps which led to the top of the tower. For a moment there was silence. Then Johnson, stepping around the turnstile in his turn, lifted a storm lantern off a hook at the side of the lift, and switching it on, flashed it up the first turn of the stairs. He said, hardly raising his voice at all, "I think you'd better come down. We're armed, and you are not. And there's really no other way out, is there?"

The answer was a shot which drilled straight through a carousel of transparencies by my right ear. Johnson's gun in my hand, I jumped to one side and fired straight at the flash. There was a scream, and then utter silence.

"Christ. *Beltanno*," said Johnson.

"We have the best grouse moors in Scotland," I said. I felt cheerful. "But a flesh wound merely, I am afraid. Your gun."

Johnson took it. Trotter closed his mouth and then opened it to say, "He's running upstairs. What's at the top of this thing?"

I said, "The stairs spiral around the elevator shaft and come out in the same chamber. It's over a hundred and twenty feet high. From there you climb a few steps to a circular walk around the tower, with a wall just chin high around it. Above that is the revolving core of the tower with the searchlight fixed to it, inside a kind of coronet of fairy lights. They don't work."

"I'll take the lift," Trotter said.

I said, "He'll get there before you."

"Not if I'm on his heels," Johnson said. The running footsteps had stopped. He raised his voice. "Doctor MacRannoch, go for the police. Quickly!"

"Right," I said. I ran for the door, banged it, and silently returned. Sergeant Trotter, in the distant light of Johnson's storm lantern, found the switch for the elevator and, stepping inside, closed the doors. Johnson, the light at arm's length, began climbing the stairs. There was a rattle, and the silence was split by the whine of the lift. There was no sound from above.

I tried to remember the inside of the tower. Mostly visitors go up in the lift with Dahlia, who switches off her normal loud slur as soon as she gets them inside and begins to emit information in short high bursts like a soprano computer: *The water is eighteen feet deep . . . rises two hundred and sixteen feet above sea level . . . view of eighteen miles all around,* ending as the lift stops with *mind the step* in the same breath. Sergeant Trotter was doing that bit, without benefit of Dahlia.

Johnson was climbing the stairs which curled left around the torn wire mesh of the lift shaft. The steps came in groups of five, joined by a short two-pace landing. At every landing the white outer wall of the staircase stopped, and there was a gap, filled by shoulder-high railings. Beyond those railings was the outer shell of the tower, lit by arrow-slit windows, and between that outer shell and the gap at each landing was nothing but space — a sheer drop from top to bottom of the tower.

The waiter knew that Trotter had gone to the top of the tower. He thought that I had left to summon the police. All he had to do, therefore, was to waylay Johnson as he crept up those stairs, flashlight and pistol in hand, and shoot his way downstairs to freedom.

He could ambush Johnson from the torn wire of the lift shaft, once the lift had risen up to the top. Or he could move to the outside of the stairs, swing himself over the railings and crouch there . . . on what? I seemed to remember there would be no trouble there. Painters' planks had been lying for weeks between the outer windows and the staircase railings at various levels. I wished I had pointed this out to Johnson Johnson.

Then I saw how Johnson was climbing the stairs — silently, flattened against the outer wall of the staircase. And as he came to each gap he stopped and listened, and slid across it with the nasty ease of an embolism. The whine of the lift stopped and, distantly, we could hear the doors rattle open above: Trotter was rightly taking his time to emerge. Then Johnson put out the light.

Silence. I corrected a full facial palsy and gripped a spanner I had found by the lift. It was difficult to know how I, B. Douglas MacRannoch, found myself here in the Bahamas, closeted in a water tower with an army sergeant, a would-be murderer, and an espionage agent. I broadened my diagnostic classification: with possibly two would-be murderers. That is, in the darkness, the waiter who had tried to kill Johnson might succeed in slipping past him unnoticed, and I might find myself grappling with him downstairs at the door.

On the other hand, Sergeant Trotter had certainly helped us pursue the man out of the club. But he was also, with Brady and

Krishtof, one of our earliest suspects from Edgecombe's collapse. He had yet to prove himself innocent. And he had knocked the gun out of Johnson's hand back at the Staircase. If Trotter were on the wrong side, all he had to do was pin Johnson down for the waiter to shoot. And then let the waiter escape.

There seemed one obvious way out of the dilemma. I banged the door again and called, "I've got the police, Mr. Johnson. We're just coming up," and ran across to the stairs. Above, a gun fired, and I could hear the bullet ricocheting; it was followed by another shot and a burst of running footsteps. Johnson's voice said, "Trotter! He's coming up!" He added authoritatively, "Doctor MacRannoch, stay down below and tell them to cordon the tower."

It was a fairly weak bluff, since anyone in their senses would have noticed the absence of car wheels and voices and general noise, but it was possible, I supposed, that a man in a panic might act on it. At any rate, I disobeyed orders and ran up the stairs, while Johnson and the waiter pounded ahead of me. There was another shot, and you could hear from the flat sound that it had been fired in the open. Then, as I raced up the last of the stairs and burst into the lift room, I heard Trotter speak. "Careful. He's above, on the struts." I crept up the steps and into the open walk which ran around the roof of the tower.

Beyond the retaining wall just beside me was the mounted telescope through which one could see the whole panoramic view of the town of Nassau: big blocks set among the green of firs and coconut palms, with the intersecting pink and white arms of the United Commonwealth there just below us. And in the distance the blue of the sea and the long furry spit of Paradise Island joined far off on the right by the long arch of Potter's Cay bridge.

Now it was all a bewildering dazzle of lights, with liners moving like nebulae across the black sea. And above, the green and white flash of the tower swung around and around, groaning, lighting up an irregular pattern of moisture — of blood, I saw, which made its way over the paving and halted, at the foot of a tall metal strut which gave access, with three or four others, to the light on the roof. Sergeant Trotter crouched at its bottom. And at the top I saw a sudden slight movement, thrown in relief as the light swept around again under its broken garland of lamps. I jumped just as the gun barked, and got to the foot of the strut, beside Trotter.

"Four," he whispered. "He had a police Colt waiting, here in the tower . . . You haven't got the police, have you?"

I shook my head. On the other side of the roof a gun fired: Johnson. It was followed immediately by two shots from above. The first did no damage that I could hear. The second, with a tinkling smash, put out the searchlight.

Johnson said sharply, "That's the last bullet. Give yourself up, you fool." There was a scrambling noise on the roof. I heard a sudden rushing of breath and realized that the waiter was above us, about to come down the ladder.

Trotter said, "Get out of the way, lady!" and left me abruptly, making for the head of the stairs.

There was a thud, as the waiter jumped onto the roof walk, and another as Johnson followed, bowling him over. You could see them twisting and rolling black against the white stone. They were both gasping and grunting.

I took two strides and lifted the spanner just as Johnson half rising, hit the man a neat blow behind the ear with the butt of his revolver. The waiter flopped. "And about time, too," said Johnson. "I feel like a dropped stitch in a circular knitting machine."

I had enough string in my purse to tie the man's legs with, aided by a jubilant Trotter. Johnson shouldered his burden. And then unshouldered it, swearing.

68

"You got burned," I reminded him. His glasses flashed balefully in my direction and Trotter, grinning, bent and heaved the waiter on one capable shoulder. We started off down the stairs.

We were a third of the way down when the waiter revived. We both saw him move. Johnson was already running to grip him when the man twisted off Trotter's shoulder. He did it on a landing, opposite one of the gaps. He was able to heel over the railing and grip it with one hand while he sought something I had noticed on the way up: a thick, free-standing metal pole, running from top to bottom of the outer ring shaft of the tower. He got one hand on it, and then two; and with his feet together below him, he slackened his hands and let himself slide down the pole.

We watched him as he got faster and faster. I don't think it even occurred to Johnson to shoot him. It was too swift for that, and it was too dreadfully obvious that the man hadn't a chance. The skin must have burned off his hands in an instant. With his grasp flayed, and no foot grip to brake him, in a matter of seconds he must lose all control.

We didn't see the moment when his body left the pole, but we heard his scream as he fell, and the flat sound as his weight hit the bottom. Trotter, straddling the rail, said, "I'll go after, poor bugger," and laying hands on the same iron pole, vanished swiftly and quietly out of our sight.

Johnson took his restraining hand off my arm. "Let him go. Haven't you noticed what a circus turn that man is?" he said.

"Sergeant Trotter?"

"Sergeant Trotter. His business is arranging international military tattoos. He's a world tattoo expert. That means he knows about dancing and marching and riding and firing and band music and trick cycling and commando exhibitions — "

"And sliding down pipes," I said. "And even poisoning, perhaps. But he had plenty of chances to kill you tonight and he didn't."

"I'm beginning to doubt that," said Johnson, giving a wriggle. "It'll be a mess on the ground floor there I'm afraid, poor fellow. Thank God I don't have to program you out of hysteria."

"I wish I could say the same of my forthcoming meeting with Dahlia," I said with some brusqueness. This type of examination is, after all, not a pleasant one to make. However, I dealt with the corpse while Sergeant Trotter summoned the police, and in due course, an ambulance arrived and all the explanations were formally made. Johnson's wallet containing, as he had said, two thousand dollars was indeed found in the poor fellow's pocket.

Much later, I ran Johnson back to my house, having said good-bye to Trotter and paused at the hospital to throw one or two things into my bag. It was five in the morning, an hour at which James Ulric is normally in bed, but I looked into the study in case. On the desk were three new box files and a pile of papers covered with his strong, undisciplined writing. The box files were all marked THE MACRANNOCH GATHERING, CRAB.

Crab Island is where the Begum Akbar has her house. I thought of setting a match to the whole thing and then dismissed it as childish. I was, however, still out of temper when I marched Johnson to my own bathroom and, stripping him to the waist, proceeded to deal with those blisters. They formed large patches on part of his upper arms, his shoulders, and back, and must have been painful. He kept up a flow of irrelevant comment, stretched on a bamboo chaise longue while I prepared the solution of flavine and soaked and wrung dry my lint. I cleaned and dressed the burns, tidied up, and took out my faithful syringe and a quarter of morphine. Second-degree burns, even mild ones, are the most painful there are.

Johnson said, "Hold it. I don't mind being micro-honed and

then made into a full-width parcel shelf with lagged edges. But I must get back to Mother Spry before morning. They've found my clothes, for one thing."

I'd forgotten he had been burgled. "You can get them tomorrow," I said.

He twisted around and sat up, fingering his bandages tenderly. I should have to get him a shirt and jacket of James Ulric's. "I'm flying to Miami in the morning," he said. "One-man exhibition in the Fontainebleau Hotel, and I'd better turn up or they'll lynch me in effigy . . . Do put down that needle. You look like a vet in a rabies zone instead of a nice girl with a hell of a family life."

I sat down slowly on the cork seat. Personal remarks of this kind I find confusing. I said, to return to professional ground, "Sir Bartholomew is being sent to the Jackson Memorial in Miami tomorrow. For dialysis."

"Don't rat out of it," said Johnson. "I said a hell of a family and I mean a hell of a family. However, we can take that up later. Look, I don't like the idea of Edgecombe traveling in public just yet. I'm chartering a Twin Otter. Would they let him come with me?"

"Without question," I said. "If you don't send them a bill."

"I won't. If you would come with him."

"He doesn't need me," I said. "A houseman would do. I should have to be away from my work for the better part of two days."

"Free transport Nassau to Miami, return," said Johnson. "For both you and Bart Edgecombe. I can't see the United Commonwealth objecting. Would you come if they let you?"

I shifted my ground. "In any case, surely it's an unnecessary precaution. It wasn't Sir Bartholomew they were trying to murder tonight. It was you."

"Wearing Bart Edgecombe's clothes," Johnson said.

71

The needle sagged in my hand. He was right. I had forgotten. To go to dinner, Lady Edgecombe had lent him Bart's tie and jacket. A distinctive tie and jacket which might well mislead someone who didn't know Edgecombe too well. Someone who assumed that Denise Edgecombe's escort that night was her husband, not Johnson.

I had another thought. "In that case — "

"In that case, we mustn't eliminate Sergeant Trotter after all from our list of vague suspects. He didn't kill me," said Johnson. "But then, he knew I wasn't Bart Edgecombe. The waiter made his mistake, we chased him, and when it became obvious that the waiter was caught and would be questioned, Trotter took him from me and mysteriously allowed him to escape. To his death. No, Bart isn't safe."

"I'll go," I said. "I'll go with him to Miami tomorrow."

"Good girl," said Johnson. I ignored the banality, but he actually looked pleased. "And you'll join us in an after-shave fizz at the Fontainebleau?"

"If my patient's program allows," I said. I shook out half a dozen barbiturates into some tissue and held out the screw. "Take one of these once you are settled in bed. You know perfectly well that there are limits to what you should do with your history."

The bifocals flashed with affront. "Bloody hell, what's this, echolocation? You were supposed to be treating my blisters, not orienteering all over my torso," said Johnson. "I'll have you thrown out of the Magyar PEN Club."

"Then," I said, "I'll publish my memoirs through somebody else."

I got him a python-printed silk shirt of my father's and matching Bermudas, ignoring his pleading, and drove him straight back to his car. On my return, I walked into my bathroom and found

72

James Ulric, in beetle-wing taffeta, on my bamboo chaise longue. He was smoking a cigar.

"My God, Beltanno," he said. "A virgin for thirty-two years and then you get laid between the loo and the bidet. Could you not move him out on the landing?"

I gathered up the litter in silence, and draped Johnson's trousers over one arm. I wondered how much my father had seen and heard; I rather thought nothing.

"No," I said. "I could not move him out on the landing. I have the landing to keep for the queue."

I walked out and took over James Ulric's bathroom, since I had to wash somewhere. His scales were six pounds under true. I reset them for him.

I slept soundly. Thank you.

Chapter 5

I WENT TO SEE DAHLIA early next morning. She knew about her boy friend already but was not unduly upset, as she had fallen in love with an Italian croupier on Paradise Island. She admitted cheerfully that she had given her water-tower key to the waiter to be copied: they kept their drafty assignations, I suppose, on the top, and much good it did the poor man. His name was Pentecost. The only other fact of interest I elicited from her (*Quis bene interrogat, bene diagnoscat*) was that Pentecost had been one of a family of four brothers from Bullock's Harbour. And Bullock's Harbour is the native settlement on Great Harbour Cay.

I meant to tell Johnson when we met at the airport, but there was no time to dwell on it. Sir Bartholomew, with his wife in attendance, a little washed out, was ushered into the Twin Otter and I followed as the ambulance drove off, with my overnight case and medical bag in one hand. From the amount of zipped pigskin luggage entering the Otter's hold, I gathered that Lady Edgecombe didn't intend to spend all her time at the hospital. She was wearing a beige trouser suit of some elegance, and even Johnson had smartened up remarkably, in a tropical suit of rather elderly cut and a long suede tie with an unclothed woman neatly affixed to the lining.

74

I may have been looking at it rather pointedly. At any rate he scanned himself searchingly as we revved for takeoff and said: "Do you like it? I have a new skinny body hug, but I thought the clients would worry."

I lifted up, without speaking, the underside of his tie, and he looked at it with bewilderment. "How extraordinary," he said. "It was a Christmas present from my agent's secretary, along with a pair of little league baseball shoes with genuine Nescohyde vinyl uppers and safety rubber cleats."

"Your agent's secretary wants watching," I said, handing him my nail scissors. He removed the lady with care. With, indeed, a regrettable artistry.

The Twin Otter cruises at 8000 feet and does a comfortable 150 mph. The journey to Miami was less than an hour and we had coffee halfway: " 'The Beautiful People eat a leisurely breakfast. Why shouldn't you?' " quoted Johnson; and Lady Edgecombe smiled while Sir Bartholomew grimaced weakly. He was looking forward, clearly, neither to his dialysis nor to the prospect of further attempts on his life. I could see the bulge where Johnson's gun (or his pipe) lay in his pocket. He gave no sign of discomfort from his invisible burns and had already suggested that I forget them.

I did. Like plucks of crabmeat, small fleshy clouds hung over the blue sea below, and ladders of fine cloud streamed past higher up. There are seven hundred islands in the Bahamas, and they lie avocado colored in a marbled green and blue sea which shoals to apricot and light apple green as it lifts to the beach. So white is the sand and so clear is the water that land and sea blend in a thin watered green, and you must stare to see the faint dermatoglyphic patterns which show you fly over water. Off Bimini, speedboats passed over the blue like smoke-tailed rockets crossing the heavens. "There's Miami," said Johnson.

And it was the Florida coast. Flat land skeined with sheets of flat water. Groups of skyscrapers white and polished as eye-teeth passing below us, surrounded by vacant stretches of plain and of water, and the stubble of acres of houses, set in palm trees and blue pools and a sparkling mosaic of cars.

"There is no reason," said Johnson, "why any one of you shouldn't have a fully sodded lot there in Leisureville."

"Leisureville is rather attractive," said Lady Edgecombe. "I was shown over it once. Or maybe it was Canongate-on-the-Links. They're very careful whom they admit."

"But you have your perfect setting, Denise," said Johnson. "On Great Harbour Cay."

"Denise misses the company a bit, off season," Sir Bartholomew said into the ensuing small silence.

I had been neglecting him. I said, "You'll be in very good hands. I shall see you settled and comfortable, and I shall be on call if they want me. You'll be surprised how simple it all is."

"I daresay," he said, and smiled at me. With his wife there, and the two pilots, nothing could be said. But he must be wondering, as Johnson was wondering, why after all these years should he be singled out for attack now? And for such sordid and painful attacks, as if personal malice were in some way involved, not simply the task of one agent to dispose of another.

Johnson said, "You've got the best of it, you fully sodded lot in Miami. I've got to go and be buddy to forty society ladies and gentlemen I've had the misfortune to immortalize on canvas. I'll expect you both at the Fontainebleau whenever you're free. Denise. Doctor MacRannoch. Ask for Timpson, my agent. Nice chap. Lives in Miami. Made of fine bonded copper with a ver-digrised patina."

It was in fact a surprisingly accurate description of the bronzed Timpson, who stepped forward to meet Lady Edgecombe and

76

myself inside the undulating white frontage of the Hotel Fontainebleau later that morning. After the cool of the hospital, the sun
blazed on the flights of white steps leading up to the two sets of
doors; inside Lady Edgecombe sighed with relief in the vast space
of the lounge with its islands of armchairs and tables on several
acres of squared marble floor. Above us blazed oval chandeliers
the size of small swimming pools; the room, if you could call it
a room, seemed crowded with American citizens in wigs and dark
glasses purring at one another, with cigarettes spiraling smoke
from their knuckle rings.

Mr. Timpson, however, was a personable middle-aged man in
a neat dark suit, with strong deductive powers: he had us singled
out in a moment, and taking my medical bag, drew us through
the heavier socializing to the back of the hall, which was on a
lower level. On the way Lady Edgecombe, I noticed, acquired
a glass of champagne, while I lifted a tumbler of iced water. I
had just noticed, through the throng, that the back wall of the big
room was a gallery, on which some forty large paintings had been
hung against velvet drapes, when I became aware of a tall, cool,
scented presence, blocking my way like a single tree trunk in a
mill race.

"Don't tell me," an English voice said with amusement — I
swear with amusement, "that you're Beltanno MacRannoch?"

"I am Doctor Douglas MacRannoch," I said automatically.
She was five foot ten inches at least, although her shoulders had
rounded with age, giving her tallness and thinness an extreme of
dry elegance. Her hair was still black mixed with gray, and expensively dressed over the prominent bones of her face. Her eyes
in particular were extremely fine and heavily made up: she also
wore a bright lipstick. Her head and all of her body were
shrouded in blue and silver silk voile, caught with a large sapphire
brooch on one shoulder. None of her rings, I should judge, was

77

worth less than five thousand pounds. "The Begum Akbar?" I added.

To rent Castle Rannoch — its staff, its shooting and fishing, season after season at James Ulric's price — requires, I have always known, a very special kind of bank balance. The kind that comes with deceased Indian princes, for example. The Begum, I had heard, had spent her brief married life in north India, far from the fields of her native Huntingdonshire, and on her husband's death had not remarried, but had amused herself acquiring houses in different parts of the globe, and surrounding herself with neurotic idiopaths like my father, whose excesses appeared to amuse her.

I had kept well out of her way. I thought of the files on James Ulric's desk and positioned myself to follow in Mr. Timpson's closing wake. "How nice to meet you," I said. "I'm afraid I must rush. Mr. Johnson is expecting us."

"I know. He told me," said the Begum. She smiled at Lady Edgecombe. She had small, irregular teeth and a firm chin, which gave her smile a strong element of attraction. Lady Edgecombe's trim eyebrows lifted and she smiled back. The Begum said, "I'm hoping you'll both come and look at my portrait. I'm the Begum Akbar, known as Thelma usually."

"I know. I'm Denise Edgecombe. I live on Great Harbour Cay. May I say," said Bart Edgecombe's wife, "how perfectly lovely your sari is."

I didn't say anything at all. I was brooding over the dishonesty of Johnson Johnson. He had said nothing to me about the Begum being here. Or of having painted the Begum for that matter. I began to wonder what else he had neglected to tell me.

"Come," said the Begum. "It is the third portrait on the left, between the duchess and the governor. The press came a short while ago to photograph us all standing beside our commissions. It's a kind of club, isn't it? The sitters of Johnson."

I was silent, and so was Lady Edgecombe beside me. I don't suppose either of us had realized what a big name he was. Presumably all the paintings here had been lent back for the exhibition, and the subjects had come too, to drink champagne and be photographed and meet Johnson again. He had disappeared again in a welter of spectacle frames; Timpson equally had vanished. The Begum, exchanging smiles and waves and snatches of conversation as she swayed through the crowd, arrived with a certain iron persistence before her own portrait and tapped the silk shoulder of a long-haired young man standing before it. "Krishtof, I won't have you study it. It gives too much away," said the Begum. "You have met Beltanno and Lady Edgecombe, have you not? Dear Krishtof is coming to stay as my house-guest."

The Turkish dancer. So that was why he had flown to Nassau. He was on his way to stay with the Begum. "I have not only met Lady Edgecombe: I have danced with her," said Krishtof Bey cheerfully. The Mongoloid face gave as little away as his hostess's: the slanting eyes smiled in a manner one could describe without whimsy as evil. His hand, when he gave it to me, was long and thin and stringy with muscle. He wore a cinnamon tunic and trousers with gold Turkish slippers and the discreet bodyguard of his friends, I noticed, was between him and the crowd. I said, "Has Johnson painted you as well, Mr. Krishtof?"

"This he is going to do," said the dancer. "In the nude, do you think, Doctor MacRannoch? Or with one small flower? 'The Après-midi d'un Faun'?"

" 'The Miracle in the Gorbals'?" I suggested.

He was not abashed. "But nothing is out with a doctor's experience! The naked man you have seen in his thousands."

"True," I agreed. "Mainly cadavers."

"And that is how you think of us?" He came very close, with

79

his almond eyes trying to mesmerize mine. "Cold? Unresponsive? Repellent?"

The Begum chuckled. Lady Edgecombe, beside me, was visibly out of patience. "On the contrary," I said shortly. "There are few things more beautiful than the blood vascular system of the grown human body. Until you have dissected two cutaneous arterio-venous anastomoses, you have no idea what elegance is."

"Give up, Krishtof," said Johnson's deep, comfortable voice just behind us. "You can't outplay Doctor MacRannoch. We've all had a shot."

Krishtof Bey had retreated slightly, but the almond eyes had never left mine. He was smiling. "Pardon, but I do not think," he said gently, "you have yet found the proper approach."

"Lunch," said Johnson hastily.

In the end the Begum took us all to lunch at the Columbus Hotel. I made a telephone call, out of duty, to the Jackson, heard that Sir Bartholomew had been successfully treated and was resting, and after a quick comb through my hair, finally joined the Begum, Lady Edgecombe, Krishtof, and Johnson on the seventeenth floor.

The dining room on the seventeenth floor of the Columbus is three quarters plate glass, and its windows look down on the streaming cars of Biscayne Boulevard and the palm tops of Bayfront Park behind. Beyond that is a blue sheet of water, crossed by the ranks of long, low white bridges which lead to Dodge Island and the rest of Miami on the horizon.

The others were ready to leave the cocktail lounge when I arrived. I told them the news from the hospital while Krishtof Bey got me a tomato juice. I carried it into the dining room, where we sat beside the scarlet swagged curtains and rhapsodized over the view.

Or rather the other four did. Sipping my tomato juice, I reflected that it resembled nothing so much as a child's cut-out cardboard picture book, brought me once by a dim MacRannoch aunt from Australia. Before us, the swing bridge opened regularly to allow handsome white yachts to speed on their way: between its arches tuna fishing boats were constantly sprinting, like foreshortened twin prams. Beyond the first bridge a sea plane skimmed down and landed, taxiing across to its berth on Dodge Island. A scarlet helicopter, buzzing past the hotel, crossed the inlet and made for the small field, air sock flying, which we had already noted on our way here. You could see the Disneyland scenic railway: the best description of the concrete complication of freeways which we had just finished crossing.

The sun shone out of a cloudless blue sky on all that clean, luxurious activity, and I drank my tomato juice grimly, thinking of Bart Edgecombe lying in the hospital, and Pentecost with the gun in his hand, and the fire swirling up Johnson's borrowed jacket. Krishtof Bey, as if he had read my thoughts, said gently, "What caused the upset to Sir Bartholomew, Doctor MacRannoch? Was it ever found out?"

It was a natural sort of inquiry. That is, I suppose it was a natural sort of inquiry. I schooled my face, but I judged my pulse rate all the same to be in the region of 80 to 90 a minute. "I don't suppose we shall ever know quite for certain," I replied. "But it seems fairly sure the fault was his own. Some sandwiches which had become tainted." I spoke quietly, out of Lady Edgecombe's range of hearing. No one had mentioned crab sandwiches to the woman who made them.

"Ah? Then do not let us dwell on it," said Krishtof Bey cheerfully. "Here is the menu."

I have felt hungrier. We had palm hearts, a matter of flaccid white tubing, followed by prime rib steak and apple pie à la mode.

À la mode in the United States means ice cream. European Plan means a bedroom reservation without meals. Modified American Plan means bed, breakfast, and dinner. Full American Plan means bed, breakfast, lunch, and dinner. I well remember my father's reply when on his first hotel stay in Nassau he was asked whether he was Modified American.

"Why so grave, Beltanno?" the Begum suddenly said. "Sir Bartholomew is better; we are eating pleasant food in good company; and the whole day and night lie before you. The hospital doesn't expect you, does it, until tomorrow? Then you are on holiday. What is your favorite pursuit?"

"Golf," I said. I felt overrelaxed. Indeed, I had to exert myself to say it quite clearly. Lady Edgecombe showed, for some reason, slight apprehension. I added, "But surely, Begum, Mr. Brady has told you of our game on Paradise Island?"

"He told me, yes," said the Begum. She hesitated, as if reflecting how to phrase her next comment. "He feared you considered the whole encounter as a means to force an introduction to your father. I hope he was wrong," said the Begum calmly. "He is an extremely talented young man, with no need to solicit his orders. Furthermore, I gather it is not at all likely that James Ulric will see Castle Rannoch again."

I was angry, but I took time to make myself clear. "It's not impossible," I said. "If his condition should stabilize. If he avoids exerting himself with large-scale entertainments, for example."

"But how dull he would find it," the Begum said, smiling. "Shall I quote René Sand? 'The place of medicine is in the stream of life, not on its banks.' And that applies not only to the MacRannoch but to his daughter. I embarrass you, Beltanno. But I wish you to be friends with my Mr. Brady. Did you know he was building a bridge for me?"

"How is it?" said Johnson.

The Begum said, "He thinks he can solve this last problem. But the currents are quite impossible, you know. Everyone has tried it. But I think he will succeed."

Krishtof Bey's almond eyes were still watching me. He said, without moving them, "A bridge? But how exciting, Thelma! Where does it run from?"

"Lady Edgecombe will have seen it," the Begum said, smiling at us all with that regal tilt of her head. "Indeed, it will be quite spectacular when it is finished. It runs from my scrap of land to the nearest large island. It joins Crab Island to Great Harbour Cay."

"I didn't know," I said slowly, "that you lived so close to Great Harbour Cay?"

"Didn't you? But then, James Ulric hates Crab Island because it has no proper harbor," the Begum said. "I couldn't build him a landing strip, but at least I could give him a bridge. Do you think he will visit me now? Will you, Beltanno?"

I looked at her. "I am afraid," I said, "that working hours don't make such trips very easy. But it was kind of you to suggest it."

"But you get weekends?" Lady Edgecombe said unexpectedly. "Bart was saying you must get weekends. He wanted you to fly back with us to Great Harbour Cay and stay awhile. We owe a great deal to the doctor," she added apologetically to the Begum.

"But of course. And then she can come visit us," said the Begum with satisfaction. "It is arranged." She signed the bill with a flourish; it went into three figures. "Now, shall we go? Johnson, you have to go back to your egocentric display?"

"I'm a working man," said Johnson. "If I weren't, you wouldn't have that historic painting to show for it. Like Doctor

MacRannoch, I have to clear my desk before I come and loll on Crab Island."

"You're going to stay with the Begum?" I said. I was suspicious. Suddenly the center of equilibrium had shifted quite away from Nassau and the United Commonwealth Hospital. Victim, suspects — all the protagonists in this threatening disaster seemed to be slipping away, to Crab Island. To Great Harbour Cay. Or nearly all. I thought of Sergeant Trotter.

Johnson said, "Krishtof Bey has asked me to paint him, and I'm tempted, but you know what a sartorial dropout I am. Do you all dress at Gina Fratini?"

"We don't dress at all," the Begum said in her calm way.

"Or just a little rose sometimes," said Krishtof Bey, slanting his faun's eyes at me.

And I made a discovery. I knew why my enunciation was giving me trouble, why my limbs were ataxic, my responses badly impaired. Like poor Sir Bartholomew, I had been forced to ingest foreign material. My tomato juice had been doctored with vodka. My tomato juice from Krishtof Bey.

I do not refuse alcohol because I cannot drink alcohol. I refuse it because it is a frivolity I cannot afford. While therefore I will not pretend that the look I cast the dancer was friendly, I rose to my feet at the end of that meal with perfect success to say good-bye to Johnson and Krishtof Bey, who were returning to the exhibition. I then accepted the Begum's invitation to attend to routine comfort in her suite. Lady Edgecombe came with us.

Since routine comfort with Lady Edgecombe appeared to entail stripping off the entire supra-coating of creams from her hairline to her jawbone and replacing it with a similar one, the Begum and I were left alone in her sitting room a long time. Mr. Frost appeared on the television. She switched him off. "Well, Bel-

84

tanno," she said, sitting down in expensive folds of azure and silver. "So you don't drink and you don't smoke and you aren't interested in people. No wonder the MacRannoch is behaving like a mad broker in a sweat-box stock exchange. Why won't you let him spend his money on you? Pride?"

I put my bag neatly between my feet and sat back. "For reasons that seem good and sufficient," I said.

"And isn't it normal in extreme cases to take a second opinion?" the Begum said.

"It is," I said. "But only from qualified persons."

She smiled. I had expected her to get up and leave me. But instead she murmured, "But James Ulric has asked me to marry him. Didn't you know? Repeatedly."

That was all I needed. A bloody mother as well. I beg your pardon. The vodka. I said, "And you've refused him?"

"I have refused to consider it," said the Begum, "until I met you first."

I sat and stared at her. Because the implications of that struck me for the very first time. My father could have no further children. The Begum, in any case, was well past the reproductive years and had no children from her previous marriage. And that meant that the combined fortunes of the Begum and my father would descend eventually to me.

No wonder she wanted to meet me. To influence me. To present me. To marry me off to some effing man. I beg your pardon.

I said, "It may help you to make up your mind if I say I have no intention of marrying."

"I know," said the Begum thoughtfully. "You're scared of not being top dog."

"I am unwilling," I said calmly, "to spend the rest of my life tied to inferior company."

"Does it follow?" said the Begum reflectively. "I wouldn't say that the company of poor dear James is all that superior. And what about Johnson?"

One of the anterolateral muscles of my abdomen, whose name I could not quite place at the moment, produced a soft thud. I said, "I am talking of viable probabilities."

"I'm talking of liking people," said the Begum. "Ah, here is Lady Edgecombe. How charming. Beltanno, all this elegance must not be wasted. Come. Get ready quickly, and leave that ridiculous bag on the floor. Lady Edgecombe and I are going to show you Miami."

The first language in Miami is of course Spanish: the shop girls discuss you in it, the cinemas advertise their program *Hoy* and the drugstores sell *perros calientes* as well as the jumbo dog sauerkrauts of everyday life. The admonitions on the freeway from the airport are however wholly American: KEEP OFF THE MEDIAN. WALK. DON'T WALK. HAVE A NICE DAY.

To be wished a nice day by a bored distributive trades employee is an American compulsion which never fails to incense me, as do the personal good wishes of junior disc jockeys relayed over the radio at home. The ultimate end of mankind is not necessarily to have itself a good day. I was not having a good day.

I was being dragged by the Begum Akbar and Lady Edgecombe through the nerve center of the Sunshine State. The impossibility of guessing from one moment to the next what would catch the Begum's fancy both heightened my blood pressure and confused my recollection of the hours which were to follow.

The infinity of possible entertainment was frightening. So were the placards: ROLLER GAMES. FLORIDA JETS VERSUS NEW YORK BOMBERS. THE BOOM BOOM ROOM. SAMMY DAVIS, JUNIOR. MINI ADULT SHOW FOR THE LIBERAL MINDED. GEORGIE PORGIE

AND THE CRY BABIES. DEAUVILLE, HOTEL OF THE STARS. MIAMI INTERNATIONAL BOAT SHOW, SUNDAY THROUGH WED. (Was that where Johnson had gone?) ADULT VILLAGE OF GARDEN APARTMENTS. (What adults, for goodness sake?)

I remember big shopping blocks like New York. I remember a freeway built over the sea, with pelicans flying like dirty washing in the blue sky, and expensive houses set among palm trees. I remember endless shops selling thin fancy clothing set among The House of Pancakes and Big Daddy's and Lum's Famous Lumburgers, and small packed hotels with sweating guests sitting out in the porch. I remember avenues of hotels and apartments which were the living prototype of every agency illustration from London to Australia: soaring foreshortened up to the sky behind their floodlit strip of bushes and palms, their banded balconies, their ribbed walls, their double-lit pierced concrete façades, their rows of twenty-foot bronze male caryatids, their buttressed porches underlit by a hundred cut lamps, with the Chevrolets, the Cadillacs, the Chryslers, the bronze soft-top Buicks nosing like ants up the drive to the steps, and groups of people in evening dress being handed in. The apartments had names: Ivanhoe, Kenilworth. The Starlight Room floated by: a galaxy pinned by a roof to the top of a skyscraper building. On the left, gleams of water with white motor cruisers lined up.

Then as the night darkened and we drove north through the red and green and blue neon lighting, Hollywood Art School design took the tourist trade over. The buildings on either side were lower and had dramatic legends and labels: *Vagabonds. Hawaii. Sahara,* with two groups of life-sized figures with camels. Floodlit fountains and jets. A stagecoach with six horses. A series of thatched buildings with green-lit jungly pools and cascades. *Two swimming pools. Air-conditioned.* French motifs. Old English motifs. *Burlesk.* More *burlesk.* Darkness.

87

"Beltanno?" the Begum said at one point. "Have you fallen into a stupor?"

I forget what I said.

They took me to a nightclub. Johnson joined us there. I stared at him in his suede tie with the threads still hanging out where he had cut off the nude, and he grinned and said: "Krishtof Bey has gone to bed with a hot water bottle. I think." And ordered us supper.

We didn't talk during supper. You can't, through two electric guitars, drums, three trumpets, and one saxophone. We were blighted with polyhedral whirling chromium balls and more ultraviolet. The nudes were dressed as sixteen Jean Harlows; in the next scene they rode motor bikes in crash helmets and boots. One of them had quite the most beautiful abdominal scar I think I have seen. I had a tomato juice. "What have you done to her?" said Johnson to the Begum.

The Begum looked at me and smiled. I paid no attention. "Given her a little concentrated experience," she said. "I think she is tired."

"All right. But I insist on one more thing," said Johnson. "Beltanno, how would you like to make yourself some money?"

My view of him was not very clear, but I got the words out all right: "What do you mean?"

"Dog racing," said Johnson.

I think I protested. I am not in principle against gambling; I simply cannot afford it. But my protests seemed to be overridden. It was in any case hard to keep track of what they were all saying in the crosslunge of American voices. *It's going to be lousy. So we should go somewhere else? . . . This real dumb blonde . . . Right? Righty . . . So I wouldn't even go there no more . . . Like I used to like candy . . . I tell you, I'm going to lose control of myself.*

That rang a bell. I thought hazily: damn it . . . More vodka in the tomato juice? But Krishtof Bey wasn't with us. *I like a tight little ass,* someone said. *She's got an ass like a tight little brick.*

"Come on, Beltanno," said Johnson.

The Hollywood dog track is a large, brightly lit family stadium between West Palm Beach and Miami. It is clean, cheerful, and well serviced, and full of merry neighborhood groups in fresh dresses and sweaters drinking cola and buying chili dogs, as a change from *perros calientes,* at the well-stocked snack stalls. Johnson got us seats in the upper tier, which looks down on the round floodlit track with a tidy green plot in the center, and got us some programs.

Lady Edgecombe disappeared to restore the natural bloom on her face. The Begum also retired, but returned with her bag full of betting slips. She and Johnson had a discussion. I focused on the program, which contained a great deal of valuable information such as WIN: *Your dog must finish first;* and less obvious things such as QUINIELA: *Your dog must finish first and second.*

I said aloud, "I haven't a dog."

Johnson put an arm behind my shoulder blades and said, "Beltanno, you are my utterly favorite suppressed doctor, but we mustn't overdo things. Choose a dog and let me place a bet for you, and then Thelma will take you down and give you some air."

I felt the Begum look at me critically. "She seems perfectly happy," she said.

"Yes, but I'm not," said Johnson. "In fact, we are due a little talk, you and I, in a moment. Beltanno, choose a dog."

I focused. "Pally Loo-loo?" I said. It was the first dog on the list, and I was simply trying to discover if it was true, but

89

Johnson took me up. "Pally Loo-loo it shall be. It doesn't need to be much. Ten dollars?"

I frowned. Ten dollars is ten dollars. On the other hand, I had two free meals to take into account. I hauled my handbag up and got out two five-dollar bills. "Right," said Johnson. "Thelma, you are a dangerous Begum."

"Not at all," said the Begum serenely. "I shall take her downstairs."

Which was how we came to be near the turnstile when the Negro rushed in from the parking lot, calling for help.

He wanted a doctor. My head had cleared enough by then to register that. I felt the Begum's hand on my arm, but I couldn't have stopped. It is a conditioned reflex, and nothing whatever, I believe, to do with one's personal ethos. One hears a call for medical aid and one runs.

So I called back and raced out of the dog track entrance after the Negro. He ran ahead through the parked cars, gesticulating and shouting hoarsely over his shoulder. Someone had been run over, I gathered. I hoped the Begum would have the sense to summon an ambulance. I regretted, for the first time, that I had left my medical bag at the Columbus.

The man disappeared around the corner of the vast car lot. I followed. For a moment I lost sight of him; then I glimpsed him far ahead, struggling through the dark mass of cars.

I had started to follow when something heavy struck me a violent blow on the base of my skull. I became quite insensible.

Chapter 6

MY FIRST REACTION, on waking sometime later in Johnson's grip, was to say, "Where is the patient?"

My second was to realize that I was lying there in the dog track parking lot, clad in nothing at all but my underwear. A pain radiated from the base of the cranium through my entire nervous system. I felt weak and surprisingly poorly.

"The patient is you," said Johnson. "The whole thing was a trick to get you out here. It took us hours to locate you. Beltanno, we're going to lift you into the back of the car and take you up to the Jackson. I don't think anything disturbing has happened, but I'd like them to check."

"What do you mean, disturbing?" I said. My voice was hoarse.

"I mean disturbing above the neck, B. Douglas MacRannoch," said Johnson's deep voice with amusement. "My God, with all that underwear, the man would need pliers."

It was, I felt, a remark in bad taste. I was still brooding over it when Johnson, with a number of helpers, carried me into the back of his car. The Begum's face, distinctly anxious, was visible in the background, and Lady Edgecombe's, bearing an appearance of anxiety which seemed to cover something quite different.

If I hadn't thought it unlikely, even for Lady Edgecombe, I would have believed her amused.

Then I caught sight of myself in the car mirror, and all was explained. She *was* amused. She was having trouble in fact not to scream out with laughter. For I had not only been divested of clothing by my attacker: my hair had been cut off in irregular bristles all over my scalp.

Vanity is not one of my sins. But I prefer, like the next person, to be brushed, well washed, and tidy. The near-bald rag doll I saw in that mirror was the sharpest blow I suppose I had ever suffered to a pride I knew very well how to protect. My face grew hot, and I dug the nails of both hands into my palms. It is possible to control every normal physical manifestation, given enough will power. Coughs, sneezes, hiccoughs. And tears.

Johnson said, "Do you mind?" and in one smooth movement passed over a bill and slid the bandanna from the neck of one of his helpers. He bound it loosely, kerchief-style around my head and said: "You've got a bad cut, Beltanno, but there's nothing science and art together won't cure . . . Thelma, I think you and Lady Edgecombe should go back to the Columbus. I'll ring you when they've had a look at Doctor MacRannoch. And no United Commonwealth for you tomorrow, my girl," to me.

But he was wrong. I shared the services of the Jackson Memorial Hospital that night with Sir Bartholomew Edgecombe, and had four stitches in the back of my head, with no serious concussive complications. By morning I was able to discuss my return to Nassau with Johnson, and also, unimpeded by all but a headache, the reasons behind the attack.

"I don't know," he said. I must have looked an odd sight, in a hospital bedgown, with a white bandage encircling a black near-bald scalp, but he paid no attention. "The *don't do it again* brigade, one would think. But why? Do they think you're going to follow Edgecombe to Great Harbour Cay?"

"Lady Edgecombe invited me," I said.

"All the same, it seems to lay a great deal of stress on your undoubtedly efficient role as guardian angel. Or are they worried not because you might save him from another attack, but because you might spot something a layman might miss? You'll note that in everything they do they are very careful not to come into the open. No overt murder attempts have ever been made. Everything has been carefully designed to look like an accident."

"I couldn't go to Great Harbour Cay," I said stiffly. "I understand you think I might be of some use, but I really cannot risk leaving my post any longer. I do depend on it, as you know, for my living."

"Oh," said Johnson, but not at all with the inflection I expected. The bifocal glasses flashed, and he got up and began in a leisurely manner patting the pockets of his now severely creased suit. "That reminds me. Do you remember Pally Loo-loo?"

I stared at him with a great deal of misgiving.

"You don't remember," said Johnson.

"No, I don't," I said sharply. "And by the way, who was it who kept putting vodka into my — "

Johnson stopped, with his hand on his pocketbook. "That's another mysterious thing," he said. "I assumed it was the Begum, but she says it wasn't. And Beltanno, how do you know it was vodka?"

I stared at him. "I don't, for sure," I said at length. "But it's the only tasteless strong drink I could think of. Wasn't it?"

"It may well have been," Johnson said. "I just wondered. Because, you know, tomato juice with sauce in it can disguise almost anything. But let's get back to Pally Loo-loo."

93

"What is Pally Loo-loo?" I said. I was becoming annoyed.

"She's a bitch," Johnson said. "Owner: Marty Stootzer. Kennel: Marty Stootzer. Trainer: Willy Emmet. Whelped: June 1964, Pally-itzy out of Pot Pot. Post weight: sixty-five pounds. Record in last six races: *Collide first turn; Steady fade; Tiring; Brief lead; Weakened; Gamely*. She's won you three thousand four hundred dollars."

"What!" I said. My stitches cracked.

Johnson finished counting green dollar bills onto the bedcover. "Three thousand four hundred. With a record like that, what do you think the odds were?"

I sat with my mouth open. I was still sitting like that when he waved, grinning, and began to go out of the room. I collected myself just in time to pack them away before the Begum arrived. I daresay my headache was still there, but I can't say I felt it.

The sari was green, embroidered with peacocks today, and the Begum's brown-shadowed eyes were, I think, quite genuinely solicitous. She sat down with not quite her usual grace and said, "Beltanno. My dear child. If only I had stopped you."

"Well. It might have been a genuine call," I said.

"The nurse tells me there will be no lasting effects. But you don't mean to go back to Nassau today?" She actually looked worried.

I said, "Really, there's nothing to keep me. Sir Bartholomew and Lady Edgecombe and Mr. Johnson are going, and I ought to accompany my patient back. I have to make my report."

The Begum said sharply, "Beltanno, this is not economy, is it? The hospital are not so short of funds that they would force you to pay your own fare if you don't take a free trip with Johnson?"

"I'm not worrying," I said, and smiled cautiously. "Didn't you hear of my windfall?"

The Begum regarded me. "From Lady . . . ?"

She didn't finish. It seemed too unlikely, I suppose. "No. From a bitch," I said, "called Pally Loo-loo."

I suppose I was slightly lightheaded. But I must say it gave me great pleasure to say it.

Before she left the Begum gave me two parcels. As I drew breath to refuse them civilly she sat down again on the edge of my bed and spoke first. "Beltanno. I gave you an unpleasant day yesterday. Some of it wasn't my doing, but I did take you right out of your depth and keep you there for longer than I had any right to. It was like watching a good car trying to run with the choke out. This is my way of saying I'm sorry. If you don't like them, don't use them. Throw them away. You've got money now to buy something else. But it would please me very much if you took them." She stopped, and smiled that sidelong, regal smile. "And Beltanno. There are no strings attached."

I smiled a little, cautiously, back. "Or bridges?" I said.

The first parcel contained a straight sleeveless dress in plain Ottoman silk with a small high collar and some interesting anatomical seaming about the bust. The other contained a wig of dark hair, the exact shade of my own. But longer and fuller, with two little sweeps over the cheekbones. I drew the curtains around my bed and slipped it on rapidly, then took it off and thrust it under the bedclothes. It was not my face. But I needed something to travel in. Already, since I awakened, I had suffered the open smiles of every damned person who had come into my room. I couldn't go to Miami Airport with the Edgecombes and Johnson and look like a freak.

I could wear a hat. But a hat in hot weather? And I hadn't got a hat.

I hadn't got a dress either. They'd searched the parking lot, and it had vanished. All I had was a good strong brassiere, a pair of sensible underpants, a girdle, a pair of 30-denier stockings, a cotton slip, and my Dr. Scholl sandals.

When the moment for discharge came, I put them all on, and the Begum's blue dress on top. My slip showed four inches below it, and so had to come off. The ridge of my girdle, invisible under my own modest dress, also showed through the silk. My girdle had to come off, and with them my stockings. I wore my wig, my underpants, brassiere, the blue dress, and my sandals, and I felt indecently exposed: a brunette Jean Harlow. I went through all the necessary formalities, and joined Sir Bartholomew and Lady Edgecombe, by arrangement, in the entrance hall.

Sir Bartholomew was looking slightly drawn but a better color, I thought, than when I had last seen him. I realized he was staring at me, and then that Lady Edgecombe was drifting toward me, after a moment's frozen assessment, like an Afghan hound sighting a color supplement photographer. I said icily, "The Begum kindly brought me some things for the journey."

Lady Edgecombe came to a halt. "My dear. I'd never have *believed* it," she said. Bart Edgecombe, just behind, put a hand on her shoulder. He said to me, "Maybe you're sensitive about the change in your appearance. But let me say it's very pretty."

He had been really a very reasonable patient. "I'm afraid I don't worry very much about my appearance, one way or the other," I said. But not too sharply.

He made a movement of acknowledgment. "Your time is valuable. Of course. But do take the trouble sometimes, Doctor MacRannoch . . . It can be very pleasant for others."

His wife smiled at him and I thought, smiling myself, that there was something to be said for taking the trouble to be diplomatic as well. It might be worth trying.

At the airport we met Johnson and boarded the Piper Twin Otter. Whether he knew of the Begum's present I couldn't detect; I rather thought not. But he merely tilted his head and said, "Very nice," and then got on with the business of helping to stow Lady Edgecombe's myriad cases. My medical bag, retrieved from the Columbus, was already there. The Begum and Krishtof Bey, I learned, were leaving that afternoon for Crab Island via Great Harbour Cay and Johnson himself was joining them shortly.

"Leaving Sir Bartholomew in Nassau?" I said.

"Don't be tart," Johnson said. "It's not our fault we like you in drag. I shall stay in Nassau till Bart gets his clearance and then fly him to Great Harbour Cay with Denise. Today, I hope. You know they still want you to stay with them?"

Sir Bartholomew had brought this up on the way to the airport. I drew breath to restate my arguments, but the engine started and the subject was dropped. Miami and its waterways sank far below us: the golden webbed dome where Flipper played skittles daily . . . the hotels . . . the apartments . . . the dog track.

I smiled. I was still smiling vaguely when coffee came, and we saw below us the white curb of sand give way to the wide purple road of the Gulf Stream. I gazed out of the window, thinking, until we landed.

James Ulric was standing in front of the long sunshine-yellow block of airport buildings at Nassau looking furious in candy-striped Bermuda shorts. As we stood waiting by the plane for our luggage, he came stumping across on his spider legs, passed me, stopped, and whirled into reverse like an egg beater. "Great Jumping Christ," he said. "The creature looks almost human."

"Thank you, Father," I said. "I am glad to hear it. I have decided, by the way, to marry Mr. T. K. MacRannoch. If the Begum names the day, we could make it a foursome."

For a moment I thought he was going to jump straight into status asthmaticus, but he relaxed out of sheer spite. "Bloody undersexed doctor," he said. "You've never met him. You wouldn't marry him. And if you did, what'd you live on? Not a penny of my money or Thelma's is going to that ill-gotten Nip."

I picked up my case. "Then," I said airily, "I'll have to start betting on dogs," and walked past him into the airport. Edgecombe had already pushed his wife off. Only Johnson, I noticed, had remained a blank spectator of the whole petty scene.

But he didn't come after me and neither of course did my father, so I got the Edgecombes into the United Commonwealth on my own. I pulled off the wig in the airport lavatory on the way. I looked freakish all right, but that had nothing to do with my qualifications. I kept the Begum's dress on because I had nothing else to wear.

The hospital of course was an obstacle course of cries and giggles and people running after me and trying to summon the courage to turn me about. You would think that after all they had seen in those wards, they would find a cropped head beneath their attention. Not so.

At any rate, Sir Bartholomew got his final examination; his clothes were collected and his wife's from her hotel, and they were seen off at last for the airport, where Johnson awaited them. He was being as good as his word. The Twin Otter would fly them all to Great Harbour Cay. And from there, Johnson would sail to Crab Island.

Sir Bartholomew stood by the car a long time trying to persuade me to fly with them. I convinced him, I think, that a doctor's job is not one which can be left indiscriminately. But I promised that I would ring him the first leave I got, and perhaps spend a weekend or longer at Great Harbour Cay. Then I went back to the hospital and was summoned before the chief medical officer, who asked what the hell I meant by coming on duty while I looked like a tough case of ringworm.

I remember looking blankly at him and saying that I felt quite all right.

"Maybe," he said. "But McGonagall, I am less concerned with your medical health than with your ludicrous appearance. In this eminent hospital, as you are aware, the nursing staff is far from stable."

"But —"

" — and far from according you sympathetic respect, is liable to ignore you while rolling about in fits of helpless hysteria . . . Well?"

"You're short staffed," I pointed out. I refrained from adding that the number of competent medical officers in my view was not very high.

He gazed at me. "No doubt we shall have to close down," he said. "But in spite of that, Doctor MacRannoch, I wish you to take ten days' sick leave."

I fear I spoke with some sharpness. "My hair will hardly have made much progress, Doctor, in ten days."

"No," he said. "But I feel ten days' peace will give us the strength to confront you. Close the door on the outside."

I had turned on my heel when he called out, "Couldn't you wear a wig?" But when I looked over my shoulder, he merely shook his head and answered himself: "No, you couldn't."

I was hungry, but James Ulric was at home. I put on my wig. I got out the Ford, and rattled down to park it off Bay Street, and went through the dark Jacobean doors of El Morocco and had a cold turkey sandwich, which in Nassau is a whole turkey with salad and bread somewhere around the perimeter. The girl, who was forty-two, overweight, and had varicose veins, pushed the bunny frill up from her brow and asked what I wanted to drink.

An advertisement in front of my nose for Grand Bahama said: COME PLAY ON THE ADULT ISLAND.

I said, "What have you got?"

I am aware that this does not sound like the climacteric it actually was. The waitress intoned a long and incomprehensible list of alcoholic drinks. I said, "What's a Bossa Nova?"

"It's a dance, ma'am," she said. "This drink's named itself after it. Rum, apricot brandy, and pineapple juice, ma'am. Very special."

"I'll have one," I said.

A man, a good-looking man, said, "Is this anyone's seat?" and I said, "I'm sorry. I'm expecting a friend."

There were plenty of other seats. Equally, it was obvious that I was halfway through my meal. He smiled and moved off. The Bossa Nova came and I drank a third of it off. I had brains, good health, and clean habits. Why the hell should these go for nothing unless I had a trendy dress and hair style as well?

I drank the second third of my Bossa Nova. It was rather good, with a deep fruity taste. I wondered how I could get hold of T. K. MacRannoch.

I drank the last of it, and pulled out my wallet in a casual way to flutter dollars onto the bill. Dollars, in the plural. I had to put a fork on top to keep them from blowing away. Then I left and got into the Ford and rattled off to the villa.

James Ulric had gone. I knew it by the singing and laughter going on in the kitchen, which stopped as I unlocked the door. Daffodil, our housekeeper, trotted in and said, "Oh Miss Beltanno, how smart you look, Miss Beltanno . . ."

I cut it short, though all the others were crushed in the doorway now, gaping. Father had packed, taken the car and gone to the airport: to fly to Great Harbour Cay and Crab Island.

Lost in slightly hazed thought, I wandered alone through the house. Daffodil brought me coffee and I took it into the study. The files on the MacRannoch Gathering had gone.

So. The Begum was on Crab Island with Krishtof Bey and

Johnson, soon to be joined by my father. Sir Bartholomew and Lady Edgecombe were at Great Harbour Cay, the next island, where Wallace Brady also stayed. Sooner or later, if I knew my father, to one island or the other would come every MacRannoch in the Bahamas and beyond.

Including T. K. MacRannoch, my father's heir. I thought of what I had said to my father. Said out of pique, I well knew: it was the single unthinkable outcome of all his maneuverings which he would never face. Through the female line, if I were to marry, all the blood and wealth of the MacRannochs would be safely transmitted to good Caucasian stock. But for me to marry his Japanese heir!

I laughed to myself, sitting there drinking my coffee, though guardedly. I remembered vaguely that alcohol is really not to be recommended after a blow on the head. It didn't seem to be having any effect. I wondered how I would strike T. K. Mac-Rannoch with my blue dress and my wig. All I knew of him was that he played golf.

I got up and looked for my golf bags. I got my old cloth suitcase and put into it three sets of clean underwear, my girdles, my stockings, my toilet bag, my pajamas, dressing gown and slippers, and my brush. I took out my brush.

Handkerchiefs. My Horrocks cotton. My Bri-nylon two-piece, which had been washed. My bathing suit, bathing cap, and towel. Two pairs of sandals and one pair of tie shoes. Two skirts and two shirts for golfing. One crepe dress with short sleeves for evening, and a cardigan, in case it was chilly. A plastic raincoat and headscarf . . . Sudden doubt. I added a small plastic hood.

The suitcase, of medium size, was quite full. I looked at it with quiet satisfaction and then with a shock caught sight of my new head in the mirror. The head didn't go with any of the clothes in the case.

Too bad, Beltanno. I shut the case and locked it, and lay down on the bed because my head had started to ache. I was wakened by the telephone ringing.

It was Sir Bartholomew Edgecombe, from Great Harbour Cay. "Doctor MacRannoch? I phoned the hospital and they say you're on sick leave. Are you all right? You are? How long are you to be off? Right," said Bartholomew Edgecombe. "Listen. A company plane from Great Harbour Cay is landing at four-thirty at Nassau. There are no tickets to buy and nothing to do. Just walk onto the plane, and you'll be taken care of. Denise and I want you here as our guest."

I didn't know about Denise, but unmistakably, Sir Bartholomew's voice was sincere. "It's very kind of you — " I began, when he broke in.

"I'm being selfish, not kind. What do you think it's worth to have my own private M.D. staying with me?" He sounded as if he were joking, but I knew that in a sense he did mean it. He added, "And if that isn't sufficient inducement, let me tell you that you won't be the only MacRannoch in sight."

I opened my mouth. "Oh?" I said.

"Yes. I had a look at the Tamboo register to see who'd arrived since I left and I see there's one of your clan dealing death on the golf course. Chap by the name of T. K. MacRannoch. Any relation? Or is it heresy to claim relationship to the clan chieftain's daughter?"

"Oh no," I said. "Father always says we should stand shoulder to shoulder, a single blood brotherhood. Coherent, that's us."

Bart Edgecombe laughed. "You certainly are, Doctor," he said. "Can we expect you then, on that plane?"

"Yes. And thank you," I said, holding the back of my head.

My emotions, to be candid, were exceedingly mixed. My life-long small-arms battle with the MacRannoch was one thing; the attempts on Sir Bartholomew's life another entirely. I was going to stay with the Edgecombes. And I had just received a blow on the head to dissuade me from doing this very thing. What was more, Johnson wouldn't even be present. Instead, I should have the company of one of our suspects. Wallace Brady, the engineer, lived and worked on Great Harbour Cay.

To protect myself I had my common sense. And the protection a doctor always carries in his medical bag. And the little Frommer, 6½ inches long, which Johnson had given me, to keep in my handbag. "Remember," he'd said cheerfully. "Aim for the right wing, in self-defense only. Corpses are tricky things to dispose of. And don't go anywhere lonely with less than two people."

Which was all very well. Then I remembered the blisters, and felt slightly penitent.

I approved his reticence. On the other hand, I supposed this was his profession. I went out for a session with Daffodil, and then placing my suitcase and two bags in the Ford Anglia, drove off to the airport to meet the 4:30 from Great Harbour Cay.

It was there already: a handsome blue and white DC–3 standing out in the sunlight, with a background of larger taxiing planes like moths on a windowpane. And standing at the foot of the steps waiting to board it was Sergeant Rodney Trotter. He wore a short-sleeved checkered shirt with a pair of smartly creased pale gray trousers, a neckerchief, and a smile of ineffable welcome.

"Doctor!" he shouted. "Here I was, getting a hang-up. Thought I was going on my lonesome."

I walked to the base of the steps before replying. "There seems to be plenty of time. Were you expecting me?"

"Yes! Sir Bartholomew said I'd have you for company. I'm on my way to the Begum's," said Trotter. He studied me with unconcealed interest. "They said I wouldn't know you, and my word, they were right. It's a sensation, Doctor MacRannoch."

I put a foot on the steps. "I'm beginning to wonder what I looked like before," I said freezingly. "Mother Goose?" And left him to heave in the luggage.

It didn't stop him in due course from sitting down on the sofa beside me. It was one of a facing pair in oatmeal with hide trim, and was equipped with three sets of safety belts. The rest of the plane was filled with single and double seats with matching small tables; the bar in white and daffodil stripes was accessibly placed in the center.

The saloon was close carpeted in maize tumble-twist with maize linen curtains to match and held about ten of us so far, I noticed. Two of the faces seemed familiar, but I wouldn't care to go further. I am not a devotee of the big or small screen. We fastened our belts and the engines increased their impact in decibels.

"Mr. Johnson mentioned the tattoo business, I believe," Sergeant Trotter roared in my ear.

The choice of subject at that moment appeared oddly capricious. I nodded.

His brown, vigorous face became wreathed with bonhomie and a certain tinge of relief. "It'll be a great opportunity," he shouted. "You know, they've never had a Highland Gathering? Never?"

Light broke. "You mean my father?"

He beamed. He nodded. The extraordinary noise slackened as we reached the end of the runway, and he was able to say in a moderate shout: "Well, the Begum anyway. She didn't want to say too much about it until she was sure of your father. But he's agreed, I'm glad to say; and here I am, off to Crab Island to plan it."

A tattoo? For the MacRannoch Gathering? On Crab Island? I stared at him in outraged disbelief. Locked in a trance of professional pleasure, he did not even observe it. "But don't you worry your head. Whatever way it's done, it'll be a sure-fire success. I've run tattoos every place in the world from gym stadia in Australia to old airfields in the back hills of India, and if anyone can get one off the ground, it's Rodney Trotter."

"I'm sure you can," I said. The engines roared painfully and we moved off. I waited until we were airborne and said, "Does the army pay you to do this, Sergeant Trotter?"

"In a way. I'm seconded," he said. "Six years in Aldershot and twenty-two years in Edinburgh: there can't be a man alive in the world today knows as much about tattoos as I do. We used to get people from all over the world — generals, even — coming to ask us how to put on a show as good as we did for Edinburgh. It got so that we hardly had time to lift our heads before someone was at us again: how do you do the seating, what do you feed the troops, how much lighting have the bandsman got to have, what do you do if it's raining . . ."

"So they decided it was cheaper to put you on circuit," I said.

"Well," said the sergeant. "A matter of public relations, they said. My brigadier does the big ones, or we do them together. And the little ones I get to myself."

"What does a little one cost?" I said. A well-made-up girl in a black dress had opened the bar and was moving from seat to seat taking orders.

For the first time Sergeant Trotter returned to the discretion of our earlier acquaintance. "Well, now; that's a matter for the Begum, once it's worked out," he said. "It was her idea, you know. Your dad had just dreamed up the idea of a Bahamian Gathering, and it was the Begum who thought of the tattoo."

"With a performance by Krishtof Bey?" I said impolitely. The stewardess bent over me and I ordered a Bossa Nova.

"I hope not," said Sergeant Trotter. He appeared to be looking at me with respect. He ordered a beer, and said, "You know why?"

"No," I said. It was beginning to turn out like Miami. Or maybe it was just a postconcussive syndrome. The drinks came, in plastic cups with large paper napkins. I took a sustaining draft of mine and said, "Why?"

Sergeant Trotter sat, cup in large hand, and fixed me with an inimical glare. "Because they go sick, that's why," he said. "Every time you've got a star performer, something happens. Like the six Arab legionnaires that was to trot their camels up and down in a war dance."

"Who got sick?" I said. "The Arabs or the camels?"

"Camels?" said the sergeant, and tipped down half his beer. "The camels never even got into the country. No license, see. So what do we do — we hire six more from a circus."

The Bossa Nova was sinking agreeably into my interior. "You did?" I said. "The army?"

"Well. The show must go on," said Sergeant Trotter. "And then one of them bloody legionnaires reports sick and they must have a reserve to go on, or else the pattern won't come right. So guess who's an Arab legionnaire."

"You," I guessed. It was easy.

He nodded violently. "All done up with black beard and nightie. And they'd sent the wrong bloody camels. There we were with saddles for one hump and the bastards had given us camels with two. We had to pad them with old socks. I've been a Canadian Mounty."

"You have?" I said.

"And a Turkish janissary. And a Danish cadet in one of them bellboy uniforms. I've been a Spahi and an American marine and an Evzone Greek Royal Guard. I was even a Gurkha once, with me bloody face blacked, but they had to take me out because I was two feet taller than the biggest of them. I've been everything but the Manchester Drum Majorettes."

I finished my drink. "In my opinion," I said carefully, "you'll end up in a psychiatric ward if you do that too often."

He finished his drink. "Do you think so?" he said worriedly. We thought about it in companionable silence as the plane circled and prepared to land on Great Harbour Cay.

I remember looking down on the island: the dense blue rippled sea blending to the familiar shades of apple green and emerald and biscuit where the white beaches ran out of the water, marked with a stitching of seaweed. The island was long, like a boomerang, with a long gently incurved golden beach above the knuckle, perfectly empty. The interior I saw only as low purple-green bushes, scored by a crosshatching of white, newly made roads and infiltrated here and there by the blue of the sea. Of people and houses, there was at first glance no sight at all.

A semitropical island paradise, the brochures had said. A splendid solitude, for those who seek it. A brilliant new sanctuary for sport. Deep sea fishing . . . swimming in warm clear waters . . . thinking long, quiet thoughts as you stroll the beach at evening. Sharpening your golf game.

We landed. "Come on," I said to Sergeant Trotter in sudden, pleasurable anticipation, and undoing my seat belt, strode along and climbed down into the hot, scented sunshine.

You see? Insidiously, the banana bird and the palm tree were already there, invisible in my subconscious. Merely waiting to integrate.

Chapter 7

THE AIRPORT AT GREAT HARBOUR CAY is neat, ornamental, and small, with palm trees, flower beds and an attractive low bungalow with a waterfall tinkling beside it, labeled H. M. CUSTOMS AND IMMIGRATION. A row of Mini-Mokes, a long green French bus, and a London taxi stood below the control tower, which was a picturesque open-plan affair consisting of a cone cedar-tiled roof set on stilts. A row of flags flapped slowly in a light breeze. A young Negro in a gray jacket with a jockey cap balanced on the flat of his nose said, "Doctor MacRannoch, ma'am? Sir Bartholomew sent me to meet you. Ain't you got no more luggage, Doctor MacRannoch?"

That was when I discovered my suitcase was missing. It took half an hour to check that it wasn't on board, and that it hadn't been mixed up with someone else's. Sergeant Trotter, his efficiency called into question, swore that he had put it into the hold himself at Nassau. It wasn't there. Someone had taken it off.

Since he showed signs of holding an immediate army inquiry, I said good-bye to Trotter and sent him off to pick up his boat for Crab Island. I elicited fresh assurances that my suitcase would be found and forthwith forwarded. I then got inside Sir Bartholomew's tropical Fiat beside my purse, my medical bag, and my golf clubs, and was driven to Sir Bartholomew's house.

Great Harbour Cay is an island just over seven miles long and less than two miles across, then undergoing transformation into a luxurious international playground for tropical sport, whose center was a private proprietary club named Tamboo. Or so the Edgecombes had graphically told me.

As we left the airport behind us and roared up the rough white shore road, you could indeed see what men and machinery were fashioning from a tropical patchwork of white beach and water and mangrove swamp, set with pine and palmetto brush, whose only life had been the decayed native village of Bullock's Harbour with its primitive school and post office and church.

The roads were there, broad, straight and unsurfaced, scoring through the green jungle: Great Harbour Drive, Royal Palm Drive, Fairway Road. The beach was there, on our right: turquoise sea and dazzling sand, and a beach club, smothered in coconut palms and hibiscus, with some villas buried in flowers beside it.

But best of all, the golf course was there. CAUTION CARTS CROSSING, said the notices, as we swept by empty crossroads with the sun beating down on our blue canvas canopy and the houseboy's black ringed hands moving the wheel. And on either side, winding in and out to the sea, one caught glimpses of flags and fairways and manicured greens, of high, close-cropped trees and bunkers and weathered boards, swinging on chains: Hole No. 4, 400 yards, Par 4, Handicap 5.

To hell with my suitcase, I thought. At least my golf clubs were all right.

The Edgecombes' house overlooked one of the fairways and was reached by road from the rising waste ground behind. This elevation 1 found unexpected. No one would describe Great Harbour Cay as a mountain. But it hadn't the fiberless English flatness of most of the rest of the seven hundred "Friendly Tropical Islands." Denise Edgecombe stood at the roadside to welcome me. She was gracious.

That was all right. I replied in the same key and we all went in, discussing the plight of my suitcase. "Let's see what I have that will fit you," said Lady Edgecombe. She was, I would guess, at least four inches taller than I was. She was wearing a pair of striped trousers with a black linen top and a lot of beads.

I said, "Don't worry. It'll turn up. Or if not, there's probably a shop on the island."

"There isn't," said Lady Edgecombe. She said it as if she were making a point of it, and I realized that we were at the door of the sitting room and that Sir Bartholomew was sitting in an easy chair just inside. "Of course, there's the pro's shop," she added. "But we find things there awfully expensive." She pushed open the door.

Like the few other houses I'd noticed, this one appeared built on stilts, in the form of a cluster of wood-clad rondettes, with a second level slung half down the hillside. The octagonal roofs, weathered silver, looked like a group of cockleshells left on a beach. A sun balcony, red and yellow with potted flowers and creepers, ran around the whole golf course side of the villa, but lay at present in shade; it must be, I supposed, at least a quarter to six. Denise said, "She's lost her suitcase. Give her a drink, will you, Bart darling? I must go and change. We're due at the clubhouse at seven. That's your room." She pointed to where the houseboy was already disappearing with my clubs and my bags, smiled cursorily, and disappeared. I was right. I was not Denise's most-wanted guest.

Sir Bartholomew Edgecombe got up and patted a seat.

"You've done a day's work. You must be tired. Come and sit down," he said. "It's good to see you. And I am sorry about your suitcase. What happened?"

He looked better. He looked, in fact, more relaxed than at any time I had seen him, with what one could recognize as authority back in his voice, and efficiency in his movements and manner. I said, "It got mislaid in Nassau. It doesn't matter: they'll send it. I'm glad to see you looking so well . . . No tomato juice, thank you. A Coca-Cola, perhaps?" Even in Loch Rannoch, we do not push things to extremes.

A moment later, standing over me with the drinks: "I shouldn't have asked you to come," he said abruptly. He sat down beside me. "Did you know it was Johnson's idea?"

"No, I didn't," I said. "I thought he'd washed his hands of us both."

"Do you think he would?" said Edgecombe. And a moment later, "You think you know him, perhaps. But . . ."

" 'Inside that elegantly simple body lurks a mountain goat of a car'?" I quoted.

He betrayed no surprise. Perhaps he had smelled the Bossa Nova. "Let's say that wearing those bifocal glasses is a personalized army assault vehicle with amphibian characteristics," he said. "He possesses both brains and tenacity, which is why he is my superior officer. All I have is an amiable nature." And he smiled at me and drank his martini.

"Why not retire fully, then?" I said. "If you don't enjoy it? Or did you, before all this started?"

He took out a gold cigarette case, offered me one, and took one himself. "In a way," he said. "You're in the center. You hold all the strings. You send in your reports and the people at the top decide what's to be done, and you see there's no trouble when they send men to do it. It's subtle, and interesting, and I never minded an element of danger. But this . . . this is something different."

. "This is murder," I said. "Do you have a bodyguard?"

He lit his cigarette and drew on it before answering. "The staff is my own," he said. "The boy you saw. One or two others. But I can hardly go about in an armored car. The very essence of this job is ordinariness. And mobility."

"Then why choose a house here?" I said.

His eyes stayed for a moment on the door through which Denise had gone; then he turned and smiled at me. "Why not? You know I have a nominal job here. We're only beginning. We have some permanent residents but most of the people who fly over are staying a week or a fortnight to look over property, to discuss buying, to try out the golf course. The company officials look after their business requirements. Denise and I come in on the social side. We live here for very little; we eat at the golf clubhouse. And no one minds if I move backward and forward to Nassau or Abaco or Miami. I still have some small business interests: investments to look after. And Great Harbour Cay is central to almost everywhere. Better than Nassau."

"And Lady Edgecombe likes the social life," I said.

He tapped the ash off his cigarette. "In season," he said. "It gets a bit boring in the heat, but then so do all the Bahamas. I send her away in the summer. She likes to go to the States."

"She doesn't know what you do?" I asked.

He shook his head. "And she won't know. I don't want Denise becoming a target for our opponents, whoever they may be." He looked at his watch. "Lord. Look, I don't want to rush you, but we thought you might like to meet some of the more public company on the island. They all foregather at the golf clubhouse as a rule for drinks before dinner. Would you like to freshen up and we'll take you?"

I looked down at my extraordinary uncreased blue silk. "Will·
this do?"

He grinned. "Of course it will. Suits you down to the ground."

Which was one thing it certainly did not do. I got to my feet
slowly. "Sir Bartholomew . . ."

"Bart. Please. If I may call you Beltanno?"

The thought of Denise calling me Beltanno flitted distastefully
over my mind. But I couldn't very well say, "*Doctor* MacRannoch, if you please." "Not at all," I said. "I was about to observe. Surely the need for secrecy has now gone? Someone knows
who you are. How can you possibly carry on with any form of
classified work now?"

He took my empty glass from me, and stood viewing the bottom. "You see," he said, "it entirely depends, doesn't it, on who
is trying to kill me. If it's an enemy agent, then certainly my
cover is blown, and I shall be out of work. But a man with a
private grudge might be a different matter. Or so Johnson says.
He also says, bless his fully automated positive thinking, that
it would be a pity to throw overboard all my skills and experience
until we have proof either way."

"And I am to help you get your proof?" I said.

He stared at me. "That hasn't been said. But whatever happens, Johnson's cover mustn't be broken."

"I know. It nearly cost him two thousand dollars to keep it in
Nassau," I remarked.

Sir Bartholomew Edgecombe grinned, and held open my door.
"Beltanno, my dear. He's a top man. He probably gets that a
week in expenses," he said. "You keep in with my friend Johnson. He's worth knowing, on several counts."

It was not advice I cared for. In fact I found my view of Johnson Johnson had hardened a good deal, when out of his company.
It was even possible that I had suffered some sort of hypnosis

from those confusing bifocals, allied to the blow on my head.

I shut the door, and taking off the wig, felt the wound on my scalp with exploring fingers. It was doing all right. So was I, I decided. I scrubbed up, redressed, and checked that the revolver was still in my bag. Then I went out to join Denise and Bart Edgecombe.

*   *

The sunset was of course quite spectacular: it dropped slowly into its own copper reflection, as we drove southwest to the clubhouse called Tamboo. I realized then what a lot of the island I still had to visit. The west side was greener and lusher than the east, and along the fairways of the golf course and beyond and behind were a great many villas, discreetly shielded by palm trees, with lights from veiled windows beginning to glow in the dusk.

"The yachting marina's over there," said Sir Bartholomew. "And the new waterfront houses, where you can park your boat on your doorstep. But just the prototype so far, of course. They're still pile-driving the quayside. We'll show you all that tomorrow."

The Tamboo golf clubhouse had a deep, grottolike entrance in a façade of natural stone. Above one could see a terrace, and a pair of architectural rooftops like twin wedges of Gruyère cheese. Inside it was cool and airy, with a haze of greenery encased in rope baskets, and a pink unpolished brick floor. Yellow and red hibiscus blossoms lay on a glass table surrounded by tall wicker chairs.

Edgecombe had gone to sign me in at the long counter. It had a register and a radio telephone set lying on it. A thought struck me, and I strolled along after him.

A tall figure uncoiled from behind one of the high-backed Italian chairs and trod softly over beside me. "If you're looking for Mr. T. K. MacRannoch," said Wallace Brady blandly, "I've located him for you. And he's right here."

And from the edge of the neighboring armchair, peeping and smiling, I saw the Japanese golfer, the man I had last seen in that foursome behind me on Paradise Island.

"Oh," I said.

"He likes to be called Mr. Tiko. The other name is a bit of a mouthful," Brady said. "You know the last time I met you, we were in the middle of a conflagration in the Bamboo Conch Club? Then you all rushed out the door like you were crazy, and I never even knew what had happened until Sir Bart here turned up today and told me. Your friends sure carry a lot of money around." His eyes, which had been struggling to keep off my hair, now candidly roved around and examined it. "Say," he said. "Am I allowed to say I think it's great?"

So Edgecombe hadn't told him about the incident in Miami. I was thankful for his discretion, if irritated with Wallace Brady's lack of it. "Thank you," I said. "And how is the Crab Island bridge coming along?"

"Oh," he said. "Oh, so the Begum told you about that? It's my spare-time baby, you know. The big job's over here, or will be till it's finished, but I couldn't resist having a crack at that little problem. I think she'll do."

"Is it finished?" I said.

He was surprised. "Hellfire, it takes a couple of weeks to fling these things together," he said. "Didn't you see it as you flew over?"

I made a mental resolution to eschew Bossa Novas and try something else. "Then how did my father travel to Crab Island?" I asked. I assumed without question that the whole island had taken part, willy-nilly, in the transmission of James Ulric from Great Harbour Cay to Crab Island. He would make certain they did.

"By boat," said Wallace Brady. He hesitated. "Your father is certainly nervous of water."

"He isn't nervous of water," I said sharply. "He's just sick."

"He was," said Brady. "In fact, we got the nurse to go over with him."

I knew the company nurse, an admirable person who flew her own four-seater Cherokee aircraft and administered to the health of the island from a spotless mobile clinic down by the airport. She was pretty. "That would stop the trouble," I said.

"It did. Come and meet Mr. Tiko," Brady said.

The Edgecombes were waiting for me, so we all got introduced together.

My prospective fiancé was slightly under my height, clean, neat, and possessed of perfect American English. He no longer worked in Tokyo, but with an investment company in New York. From the gold fountain pen, the gold watch, and the gold tie pin, I gathered he was not in any real want. Brady, clearly, had told him nothing about me, beyond my name, which was not all that uncommon, particularly as MacRannochs were presumably ready preparing to gather on Crab Island like flies.

I had intended to say nothing even about that, but as we gathered to walk up the flight of thick, green, carpeted stairs, Mr. Tiko moved over and said, "We are similar of name, are we not, Doctor MacRannoch? But I do not use all of mine. I am also doctor by university degree, but not of medicine: I am doctor of law. Tell me, it is not correct to wear formal dark suit in the evenings?"

We had got to the top of the stairs, where it appeared all the lights had gone out. I then saw it was merely part of the great American myth that everything after 6 P.M. including eating is more romantic if it is performed in the dark. I have known a fellow doctor actually walk out of a restaurant in New York because I insisted on dissecting my steak with a small pocket flashlight jammed into a candlestick. Here, I merely groped after the Edgecombes, who were each wearing a trouser suit, but not of the kind Mr. Tiko meant; and Wallace Brady, who was wearing a long coral shirt over sharp kidskin trousers. "It doesn't look like it," I said.

We progressed through a doorway into an area of still greater darkness and voluminous noise of both the stereo and Bossa Nova variety. It appeared to be a large parquet-floored room crowded with dancing, sitting, or leaning figures against a dim background of rose-geranium drapes. At one end, a large circular bar, seating perhaps twenty on tall bamboo stools, was gently lit from above by a cluster of some fifty vermilion lights in lobster pot cases. The wall behind the bar was tiled in natural bark. A girl with very long blond hair and a transparent white jumper reaching to the adductor brevis floated between us, talking French to a diaphanously clad boy. Lady Edgecombe stepped back and held me by the arm. "Did you see who that is?"

I allowed her to tell me.

"I think," murmured Mr. Tiko at my side, "I should perhaps go and remove my jacket and tie. More, with the best intentions, I am unable to do. Doctor MacRannoch." He gave me a small bow and squirmed off.

I liked him. I should have to. Sir Bartholomew said, "Over here," and we crossed to the noisiest corner of the room, where a great many irrationally dressed people were sitting drinking in black bamboo lattice chairs and beige sofas, in a welter of potted plants. The names meant very little to me, but appeared to illuminate Lady Edgecombe, who became more graciously animated than I had ever known her. The ambience appeared to be stage, screen, TV, with a sprinkling of New York and Philadelphia society. There was even an English drawl here and there. It was difficult to ask them what they did when they all obviously assumed that one knew what they did, so I contented myself with ordering a Yellowberry and listening to a long item of scandal closely connected with a patient I had once operated upon. I had no idea what a Yellowberry was, but my companion, a lusty athlete with golden sideburns and a diamond locket over his suntan, had just ordered one and I hoped he was used to it, and even that it might be responsible for his present splendid condition.

It came, and was indeed yellow, and smelt of rum, banana liqueur and fresh orange juice. Sir Bartholomew, straining out of the gloom, called smiling, "I thought sensible doctors only tippled tomato juice."

I called back, "I've gone off tomato juice," and felt a little contrition. It might, after all, be quite expensive. There was a cloud of Brut and the diamond locket suddenly swam into my field of vision. "I didn't catch your name. You're English?"

"Scottish. Beltanno MacRannoch," I said, and counted. I can't help it if it sounds like a war chant. At five he said, "I beg your pardon?" and I said, "Never mind. Miss MacRannoch. It's a Scots name."

"Ah." He looked nonplussed; I wasn't sure why. Doubts, perhaps, about speaking my language? He said, "I thought from what your friend said that you were maybe a doctor."

I sat there, quiet as an overstuffed washing machine, and ticked over the options: Say, *no;* get up and move off; say, *yes, but I prefer not to talk business;* say, *what free advice you after, brother?* I pressed the button and slid the disc on the line. "Yes," I said. "I am."

"Say!" His smile really was breathtaking. He looked me up and down. "I'll say you don't look it."

This, note, was a compliment. "You don't either," I said.

The brilliant smile gathered hazed overtones. "I'm not," he said.

"I thought you couldn't be," I replied.

Sir Bartholomew Edgecombe, who had not become an ambassador somewhere for nothing, leaned over smiling again and said, "Beltanno is one of the senior medical offiers of the United Commonwealth Hospital at Nassau, Paul. Don't let her faze you."

"You are?" Three other faces joined the diamond locket and two other conversations began to break up. A girl in a white satin Tom Mix outfit said, "You mean you're fully qualified and everything, the same as a man nearly? Isn't that marvelous?"

"It brings its own sense of wonder," I said after a moment. I was, after all, Edgecombe's guest. There was a strangled laugh somewhere behind me which I thought, but was not sure, belonged to Wallace Brady.

"Dedicated," said the diamond locket called Paul with some reverence. "That's it, isn't it, Doctor? Dedicated to suffering mankind? In Britain anyway," he added, his tone darkening slightly. "In Los Angeles, my God, they're a heap of loot-grabbing horseshit."

"Oh," I said. "In Britain as well. We're allowed to charge a pretty stiff price for consultations in private. You'd be surprised."

There was a brief silence, cut short by three voices speaking, and someone asked someone else to dance. The girl with the fringes got up and struggled off into the gloom, bearing her starvation-induced anaemia, I judged, with her. Diamond Locket, who had eased off slightly, leaned back and said casually, "You know, it's a funny thing about feet."

It *is* a funny thing. Nine times out of ten, you can count upon it, the trouble is feet. Sir Bartholomew said, "Dance, Beltanno?"

I don't dance, and he knew I didn't dance, but I got up and worked my way through to him, and then into the center of the large room where the crowd was so thick that we merely stood face to face with our hands clasped, rocking gently. "Can you forgive me?" he said. "If I hadn't been such a damned idiot, they'd never have known."

"Oh, well. It gets around. They would have found out by tomorrow anyway," I said. "It's odd. I wouldn't go up to a stationer and ask him for a free fountain pen."

"But that is a material possession, and sacred," said Edgecombe. "Intelligence is fortuitous, and to be distributed as the air."

"Please?" said someone cutting in. "Is it permitted?"

It was Mr. Tiko. "Of course. If Sir Bartholomew doesn't mind," I said.

He was only half a head smaller, and looked less than that with his stiff white collar open. We clasped hands and rocked. "I forget to say something," he said.

You forgot to say, I thought sadly, that you are the next chief of the MacRannochs after James Ulric, my father.

But he hadn't found out. "I forget to say," said Mr. Tiko, "that it is as well you do not use your name Doctor in the clubhouse. I never do this, even I with my law degree. There are some who will not cease to pursue you for free advice."

I looked warmly upon him. "That's very kind of you, Mr. Tiko, although too late, I'm afraid: they've found out. Tell me, what sort of free advice do they ask of a lawyer?"

"Ah, wills," he said sadly. "Always wills. Is it not funny?"

The rest of the evening is slightly blurred in my recollection, although not sufficiently at the time to make me foreswear Yellowberries, to which I was becoming quite partial. But I did recall with absolute clarity that I had promised to play a round of golf with my fiancé the following morning.

Not that he knew he was my fiancé yet, of course.

Chapter 8

NEXT MORNING the housemaid, trained by Denise, brought me in early morning tea and drew the curtains; and Denise herself knocked and came in while I was still drinking it, and before I put on my wig.

"Oh, your poor head," she said, but without conviction: she was thinking of something else. "Did you sleep well?"

I had. The bed had fine American cotton percale sheets like silk, and all the furniture was white bamboo with blue and green and white floral upholstery and a positive tattoo of drum-lamps. Denise sat on the empty twin bed and said, "I hear you're playing golf with Mr. Tiko this morning, and I wondered if Wallace Brady and I could join you."

Poor Bartholomew Edgecombe. I hadn't thought of her as a golfer. But looking at those calf muscles again, and those sinewy arms, and that brittle, determined jaw, I realized suddenly that of course she was — and most likely a good one. I cannot say I was overjoyed at the prospect of watching Lady Edgecombe and Wallace Brady get to know each other better over eighteen holes in my company, but I could hardly refuse.

At the door she stopped and said, "Oh, by the way: Bart had word from the airport about your suitcase, dear. I'm afraid there's no sign of it at all. Shall I see if something of mine will fit you this morning?"

I have already spoken of the size difference between us. I need only say that at this moment Lady Edgecombe was wearing a boudoir cap of white frilled lace scattered with rosebuds, and a frilled negligee of white spotted net, and it will be clear why I declined.

"Then perhaps you should look in at the pro's shop when we go over for breakfast," Lady Edgecombe suggested. It was not, obviously, of passionate moment to her; she only wanted to make sure that I should not be prevented from playing golf by the exigencies of my attire. I said I would.

Indeed, after she had gone, I got up and padded over the carpet to examine myself in the vanity mirror, which was surrounded by fourteen ormolu make-up lamps with a total burning power of what felt like two thousand watts. My feet sank three inches into the blue and green fitted carpet, of the variety known as deep shag, which wouldn't show if your dog buried his bone in it, and for all I know he frequently does. My headache had vanished. My face was brown and clean and healthy and, once I had my wig on, looked better than Denise's.

Outside the veiled window a crane lowered its jib, from which dangled a palm tree. I went over to look. The incline of waste ground was no longer an incline of waste ground but a garden of flowering bushes, interspersed tastefully with groups of live coconut palms. A gang of men were unrolling a carpet of grass. And a boy in a floral shirt and a fancy straw hat had got down from a tanker and was watering it.

The Edgecombes had a garden.

It wouldn't happen in Scotland.

I went in to shower, singing cautiously, dressed, had a word with the Edgecombes, and borrowing their windowless Fiat, drove off to the Tamboo golf clubhouse.

The pro's shop was upstairs, near the bar lounge of last night's exotic encounters. I walked past the glass doors and some satin steel furniture and a selection of metal-reeded chairs like diabolos to the double timber doors of the shop, and I stood for a long time and looked in the windows.

For that time in the morning, it was fairly dazzling. Stacks of cellophaned cashmeres and floodlit rows of hide golf bags in green and yellow and cream. A carousel of slacks in cream and coral and primrose; drawers of suntan oil; shelves of white balls like nest eggs. Around the corner, I knew were tunics and bathing suits and sunsuits, bikinis, pant suits, divided skirts, sandals . . .

I walked past the cashmeres and stopped in front of the slacks. Then I opened my bag, pushed the revolver out of the way, and took out all Pally Loo-loo's remarkable dividend.

I have no trouble making decisions. Half an hour later I was back at the club and able to join my host and hostess for breakfast. I had on a culotte dress in green linen with a see-through matching jacket and square-toed green canvas shoes. Lady Edgecombe had sprigged pants and a pink cotton shirt pinned with an Indian brooch at the navel; Sir Bartholomew merely his old Bermudas and a fresh shirt. He grinned, stood up, and gave me a full bow as I came to the table. "Beltanno, I can tell you one thing," he said. "By this evening, they'll have stopped bringing over their feet."

"And started bringing over their wills, perhaps," I said. I felt remarkably skittish. "I say, that would be something."

I had fresh orange juice, coffee, a small hot fluffy roll like a bread cake, and an individual packet of corn flakes, served already perforated across the abdomen like a prepared case of peritonitis. Afterward, Sir Bartholomew took me out on the high apron sun deck at the back of the clubhouse and we leaned on the railing and looked at the prognosis for the dream called Tamboo.

Below us stretched the club's own private patio, edged with tropical flowers and trees and scattered with yellow beach chairs around a swimming pool lined with baby blue tiles, and filled with baby blue water. Built on the same ridge, but divided from us by the steeply undercut road to the marina were the clustered rondettes belonging to the guests of the golf club: smaller timber-clad rondels like Edgecombe's, still with their feet in scrub and piping and rubble.

But they were complete too and occupied, most of them. Coming to breakfast that morning I had seen Diamond Locket and the French screen star among others crossing the overpass which stretched from the rondettes to the clubhouse and golf course. Below the bridge rumbled the trucks carrying the plant and work gangs and tools to the marina. You could see it there, blue in the distance, marked by the white of the shining new jetty; the squat red and gray shape of the pile driver; the huddle of cranes. Beyond on one side, the walls of the first waterfront townhouse condominium had got up to two stories high in front of the rough green slope of the hill. On the opposite side, I could distinguish the red pantiles of the first house in a Portuguese-style fishing village. Around the corner in the Bay of the Five Pirates a yacht club was scheduled to rise. Elsewhere unborn were Tamboo Village with international shops, roof gardens, and patios. The discotheque in the Lighthouse Pavilion. The tennis courts. The beach club and swimming pool. The private luxury houses for single and multiple families. The Condominium Club. All that in the future; and the future was becoming the present with the speed of Sir Bartholomew's garden.

Beyond the walls of the swimming pool near the uncleared bushes, where the stagnant swamp lay below, an excavator was working. Tractors crawled by; trucks with gravel; smart cars filled with dark-skinned talking men in caps and bright shirts.

Below the overpass a crane bearing an uprooted tree backed into sight, slowing to allow a mechanical grab to pass, followed by one of the ubiquitous water lorries.

Generators throbbed. The whole island hummed and muttered with the mechanized voice of creation. Swarming, single-minded over each growing point, the builders, the planners, the developers paid no attention to the socialites, the holiday-makers, the investors, bronzed and sunglassed, driving one-handed amongst them, bathing trunks and towel in the back seat, hissing past on the shore in the ski boat, sending buckets of balls down the practice drive with a flick of the wrist.

Sir Bartholomew raised a hand and pointed beyond the marina, to a strip of road on the near horizon. "That's the way to the native settlement. Bullock's Harbour," he said. "We must take you there sometime. It's not in the development, of course, but most of the men work for the company now. It pays better than fishing."

It reminded me that I meant to go to Bullock's Harbour too, but not, thank you, before I'd had my game of golf. Johnson had had no qualms about inducing me to come here. He could therefore accept my services in the order in which I elected to offer them. As it happened, Johnson was unaware where the dead waiter Pentecost came from. Or for that matter that he had three brothers still here. But that was Johnson's fault for going to Crab Island instead of Great Harbour Cay.

Wallace Brady and Mr. Tiko joined us at that point. We left Sir Bartholomew to return to his house and followed Lady Edgecombe out onto the terrace which swept down through coconut palms to the brilliant green of the No. 1 tee. There was no need to inquire whether or not there were caddies. Here the main route was joined by a path from the clubhouse. And in motionless file on that path, two by two like black-nosed creatures about to descend from the Ark, were three dozen baby blue and white golf carts with white seats and cocked white and blue sunshades.

To one of them Lady Edgecombe's houseboy was already strapping her olive green hide bag, and to the next my secondhand one glazed with rubbing. Wallace Brady, in pale pink sweater and white slacks, heaved his own bag beside Lady Edgecombe's. His woods were protected by thick plushy socks. Beside mine he also strapped Mr. Tiko's bag, the most immaculate of all, with each of four woods and ten irons encased in its own quilted anorak, and his initials on his hide bag in gold. Mr. Tiko, in a blue tunic shirt and blue trousers, had been patronizing the pro's shop this morning as well.

I gave him a smile based on fellow-feeling and a considerable body of unvoiced good intentions, and said: "It looks as if Mr. Brady is going to drive Lady Edgecombe. Do you know how these things work?"

He was happy to show me. Lady Edgecombe's houseboy had already paid our ten dollars and the meter key was turned in front of the seat. Mr. Tiko settled beside me, grasped the wheel, and pressed his left foot on the long flat accelerator. The cart moved, and so did Wallace Brady's beside us. Side by side, at a gentle five miles an hour, the four of us drove down the path and onto the perfect green sward beside the first tee.

To slide the driver out of your bag and stand facing the first of eighteen beautiful fairways, your feet planted apart and the wind in your hair — what satisfaction is there like it in Scotland, with the sandy ground under your spikes, and the sea roaring there on the shingle and the cold trying in vain to penetrate your woolen stockings, your tweed skirt and pullover?

What, then, is it like sleeveless under a warm, cloudless sky, with five hundred yards of green velvet unrolling before your eyes, surrounded by low palmetto brush jungle? When the double bunker ahead is guarded by a coconut palm? We tossed for first drive from the women's tee. Lady Edgecombe won and hit her first ball without preamble a good third of the distance, nicely placed for a wood shot fairly close to the green and well clear of the white sculptured traps. She had, as I suspected, excellent muscular control.

So had I. I drove off deliberately with the whippy crack which means distance; and meant, incidentally, the devoted practice of nearly every off-duty hour since I came out to Nassau. The sun was in my eyes. But I watched my ball with satisfaction take the straight line Lady Edgecombe had avoided, to fly over the first pair of bunkers and lie safely beyond. She smiled at me with her carefully drawn mouth and said, "Well done, Beltanno!" but she hardly watched Brady or my Japanese namesake drive off. I thought, there are few things she does naturally well, and this is one of them. This is one field in which she is secure. A psychiatrist would suggest that it would be wiser, for her sake, not to trespass on it.

I am not a psychiatrist, and I believe that cures are effected by people being made to confront their own weaknesses. I watched Brady give a competent and Mr. Tiko an excellent opening shot, and then trundled off with my partner to watch Denise play her No. 3 wood. She drove it crooked, almost out of the fairway. Mine brought my ball neatly just below the lift of the green. Par was 5. It seemed very likely I was going to start with a birdie. Brady placed his next shot beyond mine, but on the lip of a trap; Mr. Tiko, with care, sent his ball close beside me. With mutual smiles, we entered our cart and drove off. "You play golf a great deal?" he asked.

"Well. I did my training with six first-class golf courses within half an hour's drive. But you learned in Japan, Mr. Tiko?"

"I learn to drive, yes. I have a good drive," he said. "But

the rest I learn in America. Lady Edgecombe is good, is she not? But it is a game like chess: one must not allow oneself to be put off."

"I can't imagine anything putting you off, Mr. Tiko," I said, getting out. Denise had failed to get her ball near the green.

He gave a miniature shrug with his miniature shoulders. "An excess of alcohol, perhaps, or too little sleep, were I to be self-indulgent. But little else, I venture to hope. One must discipline the inner self as one would preserve any implement."

It was a philosophy with which I found myself in perfect agreement. A five iron pitch and run brought me within two yards of the pin. Both the men followed onto the green, but neither remotely so well. I got my birdie.

It was a pleasant moment of success. The sun blazed down; the white fringe of the cart canopy moved to the faintest of sea breezes. Ahead, triangular against the blue sky, was the roof of the airport control tower; behind us, on the ridge, one could just see the twin sloping roofs of the clubhouse. Brady dropped back the yellow flag and we resumed our seats. The two carts side by side set themselves into motion, and crossing Santa Maria Drive, we turned uphill past a low scrubby wood to No. 2 tee.

The condition of the fairway and greens was a joy. Ploughed up from jungle and swamp, the course had been designed and then sown by blowing machine, the sprigs raced here by barge from their seed farms in Georgia. Turf, I knew, had come in the same way, rolled like carpets the way I had seen it, and even the coconut palms, their roots wrapped in polyethylene, had been imported by the bargeload, the tugs dragging them across from the Florida coast. For no coconut palms grew on Great Harbour Cay before the development. Nothing grew. The islanders fished for sponges, and when that failed, for lobster and crawfish. Now, down on the road we saw the trucks going by from the big netted nursery off Royal Palm Drive. Trucks full of potted tropical plants, and bags of horticultural perlite, and Canadian *Sphagnum* peat moss. The grass on the fairways, cut weekly one inch in height, was like the grass on the greens where I used to play near Loch Rannoch; and the grass on the greens, three sixteenths of an inch and shaved daily, in green powderings which lay in small heaps on the roads, was like heavy green suede.

We moved around the course in the sun, like children on a toy railway, stopping and starting, pretending to play plastic golf under the perpetual hot sun of childhood. An inlet of sea water ran past the second green, its beaches white, a rocky island of gray and yellow stones in the middle. The third fairway led up to the airport: beyond a banking of white limestone the line of flags showed, and as we played a Dakota flew in slowly from the left, skimmed our heads, and landed. You could see the passengers disembark. I watched Lady Edgecombe scanning the numbers, and she played well at that hole. Reminded of her status: reminded that if the company at present did not come up to her expectations, there was more and better elsewhere.

Not that she seemed disappointed in Brady. He had good American manners, and he was polite as her rank demanded, although he was unable, I saw, quite to get her measure. I guessed this was one of many attempts on her part to draw him into their circle. I guessed she would get tired of trying, again, as she had, petulantly, at Nassau.

In the permanent company lodged on the island, there were probably few enough whom she felt might amuse her. And Brady's style, one had to admit, was engaging enough. He played an even game, without rancor, and cracked one or two mild jokes; then ceased to crack them when Lady Edgecombe leaned on the theme just a little too long. Mr. Tiko, ever polite, merely smiled and made congratulatory remarks. To me, in the cart, he talked a little about the game in Japan and put one or two gentle questions about courses in Scotland. He was no trouble.

For the fourth hole we recrossed the Santa Maria Drive, busier now: trucks rumbled around the white dusty corners with their loads of men and machinery. On the fairway however it was quiet; the twitter of an unknown bird came from the small wood beside us. A small red service cart with two Negroes sitting relaxed side by side moved almost without sound down the next fairway. Ahead, a spray was working, jets of water rising in pulses as if a small monkey engine were throwing up steam in short bursts. It swung slowly and left on the slope of the green a long sparkling bloom of pale blue, the beaded grass reflecting the sky. Wallace Brady had shown me the red metal caps, sunk in scores around the tees, greens, and fairways, from which emerged the sprinklers at night, set to spray in rotation all through the darkness and keep the turf perfect under a tropical sun. We played down the fifth and crossed the Harbour Drive to the sixth hole, and the first set by the sea.

The Fiat was sitting at the side of the road, and in it Sir Bartholomew, waiting for us. He waved to Denise. "It's all there according to orders when you're ready. Who's winning?"

"Doctor MacRannoch," said his wife brightly. "She's beating us hollow. Lots of Scotch perseverance." I noted I had been demoted from Beltanno again.

We played the hole, and then joined Sir Bartholomew on the beach. The last thing I want, I suppose, when playing a competitive eighteen holes against unknown opponents, is to break off a third of the way around for refreshments. For one thing, it takes quite some effort to collect one's concentration and rhythm again. I had a feeling that Brady and Mr. Tiko, although agreeable as ever, felt much the same.

We stepped down to the beach through a thicket of gray-green cactus and water-lily-like mangrove, sprawling over ridged layers of crumbling white rock. Beyond stretched the dazzling white sand with the sea hissing transparent upon it, and changing as it deepened to all the brilliant aniline shades: greenish chrome to pure turquoise to cerulean, to hazy grape blue on the horizon. Someone had put out long beach chairs and umbrellas just here, and Sir Bartholomew was unpacking a hamper with tins of soft drinks and a big flask of coffee. There were also some biscuits and fruit. Lady Edgecombe unstrapped her golf bag and drew a neat thermos from one pocket. "And this."

Sir Bartholomew looked at it. I said to Mr. Tiko, "Look. There's some fan coral." The beach was like white silk, weathered into tissue by the unceasing water and mapped with spidery black curves, skeletons of dead waves.

Sir Bartholomew said, smiling, "Well, for before lunch, Denise. Don't let's put everyone off their superb strokes."

She uncorked the flask without listening. "I don't suppose Beltanno has tasted Planters' Punch. Don't be a spoilsport, darling," she said. She started to pour.

"Not for me," I said, turning quickly.

Lady Edgecombe smiled at me. "I dare you," she said. "You're afraid of losing that lead. Confess, now."

I looked at Sir Bartholomew. "All right," I said. Brady and Mr. Tiko both held out for coffee, and she didn't press them. But her husband, I saw, also took Planters' Punch. It left less in the flask. But not little enough.

It was hot now. I was glad of the green linen dress, lying back on my chair, glass in hand, one finger trailing in the glistening sand. It was full of treasures: white sea urchins, transparent shells so small and perfect that I wished I had a microscope and some means to identify them. The sea rim hissed and withdrew, leaving the sand like satiny porridge patched with sparkling patterns of froth. Seaweed stirred like gray snippets of ribbon, and a dog bounded by, followed by a splashing group of sunburned young men and women — the visitors, or some of them, who had been at our table last night. They stopped to call greetings and ask after Sir Bartholomew. Denise, drawling and languid, offered a selection of amusing remarks, fanning herself with the tie of her shirt. Diamond Locket, in python bathing trunks, said to me, "Are you swimming?"

"Don't be frivolous, Paul," said Lady Edgecombe gravely. "Doctor MacRannoch is playing an awfully scientific game of golf." She managed, with clarity, to the end of the sentence.

Wallace Brady stood up. "And I think we'd better get on with it," he said. "Unless anyone's tired? There might be someone on our heels, don't you think?"

Lady Edgecombe shook her head. "No one on that plane who plays golf. No. We have the course to ourselves. Finest course in the world. Isn't it, Bart? Good, clean, healthy living. No gambling, no blackjack, no roulette, no casinos. Nothing to do but swim and fish and play tennis, when the tennis courts have got themselves built, and sail, when the marina is built, and go to nightclubs when the nightclub is built, and make love . . . when . . ."

Sir Bartholomew put a hand on her arm. "Look out. Your nice brooch is slipping."

It stopped her, and she looked down. Mr. Tiko had already moved off, returning the collected glasses to their basket; Wallace Brady was gazing, eyes shaded, at the reefs out to sea. Bart Edgecombe said gently, "Take it out and put it in your pocket; then it won't get lost. Or would you like to call it a day? We could go back and see who's in the clubhouse."

She drew up her brown, middle-aged muscular body, throwing off the arm he had placed around her waist. "When I'm doing something exciting, I want to finish it. You go and rest. You haven't been well. We're doing splendidly. One for all and all for one!" said Lady Edgecombe, sportingly if rather confusingly, and set off back to the fairway. I caught Wallace Brady's eyes on me and we exchanged glances; then he went on to take Denise by the arm. Sir Bartholomew passed me on his way to the car without saying anything. As he went by, one of the red service buggies drove up and stopped by the crossed rakes at the edge of the green; before we were out of sight the hole was being manicured back into pristine perfection again. We gathered on the seventh tee and set off again.

I played the rest of that round with a sense of unease, which was not due to Lady Edgecombe's new and lighthearted approach to the game. It was, I think, because I had forgotten Bart Edgecombe's danger. Or, seeing him at home, with wife and servants, or among familiars in the clubhouse in a closed society, on an island in which every guest, every stranger was known, it seemed the danger must be less than in the unconfined rat race outside.

And now, seeing him walk alone to that light open car, and get in alone and drive off alone, I wondered what protection Johnson thought he was offering him from the shelter of Crab Island. Or was I his protection? And what did Johnson suppose I could do if an excavator turned that corner and drove headlong into the Fiat?

I sliced my drive and Wallace Brady gave a cheer and said, "The first crack!" I grinned back, but I was thinking still. Of all our suspects, only Brady was on Great Harbour Cay, and he was here beside me. But that meant less than nothing. Whatever induced Pentecost to attempt murder in the Bamboo Conch Club could buy exactly the same sort of services here. If Bart Edgecombe was going to be killed, it would be at second hand, by somebody whose employer was very likely not even here on the island. Crab Island, after all, was only twenty minutes away by fast speedboat.

I lost that hole. Progressing along the course, I was struck not only by its superb condition, its peace, and greenness, but by how much lay near it which could be used by a killer. Here on the seventh the green overlooked a large sandy dip full of blue water; a flock of white egrets with swan necks and spider legs dangling rose as we approached and circled until we had gone. The water looked deep.

The fairway for the eighth lay between two half-made reservoirs. You could hear the soft roar of the machinery before driving off; then on the right loomed the raised lake, with yellow hopper and red chute in full operation. On the left, a sunken yard dug from the limestone was filled with machinery and equipment: hoppers, stacks of timber, bundles of pipes, red oil cans, and big silvery drums of gas. A three-sided warehouse held more plant and tools and some cars; rows of spares for the sprayers; rows of the long fan-shaped brushes I had seen being used on the greens. They were marked *Little Helper*.

We holed out and moved on. The ninth led to another lake. On the left rows of stilted rondettes were in the process of roofing; the air was filled with the dry, pleasant smell of sawed wood. The tenth was beside the new embryo tennis courts, but from the fairway to the skyline on all sides was palmetto scrub. High on the left someone had built a crow's nest, a look-out platform for condominium clients, or snipers; another lake. The eleventh: harmless, secluded, with the sun blazing down on its greenness; the only shade in the center, from a single buttonwood tree, low and wide with its gray scabbed bark and dark green willowlike leaves. Mr. Tiko went off to study a strange yellow butterfly; Lady Edgecombe was playing silently and not very well; Wallace Brady was winning.

Across Fairway Road and more heavy traffic. Workmen swarmed over a half-finished house; heavy tools lay about. The twelfth, and past Edgecombe's own house. Seen from the golf course the red poles on which it stood looked all of twelve feet in height. They had put in more hibiscus; the villa perched with its feet in palm trees and flowers, with the hum of its generator coming plainly down from the hut on the right. From the balcony, before the picture windows with their elegant curtains, Sir Bartholomew waved from his chair. Isolated, overlooking the whole empty fairway and the jungle of low trees and bushes set around it. A killer need only lie there under the bushes at night and then, if he were agile, climb up the poles.

Brady waved back, and so did I. Lady Edgecombe gathered herself and drove one excellent shot, the best for several holes, down the heart of the fairway. We sat in the carts and drove on.

The thirteenth: a raised tee and on its right a deep dry excavation for a reservoir; the sides scored with the wide ladder marks of caterpillar tractors crossing and recrossing. At the bottom lay an unattached green harrow with spikes on its wheels. Why should I think of Johnson?

Ahead, the pale green of a new lake in a deepish cut; the roofs of one or two other houses; the sound of dogs barking. Peanuts and Popcorn, perhaps, the pro's chocolate poodles. And the fourteenth, turning back. We were on our way home; the sea, invisible, must be on our left. Then across Great Harbour Drive for the fifteenth and there was the water, pale turquoise ahead; to the right an unexpected deep cutting and more machinery; another house, its roof newly timbered, its walls not yet completed. The sixteenth: separated from the sea only by a strip of flowering bushes, and the occasional pine.

We stopped there, while Denise waded over the scrub without speaking, and went to stand alone on the beach. She gazed out to sea. Mr. Tiko, who had played an unvarying average game with placid good humor, waited patiently. Wallace Brady walked over to me. I said, "I don't want to play it out, unless anyone else does." He was four strokes better than I was; Lady Edgecombe poorest of all.

Brady said, "I don't mind, either way. The last two are a straight walk back in to the clubhouse. We have to go that way anyway." He hesitated and said, "D'you think we should all ease up?"

"Good lord," I said. "What good would that do?" Giving Lady Edgecombe the game wasn't going to improve her ego. Only a dramatic improvement in her golf would do that. I don't know what Brady was going to say, but just then Lady Edgecombe said something aloud.

Mr. Tiko, who was nearest, walked politely toward her. She repeated what she had said, and this time we could hear it. "She's lost the brooch out of her pocket," I said. "End of game, end of problem. Leave things long enough and they'll find their own answer."

"It worries me," said Wallace Brady, "to think that you think I'll swallow that. Maybe you forget that civil engineers don't get to be civil engineers with that kind of philosophy, any more than doctors do."

"But lady ambassadresses can," I said. But under my breath. Mr. Tiko was volunteering to tramp back and look for the brooch. Brady, putting a good face on it, walked up and offered to do the same; so did I.

We were about to split forces when Lady Edgecombe said, "No, you mustn't, Beltanno. All that stooping with your poor head." I had forgotten my poor head and so, I swear, had she until that moment. She said, "Look, someone must go and tell poor Bart. He'll be up at the clubhouse in a few moments, patiently waiting. Suppose Beltanno takes one of the golf carts, and leaves us here with the other."

136

I didn't mind if she wanted the company of both men together. They were arguing who should go where, as I got into the cart and drove off.

It was the first time I had operated one of those things. On my salary you don't hire them lightly. The brake was fiercer than I had expected, but the thing was stable enough, so long as one didn't ask the impossible on a steep or an uneven gradient. I steered sedately over the road and along the seventeenth and eighteenth fairways, finding on my left one of the big rubber-lined reservoirs from which the underground pipes could be fed. An ingenious system.

I had had, as I reviewed it, an excellent morning of golf. A piquant round of great comfort. Not one for tricks or nasty surprises or any of the crude and unpleasant hazards which tax one to extremity, in sport as in life. But a good game of golf.

Sir Bartholomew was waiting, as predicted, on the patio of the clubhouse. He wouldn't hear of my going back but pressed on me instead his beach towel and his chair, ordered me a fruit juice, and suggested that I should pass the time with a swim.

He didn't need to explain his gratitude any more than I my commiseration. I changed, thankfully, into the new bathing suit and beach shirt I had left in my locker, picked up my bathing cap for dewigging with later, and made my way back to my tall, ice-filled drink by the pool.

It was too hot to talk. In the baby blue water a long-haired girl swam showily and then got languidly out. The palms in front of the clubhouse were motionless and the sea grape in the corner hung its leaves like unpolished green sequins. Around the pool, the slatted beach chairs lay straddled like spiders, each with its burden of naked bronze flesh. Someone said politely, "You need to be oiled, lady, or you'll get awful sore."

It was Paul, of the locket. I said, "Thanks, but I should be all right. I've been quite a lot in the sun."

He flashed his snowy, capped teeth and waggled a finger. "Not there you haven't. Call yourself a doctor, as well?"

He was correct, I was annoyed to discover. The shape of my present bathing suit produced problems which were undoubtedly novel. "Now just you lie there," he said; and before I could stir, a large warm hand lapped in liquid spread itself over my central vertebrae and proceeded to massage, ably and hard. I gasped, and turned my head to one side in order to read his expression. He winked and continued unpausing. Feet had not even been mentioned. His impulses were entirely benign.

Someone, three chairs away, was grumbling softly about something; someone else somewhere was laughing. But quietly. Everything was quiet. In the pool, empty now, a string of colored floats moved with the air on its satiny surface, hand in hand like a dream line of children. A brush hissed. A black boy, in a black lace shirt with pearl cuff links, was spraying the bushes at the back of the open-air bar; his sneakers squeaked below bare brown ankles as he moved gently along. The sound mixed with the organ note of a plane coming in, the giant cricket hum of the generators. A whining buzz came from the cart room, where the sixty unused golf cars sat in canopied rows, feeding umbilically, each from its meter. Paul said, "You've got a cute little figure. Ain't no one ever told you before, Doc?"

The girl from the reception counter, running out on the back steps with the radio transmitter box gripped in her hand, stood and screamed: "Doctor MacRannoch! Are you there! Doctor . . ."

I was up and running, the beach shirt whipped over my shoulders, before she got another word out. She stood and stared at me gasping, her face stiff and the color of yeast. I said, "Give me the transmitter. Take a deep breath. Now, what is it?"

But I knew. I could hear the hubbub behind: people wakened,

talking, asking; even Paul's naked feet padding along, a late starter behind me. I knew it. I knew it. I knew it.

The girl was still choking. I gave her a rap on the shoulder. "Come along. What is it?"

She said, "That was the car from the beach. To say they've gone for the nurse. And Mr. Brady said you're to go, too. They were looking for something . . ."

"A brooch. I know. What happened?" I said.

"They didn't find it. And Sir Bartholomew said to call off the search. And they called Lady Edgecombe, but she didn't answer. And Mr. Brady went off to look. Then Mr. Brady called from the thirteenth that he'd found her."

"Well?" I said. My voice was calm, I trust, but I couldn't believe it yet, the thing she was going to say.

"Lady Edgecombe was dead," said the girl. "They say her neck's broken."

Denise. Not Sir Bart but his wife.

Chapter 9

"So she was gassed," said Johnson. "And deliberately, you fancy, Beltanno? Not a victim of environmental pollution?"

"It would be hard to prove it," I said, "but I think a pad was pressed over her face."

"And then she was flung into the empty reservoir," Bart Edgecombe said. His two hands were still clenched in front of his face. "Instead of me."

In forty minutes after it happened, Johnson had been there. It was the first thing I thought of, to summon him. He was known as a friend of the family; it seemed natural enough, I had hoped. I waited until the special constable came from the village and left him beside Bart, kneeling beside that sad, covered body; and then got a lift in the company car up to Hilltop, the little restaurant which was also the transmitting station to the outside world. Official messages had to be sent: to the hospital, to the Criminal Investigation Department at Nassau for a plane to come over.

Crab Island didn't have radio transmission, but *Dolly* had. I pinned my hopes to the fact that Spry would have sailed her from Nassau, and that Spry would be on board. He was; and I spoke to him, while in the coffee bar next door, people who hadn't heard the news laughed and chattered under the ceilings and walls

140

covered with autographs from the Americas and all over Europe: *Surfside, Massachusetts; Sundsvall, Sweden; Provo, Utah; Brighton, England; Vreeland a/d Vecht, Holland; Caracas, Venezuela; Hollywood, California.*

Brady and I met Johnson by the workers' camp on the pier which the cargo ships used. We heard the engine before *Dolly's* launch came in sight, low and white and extraordinarily fast. Johnson was alone at the wheel. The boat cut an efficient arc through the water, reduced its power, and murmured up to a mooring. In a moment he was ashore, and we were moving off in Brady's Javelin SST.

No one could have faulted my friend Johnson's behavior. Consternation, and a mild stimulation—so characteristic of sudden death, so identical with the feverish atmosphere of the clubhouse I had just left that it deceived even me for a moment. Then Brady dropped us at Edgecombe's house, and I realized as we walked up the path that all those questions had had a point; and that although his greeting of Sir Bartholomew, huddled inside, might hold genuine feeling, it was merely the preamble.

The chairman of the board had arrived, and whether we wanted it or not, we were about to hold a post-mortem in the fullest and ugliest sense of the word.

It helped Edgecombe to talk. I had heard it before: Mr. Tiko had gallantly tramped back to tee No. 7, where Denise had put the brooch in her pocket, and volunteered to search the next three holes. Brady had begun from No. 10, and Lady Edgecombe had begun walking backward from the sixteenth where she had discovered her loss. Sir Bartholomew, starting much later, had taken a golf cart from the clubhouse to No. 10, and had caught up with Brady at the twelfth. They walked on from there together. It was Brady who had noticed the footmarks at the edge of the great white excavation to the right of the green, and had called Sir Bartholomew over to look.

I had seen it as well. Unrolled like a ribbon over the crossed caterpillar tracks down the side of the chasm was the smooth undulating mark of a falling body, with the small rubble kicked up alongside. Lady Edgecombe lay at the bottom, where the harrow had been left with its sharp turning spikes. Luckily, most of what had happened to her was obliterated by the folds of a dusty tarpaulin.

I was the only person who had picked up the tarpaulin and sniffed it. The smell of gas was then perfectly clear: the exterminating gas, and something else so faint I was unable to name it.

"Chloropicrin. They use it to fumigate the ground, don't they?" said Johnson. "If they're replanting, or relaying turf on old ground. It kills the weeds and removes the bacteria. Were they planting there?"

"Yes," said Sir Bartholomew. He removed his hands. Beneath his face had aged a great deal. "They were creating a border of plants between the tee and the new lake. The tarpaulin was there when we passed earlier on. We think she picked it up . . ." He stopped.

"It was wet," I said. "We believe the sprinkler was on. In fact we know it was: the grass still had a big silver-blue patch where the spray had just fallen. We think the brooch must have lain in the path of the spray, and Lady Edgecombe picked up the tarpaulin and slung it over her head before running in and snatching it up. She got as far as that, anyway, before the gas overwhelmed her. We found the brooch where she dropped it again, probably when she started coughing and choking near the edge of the quarry."

For a moment Johnson was silent, the bifocals in impersonal communion. Then, "If the victim was supposed to be you, Bart," he said, "why should they trouble to do anything more to Denise? Or do you think she genuinely fell over the edge?"

"I think she saw whoever it was," Sir Bartholomew said, his voice rough. "I think the killer was there, ready to finish the job. Beltanno says unless you were trapped under that tarpaulin for any length of time, the gas wouldn't kill you. But it would choke you long enough for a determined man to do anything with you he wanted."

" — Such as press a pad of ether or chloroform or whatever you like over your face and suffocate you before you went over," I said.

"In the open air? In daylight?" Johnson's voice was merely clinical.

I said, "Go down and look at it. There's palmetto scrub to the horizon on every side. You can just see the sea on the right, and if you look back, you can just see the triangle of the airport control tower. But it's secluded as three quarters of the fairways on this course are secluded. The only possible interruption might have come from a service cart; there were plenty of them about. But if he used the tarpaulin as a shield, he might appear only to be sheltering Lady Edgecombe."

"Or he might have been in a red service cart himself," Johnson said. " Or in a golf cart. What's your view of Wallace Brady now, Bart?"

"Only that I don't want to see him again," Edgecombe said. He was beginning to lose his precarious poise. I caught Johnson's eye, and he ignored me.

"Have you found out any more about him?" Johnson said mildly. Edgecombe put down his fists.

"Have I found out anything? I've told you what I know. He's American; he comes from Virginia; his family seems authenticated; he is a genuine engineer, and good at his job; he's been here six months and expects to spend another three on his part of the development. He's going on after that, I believe, to Caracas. He works all over the world. He has never spoken out of turn or given the least cause for suspicion. In fact, he was good to — " He balked at the name.

He said, staring at Johnson, "What the hell more do you want from me? You're the top man. You're the big shot with the money and resources. All you have to do is radio around your pals and you can find out what toothpaste he uses. But you didn't bother to do it, did you? You didn't check; you didn't call in protection; you didn't even trouble to keep an eye on the matter yourself. You were too damned keen to get off to Crab Cay and your latest . . ."

"Actually, the Begum is James Ulric's property," Johnson said. "But I'll admit to a crazed liaison with Sergeant Trotter, if it'll make you feel any better." He paused, and said quietly, "Brady has been checked out, of course. He's clean, or appears to be. So are Krishtof Bey and Sergeant Trotter for that matter. All it means is that so far, no one has traced any misdemeanors they may have committed. Brady could have killed Denise. So could Mr. Tiko. So could any one of several hundred men of the island's labor force, if suitably paid. Do you honestly think she would still be alive, Bart, if I had moved in beside you with a revolver?"

Edgecombe muttered something. I heard only "protection."

Johnson looked up. He said, "But you don't get a wet nurse with this job. You don't even get good toilet and canteen facilities. You get permission to kill and be killed, with no questions asked. You've the training we all have, and the weapons we all have, and a fair number of your housestaff, I expect, are in the Spoonmakers' Union as well. What the hell more do you want?" He got up and stood over Edgecombe, his hands in his pockets. "If someone's killing you because he doesn't like the shade of your socks, that's too bad: that's natural wastage. If someone's killing you because you're an agent, then he's lying out there taking his time about it for a very good reason. He wants to see who else is going to drop off the rock face and sprint for the play area."

Johnson moved across to the drinks table, and uncapping the whiskey bottle, began to pour three neat doubles into three heavy tumblers. "You may have blown your cover, Bart," he said crisply, "but I'm damned if you're going to blow mine."

"You've made your point," Edgecombe said. He paid no attention to the drink Johnson laid by his side. Edgecombe said, "I suppose I can't expect you to come to Nassau for the funeral? There won't be anyone else." His eyes were bloodshot as if he had had a blow on the head, but I thought his training showed, if nowhere else, in the remarkable grip he had taken again on himself. Johnson offered me a whiskey and I snapped a refusal. I wasn't in the bloody Spoonmakers' Union.

Johnson sat down. "Doesn't Denise have any relations?"

Edgecombe shook his head. "A few distant ones in the south of England. They couldn't afford to come, and wouldn't care anyway. She . . . she'd made her life with me."

"But you left her alone a good bit, didn't you? Didn't she resent that?" Johnson said.

Edgecombe shut his lips and put the back of his hand to his mouth. I walked across and standing between Edgecombe and Johnson, put my hands on my hips. "What possible business is it of yours?" I said to Johnson. Pleasantly, I trust.

Edgecombe said, his hand still over his face, "He gets twenty-five thousand a year for asking that sort of question. At this sort of time."

"Was she alone a lot?" Johnson repeated. He might not have heard me.

"Yes. But she had friends," Edgecombe said.

"Did you know who they were?"

"Not all of them. I couldn't," said Edgecombe with sudden

145

bitterness. *"Go here; do that; we want this code broken by Monday* . . . You know this business. I had a wife. I'm sorry. It was a mistake. But I'd had her a long time — long before I entered your stainless profession. I loved her . . ."

"Did she love you?" said Johnson. "Or was she bored and resentful, and open to suggestions by anyone with enough money? Suggestions which would make her a comfortable widow . . . except that she didn't live to become a comfortable widow. Because Denise talked too much when she had had too much Planters' Punch, didn't she? Who made up the crab sandwiches you took to New York, Edgecombe?"

Edgecombe's big, well-groomed face had gone white to the lips. I said sharply, "Drink this!" and gave him the whiskey Johnson had poured. He started to speak, and then as I looked at him, drank it off in one gulp. He put it down and got to his feet and stared at Johnson, until his breathing allowed him to speak.

Then he said, "All right. You said that, with Denise lying dead in that diabolical quarry out there. She fell on a harrow . . . can you imagine that? I expect you can; you've seen plenty of violent deaths in this job. Before that she was suffocated — by gas, by a cloth — it doesn't matter. You can imagine that, too. I'd like you to. You can further imagine that we slept here last night, Denise and I, and had breakfast together this morning. I shaved, she dressed. We talked of the day, and our plans for tomorrow . . . She was looking forward to her golf . . ."

He stopped, still breathing hard. I made a little movement, but he waved me off. "Beltanno was too good a player. I realized what had happened. Denise wasn't strong willed. She didn't need to be. She had me . . . most of the time. She knew her own weaknesses, and we supported one another. She wasn't spiteful, she wasn't anything but a nice, pretty woman who was perhaps a bit vain . . ."

He looked straight at Johnson. "She doesn't deserve on her deathbed to be accused of murder and treason. I don't deserve that the first posthumous words I hear of my wife are the suggestion that she wanted to kill me." He stumbled, and I put my hand on his elbow and kept it there. "You may withdraw your attention from Great Harbour Cay," said Sir Bartholomew Edgecombe. "As from this moment, I have resigned from your service. Whatever interest you have kindly heretofore taken in me, I deserve none of it now."

Through it all, Johnson had not even moved. His glasses, motionless, reflected the chair, the table, Edgecombe's pale face and the blue of my beach shirt, as I stood and supported him. I had forgotten I was still in my swimsuit. The anger I was suppressing became a strengthening pain in my stomach. I controlled myself. Johnson said levelly: "As soon as you are exposed as an agent, your career as an agent is ended. Nothing has changed."

"Something has," I said with satisfaction. "I put a strong sedative in Sir Bartholomew's whiskey, Mr. Johnson. If you want to distress him still further, I suggest you come back in two hours."

Johnson said, "Is he distressed?"

I had Edgecombe's pulse under my fingers. I said, "Would you like to come and feel this?"

Johnson shook his head. He was looking at Edgecombe. Sir Bartholomew stared back at him. I could feel his weight press on my arm as the drowsiness gathered. Edgecombe said, "I told you the truth." The rancor had gone out of his voice.

"I know," Johnson said. "But I had to be sure. We swear loyalty ten times over to our employer, and mean it. But we cover up for the person we love."

Edgecombe said, his voice gentle, "She wasn't mixed up in anything. Not Denise," and Johnson, walking forward stopped, ignoring me, and took Edgecombe's other arm, turning him toward the shut bedroom door. "You would know. I accept that," he said. He walked Edgecombe to the door and opened it on the empty bedroom. "I never apologize for the inexcusable," he added.

Sir Bartholomew put one hand on the doorpost and with the other patted my shoulder. "You see? Brains and tenacity," he said. "Should I accept his apology?"

"He didn't offer one," I said grimly.

"Oh. My mistake," said Sir Bartholomew vaguely. But he smiled at Johnson before he turned in the door, and closed it gently behind him. And below the bifocals Johnson's lips, I saw, stirred in an answering smile.

It had disappeared when he turned toward me. "That was interfering of you, Doctor," he said. "But not as disastrous this time as it might have been. If you could take a moment now to veil your splendid nubility, I should like to see where Denise Edgecombe died."

I didn't speak to him even after I dressed. I cannot remember addressing a word to Johnson through all the dreadful, drawn-out proceedings of the long day. The police came, and another doctor, and questions were asked, but in a climate of reverent pity. Lady Edgecombe had died from a fall, after being made dizzy by the inadvertent use of a gas tarpaulin. So all the experts said, and who were Johnson or I to contradict them. Or perhaps it was because of Johnson, behind the scenes, that the formalities were so smoothly completed.

Denise, taken from her resting place in the nurse's tidy white trailer, was flown at last to Nassau, her husband beside her. Johnson let them go, and restrained me also from following. "There is nothing you can do. He will be under the eye of the hospital, and besides, he can take care of himself."

"I want to go to the funeral. I was their guest," I said. They were the first words I had spoken to him directly, since that sadistic discussion that morning.

"He doesn't want you. I'm sorry, but that is the truth. He doesn't want anyone. And I wish you to come to Crab Island," Johnson said.

We were back in Bart Edgecombe's empty house. I was watching his maid pack up Denise's things, and Johnson, French windows open, was standing on the sun deck over the golf course, absently filling his pipe. "A splendid idea," I said. I picked up an ashtray and marching out, placed it on the table beside him. "A big, cheerful party with the Begum and James Ulric, and who? Krishtof Bey ogling and Sergeant Trotter giving his famous imitation of a Royal Canadian Mounty on top of a camel. That'll soon cheer us up."

"You'd find it compatible compared with the clubhouse," he said. "Stage people hate death."

"Who doesn't?" I said. I badly wanted a quarrel.

"Some people come to terms with it," Johnson said. "The Begum, for one. And your father, for another . . . Why didn't you tell me about Pentecost's family?"

"I meant to make some inquiries myself," I said brusquely. And so I had. Only there had been so little time. I said, "Who told you? Dahlia?"

"Eventually," Johnson said. "She disappeared after you saw her, and my people only found her this morning. By then it was too late."

"How?" I asked.

"The family had gone from Bullock's Harbour. Someone put two and two together and guessed that the water tower would lead us to Dahlia. They left yesterday to go work on Abaco. So they said. Of course, now there's no trace."

I was silent. I had meant to do that myself, when I first set

149

foot on Great Harbour Cay. Instead I had swum, and bought myself clothes, and listened to the doctorbirds in the hibiscus bushes. And had lain on a beach chair with Paul's warm hand massaging my spine, while Denise Edgecombe fell to her death. Johnson said, "I know Bart asked you to stay here. But it would send you crazy, Beltanno."

"So would Crab Island," I said.

"It won't," he said. "Or if it does, I'll bring you straight back to this house. Or to Nassau. Or anywhere else you want to go." He paused, and then said, "I'm taking Wallace Brady over with me . . . Do you know, Beltanno, what it means to finish a job?"

And I understood that. No apologies for the inexcusable; no reference to what had happened that morning. No further reference, either, to Pentecost. I thought of Brady's voice indignantly refuting my own ironical suggestion. Leave things long enough and they'll find their own answer.

Whatever one thought of Johnson, he was concerned at the moment with bringing the author of two deaths to light. And for that he wanted my help. I didn't want to go to Crab Island. I wished to avoid the Begum, more than ever in the company of my father. The friends she surrounded herself with, I did not know. The three I knew, Brady, Krishtof and Trotter, were each still men of mystery — figures of unproved suspicion. And Johnson himself I distrusted, after this morning.

He had been watching me, while lighting his pipe. He took it out of his mouth. "Have you ever seen," he said, "a bronchial patient being lambasted out of a spasm? Perhaps you've had to do it for your father."

I had, twice. I didn't say anything.

"It isn't pleasant," he said.

The maid had finished. I walked back into the room and turned on one of the lamps. I thought of my own lapse with Pentecost. "Sometimes," I said, "it may be necessary."

He came in and stood in the doorway, the lamp igniting the bifocals, the pipe glowing red in his hand. He had extraordinarily thick dense black hair, with no hint of gray. But he was older, of course, than I was. "Sometimes it shouldn't be," he said unexpectedly. "Denise Edgecombe should not have died."

I looked at him. "You said so yourself. Who could have stopped it?"

"I could," said Johnson. "I personally, Big Daddy, could. But I didn't."

"Why not?" I said. He had had, I think, a shade more whiskey than even a top person could carry with no sign at all.

But he had not had as much whiskey as that. "Probably because you had that blue thing on at the airport," he said, sticking his pipe in his mouth. "How many inches above the knee did it come? Ten? Twelve? . . . I want you to wear the blue thing on Crab Island, Beltanno. And the bathing suit. And everything else you've got. Don't become a case history. Mix your professions like me."

"Do you need me on Crab Island?" I said.

I thought he was going to quip for an answer, but he didn't. "Yes," he said.

"In the Spoonmakers' Union?"

"In close affiliation to it. A tong, perhaps."

"All right," I said.

*   *

We dined briefly in the clubhouse, beleaguered at a table with Mr. Brady and Mr. Tiko, to whom with some misgivings I introduced Johnson Johnson. I had no need to worry. Johnson, it was clear, had not heard of the heir to the MacRannochs. Mr. Tiko, on the other hand, had heard of Johnson Johnson. They discussed Japanese painting, to the confusion of the long chain of well-wishers who came to commiserate with us over Lady

Edgecombe's sudden death, and to inquire in the nicest possible way into her domestic circumstances.

We separated early, Johnson to sleep in a rented rondette for the night, I to retire alone in the Edgecombe's silent big house. But first, he came in and watched while I checked the mesh frames at every window, and locked the French windows. I had my gun by my bed.

"I fancy you're safe, with Bart away, but it doesn't do to take risks. Nervous?" he asked.

I shook my head, as near truthfully as makes no difference. One takes one's precautions. Then it is merely a matter of will power.

"Good girl," said Johnson.

"And Bart Edgecombe?" I said.

"I give you my word," said Johnson. "Nothing will happen to him in Nassau. And after it's over, I'm bringing him back to Crab Island with me."

I remember concealing my rising horror, and tackling instead the more domestic connotations of this statement. "Heavens," I said. "How big a house has the Begum?" For *guests* with the Begum Akbar never meant seven blow-up mattresses on the sitting room floor. It meant seven bedrooms with full, personalized plumbing. We, who had been forced to put in all those extra bathrooms in Castle Rannoch, were sorely aware of it. Crab Island was a half-mile across. "And the sewage!" I added, as my stream of consciousness began to run faster.

But Johnson Johnson merely gazed at me through his bifocals. "Good night, Doctor. I won't spoil the surprise. Wait," he said, "till you see it."

Chapter 10

WE SET OFF for Crab Island next morning, Wallace Brady and I, in *Dolly*'s white 50–mph Avenger launch, Johnson at the wheel. Brady, neatly and rather formally dressed, was not in a talkative mood; and neither was I. I noted that the approach road and first span of Brady's bridge were already in position not far from where we embarked. The outline of Crab Island was quite visible from the shore of the larger island, and we followed the line of the new bridge all the way, tying up where the piles at the Crab Island end already stood in the water. There was a small jetty, without a great deal of weather protection, off which *Dolly* rested at anchor.

We climbed out of the speedboat onto the jetty, and into a green Daimler convertible, which was waiting there empty. Johnson again took the wheel. "Green is the Akbar color," he said. "And philanthropy their habit. You should see the Akbar elephants campaigning for family planning. There's been a population explosion of tigers, because the elephants are all pooped with handing out condoms."

The jetty ended. A uniformed man at the entrance to a low modern bungalow unlocked a pair of wrought iron gates and saluted, and the Daimler swept onto a broad metaled road edged with Japanese fuchsias, Royal Palms, and oleander bushes. We passed a man in two shades of green, spraying them. A large scarlet butterfly trembled past.

Brady said, "That's a — " and Johnson lifted one hand from the steering wheel and waved with it. "It is. They buy them in and release them. Same with birds. Ever seen a doctorbird, doctor bird?"

"Frequently," I said.

"They're a damned nuisance, aren't they?" said Johnson. "Whoa."

The Daimler came to an expert short halt. Overhead were tall pines, their spaced and interleaved branches like fruit espaliers, each feathered in dark silky green hair. In front of us, crossing the road with their salmon necks looping, was a small flock of flamingoes. They stepped with great deliberation, their elbows like pink coral beads on pink needles. Their feathered bodies could be worn with an eye-veil at weddings. One came close and gazed pupil to pupil with Johnson, its yellow whorled eyes glistening over its thick black-tipped beak.

"*Forsan et Haec Olim Meminisse Iuvabit*. Virgil," said Johnson.

"The kiss of the sun for pardon,
The song of the birds for mirth,
One is nearer God's heart in a garden,
Than anywhere else on earth.
"Dorothy Frances Gurney," said Wallace Brady, surprisingly.

I'd been to the Ardastra Gardens too. " 'These flamingoes are the unique gems of the tropical bird world,' " I said helpfully. " 'Mini skirts and midriffs are not allowed. Lack of modesty breeds contempt.' "

Johnson took the bird by the beak and turned its head firmly away. "That wasn't contempt. That was just one of the dirty

154

old men of the tropical bird world," he said. "I could see its Polaroid camera."

It was, I suppose, a short dress. Wallace Brady gave me a hesitant smile. I hadn't the strength of mind not to smile back. And yet, what shaft of brilliance had called forth this tribute of manly comradeship? In a nutshell; my knees.

The drive continued between flowers and trees for a considerable distance, considering the size of the island. Johnson reassured us that it was all done with mirrors, and we were still back to back with the Ghost Train. He seemed to have forgotten Lady Edgecombe's death in the thrills of forthcoming reunion with Trotter.

We passed a gazebo, a fountain, a bridged pool with duck, a dovecote, and two marble statues. "Mini skirts and midriffs are *not* allowed," said Johnson chidingly. Stables, tennis courts, shuffleboard. The glimpse of a pool. The roofs of staff houses, discreetly tucked away behind a landscaped wood of coarse orchids. An avenue of firs, which turned with a sweep at the end. "Shut your eyes, Doctor," Johnson said.

Nonsense.

A moment later he looked in the mirror and said coolly, "What are you scared of?"

I shut them.

The car turned the corner, slowed and ran to a quiet halt. "Open them, Doctor," Johnson said.

I opened them.

In front of us rose the Begum Akbar's house on Crab Island. I didn't examine it, floor by floor and window by window. I didn't even speculate on the number of rooms she had, or what promoted the unique and unusual ground plan.

I didn't need to. The Begum's house on Crab Island was an exact copy, turret for turret and stone for stone, of Castle Rannoch in Scotland. She had built James Ulric a second home here in the Bahamas.

Beside and in front of me, there was silence. Johnson, of course, knew the house. Brady had probably helped her to build it. They were waiting with unconcealed interest to see what I would do.

There was quite a number of things I could do, including make a fool of myself. I regulated my impulses. I said patiently, "I do manage to take your point. So far as I know, no patent was ever applied for. I suppose this makes my father the only clan chieftain to lodge in two seats. One for each buttock."

The bifocals dwelled on me for a long, lingering moment. "Beltanno," said Johnson, "the steel industry needs you." He turned to Brady. "And you know what she thinks? She thinks they're all lying around in there wearing beads and stoned out of their skulls on French Blues or Black Bombers or one of the lighter character rums."

Wallace Brady turned his pleasant, suntanned all-American gaze on my knees, and then smoothly, up to my face. "The intelligent rich don't do that," he said. "The intelligent rich play children's games and tell each other true ghost stories prior to going to bed with each other. Other stimuli they do not require."

"They don't play golf?" I said. I wondered if it was Johnson's company. Wallace Brady hadn't talked like that on Great Harbour Cay.

"You and I play golf," said Brady. "Golf is played by the intelligent candidates for ascendancy."

I thought of the price of those golf bags. "A few seem to have made it," I said; but Brady shook his head firmly.

"First-generation tyros. Until you see a man playing a children's party game, you may know he doesn't belong to the real aristocracy of wealth."

The car door was opened by a manservant, who directed a

black boy to take out our suitcases. I walked up the steps and entered, with more than a few misgivings, the dark and echoing hall of my own home. Her footsteps padding through what appeared to be a series of vacant apartments, the Begum appeared smiling, her hands outstretched. She wore a dark blue sari of floating organza. "Beltanno! Wallace!"

She stopped and lowered her hands. "Johnson. What are you looking for?"

"Paper games," said Johnson. "Or Monopoly would maybe do. Or three-D ticktacktoe?"

The Begum looked at him critically. "You have that stuffed and smiling look," she said. "Like a piece of hand-carved ethnographica. What are you doing? Auditioning for Mensa?"

The glasses glittered. "You're not far off it," said Johnson admiringly. "Actually, it's an IQ and stock-holding index. No doubt your half-year figures were buoyant?"

"They were," said the Begum Akbar calmly, leading the way into the morning room. She appeared in no way amazed.

"And your intelligence is undoubted. Therefore . . . Ah!" He pounced.

"We think it's the meeting of Solomon and the Queen of Sheba," said the Begum serenely, "but the club never gives you a subject and they won't answer letters, damn them. Coffee?"

"Yes, please," I said. Brady, grinning foolishly, had followed Johnson to the immense baize table set out in the window with the largest jigsaw puzzle I have ever seen.

"Thelma," said Johnson.

"Damn you, darling," said the Begum in her careful, mannered English voice. "It's the Queen of Sheba. Krishtof recognized the cut of her trousers."

"She's smoking a cigarette," Johnson said. He slid another piece into place and surveyed it.

"She was in advance of her time," said the Begum calmly. She opened the French windows and called into the bushes. "James! Your daughter is here."

A lithe Turkish figure in a gold necklace and a pair of green cotton beach pants stepped out of the hibiscus and did a mild leap into the morning room. "He's paddling," said Krishtof Bey. "Bloody hell!" He stood rigid over the table.

"She's smoking a cigarette," said the Begum placidly. "Black or white, Beltanno?"

"White," I said.

"It's a lie!" said Krishtof Bey furiously. "It doesn't fit!"

"It does," pointed out Wallace Brady. I admired him for the way he was keeping his head.

"So do the trousers," said Johnson.

"It's Rita Hayworth in *Salome*?" said the Begum tentatively. Krishtof Bey snorted. "She didn't smoke a cigarette in *Salome*."

"She might have, off set," said the Begum helpfully. "James? Does Rita Hayworth smoke?"

"Is she on fire?" said my father, appearing dripping in the window, cackling. He looked like Picasso. He emitted a roar. "Who put that damned fag in her mouth?"

"*His* mouth," I said.

They all turned and looked accusingly at me. The Begum stirred her coffee.

"They all want to know how you know." She looked around. Sergeant Trotter, in a clean shirt and white trousers, came hesitatingly into the room. "Rodney! Some coffee," said Begum. "The Queen of Sheba's a man."

Sergeant Trotter stopped looking hesitant. "Get along with you," he said. "With them trousers?"

"Unisex," said Johnson. "Or how Solomon got wise. I agree with Beltanno. You are looking at two virile forms. Krishtof, tell us who dresses like Turks, apart from Turks?"

"I thought Turks dressed like Indians?" I said innocently.

"English dress like Indians," the Begum pointed out, with justice. She thought. "Racing car drivers dress like Turks. And old Harrovians. And men from pirate radio ships. And antique dealers. And fashion photographers."

Johnson picked up another piece of the jigsaw. "There's a dog here," he said.

The room was plunged into gloom, broken by the chinking of coffee cups. The Begum put hers firmly down. "I will not have my day controlled by ten thousand interlocking pieces of wood," she said. "Johnson, I wish to break into light conversation. Who killed Denise Edgecombe?"

She was an irresponsible woman. I had always suspected it.

There was a cracking silence, wrecked by the clatter as Sergeant Trotter's cup jumped in its saucer. Johnson's bifocals and eyebrows, I was glad to see, had parted company. For a moment he looked like the rest of us: frankly subnormal. Then he said, "Who do you have serious conversations with — morgue attendants? So far as the police know it was an accident."

"Oh?" said the Begum. "Wallace, do you think it was an accident?"

Wallace, a devotee of good taste if ever I saw one, was markedly reserved. "If you had seen the poor lady in that quarry, Begum, you wouldn't have any doubt. Of course it was an accident. Why should anyone want to kill Lady Edgecombe?"

Even my father, I was glad to see, was staring at his soulmate with extreme disapprobation. "What did you want to say that for? Pretty woman. Nothing wrong with her."

"Except boredom," said Krishtof Bey surprisingly.

"Not when you danced with her," said Wallace Brady. I had forgotten that.

"No. She had been a good dancer. Not an easy thing to give up," said the Turk. He moved across to the coffeepot, executing a swift half-dance step as he went, reminding you what an agile body he undoubtedly had. "It gets into the blood. Better to produce, to teach. Hard to leave it altogether."

"Sir Bartholomew understood it, I think," I said. "He was most gentle with her."

"Yes. The slightest touch of patronage, don't you think?" said the Begum. "I am sorry no one will take up my scandal. My theory was that Denise poisoned her husband, and then killed herself, hoping to land him with the blame. No supporters?"

"Like the Queen of Sheba," said Johnson, "it's a novel idea. Could you play thirteen holes of reasonable golf just before killing yourself?"

"My dear man," said the Begum. "I can't play golf. I thought it was like making love. If you were enthusiastic, you could do it anywhere, no matter how adverse the circumstances."

"You can," said Johnson, seated with his tobacco pouch on his knees. "But golf takes a lot longer."

"Attend," said the Begum, and reaching out a leisurely arm for the soda syphon, depressed a squirt accurately into his pipe. "I will not be balked of my fun. What if they are both killed, Sir Bartholomew and Denise Edgecombe? Could someone be attempting to wipe out this family?"

I avoided looking at Johnson. Krishtof Bey, with a fresh cup of coffee, was doing a slow *glissé* prowl back along the edge of the carpet; Sergeant Trotter, sitting poker backed on one of the Begum's most comfortable armchairs, was looking bored and uneasy; Brady was trying to catch one of Johnson's eyes. I had been attempting for some moments to impound the other.

Johnson shut his eyes, thus eluding us both. My father, who had been padding about for some time, leaving wet naked footmarks on the parquet, said, "Where's that damned paper, Thelma? Who should want to dispose of the Edgecombes? Played a perfectly rational game of contract, both of them."

The Begum's large long-sighted eyes rested on me. "Your father holds the theory that, against a sure knowledge of cricket and bridge, the criminal classes are powerless," she said. "He is wrong. It is the man with the brown ale-making set and the night tidy who will attract violence. Suppose Sir Bartholomew was poisoned by the food or the drink he had at the airport. Suppose he was poisoned again when he became worse on the plane. Suppose Johnson here, who was so neatly set alight at the end of Leviticus' drum solo, was singled out because he wore Sir Bartholomew's jacket? Suppose Denise was gassed and pushed down that slope?"

Wallace Brady looked across at me. "I told you," he said. "Paper games."

"Well, Beltanno?" said the Begum; and they all, even my father, who was searching inside the harpsichord, looked around at me.

I breathed slowly and steadily, avoiding a second glance at Johnson, whose despicable eyes were still shut. I said, "It sounds dramatic, but I think you should look at the probabilities. Who had anything to gain, as my father has said, from killing the Edgecombes?"

Sergeant Trotter said, "Well, it usually boils down to money. Who gets the nest egg?"

"There wasn't any," said Johnson. He sat up, opening his eyes, and taking out a clean handkerchief, began to dry the blackened bowl of his pipe reproachfully. "They were comfortable, but far from the top of the cheese trolley. No heavy insurance either, and no family."

"No Queen of Sheba either, Thelma," said my father, and cackled. He appeared to have found what he wanted; he sat down in another chair with a thick file of papers on his knee. "You're on the wrong track."

The Begum stretched her elegant legs on her lounge chair. The furniture on Crab Island, I had to admit, was lusher than Castle Rannoch had ever possessed. "There are other reasons for murder. He was in the diplomatic service abroad. What about you, Rodney? Did you get cashiered in Aden for selling cut-price juke boxes to oil sheiks? Does Sir Bartholomew know the secret of your horrible past?"

Sergeant Rodney Trotter was a little man in quite excellent health. But for a moment the veins stood out on his cheeks, and I thought his upper plate was going to drop. He said, "Why me?"

"You were at the airport and on the plane and in the Bamboo Conch Club," said the Begum. She was clever. And idle. And enjoying herself.

"I wasn't on the golf course," said Trotter.

The Begum stretched herself luxuriously. "If you could pay a waiter at the Conch Club, you could pay a groundsman at Great Harbour Cay," she said.

"Then why pick on me?" said Sergeant Trotter. He was becoming angry. "It might have been anyone, by that reckoning. Anyone else on that plane. Someone on the BOAC staff."

"But I gather," said the Begum gently, "no one else knew Sir Bartholomew, or had any dealings with him, or indeed was likely ever to see him again. No one else in the Monarch Lounge was going to stay on or near Great Harbour Cay. Except, of course, for Mr. Brady."

More sophisticated by far than Trotter, Wallace Brady had of course been waiting for it. He grinned at the Begum, his hands clasped over his pale cotton stomach. "I've been here six months, and I'm going to be here a good few months yet. If Bart Edgecombe knew any dirty secrets from my past, I feel we would have slugged it out long before now."

James Ulric, hugging his file, produced an actionable grin.

"Maybe it wasn't an old blot in the games book, Brady. They tell me you were seeing a lot of Denise."

Wallace Brady got up. "Begum," he said. "Enough is enough. The lady we are talking about is dead, and you're acting like it was a game. The Edgecombes were neighbors of mine, and I did all a good neighbor would do. That's all there ever was to it. And now, if you'll excuse me, I'd like to take Beltanno out and show her the gardens."

The Begum got up, but James Ulric didn't stir. He nodded at me. "Some day that girl will be worth nearly three million dollars," he said. "You should get your hooks into her, now Denise is out of the way. Although she tells me she's going to marry an effing Japanese . . . Have you asked him yet?" he demanded.

I stared at him and said, "No. But I shall."

"Who?" said Wallace Brady. He was looking at me as if I'd just knocked down his hamster on a Suzuki 120.

"Mr. Tiko," I said.

"Great jumping Jesus," said Wallace Brady.

"I suppose," said my father, "I should ask him to the Gathering. We are having a Bahamian Steel Band leaping through flaming circles on motorcycles. Since accidents are so plentiful, no doubt he could have one."

"I shall arrange it," said Krishtof Bey.

We had forgotten him. Even the Begum turned around sharply, and he smiled up at her from where he reclined on the carpet. "Am I not a suspect too?" he said. "I have been in all the right places at all the right times, although I have not yet found a motive. The lovely Denise? But I barely met her. A sordid event in my past? But all dancers have lascivious pasts: it is expected of them. No one can blackmail a dancer."

"Let's pretend," said Johnson suddenly, "that you were wanted for some major crime, say in Turkey, which would involve a long prison sentence. A top dancer wouldn't remain a top dancer, would he, if he had to spend ten years breaking stones in a quarry?"

Krishtof Bey put both hands to his head, spun around, and fell full length, with a light thud, at Johnson's feet. "Save me! Save me!" he screamed.

I gazed at the magnificent lumbar area of his vertebral column as the Begum said, "Foolish boy. No one suspects you. You haven't the application."

The dancer rose compactly to his feet, his face rigid with hauteur. "You say no application to me? When I practice seven hours a day?"

"You don't practice hate seven hours a day," said the Begum calmly. "That is a European trait, Krishtof. Besides, you would kill with a knife."

"And you?" said the dancer. He tossed back his long hair and seizing her chiffon scarf from a chair, draped it swiftly over his head and shoulders, one slender hand holding it in place. His walk and carriage had changed: he was the impudent replica of the Begum herself. "You, Thelma, have been much in evidence. What did Sir Bartholomew and his wife know of you that you preferred the MacRannoch and his daughter should not know?"

For a moment the beautiful, ageing face was quite still; then she drew the scarf from his hands and flicked it lightly around his throat. "That my friends don't play cricket or bridge. Who are the false eyelashes for?"

"Johnson," said the dancer immediately, his faun's mouth lifting. He had quick wits. Nor did the lightly accented voice have any trouble at all with its English. I saw with misgiving that his eyelashes *were* false. He gazed through them at Johnson's Aertex shirt and shambling trousers. "He is going to paint me, is he not? In the sun, in my natural state. An animal, a leopard. Lithe and lordly. Pan leaning against a tree trunk. A hibiscus flower here and there?"

Johnson looked uneasy. "I'm a rather splashy painter," he said.

The Begum drew her veil lightly from Krishtof's throat. "Are you trying to shock Johnson?" she said. "You won't." The brittle gaze, wavering around, rested on the impassive bifocals. "You boring, smug little man," she said. "I was hoping for a colorful morning. And now you say all these events are pure accidents."

"I don't," said Johnson. He was filling his pipe. The muscles of my abdominal wall recoiled like a spring and I choked. No one noticed.

"You did," said my father. "You said . . ."

"*You* said they were accidents," said Johnson. "Actually, Sir Bartholomew was poisoned with arsenic, and his wife Denise was undoubtedly killed. Beltanno will corroborate." He struck a match and puffed at his pipe.

Everybody stared at him. The Begum sat down, and after a moment Krishtof Bey slid to her feet. My father remained seated, his bony finger still keeping the place in his unspeakable papers. Trotter and Wallace Brady, by contrast, both slowly rose to their feet. No one spoke.

Johnson wagged the match, dropped it, and took the pipe comfortably out of his mouth. "All right, Thelma?" he said. "Status redeemed? Pumped up the prelunch adrenalin?"

Someone let out a long sigh. The Begum half relaxed, still staring at Johnson. "You hideous creature. You are trying to reenter my good books?"

"Not at all," said Johnson. "I never touch a good book before lunchtime. It *is* nearly lunchtime?"

165

"Then they were accidents?" Brady said. He was still standing.

"Beltanno says not," said Johnson blandly. "She took stomach tests, which the hospital didn't. And she's got signed papers to prove it. It was arsenic."

Sergeant Trotter's parade-ground voice, though muted, was still cold and carrying to a degree. "Then why don't the police know?" he said.

"Because Sir Bartholomew asked Beltanno not to tell them," said Johnson; and they all turned again and looked at me.

A large number of well-adjusted persons go through life ignorant as a cabbage of their own likely reactions in sudden emergency. Mine are not only within my awareness; they are timed and graded according to the emergency. This I would rate as an acute abdomen. I thought with commensurate speed.

I said, "I did take tests, that's true. Sir Bartholomew was given a dose of arsenic both times, by whom I don't know. I need hardly say" — I looked at Johnson — "if the police get to hear that I've concealed the fact, it'll be the end of my career."

"We won't tell them," said Johnson soothingly. "Thelma, you can vouch for everyone here? We don't want Beltanno in trouble."

"Speak for yourself," said James Ulric suddenly. My dear, doting old father. "But why didn't Edgecombe want the police told? And why did Florence Nightingale here agree not to tell them?"

"Tell them," said Johnson through the haze of his pipe. "You won't believe this, Thelma, and I'll thank you to remember it the next time you accuse me of boring you, although I must remember in future not to raise these matters just before meals. Beltanno, tell them what Bart said that his job was."

It was like double talk in the operating theater when the patient is only partly anaesthetized. I kicked the Spoonmakers' Union mentally in the teeth and gave my answer, right or wrong, but bang on the cue. "He said he was a member of the British Intelligence service," I said. "He persuaded me, too."

Like a handsome doll in her robes, the Begum was staring at me. "You're making it all up. Johnson, what are you teaching this girl?"

"Listen," said Johnson. "No one has anything to teach Doctor B. Douglas MacRannoch. She believed Sir Bartholomew Edgecombe, and I believe her. And what's more, I'm keeping my mouth shut about it. If the espionage network is gunning for Bart, then the counterespionage network can get on with gunning right back without help from us."

Four people said, "But — " and I swear you could hear their ectopic cardiac beats chiming like clocks.

My father said, "In that case he's not coming here. Thelma, I forbid you to invite Sir Bartholomew Edgecombe here. Johnson here was once nearly killed in mistake for that man, and his wife *has* been killed. Which of us might be next?"

"Really, James," said the Begum with interest. "You mean you think the killer is here?"

My father is not one to boggle. "If he isn't here, he could get here without blowing his mind. How many people are coming from Nassau for this beach barbecue next week?"

"Seventy-five," the Begum said serenely. "Most of them MacRannochs, darling."

Krishtof Bey, his face solemn, shook his head slowly. "This is bad. Even registered breeds have their deviants."

I despised them all, and especially Johnson. I said icily, "I cannot imagine that Sir Bartholomew returning from his wife's funeral will wish to attend a beach barbecue. May I invite Mr. Tiko?"

My father shouting "No!" clashed with the Begum answering "Yes." She went on firmly: "Of course Sir Bartholomew need not come to the barbecue unless he wishes. But I will not throw this poor man to his attackers. He will stay safely here on my island as long as he wishes. And so far as the Asiatic forty-sixth chief of the MacRannochs is concerned, the answer is equally simple. Beltanno will tell you. The quickest way to make anyone immunologically competent is to expose them freely to the disease."

It was a layman's imprecise grasp of a precise physical law, but I overlooked it. If I was an emotional midget, the fault was my father's, tramping through all my nascent relationships to visit his traplines. This time I was setting my own gun with the Begum's assistance, and James Ulric wasn't going to keep Mr. Tiko away. I wanted to see Mr. Tiko's face when he found out I was the MacRannoch's sole daughter. If I lived long enough, that is to say.

The lunch gong sounded as the Begum's butler was handing around drinks and everyone was in the midst of exclaiming and speculating about Edgecombe's precise function in the unbelievable and slightly ridiculous world of espionage. During all the boring repetition of events at the airport, at the club, and elsewhere, it was remarkable how earnest was the conversation and thoughtful were the theories of the three men most closely implicated: Brady, Trotter, and the dancer.

Since the Begum's fantasy had turned into cold fact, no one had had the bad taste to refer to the favored position of these three in the list of suspects. No one either appeared to notice that Johnson had done the very thing he had warned me against in Nassau. He had warned the murderer, if the murderer were one of these three, that I alone had the physical proof that Bart Edgecombe had been poisoned.

My irritation with James Ulric evaporated. Even my plans for Mr. Tiko began to appear somewhat flat. If anyone in this house was laying traps, it was Johnson Johnson. And the lure, 126 pounds deadweight, was me.

Chapter 11

I REMEMBER VERY LITTLE of that lunch, except that during it I decided to apply for a Heinz Fellowship in Zambia. After coffee the Begum announced that the immediate hours of heat were to be spent, by order, in siesta and that we should foregather later by the swimming pool. Having tried to catch Johnson's eye yet again and been repulsed by those despicable bifocals, I walked upstairs to my room and locked myself in.

I took off my dress and lay on the bed. Without slip and girdle, I had to admit, my pores functioned more freely. There was a pink patch, from the second rib down to the navel, where Paul's oiling yesterday had ameliorated the effect of the sun. Above my head a fan moved like an aircraft propeller, stirring my wig and rustling the long blossoming stems in a Chinese vase in the corner, across an unthinkable expanse of white, fitted bearskin. The air conditioner hummed.

It was peaceful, as under a hair dryer. In long cedar cupboards, my new clothes hung out of sight. Beside me on a low table were a Chinese lamp, some new books in glossy dustjackets, cigarettes, a lighter and ash tray, and a vacuum flask of iced water. No telephone. No telephones on the Out Islands of the Bahamas. No telephones or radio transmitters on Crab.

The branches stirred, pale pink against the taffeta of the drawn curtains. A frivolous dusk enfolded the room. It was the same shape as my room in Castle Rannoch, but my room at home had no cedar wardrobes and only one deep-set window, looking onto the sea. The cold sea and the rain. I closed my eyes.

No fitted carpet either. My room in Castle Rannoch had a gray stone-flagged floor, with an old and valuable rug. One of the first tests of a candidate had been his response to that rug. The boy who had taken me home from the Oban Gathering had offered to get an uncle to mend it. Last seen of that boy. Last seen of any boy worth a damn.

I opened my unwilling eyes. The curtain billowed. This room is just like my room in Castle Rannoch except that everything in it is in perfect condition, save for B. Douglas MacRannoch.

Query: What did I have to drink at lunch?

Answer: Tomato juice.

Addendum: Krishtof Bey was at table beside me.

My room at Castle Rannoch connects with a dressing room used as a bedroom by my succession of nurses. At Castle Rannoch the doorway would be behind that pink curtain.

The pink curtain billowed.

Even when on automatic pilot, my reactions, I am happy to say, are faster than most people's. I snatched the gun from my pillow before the silk had dropped into place and fired one, two, three times. Three neat holes appeared in the pink. The stacked branches of blossom dropped like corpses, rigid to one side of the vase. And the vase itself began moving slowly toward me.

I raised the gun, and someone beside me plucked it neatly out of my hand.

"Stop," said Krishtof Bey. "It is Tang, and the director of the Metropolitan Museum of Art would ill-wish your next elective abortion."

I sat there in my underpants and brassiere while the rest of him came out from under the bed. He had my gun in one hand, and a long lasso haltering the Chinese vase in the other. He was still wearing the gold necklace and the pair of green cotton beach pants. He said, "Dear Doctor MacRannoch. My iman says my fate is not to be shot. I thought you might have a gun."

I will not pretend to be calm. A mentally subnormal patient subject to hypomanic attacks is good humored, requires little sleep, and is always complaining of hunger. With my larded midriff maintained as upright as the bedding made possible, I said with gentle authority, "I never shoot a man who is sick, Krishtof Bey. I try to help him. Would you like a biscuit?"

The Tartar face tilted and shook slowly in thought. "I hadn't thought of it. Have you got a biscuit?" he said.

I smiled warmly. "In the pocket of my coat. Over there, you see, with my dresses."

The gun did not waver, but I had puzzled him. "Do you always carry biscuits about in your pockets?" he said.

Vodka, I thought. An alcoholic with an acute anxiety neurosis may break at any moment into psychotic episodes. "I get hungry," I said. "In the other pocket you'll find a flask of Scotch whiskey."

He lay on the bearskin regarding me, his elbow holding the pistol resting quietly on the edge of my bed, and the ends of his hair stirred on his shoulders as he shook his head yet again. A trace of anxiety appeared and vanished. He had, as they all do, a strong streak of cunning. Even his voice had become soft and gentle. "Try to relax," he said. "Forget the gun. Just lie back, Doctor MacRannoch, and I will bring to you the whiskey flask and also the biscuits. Close your eyes."

It wasn't quite what I meant, but it would do. My distress score rating — o for calm and 100 for panic — dropped to around

25 and oscillated at the ready. I closed my eyes and he got up from the bearskin and moved over to the sliding doors of the wardrobe.

I made a single athletic bound for the door.

Krishtof Bey made the kind of leap I am told Nijinsky performed as a large Hybrid Tea, and hooking my ankle, brought me down on my brassiere *thud* on the white bearskin carpet. He then flipped me over and with three turns of his lasso, bound my wrists together before me.

I was not inactive. I have felled a full-scale chromosomal aberration before now; I have brought a six-foot YY syndrome to his knees. But never before had I fought a Turkish ballet dancer in full command of his unsuppressed senses. When I found myself at length, hands bound and flat on the carpet, I felt like a foam-rubber prototype in an ergonomics laboratory. Krishtof Bey, his respiration barely stirring his necklace, tossed the gun in the air, caught it, laid it on a table and said, "Were you hoping I was a nice, easy manic depressive? I'm not. I just wanted to ask you, Doctor B. Douglas MacRannoch, about that arsenic poisoning." And he sat on my feet before I could kick him and added sweetly, "And I dare you to scream."

It wasn't rate 100 yet; but it wasn't too far away from the 90s, at that. The oblique, cynical eyes smiled down at me. All right. He didn't have the gun. But with muscles like those and speed like that he could choke the life out of me long before any scream of mine could be heard beyond those thick walls. And I knew just how thick those walls were. I cleared my throat. I said, "Tell me how you did it."

I hadn't expected him really to talk, and he didn't. He smiled. "Tell me what happened to the results of those arsenic tests. Did you write them down?"

"Yes," I said. A sound idea had just occurred to me.

"And where are they?" said Krishtof Bey. His voice was over-friendly and feline.

"Johnson Johnson has them," I said. "And if you kill me, he'll hand them straight to the police."

"Exposing Sir Bartholomew Edgecombe as an agent?" asked Krishtof Bey. Reclining picturesquely beside me, he was stroking the area of my lower diaphragm with a speculative finger. "Poor darling."

He was not referring to Sir Bartholomew Edgecombe. My skin twitched. I said, "Of course. Well, the murderer at least must already know he's an agent."

"Suppressive therapy," said Krishtof Bey thoughtfully. "Against men. Did you take a course, Beltanno? What did they do, inject a nausea response to after-shave lotion?" He picked up my tied wrists, damn him, and impudently felt my pulse. "Then why haven't you or Johnson told the police already?" he said.

I quelled a strong impulse to tremble, and tried to concentrate my intellectual powers. If I didn't watch, I was going to blow Johnson's precious cover, as the jargon regrettably went. I wasn't at all sure whether I cared. I said: "Johnson didn't want trouble. And it was just possible that this was a personal feud against Edgecombe. But if anything happens to me, even Johnson won't hesitate. I promise you that."

He grinned. He was still holding my pulse. I said, "Why do you want to kill Edgecombe? Was Johnson right? Does he know something about you?"

Krishtof Bey rose to his feet like a milk-pouring commercial run backward and struck the fifth position, brown arms outflung. He relaxed, and gazed down his torso at me. "Everyone knows about dancers," he said. "Am I not a magnificent animal?"

"So are laboratory chimpanzees," I said. "And you should see *their* psychoses."

He bounced lightly and lay on the bed, looking at me. "In Izmir at this moment two secretaries are answering my love mail. Letters from ballet-sick ladies all over the world, with their photographs, Beltanno. In Copenhagen, where I am dancing next month, they will put up the crash barriers and give me a police escort from the house of my host to the theater. In my diary I have invitations from multimillionairesses, from film stars, from royalty. Today, in a hundred places in the world, someone is saying, 'Where is Krishtof Bey? What is he doing? Will he come to my costume ball? Will he agree to dance in our opera house? Will he come and make love to me if I send him a diamond link-belt, or maybe a Cadillac?' "

His dangling arm drifted down to my thigh and I watched it, my calf muscles bunched. He withdrew it snappishly. "Beltanno, *will you relax?*"

"How can I?" I spat back at him. "Until I find out whether you're going to kill me or rape me?"

"Oh," he said. A charming smile spread over that conceited, deceitful, gorgeous Tartar face. Slow as a crêpe-de-chine scarf, he began to slide over the edge of the bed, paused, smiled, and landed with a thud on my struggling body. He kissed me.

"Beltanno darling, I'm not going to kill you," he murmured.

In all my medical reading I have found no clinical description of the kiss which he then pressed upon me. I stopped struggling. After four minutes the kiss moved down my neck and lingered here and there around my clavicles.

In fact I had closed my eyes when I became aware that Krishtof Bey had detached himself and was sitting back on his heels, viewing me thoughtfully. "Don't let's rush it," he said. "There's no hurry."

There was something wrong with my attention span. After a long time I said, "Don't rush what?" I was still lying on the floor. It was very comfortable.

Krishtof Bey rose to his feet, floated around to my bedside table, and poured out two glasses of iced water. He put one on the bearskin beside me and untied my wrists. "To counteract the vodka," he said. "It is true. I could not believe it: you have never been kissed before? A nice woman doctor like you? Not even in *medical school?*"

I was dissecting male Blumer's shelves while the others were kissing in medical school. In my year there was one Sohrab, five Abduls, and sixteen Mohammeds, but no Krishtof Bey. He brought across the white bathrobe, which was all I had for a dressing gown, and I put it on and drank my iced water, sitting in a deep furry chair. I was still fairly comatose, although I wondered why he had stopped kissing me. I even wondered, I believe, if I had done something wrong.

The word *vodka* was borne in by some kind of slow-release capsule. I said vaguely accusing, "You did put the vodka into my tomato juice?"

"Begum's orders," said the Magnificent Animal succinctly. He vanished for a moment behind the pink slubbed silk curtain and reappeared with a tape recorder slung from his fingers. It didn't even occur to me to get up from my chair. I frowned.

"Begum's orders?"

"Yes. Don't ask me why." He was fiddling with the tape recorder, which gave out a long passage of chirrups. Then he got what he wanted and looked up with that slow, catlike smile. "You didn't really think I was going to kill you?"

"You tied my hands," I said. I drank some more iced water. I do not know what was the matter with me.

"True. It is the first time I have had to immobilize a woman before I have kissed her," said Krishtof. "On the other hand, it is the first time also she has tried to shoot me." The tape recorder, at full volume, had burst into a ninety-piece orchestral rendering of the Breadcrumb Fairy variation from *The Sleeping Princess,* and he rose on the points of his slippers and did a few desultory steps while he was talking. It was very confusing.

Despite it, however, I was coming to myself. I said, "Why did you hide in my room? You wanted to know what I had done with the arsenic tests. You didn't want to kiss me. You wanted to find out how much I knew."

"I wanted to find out how much you knew about kissing," he said. He stopped and wreathed my face with his hand in the ballet symbol for affection, as explained in the Covent Garden programs. He moved off, crossing his knees in an unlikely manner. "It was a joke, my dear Doctor MacRannoch. So correct. So unapproachable. How to kiss you? It was easy. I make you drunk, and I make you frightened."

"I don't believe you," I said.

He turned and *bourréed* back over the bearskin, ending in a charming half hitch. "You don't believe me because you have no confidence in yourself," he said. "You are very kissable, Doctor. You have a body that might be a dancer's, a little ruined by golf, but one could soon set that right. You have strength and precision . . . Listen, does the music not move you?"

If it didn't move me, I thought, the walls were shortly going to fall out backward. It had moved on to the Polovtsian Dances from *Prince Igor,* who could obviously afford a larger orchestra than the Breadcrumb Fairy. The ice-water glasses were chattering and the fan over my bed started to stagger. "Come!" said the Magnificent Animal, and pulled me onto my feet.

I am not, as I have reported, a dancer. Neither am I a Hungarian acrobat. As I went over Krishtof Bey's shoulder and under his arm in a type of cloverleaf system, I had time to thank God for the bearskin. Whatever happened to my wig or my intervertebral discs, I should fall soft.

In the end, I pinned down the technique. Dancing consists of a number of simple binary decision points: whether to stand up or fall down. As we emerged from a back-to-back spin, I would begin to fall down, and Krishtof would raise me with a hand under one thigh and throw me onto his shoulder. I would begin to fall down again, and he would catch me and switch me like full dairy cream by my own upraised arm, while I stood up. He would then plié around about me until I fell down again.

I began to fear for my air passages. Rimsky-Korsakov was molesting my eardrums. Basic intestinal disturbances began to threaten my vodka. My wig was going to come off.

I yelled "Stop it!" and kicked him viciously behind the left knee. He sat. The tape recorder, which was underneath him, went off. In the abrupt silence a patient tapping at my door made itself heard. The Begum's calm English voice said, "Beltanno? Don't be lazy, darling. The water polo has started, and it isn't fair to leave Rodney one swimmer short."

The sweat showered into my bathrobe. I took a temporary grip of my respiration and said, "Krishtof Bey would swim better."

"I dare say," said the Begum. "But there's no response from his room."

His necklace heaving, I was delighted to see, the Magnificent Animal rose to his feet and, the oblique gaze on me, was retreating slowly toward the door behind the pink curtain. "Try again," I said. "I'm sure I heard him a moment ago."

"Right," said the Begum. Krishtof and I stared at each other. "I'll try him. But get up, darling, won't you? I want you to enjoy meeting people."

He had got to the Chinese vase with the blossoms. Without looking down he broke one off, kissed it theatrically and cast it into the room mournfully, as from Armand to Marguerite. Then the door between our two rooms fastened softly behind him. In

178

a moment I heard the Begum's knock on the outer door to his room. I couldn't hear what he answered.

I remained perspiring, my sympathetic nervous system all shot to hell. He was not only a murderer; he was an irresponsible murderer. To what he had just done to me, I would not subject the fittest man in my acquaintance.

I was not myself. I sat down on that bearskin and lamented.

*   *

In the end, I did go down to the pool, largely because I wasn't going to stay too long in that room alone. It took me some time to get ready. On my way out I found and delivered a cavalry charge on Johnson's modest oak door, but he didn't answer. When I got out into the garden in my sunsuit, sandals, and wrap-around glasses, I discovered the reason.

He had begun to paint Krishtof Bey. Since presumably one cannot swim in bifocals, he was fully dressed in an old crew-necked sweater and what looked like cook's trousers. Krishtof, sitting behind the collapsible easel, was perched on the shady steps of the Begum's thatched bar. He had changed into a thinner gold chain and a pair of pale tailored trousers. His stringy hands, clasping one knee, formed a pattern of light and shade against the spectacular torso, brown and lightly relaxed. His face was observant. Indeed, one could not disagree with anything about either his clothes or his posture. The taste was markedly Johnson's.

Beside them Trotter, Brady, and an assortment of muscle-bound newcomers were splashing about playing water polo, watched by the Begum and my father on deep-buttoned reclining chairs in brilliant colors.

Krishtof Bey said, "Is it permitted to wave to a girl friend?"

"No," said Johnson, continuing the motions of window cleaning with a long, pale-handled brush. "Waggle your ears. Hullo, Beltanno. Not swimming?"

Not with two potential murderers; not in that pool. "I may have pulled a muscle," I said. "I thought your sitter was to play water polo?"

"He may have strained his knee," Johnson said. The glasses bent over his palette. "You should take your muscle to Trotter. Trotter used to be the muscular therapy adviser to the London School of Oriental Studies. The whole of Zen Buddhism would have fallen down without Trotter."

I assumed he was joking. The water polo was ending. As I watched, Sergeant Trotter himself nipped up the diving board and executed a swan and somersault. It was impressive. "Flaming hoops next," I said. I was trying to exercise telepathy. Johnson's hand continued to scrub at his canvas.

"Flaming hoops next," said my father's voice, and I looked around icily but he hadn't even heard me. Then I saw they *had* flaming hoops, or at least a pile of bamboo circles wrapped in swathes of wet cotton. The pool boy, whose given name was Louis B. Mayer MacRannoch, lit one and spun it up through the air. Sergeant Trotter, reappearing at the top of the diving board, swan-dived efficiently through it.

I couldn't believe it. "The Bamboo Conch Club," I said.

"No, dear. The MacRannoch Gathering," said the Begum's cool voice. "Come and sit down. Hank, George, Missa, Louis, and Jake. That is Catherine. And that is Wallace Brady climbing up to dive through the hoop. Can he dive? He shall soon know. I beg you to watch him. He is risking his handicap solely for you."

Wallace Brady, a nicely built American figure in maroon striped bathing shorts, took off from the platform and plummeted successfully down through a hoop.

180

A respectful voice said, "Doctor MacRannoch? I hear you've muscular trouble." It was Sergeant Trotter, a well-hewn example of Canadian redwood.

I said, "I thought you were practicing for the MacRannoch Gathering."

"Oh, no. A little touch of afternoon entertainment," said Sergeant Trotter. "And it gives the boy practice, you know. Where is it, then? Back? Turn over. I'm a trained masseur, no need to worry." Fingers like heavy-grade forceps flipped me over and a red-hot poker struck me hard behind the left shoulder blade. I gasped.

"I knew it," said Sergeant Trotter with quiet triumph, withdrawing his fingers. "Golfers, they always get tightened up there. Take up running, I tell them. Swimming. Loosen up. You ought to know that, you being a doctor," he said to my suffering back.

My spine was rising and falling like dough on a rolling pin. As my face shifted up and down the deep-buttoned plastic I observed, "I am much obliged to you, although I feel it needs very little. I understand Mr. Krishtof has quite a painful left knee."

"Yes?" said Sergeant Trotter, pausing with interest.

"Afterward," said Johnson. He took a pound tube of flake white and leaned on it, while a low glistening hill formed on his palette. Krishtof Bey said feelingly, "Afterward may be too late."

"Middle Eastern soft-bellied dropout," said Johnson pleasantly.

"Pavement artist," said Krishtof Bey.

There was an amiable silence, broken by the rasping of Trotter's thumbs on my back. People splashed in the pool. I could hear James Ulric conversing in a creaking cackle with Missa or Catherine or Louis or Jake on his other side. My muscles began to warm up and spread out, like treacle. I allowed my eyelids to close against the dark glasses.

Sergeant Trotter said, "I reckon Mr. Johnson ought to burn them arsenic notes of yours, if he has them."

In a trice my fibers had sprung into their natural bunches again like strong gutta-percha. "I beg your pardon?" I managed.

"Mr. Krishtof mentioned Mr. Johnson had those tests," Sergeant Trotter explained. "Mr. Brady was of the opinion that they ought to be destroyed, and I must say I agree."

"I think you're probably right," said Johnson. He stepped back, stuck a brush in his fist and pushed his glasses up his insignificant nose. The picture, pale and stylish with no third dimension as yet, was undoubtedly that of Krishtof Bey, tinted and drawn by a draftsman. He said, "I'll put a match to them sometime. I can't remember which book I put them in. Or were they in that grip they mislaid for me at Coral Harbour?"

I said, "You were lucky, you got yours back . . ." and stopped what I was saying. Of course. That was why my case had been taken. For the same reason as Johnson's. "I lost mine, too, between Nassau and Great Harbour Cay. Someone wondered what we might have committed to writing," I said. I added impatiently, "You must remember what you did with the papers."

I have no patience with crassness. Willful crassness. Did he not realize he was endangering not only my life but his own? That between the covers of *Portnoy's Complaint* lay the seeds of a premature death?

"Oh, it'll turn up," said Johnson. "They call it information retrieval among console computers."

"It's a pity we haven't a console computer," I said. "An integrated data-processing system could find some work to do here and there."

The bifocals turned, elevated the lower lenses, and then reversed to gaze on the canvas. "I would have you know," said Johnson comfortably, "that I am multiprogrammed with impeccable software. What about you?"

"I am a small, edge-punched component," I said bitterly, "whom nobody wants." And closing my eyes, I allowed Trotter to resume kneading my back.

No accidents befell me over the rest of that day, largely because I spent every waking minute taking precautions. I would have been suspicious of Arli, the Wonder Dog Who Types with His Nose. Now Krishtof, Brady, and Trotter all knew that I was a witness to the fact that there had been an attempted murder, and that I was a prosecution witness in potential. They also knew that there was evidence of this, and that it was in Johnson's possession. That afternoon, I had regarded Krishtof Bey as a confessed murderer. By making Johnson's share in this public, he had later strengthened my suspicions. If anything befell Johnson or my notes, neither Brady nor Trotter could claim total ignorance. They were bound to fall under suspicion as well.

On the other hand, Krishtof might have been speaking the truth.

If I believed he was speaking the truth, I had to believe that he had questioned me, snatched my gun, and hidden under my bed in order to prepare me for a major onslaught of passion.

In my experience, there was no precedent for this.

I spent a number of cogitant hours in the undemanding and, it must be said, amusing company of Missa, Catherine, Louis, and Jake, as well as the Begum and my father; and at bedtime followed Johnson upstairs like an empty chair on a ski lift. At his closed door, he turned and confronted me. "Beltanno."

"Yes?" I said, stepping backward.

He sighed. "All right," he said. "Come in and tell me about it."

The door, I noticed, following him in, was not even locked.
The lights were blazing as well.

And every drawer, shelf, and cupboard in the room had been swept as clean as a whistle, and all their contents dumped in the middle of the floor.

Johnson, his arms dangling, stood beside me and surveyed it. "Dear, dear," he said.

"Are you surprised?" I said bitterly.

He thought about it awhile. "No," he said. "I wonder if your notes have gone. Actually, I did remember where I put them. In this drawer." The drawer was empty. "They've gone," said Johnson.

I was silent in my disillusionment.

"Someone else had the random-access device. Who, I wonder? It could have been anyone. But they might," said Johnson, "have folded the stuff and put it back in the drawers." A large moth rose groggily from a larval pile of old socks: Johnson smacked his hands on it and stooping, gathered an incohesive clot of his possessions to his bosom. The lights went out.

"Oh," said Johnson.

I didn't say anything. I was no longer relying on the leading luminary of Britain's Intelligence services abroad. I got the gun out of my bag and pointed it into the darkness. Now the killer had made off with the evidence, he was half safe. All he had to do to be wholly safe was to get rid of us. I said, "Johnson?"

"Beltanno," said Johnson. His voice came out of the darkness on the other side of the room; I could hear the sound of socks dropping. He said, "Can you clap your hands?"

"I've got a gun," I said, speaking slowly and clearly. "Johnson, who has the room on the right?"

"Your right or my right?" said Johnson. There was the sound of more socks dropping. He said, "Listen. Clap your hands."

"My right," I said. "Remember this is a copy of the castle at home? There's a concealed hatch to the right of the fireplace. It leads straight into the bedroom next door."

"Clever," said Johnson. "Who has the bedroom next door?"

I said, "That's what I'm asking you." To the right of me somewhere, something was creaking. I was sure of it. I took a fresh grip of the gun and turned slightly, facing the sound.

"All right," said Johnson obligingly. There was a pause, during which I heard the creaking again clearly. Johnson said, "Two senior members of Frei Korper Kultur from Sylt?"

I said "What? I'm going to fire. Stand still, or I'm going to fire."

"I *am* standing still," said Johnson's voice from the same place, touched with anxiety. "But who *was* in the next bedroom then?"

I was listening. I then said as lucidly as my engorged vascular system would allow: "Here. Who has the next bedroom here?"

"I *wish* you would clap your hands," Johnson said with some wistfulness. "I don't know. Wallace Brady, I think?"

"Yes," said a third voice, a soft voice out of the darkness on my right. "Wallace Brady it is."

I fired.

The lights came on. In front of the hatch by the fireplace stood Wallace Brady, his pale irises surrounded by an even paler rim of shocked scleral tissue, his shoulders straightening after a duck. Behind him on the plaster was a wide splintered hole. "You shot at me!" he said.

"Marvelous!" Johnson said. He dropped the rest of the woolies, and moving forward, laid a hand on Brady's limp arm. "I must say," he said, "I didn't expect it. I told her to clap."

"I wish she had," said Wallace Brady. "I didn't expect it either."

The glasses turned to where I stood transfixed, the smoking

185

gun in my nerveless right hand. "Go on, Beltanno," said Johnson. "Do it again."

"Hit him?" I said, unexpectedly in the top third of my register. My knees were trembling. I could have sworn he was sober.

"You can't hit a civil engineer," Johnson said. "They never stay still long enough. Try the ceiling. Or clap."

I was alone with a drunk and a murderer. I went along with it, playing for time. "I can't clap with a gun in my hand."

"Give me the gun," said Johnson impatiently. He took it and stood twirling it between us and waiting. "Now go on. Clap."

Foolishly, I applauded. The lights went off, came on, went off, came on, and went off.

There was a short silence. "Again," said Johnson's voice impatiently. I clapped. The lights came on.

"Lovely. Wasn't it?" said Johnson. "Acoustic switches are my absolute buzz. Come in and have a drink, Wallace. I've got some Glenfiddich somewhere, I think, if the bastard has left it. Did you wonder where that hatch was going to lead you?"

"I knew where it was going to lead me," said Wallace. "But thanks for the let-out. I was just too bloody nosy for the good of my skin." He looked at me. "I suppose you thought I was a burglar?"

"She thought you were whoever has just slithered off with her arsenic tests," Johnson said. He gazed at Brady and Brady looked down, embarrassed. "My God," said Johnson with interest. "Did you think we were conducting an orgy in four-ply? We just came in, and the room was like forget it. Hallelujah!" He pounced. "The survival kit."

He put the whiskey down, assembled the glasses, and disappeared into the bathroom for ice. I clapped my hands slowly, twice. The light went out, lingered, and came on again. Wallace Brady was sitting in an attitude of extreme discomfort, looking at me. He said, "I want to apologize."

"Not at all," I said. "It must all have sounded quite extraordinarily odd."

He said, "You can hear quite clearly behind that damned hatch."

"I know," I said.

Brady said, "Do you think I took the papers? I could have."

"So could Krishtof Bey and Sergeant Trotter," I said.

Johnson came in with the ice and Brady walked over to him and said, "There's something I'm just not too clear on. You said downstairs this morning that all this wasn't an accident. Then you told us all that Beltanno had proof that it wasn't. I just wanted to ask you why you had to shoot off your mouth about Beltanno? Doesn't that expose her to attack by the murderer?"

"How funny," I said. "I wanted to ask him that too."

Johnson handed around the drinks, sat down, and looked at him, his bifocals twin circles of blankness. "I'm being paid by Mr. Tiko," he said. "So that he can inherit three million dollars."

For a moment I think Wallace Brady believed him. I was almost more irritated with him than I was angry with Johnson. "Don't be stupid," I said snappishly. "Mr. Tiko inherits the chieftainship, and I'm quite sure my father will see that's all there is to inherit."

"Even if your father marries the Begum?" said Johnson. He put down his whiskey and began comfortably filling his pipe. "That's quite a lot of loot to get rid of, even if he invests in government stock. Anyway, who's complaining? You sold me up the river to Krishtof Bey and look what happened. My underwear is exposed. And we are both sitting targets."

"Tell the police," said Wallace Brady.

It was good advice. Good, sensible layman's advice which Johnson was in no position to take. I thought of that row with Edgecombe yesterday, at Great Harbour Cay. *If someone's after you because you're an agent, then he's taking his time about it for a very good reason.*

Edgecombe was the sprat. Johnson, if not the whale, was at least the halibut. I watched Wallace Brady, who was sitting sipping his whiskey with his pale eyes on Johnson. Johnson said, "I'm not going to get mixed up in it, children. Bad for business. You tell them, Brady."

"Right. I shall." Brady got to his feet, kicking a space in Johnson's dog-eared possessions. He wore, with some distinction, the Bahamian undress dress uniform of casual silk shirt and light trousers.

"But you'll have to wait until four-thirty tomorrow," Johnson said.

It doesn't do to underrate Johnson. Of course: No telephones, and fixed-schedule radio telephone facilities.

It didn't do to underrate Wallace Brady either. "That's all right. I'll borrow the launch first thing in the morning," he said. "And do it from Great Harbour Cay. Or I could fly to Nassau if necessary."

Johnson, peacefully smoking, was still undisturbed. "So you could," he said. "I wish we had the evidence to send with you. But you could take Doctor MacRannoch. After all, she's got to explain why she sat on it for so long."

Brady said slowly, "I'd forgotten that."

So had I. I must stop drinking alcoholic drinks prepared under doubtful conditions.

Wallace Brady kicked a couple of shirts out of his way and strode across to stand over Johnson. "You don't want the police, do you?" he said. "It would spoil the leisurely high-society image. Dirty little men running over the Begum's nice holiday island; maybe taking you off to a crowded hotel room in Nassau, or forcing you to stay and give evidence in some stuffy court. Beltanno doesn't matter. Or Edgecombe."

"Well, honestly," said Johnson, taking the pipe out of his mouth. He looked slightly pained. "If Edgecombe's an agent, then the last thing he wants is the police. We know that already. And if I don't testify, and Beltanno testifies without evidence, your rushing off to Nassau will do precisely nothing but create an unholy mess, for Edgecombe and Beltanno most of all. Particularly if Edgecombe denies he ever told her he was an agent, as he is extremely likely to do. You see, there's no solid proof."

"Yes," said Brady. He was pallid with suppressed anger. "There's no solid proof. I didn't take Beltanno's arsenic notes, Johnson. What if Krishtof and Trotter didn't steal them either? What if you emptied your own drawers and scattered your own papers just to save yourself trouble? Where are the notes, Mr. Johnson? In your pocket?"

"Good God," said Johnson. He rose slowly, pipe in hand, to his feet. Wallace Brady was half a head taller.

"Turn out your pockets," said Brady. "Or I'll turn them out for you."

Johnson put his pipe down. "Look," he said. An expanse of exasperated glass turned first on Brady, then on me. "A minute ago everyone was urging me to burn the damned things. I've just told you. You can't use them without harming Beltanno."

"I know. I don't want to use them. I just want to show you up, Johnson Johnson, for the selfish British bastard you are," said Brady. I couldn't believe it. It didn't make sense, any of it. It didn't make sense, unless Brady wanted these papers himself. And had looked for them. And had failed to find them.

I stared at Johnson and Johnson, bemused, stared back at Brady; and Brady, with a grunt of exasperation, lifted his strong golfer's right hand and lunged.

I clapped my hands.

For a moment the instant darkness took them both by surprise. Then I heard the *thwack* as their frames interlocked.

189

Grunts, like whispers, are impossible to identify in the dark, and so is hard breathing. I retreated to the fireplace and listened as the struggle unrolled its course over socks, trousers, and papers, yelpingly up to and over a drawer and momentarily into the base of a lamp. There was a crash, but clearly of the wrong caliber. Brady used a short, pithy word and I heard Johnson laugh annoyingly. Then the bumps and wheezing started again.

They must have been evenly matched. Neither ever got disengaged for long enough to manage a clap. But one of them contrived to get a single hand free.

They were close to me, on their feet and still pantingly wrestling when the pistol went off. As the light came on I saw it drop from Brady's right hand, but he wasn't quite quick enough. Before he could bring his fist up to defend himself, Johnson had hit him.

It was nicely judged. I wasn't going to have a broken jawbone to deal with. Wallace Brady merely followed one shoulder down into a pile of old Pringle sweaters and lay there, while Johnson went through his pockets. He got up, his respiration fast but quite even and observed, "He hasn't got them either. All the same, he made an awful fuss to cover up not going to the police, I thought. Didn't you?"

"I was too busy dodging," I said. There was a fresh bullet hole to the right of the fireplace, just a foot above where my head had just been.

"He just wanted the light to come on," said Johnson blandly. I could see his eyes. They were ordinary, with white circles around them. I said, "He's smashed your bifocals?"

"What? No! No," said Johnson, and fished out a maroon leather case from his pocket. He extracted and put on the lenses. He added, "I take my teeth out as well." I would have respected him had I not been well aware that his teeth were his own. It struck me to wonder how in the course of that fight he had found

190

time to case up his glasses. I remembered why I had followed him to his room. I said, "Right. I have something to say to you."

Johnson knelt and correctly rolled up Wallace Brady's left eyelid. Nothing was taking place under it but the doll's-eye movements of the deeply unconscious. Johnson got up, put his pipe in his mouth, and wandered over to sit in a chair. He struck a match. "You want to know why I told all, after we had agreed that we shouldn't," he said.

I said, "I don't need to be told. You're using me as your ready-rigged bait."

"Bright girl," he said, without so much as taking his pipe out of his mouth. "All right. Now suppose you triumph over hysteria and enable us to move on to a stable host-parasite relationship. What, so far have we hooked?"

I looked at the wall over my head and sat down with deliberation. "Wallace Brady," I said. "You know all I know about that. And Krishtof Bey. You will find it extremely hard to believe the latest news there."

"You know me. I'll believe anything," said Johnson. "Tell me all you think I'm fit to be told."

But he wasn't disturbed. At the end of my pungent if expurgated recital, he merely said, "Yes. That's more or less the scene as I heard it."

I don't know how I got on my feet. I said, "What the hell do you mean?"

"What you think I mean," Johnson said. "You're bugged, your room's bugged, and there isn't a move you make around the house or the garden that Spry or I aren't watching. You may be bait, but you're barbed bait. Don't worry, Doctor. All you have to do is enjoy yourself."

I thought of the four-minute kiss. I said, "You bloody little cold-bellied *stinkpotter*."

"Oh no," said Johnson, looking hurt. "Blowboater or rag-wagoner if you must." He got up and pressed the hatch and began lugging Brady's inert body toward it. I suppose he was going to search Brady's bedroom as well.

I stood and watched him. I could go to the police. I could go back to the hospital. I could leave.

I couldn't do anything and still remain Dr. B. Douglas Mac-Rannoch. I was a responsible citizen who had been enlisted by a high-grade professional. On the other hand, if he was painting Krishtof Bey by the pool, how the hell did Johnson expect to hear what happened or didn't happen all the time in my bedroom? I stopped dead with my hand on the door and said, "A *tape*?"

Johnson was watching Brady's non-slip composition soles and heels smoothly recede through the hatch. *"Rolls out on wheels for easy clean,"* he observed. He straightened. "Yes, a tape. But I edit it," he said. "In fact, some bits of it I really don't hear at all. And whatever else I have done or not done to you, Doctor B. Douglas MacRannoch, I think I have shortened your shelf life."

I slammed the door, but being the Begum's door, it closed with a click.

I couldn't find the bug. I undressed with the radio roaring and fell asleep to the strains of Tchaikovsky. I will narrate none of my dreams.

Chapter 12

FROM THAT MOMENT until Edgecombe's arrival five days later, I contrived to remain, with some trouble, intact. The social life in fact became so prodigious, it was quite hard to keep one's attention on murder.

The house filled up and emptied and filled up again. The Begum seldom had fewer than twelve bedrooms occupied, and parties of twenty or thirty were common for lunch, the visitors flying over to Stirrup Cay or Chub Cay or Great Harbour Cay and being met by the Crab Island launch. In the afternoon they would swim or engage in some other form of sport; in the evening those who were not staying returned after dinner. They came from New Providence and Miami, Eleuthera, Andros, and Abaco. Occasionally a friend would fly up from Jamaica or Antigua, stay a night, and return. My father, I saw with amazement, organized their entertainment with the same single-track vigor he had always displayed toward the MacRannochs. Many of them, indeed, were MacRannochs. He showed no hint of bronchorestriction.

As I have perhaps mentioned, I have myself little time for trivial chat. The European group tourist and the American convention component I had found it best at all costs to avoid, unless lying before me on the operating table. The young and fashionable I had also found suspect. In fact, I had a number of theories I thought it better to keep to myself.

At James Ulric's level, the level of Coral Harbour and Lyford Cay and Grand Bahama and Great Harbour Cay, the Bahamas are an expensive holiday playground. If you can afford it and are young, I would observe to myself, it is often because your wealth derives from your physique, which seldom makes for intellectual sparkle. If, on the other hand, you have made your fortune by unremitting juvenile industry, you are unlikely to have had time for anything else. Few self-made young men of twenty-three are entertaining outside their own subject.

There remain the offspring of the rich: the unattached and young marrieds who holiday in the Bahamas at the homes of their parents, their aunts, and their godmothers. These, I always found, cultivated a wide range of interests, like mustard and cress, on grounds about as profound as wet blotting paper.

I avoided them. I avoided the middle-aged rich from both business and society. These stayed with private hostesses or built luxury holiday houses, in which they entertained the same friends as at home, mixing tropical sport with drinking and horse racing, bridge and canasta. Some of these I had occasionally been persuaded to partner at golf. I had seldom been disappointed when the relationship was carried no further.

All these came to the Bahamas in high season only. Among the permanently retired, stultifying in the sunshine at a low regulo setting, I had found nothing in common. Indeed, the only human vigor I had ever been able to find had come from those, native or incomers, who worked on the islands: The bankers, the doctors, the tradesmen, the seamen, the vast teams of engineering contractors who were creating islands such as Great Harbour Cay.

I had, I believe, mentioned all this to Johnson when he first suggested visiting Crab Island. He had denied none of it, which raised him a degree in my estimation. Indeed, I hardly know when I began to notice that my pilot groups had perhaps been too small.

Brady, of course, if not a murderer, was an American engineer engaged in his profession. He played golf. He was quiet, entertaining, and had at least attempted to black Johnson's eye on my behalf. In fact he had been more than cool to Johnson ever since.

My feeling was that if Johnson's elaborate protection had begun without my permission, it could proceed without my cooperation. It was up to Johnson to keep me out of danger. So when Wallace Brady asked me to play tennis with him, I played tennis. I swam. I allowed myself to be taught several card games. Flexibility could go no further.

Krishtof Bey was also a professional. He had made money early but he was also intelligent and of varied interests, possible subversion apart. His advances continued, but were in the nature of flattery and not alarming to handle. I was a little careful when Krishtof Bey sought my society, but not because I was afraid he would kill me.

By the same token, if Rodney Trotter was a murderer, I have never yet met a better masseur, nor a man who with greater clarity could teach me to water-ski. He even got aqua-lung equipment and wanted me to go scuba diving, but Johnson, whose launch we were using, regretfully vetoed it. I saw the point, even if Trotter did not. But I made a reasonable success, for a beginner, at skiing.

The Begum's other guests astonished me also. The first rich young socialite I met was an international skier and also a banker; the second had launched a chain of dress shops and just held her own one-woman painting exhibition. Among the self-made was an actor now equally known as a novelist; and a folk singer who has also made some excellent short films.

There were almost no mustard and cress, no juvenile millionaires, no elderly playboys. All were engaged in some form of creative work with several others usually running it close. All could talk. Among the older men and women were dramatists and businessmen and art collectors, farmers and landed proprietors actively and experimentally involved with their property; an American medical specialist I had long wanted to meet. Members of the administration from Nassau and the other islands came out to visit the Begum, and she blended them all into a comfortable mélange in the warm sunshine so that they talked and swam and relaxed, comparing notes and exchanging ideas, and at the end of it, left the island themselves in some way enhanced.

Conversation, to my surprise, was not arduous. None displayed any but a literary interest in my given name of Beltanno. By evening each day, instead of being footsore and exhausted, I was physically relaxed and mentally fresher than ever. My skin became brown around the new shapes of my swim and sun suits, and between my tie-on tops and my hipsters. In the evenings we had drinks: daiquiris, Tom Collins, rum punches, and long, slow dinners by candlelight out on the terrace with French wines instead of iced water, and music, and paper games, and dancing. Krishtof Bey and Johnson between them taught me how to dance in time with the music and then how to dance out of time with it. No one mentioned his or her feet.

I remarked on that once to Krishtof Bey as we walked along the white beach after dinner, having sent on its way another launchful of the Begum's departing houseguests. He said, "Perhaps the Begum's friends do not need free advice."

It was warm. In the dimness, the thin waves breathed in and

dwindled on the smooth sand. I said, "No. That isn't the difference. People who want free advice almost always earn far more than I do."

"But you frighten them," said Krishtof. He stopped, his voile body-shirt glistening in the dark. "People who are not articulate, how are they to know what to say to a woman doctor? Especially a woman doctor with a stern face, who plays golf, and does not wish to be kissed?"

I realized I should not have let him walk me away from the others. But one cannot really remember to be cautious all the time. I said, "Of course, I always tell them that as soon as I meet them."

"They sense it," said Krishtof. He ran the back of his hand down my arm and my reflexes bounded. "So they think, what will interest this so austere woman? Only her own business, medicine. What can I say that will interest her, and will also be of some interest and benefit to myself? Ah. This remarkable and unusual symptom, they say, that I have observed in my feet . . ."

I said, "You flatter them." The drifting fingers were caressing my neck.

"No," said Krishtof. I wished he didn't use quite so much Monsieur Balmain: it was making me dizzy. "No. You despise and therefore underrate them. I do not agree, this rich diet the Begum is giving you. How will you have patience, when you go back? Not everyone is witty and fluent. Some are just nice, inarticulate people."

"Like you," I said. I tried to move away slightly but his other arm had gone around my waist.

"You wish to be sarcastic. But I am nice," said Krishtof Bey cheerfully. "I do not rape you when we first meet. I wait."

I said, "I appreciate that. I think we should go back to the house."

197

He had stopped walking, but the hand around my waist had not relinquished its grip. "There are people at the house."

"I know."

"But I do not wish to rape you before people," explained Krishtof Bey.

"That," I said firmly, "makes two of us. Back to the house."

There was something magnificent about that man's psychosexual development. He didn't trouble to answer. He merely tightened his grip and shifted his system of leverage so that I fell slowly backward on the white sifted sand, my bare shoulders cool in the surf. Then he kissed me.

"Hullo," said Johnson.

I did not at first hear him. As before, rapid chemical and psychological changes appeared to be happening. Certainly I was beyond responding to quite painful stimuli, and uncoordinated eye movements were threatening. Krishtof Bey's open mouth continued to adhere to mine, although I could hear he was growling. A minor wave washed over both of us sideways and splashed Johnson's moccasins. He said admiringly, "Steam."

I could feel Krishtof preparing to get up and hit him. Johnson said mildly, "Don't stop unless you're inclined. The tide turns in an hour and a half. Actually, the Begum and James Ulric are coming along just behind me."

Krishtof Bey got up and gave me a hand to rise to my feet, but all the time the slanting black eyes were on Johnson, and he was smiling. I distrusted that smile. So apparently did Johnson. I can give no precise account of what actually happened, but one smooth movement followed another smooth movement, and Johnson entered the ocean in a dim shower of spray, followed immediately and without premeditation by Krishtof Bey.

The Begum and James Ulric walked by as they were picking themselves up. "Beltanno!" said James Ulric sharply.

"Yes, Father?" I said from the shadows.

"Are those two lay-abouts falling out over you?"

Krishtof Bey and Johnson, rising with uniform dignity, could be seen making their way out of the sea. All at once it seemed purposeless to withhold the truth. "Yes," I said.

Moving up, my father peered closer. "Are you drunk?"

"No," I said.

"What happened to that fellow Broody I offered seventy-five thousand to marry you?"

"That was Wallace Brady," I said. "I told you. He's somewhere about."

"You're drunk," said my father grimly. "You're high. You're out of your mind. You think you've got so many dangling you can afford to let two of them *drown?*"

"Why not?" I said. "I've got Mr. Tiko."

"I'll believe that," said my father, "when I find myself inside the Silver Bells Wedding Chapel, Reno, toasting you both in Gold Nikka. I warn you again. You marry that bloody Nip, and I'll cut you off with a yen."

"He's a MacRannoch," I said. The moon had moved around a trifle, but I didn't care. I was drying off a bit, anyhow. I didn't know where Johnson and Krishtof were. The Begum stood smiling but offered no comment. She didn't need to, with James Ulric batting.

"In bloody name only," said my father, between his straggling teeth. "They eat raw fish. They speak Japanese. They all bathe together, with geisha girls scrubbing their wee yellow backs. They have bad eyes and lead unhealthy lives."

"Mr. Tiko plays better golf than you do," I said.

There was a silence. "That's a lie," said James Ulric.

"It's true," I said. "Wallace Brady will tell you."

Wallace Brady, the builder of bridges, like all builders of

bridges, was sacrosanct. There was another long silence, and then my father started to wheeze. I had to go into the house for his isoprenaline, and his Forced Expired Volume per second had gone up by a quarter already. It was the first attack that he'd had since the winter, and I thought it a pity. Because I couldn't hypersensitize him against Mr. T. K. MacRannoch.

Sir Bartholomew Edgecombe arrived the next day, which was Friday; and, although excessively quiet, was at pains to merge in with the household and to make no demands on the Begum. He spent a good part of the evening ruminating over the jigsaw, in which the Queen of Sheba was now seen to be stepping out of an Alfa Romeo. Afterward he went off to bed rather early, although I noticed he called on the way at Johnson's door, and was there a long time. I wondered what they were hatching. Whatever it was, Edgecombe looked tired when he came out. He had lost a lot of color and weight in the last week, and had had his hair cut. I suppose it was Denise who had thought it dashing, hanging over his collar.

I make no apology for taking a close invisible interest in Sir Bartholomew Edgecombe. I had no doubt by this time that whatever was going to happen to him was going to happen to me. And with his arrival, my available protection was halved.

But what everybody appeared to have forgotten was that I was due back in Nassau on Tuesday. After three more days no one could use me as bait or anything else. I should be away from the scene. I should be Dr. B. Douglas MacRannoch, Scotland's contribution to Unisex.

Three weeks ago, I wouldn't have known what that meant, far less bringing myself to apply it.

I wish it were three weeks ago.

No, I don't.

*   *

Next morning a small extra briskness in the calm air of the house was the only sign that the Begum was expecting seventy-five people for an afternoon beach party and barbecue. My father, who had quarreled with her over the guest list, locked himself after breakfast in the study, from which sounds of industry emerged from time to time. The original box file marked THE MACRANNOCH GATHERING had now bred a stack of fat folders, with titles like CABER, STEEL BAND, HIGHLAND DANCING, CHEROKEE INDIANS, PIPING, COMMANDO RAIDS, COLUMBUS, COMMUNITY SINGING, and FIRE DANCERS ON MOTORCYCLES. The date, I had noticed, was now only five weeks distant, and the guest list ran to three thousand names, with mine at the top: *Beltanno*.

He must have been stoned out of his crust.

Krishtof Bey never came down for breakfast. I had mine. I asked the Begum, who was lying in a lounge chair, if I could help with the barbecue, but of course with a staff like the control center at Cape Kennedy she said no and meant it. Rodney Trotter suggested fishing and I got my swimming things while he collected some live bait for amberjack.

By the time I got back, I discovered two other people wanted to go, and Johnson had volunteered to take us in *Dolly*. Spry ferried us out in the launch: myself, Trotter, a picturesque investment broker from Nassau whose first name was Harry, and a middle-aged beautician in a wide floppy hat who was referred to simply as Violet of New York.

Climbing *Dolly*'s companionway behind her broad, Paris-dressed pelvis, I wondered privately who was supposed to be standing guard over Sir Bartholomew Edgecombe while Johnson, Spry, and myself slaughtered amberjack. Johnson himself responded to my hints and raised eyebrows with an expanse of impossibly vacant bifocals. I held my own embittered counsel and was rewarded ten minutes later when the launch departed and returned to *Dolly* once more bearing Edgecombe.

With him, in zebra-striped surf shorts and towel, was my friend Wallace Brady. So Edgecombe was with us, but also with two of our suspects, Trotter and Brady. In which case he might have been better off alone with Krishtof on Crab Island. I wondered which of them had persuaded Sir Bartholomew to come: Johnson or Brady.

The anchor came up. Johnson put the big six-cylinder engine into gear and we began gently to motor out of the anchorage. Then he turned her into the wind and the sails ran up as Spry broke them out, helped by Sir Bartholomew Edgecombe and Trotter.

But for my father's paranoia, we should have had a family yacht at Loch Rannoch. It seems odd to spend all one's childhood on a rock in the sea and know as little as I did about sailing. But at least I knew how to fish. And to shoot.

The seventy thousand square miles of Bahamian waters are full of extraordinary fish, from striped grunts to queen triggerfish. Or take the wahoo, if you can catch it. It can manage 40 mph on a good day, and the world record is 149 lbs. "I once caught a wahoo," said Sergeant Trotter dreamily, as *Dolly* lay on her side. "But I'd rather have bonefish. A nice quiet afternoon in the shallows, lying flat in a skiff with the sun on me plumbago . . ."

The silence, after the pounding of the Mercedes-Benz engine, was like the bliss of a warm water bath to a cripple. The sea lay clear as shellac underneath us, jade and turquoise; cerulean and peacock, sheared white by the blade of our bow. The island skeined past, low and green and feathered with palms. A sea bird flew by. The light from *Dolly*'s mainsail, spilled straight from the sun, ached into my eyes, and I put on my dark glasses. We had all moved, redisposing ourselves in the sun and the air and the silence, our voices sounding small and lonely and clear. Harry the broker was already oiled and stripped to his trunks, lying prone on the foredeck; and I saw that Wallace Brady had settled beside Johnson and was untangling a fishing line in long, muscular hands, without speaking. In his tanned face, his strange light eyes remained pale as a fish's.

We had passed his bridge, its white caissons glittering in the sunshine: the thump of the generators traveling over the water, and the distant voices of men from the pile driver and supply boats on the far side. Brady had stood up and waved, and someone waved back. Where he sat now, I saw he still had a bruise on his chin where Johnson had hit him. On the other hand, I noticed Johnson had a cut lip where Krishtof Bey had followed through first.

The walking wounded were insensibly growing. If you counted James Ulric's asthma, the only unblemished scout in the Save Edgecombe Club was the Begum.

Now I can realize how far I had been reduced, deliberately reduced, below my own high intellectual watermark. Then I merely felt pleased that I had exchanged my wig for a neat cotton turban, and holding my face up to the sun, listened to Violet of New York discoursing about the glandular troubles of civet cats, while Bart Edgecombe made conversation with Trotter about his tattoos.

Then Edgecombe turned his gray head to me and grinned, and said, his voice public, his eyes conspiratorially private, "I rather like the way Johnson keeps throwing us together. Or is it you and Wallace Brady he's throwing together?"

"I can feel thrown together," I said heavily, "without any outside help whatsoever." I dislike double talk. I dislike haphazard danger. I dislike not being in anyone's confidence.

I asked Johnson how he felt after his sea bath, and he said fine. I turned my back on him. Someone switched on a stereo cassette of that cello piece by Saint-Saëns and all the men started to warble it. Spry came around with Royal Hawaiian Macadamia nuts, fifteen shillings for three and a half ounces, and a tray of strong Planters' Punch. I helped myself freely to everything and watched *Dolly* run gently north and west before the soft southeast wind to the fishing ground.

It was a short sail, as we had to be back. Edgecombe guided Johnson into the currents, their heads together over the chart, and too soon for the sluggards *Dolly* went about and, idling, dropped all her canvas. Then we were lying in the full sun again under bare poles, and Spry was handing out fishing tackle and lures. Violet, holding onto her hat, went below and returned with a jam jar of shrimps and Rodney Trotter, who had brought his own rod. The handsome Harry, now sitting beside me, was gazing speculatively at the undynamic figure of Johnson.

"Now who," he said, "would have expected such mad efficiency?"

The bifocals turned and got him into alignment. "I only look like this," explained Johnson, "because there wasn't enough zinc in my egg."

Bart Edgecombe, baiting his hook, grinned without turning. "And he only looks efficient," he said, "because *Dolly*'s a cow. A cutter for imperious youth, a yawl for respectable middle age, and a ketch for the old and feeble. Old Balinese proverb."

"My ethos can stand it," said Johnson. "Is this tub drifting too fast? We're just about at slack water."

"The wind has freshened," said Brady. "Does it matter?" And indeed, we seemed in no need of sea room: the 200-foot mast on Great Stirrup Cay was the nearest sign of the Great Harbour Cay group of islands, far on our left as our bows pointed upwind and south.

I stared at it through my dark glasses and said, "What is it? A radio mast?"

"The tracking station," said Edgecombe mildly, after a moment. I hadn't heard of it. I suppose it was public knowledge that one of them lay in these islands. But I realized now why Bart Edgecombe had chosen to live where he had. And remembered afresh, as we gently rocked there on the warm turquoise sea, that somewhere there was a gun at his head.

Brady said, "We *are* drifting." And Johnson, who had pulled out the chart, said: "Yes. I think the anchor. Come on, Bartholomew. You've got to work for your bloody beads and striped blanket. Is this the right place?"

"Yes, but Brady's right. There are shoals to the northeast back there, and some coral heads beyond that, and out west. If the tide's on the turn I should watch it, but you'll be perfectly safe with your anchor. Anyway, the chart'll give you your bearings."

"All right. Let it go," Johnson said. His pencil, poised, made a mark on the chart among several beer rings. Spry moved forward, but Edgecombe, already in the bows, had picked up the anchor. Brady and Trotter, in the cockpit, were arguing about British and American scarphing. They both sounded knowledgeable.

The second anchor for this kind of ketch weighs about ninety pounds, so Spry told me later, and when it is heaved overboard, the three-quarter-inch cable for it comes flying up from the fo'c'sle through navel pipe and fairleads and over a chain gypsy, which spins it out over the stempost. Even when performed with precision, in a well-maintained boat with greased winches, it is not an exercise which is ever quite foolproof. The chain can cross link on its way up from the locker, or as it is rendering around the chain gypsy. A projecting shackle pin can cause an abrupt jam. Coming into a crowded anchorage, you can find your anchor stuck, halfway to the bottom. Or jammed higher up, and kicking a hole in your hull. Or pulled up short as it flies through the air so that it plunges rolling back toward you and the deck, its iron flukes twisting.

That was what happened to Bart Edgecombe. The chain jammed and then somehow ran back, almost before the anchor got over the side. It kicked back; and in a moment those ninety pounds of galvanized iron would have been down on the deck and scooping Edgecombe's legs over the side.

He didn't have time to escape, but he did what anyone would have tried to do: he fended it off with his hands. I heard him shout and saw the blood spurting. The anchor crashed on the deck. Brady jumped out of the cockpit and in two strides got hold of Edgecombe's arm; he had a handkerchief out, already scarlet with blood. Trotter followed, looked for me, and choosing his priorities, dropped and began grimly to tear at the windlass. Spry, after a movement from Johnson, went forward to help him.

By that time, I was beside Edgecombe myself. I think my main preoccupation as I took his arm wasn't the long open wound, tearing through the fascia and anterior brachial muscles and ending around the base of the thumb; even though I registered that it had somehow missed a main artery, and equally that it would be as ugly a scar, at the very best, as any arm lesion I ever had seen. It was the fact that in this disaster-fraught climate, pure accident could claim its share. No one had pushed Edgecombe; no one had been anywhere near him; no one could have caused the fault in the chain. It was, as usual, merely Fate kicking.

But nothing was said, or could be said: thought was for later. Meanwhile the medical box was produced, and aided — surprisingly — by the face-lifted Violet, I made a workmanlike job of the tear. The medicine chest was impressive and included surgical needles and silk in a stoppered glass tube, as well as dressings and mercury sublimate. Johnson produced a blanket and bowls of warm water and brandy. He also had ampoules of morphine and three new syringes wrapped in foil, but I shook my head and he packed them away. Edgecombe didn't need them, and there was no need to advertise their existence. I wondered what other scenes, in other ports, *Dolly* had survived with the help of that competent chest.

Spry made some tea while we cleaned up, and Edgecombe and Johnson had a brief talk in the saloon, Edgecombe's bandaged right arm cross-slung before him.

Trotter appeared suddenly at the top of the companionway and said, "We've freed the gypsy. Do you want to get under way? She's still drifting."

"You haven't had your fishing yet. Beltanno and Violet . . ." Edgecombe was getting over the shock, although his face was still pale under the bright reddish tan. "I couldn't have done better if I'd been run over by a trolley in Guy's. Look, J.J., there's no need for a fuss. I'm as comfortable here as I'd be anywhere else. Get your anchor out and go on with your fishing."

Johnson looked at me. I said, "No, I want him back. He'd better have an antitetanus shot, for one thing. And he ought to rest properly."

"Then I'll go back in the launch," said Bart Edgecombe wearily. It was, I suppose, what they had planned. It left both Trotter and Brady on *Dolly*. And only Krishtof Bey to worry about at the castle.

I said, "That's a good idea. And it's faster. I'll take him, if you'll show me what to do."

"No, the launch is heavy. It needs a man," Johnson said.

Trotter, waiting patiently at the top of the companionway said, "I'll steer, if you like. Provided Sir Bart here can pilot."

Edgecombe looked quickly at Johnson and said, "I don't mind, but perhaps Harry or someone would be better. They get more chances for fishing than Trotter."

Trotter looked surprised and a little impatient. "No, I'll take him," he said. "No trouble at all. I'll help Spry to get the Avenger unshipped." He disappeared.

We couldn't talk because Violet of New York was still there, screwing rings onto the pegs of her fingers. Johnson said to me, "Beltanno, you'd better go with him. Maybe one or two of the others would like to get back as well. Violet?"

"You want me back," Violet said. She had repowdered her face, which had the fine texture of hospital rubber sheets; her eyelashes were painted dark blue. She didn't fuss. She picked up her jar, and said philosophically, "I guess that's the sort of life that shrimps have. You want them, Beltanno? They taste real good on toast with a little sesame seed."

I took the jar and she smoothed down her hat and followed by Johnson led the way up on deck. There was a heavy splash, and then a rattle from the fo'c'sle as the anchor chain ran out. I could hear feet overhead and pulley blocks squeaking as the launch was winched down into the water. I put the jar on the table.

There was no doubt that Edgecombe ought to go back. His pulse rate was higher than I had hoped for, and he was lying inert with his eyes not quite closed. The man called Harry appeared silently on the stairs, and I said, "How fast is that launch?"

"It's fifty miles an hour, dearie. He'll be on Crab in ten minutes," said Harry. I could hear Johnson's voice above, talking to someone persuasively. He could be very persuasive, could Johnson. Harry said, "Listen, dearie. Would you rather I went back with Sir Bartholomew?"

It was one way, I suppose, of finding out which of the men I was interested in. Or maybe he thought that he knew. I said, "No. It's all right," just as Brady appeared on the steps and said:

"We're ready, if you can show us how to carry him. Violet's going."

Edgecombe roused at once and got to his feet. Between us we got him on deck and down the gangway into *Dolly*'s white launch. Violet was already ensconced there, her face tucks showing in the clear light. Brady got down beside her and steadied Edgecombe as we lifted him down.

We were still in the slack of the tide and there was a slight jopple, enough to make the boat lurch more than it should. Edgecombe arrived in the well of the boat, stumbled, and put out a hand. Brady, not expecting it, lost his balance and saved himself by gripping the engine casing. There was a roar, and the engine, which had been idling, went into gear.

We saw the launch shoot backward, graze *Dolly's* virginal sides, and then as Brady frantically grabbed at the lever, stop and plunge nose outward away from the yacht. The lashing on deck unfurled like gray smoke and vanished. We saw Violet's arms batten her hat, and Edgecombe fall, and Brady, his eyes white with fright, try to regain his balance and wrench at the launch's controls. He throttled down, and started to bring the launch back. I saw Edgecombe move in the bottom, and Violet straighten her hat.

We stopped shouting. It had happened so quickly; but I suppose there had been no acute danger. Spry, beside me, had a line ready to throw them, and I stayed on the gangway with Trotter, whose language would have enchanted an army anaesthetist.

He grinned at me. "If you ask me, that lad needs some help with his steering," said Trotter. "Don't worry. I'll get you on."

But neither of us got on. As the launch came within earshot, we could see Edgecombe had struggled up and that he and Brady were talking. Then Brady stood up and hailed us. "We won't come back . . . Now we're off, Sir Bart thinks we should just carry on without spoiling your fishing. Save us a nice, sixty-pound grouper."

He gave a cheerful wave and stood down to the wheel. The throttle opened and the white launch, turning sleekly in the blue water, heeled and made off, gaining speed, southward.

Harry had found Violet's shrimps, but I think the other four of us stood staring at the boat until she curved out of sight; and Johnson had his binoculars on her to the end. Then he said flatly, "Poor Bart. I'll go and radio the nurse to expect them. You might as well start fishing, Beltanno. Harry and Spry here are the experts. What about you, Trotter?"

His hand shading his eyes, Trotter was still watching the spot where the launch had disappeared. I wondered if it were Brady's erratic steering he was worried about, or Brady's interest in Edgecombe. He turned back and said, "Fishing it is. Mind you, I don't know much about it, but I don't suppose your amberjacks go much for launches. Would it be worth moving somewhere there's been less commotion?"

Halfway down the companionway, Johnson glanced at his watch. "I'm not sure actually it's worth moving anywhere," he said. I knew he had promised the Begum to bring us back in good time for lunch. I said, "If you want to start back, I don't mind. We can fish another day."

"Wait," said Johnson; and went forward to the R.T.

Trotter said, "I'm not much on for amberjacks either. I'd rather get back and see how the old fellow is." There couldn't have been ten years between them. It was merely the reaction of an active man to a stricken one. Poor Bart indeed, I thought.

I said, "Harry?"

Harry, shirtless, shrugged his shoulders tanned by several seasons of Great Harbour Cay sun. "Go ahead. I can fish anytime."

"Majority decision," said Trotter. "Come on, Spry. You start her up and I'll winch up the anchor."

Johnson came up as Spry pressed the button and the engine spluttered, hesitated, and caught. Spry said, "They want to go back, sir."

Johnson said, "You could sail and trawl, if you like." He looked preoccupied. His impulse, no doubt, I thought, was to race *Dolly* home. But whether he speeded or lingered, the launch with Edgecombe, dead or alive, would be home long before us.

No one wanted to trawl. *Dolly* moved. Spry and Harry went forward, so far as I remember, while Trotter and I sat in the cockpit with Johnson, who had perched on the coaming, chart on knees, moving the wheel with one canvas-shod foot. He had changed his bifocals for black Polaroid glasses which made his face even more unreadable. The warm, forced air hardly stirred his black hair.

Trotter said, "No records broken today. Poor old Sir Bartholomew ain't got his troubles to seek. He won't get to the barbecue now, will he?"

I had forgotten the barbecue. And my (prospective) fiancé.

Trotter said, "We had a little accident like that in India once. The Bengali tattoo. *God Save the President of Poland!* in fireworks, and the exclamation mark fell off on this fellow's turban. Near burned to a cinder, he did."

I said, "Do they have exclamation marks in Hindi?"

"They have in Polish," said Trotter quickly. He half rose. "That's funny."

"What?" I said.

"There," said Trotter. "On the horizon, on the left of the bowsprit. A boat, coming toward us. It isn't the launch, coming back?"

Johnson said, "Take the wheel, will you?" and in two moves

was standing up on the cabin roof, his binoculars to his eyes. In the same moment Spry's voice came from the foredeck. "Something coming toward us up from the south, sir. It could be the launch."

"It's white," Johnson said. He glanced down at Trotter. "Keep her well out to starboard, will you? There's hellish shoaling out on the left. Spry, what do you see?"

Spry looked back. "I think it's the launch. It's the right size. And it's coming straight for us."

Johnson looked at the chart in his hand. "I suppose it could have dropped Edgecombe and turned. It's in the right region for Bullock's Harbour."

But his voice was deliberate, as Trotter's had been, telling that story. We were all on edge after the mishap, and Johnson with more reason than most. I wondered what disasters befell senior officials who allowed their colleagues to be assassinated under their noses. He stood watching for some time, the binoculars still in his hands. Then he said suddenly, "It isn't. It isn't the launch . . ." and lent me the glasses to look.

It was not the launch. It was a long, shallow boat approaching at speed, and steering for *Dolly*. Johnson sprang down and, taking the wheel over from Trotter, boosted the engine. He then turned the wheel very slightly to starboard. After a moment, the other boat altered course also. There was no doubt she was coming to meet us. Johnson turned the wheel back and gave it to Trotter again while he stepped up on the roof of the cabin and studied her again through the glasses. All at once, he said, "Spry?"

In a hospital one always looks placid. Even in a hurricane case, an illness which degenerates within moments, one never runs or raises one's voice in the wards. But one learns to know one's consultant. The pitch of the voice that means trouble. The inflection which says *this is terminal*.

I knew what it was like, to be in danger with Johnson, and the pitch was there, in his voice. He said, "Spry. Who's steering?"

There was a second's silence. And then Spray answered unemphatically, "I can't see anyone, sir."

Johnson said, "Give the glasses to Harry. Trotter, take mine."

They changed, and for a moment, no one said anything. Then Harry spoke. "There isn't anyone steering. The boat's loaded with cargo, but there isn't a helmsman. There isn't anyone on board, I should say."

"He's right," said Trotter. "Unless they're lying in the well of the boat with their feet up." It was a good effort, but his voice wasn't quite normal. "*Marie Celeste,*" he added. "She must've got loose from her moorings. Should we catch her, do you think?"

I relaxed a little, I believe. It was eerie, but the explanation was probably simple. One of the boys had overbalanced, starting her off from the quayside, and she had driven out of harbor under her own steam. At any rate, it wasn't the launch with the dead body of Bart Edgecombe inside it.

Johnson said, "She's going too fast to get hold of. She'll run out of gas: we'll report her once we get a look at her name. Meantime, let's give her a nice lot of room just in case the sea kicks her rudder."

He had turned *Dolly* sharply to starboard, and instead of the bows, the white flank of the other boat began to appear.

Trotter focused on it with the glasses. "It's the *Hay* something," he said. "Hell?" He brought the binoculars down.

Harry, Spry, and I looked at him and he looked at Johnson's black Polaroids.

"Try again," said Johnson mildly, and this time turned the wheel hard over to port. Ahead, I could see the flash of Spry's anxious face, and then the two pairs of binoculars were lifted again. This time I stood up and watched, hanging onto the boom.

It was remarkable in that short space of time how much closer the white boat had come. Even with the naked eye it was perfectly obvious that she carried no crew and no helmsman — merely a large rectangle of unspecified cargo lashed down with tarpaulin.

For a moment the white beaked bow far over the water faced us directly. Then as *Dolly* veered left, answering Johnson's pull on the helm, we began to expose the other boat's shallow white flank and the name, which to the binoculars must now be quite legible. Then as I looked, the flank foreshortened; the name slid out of view, and we in *Dolly*'s stern were again facing the other boat across a lessening distance of water, and looking straight at her bows.

Trotter lowered the glasses very slowly, and his face had lost a lot of its color. "She's the *Haven*," he said. Both Spry and Harry had dropped their glasses and were also looking, without speaking, at Johnson.

"Once more," said Johnson, and turned the helm hard over to starboard.

I hung on. We heeled. The sun slid to our port quarter and above me, the halyards whipped the bare poles. I saw that Harry's shoulder blades were catching the sun: he pushed his arms into his shirt without looking. My cheekbones stung. Engine beating, *Dolly* settled to her new, angled course.

Haven took a moment or two to adapt, but not very long. The view of her flank opened, and closed. Behind her, the scar of her wake, white on blue, began to lean outward. We were moving fast. But *Haven* was moving still faster, swinging around, adjusting. She was on course in thirty-five seconds. In thirty-five seconds we found ourselves looking straight into the beak of the oncoming boat as if into the stare of a predator.

A hawk. A familiar. An enemy. A pilotless ship following us as the barracudas below follow blood.

This time Johnson held the helm down. The bows continued to swing. "The *Haven*?" he said to Trotter. "Who is she?"

"The construction teams use her," said Trotter. "She runs between various jobs." He halted. Ahead Spry and Harry, signaled by Johnson, had left the foredeck abruptly and were scrambling past the saloon roof toward us.

Johnson said, "Yes?" It was like winding up an automaton.

Trotter's face had gone rather pale, and he was perspiring. He said, "Brady had her loaded some days ago, ready to call at the Tamboo Marina."

He stopped again, staring at Johnson, and Johnson stared back and said slowly, "I see."

None of the rest of us saw. Harry said, "What is it? What's the matter? Is she going to crash into us?"

"She's going to crash into us," Trotter said. His face was glistening, but his voice was quite firm as always. "She's steering by radio — yes, Mr. Johnson? — beamed on a homing device hidden somewhere on *Dolly*."

"And?" I said sharply.

The bows had swung around. We were going due north now, the sun blazing behind us. The white boat settled undeviatingly on our tail and began to creep forward.

"And," said Trotter, "she's full of explosives."

Chapter 13

"YOU'VE GOT to be kidding," said Harry.

Johnson changed course. He said, without looking at Harry, "Wrong mammal, wrong gender. I wish that I were. The transmitter'll be in the bilges or under the hull. We can look for it later, but I doubt if we'll find it. Meanwhile, *Haven*'s faster than we are."

Harry said, "What'll happen? What'll happen if she overtakes us?"

Johnson changed course by forty-five degrees, and in our wake, the white boat changed course also. Johnson said, "She won't overtake us. She'll crash into us, and if she hurries, we'll make the one twenty-five news after 'Peyton Place.'"

"You're zig-zagging?" said Trotter.

"Righty," said Johnson. "In the classical phrase. *Haven's* rudder is giving a thirty-five-second delay on the turns, and so long as our fuel lasts, we may hold her until help arrives."

Trotter said quickly, "Could we explode her? A rifle?"

I had already thought of my Frommer. Johnson said, "I haven't a rifle. In any case, whatever the range, the explosion would wreck us. You don't need to tell me it's a pity we've lost the Avenger."

He had changed course again. Harry, wrenching his gaze from the *Haven*, said breathlessly, "We could jump."

Around us the sea stretched, blue and empty. "We could," said Johnson. "Sharks permitting. But I don't think we should get very far. And the explosion would still take place very close to us."

Spry came up quickly from below and said, "I can't see anything, sir. Shall I send an S O S on the radio telephone?"

"Yes," said Johnson. He began to say something else and broke off suddenly. I realized the engine had altered in tone. Spry stopped dead.

"Well?" said Harry.

The engine hesitated.

"Intermittently well," Johnson said. It was time to change course. He turned the wheel steadily. The even tone of the engine changed, broke off, and resumed instantly again. Harry said, "My God, is the tub breaking down?"

The engine stopped. "The tub has broken down," Johnson said. His eyes on Spry, he had a hand on the starter. The engine coughed and was silent again. Spry disappeared suddenly below. We heard the hatch open which gave access to the engine under the floorboards. *Dolly* pitched in the silence, the advancing waves slapping her bows with a cluck. "All right. Let's sail," Johnson said curtly. "Mainsail with me, Trotter. Harry, mizzen. Beltanno, take the wheel and bring her into the wind when I tell you. Spry!"

"I heard you. You'll want the spinnaker," said Spry from the ladder. "The fuel pump's choked. Sugar, I think, in the tank."

Sabotage, as they say. I didn't even take it in. The wheel was thrust in my hands and obeying the clear, ceaseless stream of Johnson's instructions, I brought *Dolly* around into the wind. Into the wind, stationary, and full in the path of that white, onrushing arsenal.

It had to be done, to allow the sails to break out. And the sails were our only means now of escaping: those square yards of canvas Spry and Trotter and Harry were hauling up by main force while we rocked there in silence.

They worked as fast as they could. The heavy blocks rattled. I could hear the men's breathing as their arms pulled in rhythm, their throats exposed to the sun, and then masked by the lifting dark of the canvas. Johnson was everywhere: issuing orders, guiding, pulling, belaying; watching the wind, the spinnaker bent on the foredeck with Spry kneeling beside it, the *Haven* rushing toward us.

I watched the *Haven* as well. I could see her quite plainly. I could see her windshield and the neat, taped tarpaulin. I could see the empty seat and the empty wheel, turning a little, delicately, to left or to right, correcting her rudder, keeping a straight course toward us as she crossed the spent white expanse of our wake.

She was as near as that, and my hands were wet on my own steering wheel when Johnson said, "Right. Beltanno. Ready to gybe . . ." And I turned the wheel as the main topping lift was belayed and the mainsheet freed and held at the winch.

The mizzen slid up and pulled taut and, as *Dolly* swung around, the sails both bellied full, boomed out to catch the following wind. Then with a great huff of sound forward the spinnaker filled, a shining and fragile balloon, lifting the boat from under our feet with its pull, and Johnson vaulted down and took the wheel from me, his eyes on the sails. "Further out, Spry . . . What about this one? No. Clew up and leave it. A point or two for the mizzen . . . That's it. Now . . ."

Now we were sailing. I had never traveled as fast as this on a yacht under canvas. The seas hissed beneath us: the sun, the shadow, the whirling draft of the sails made the escape a live thing — as personal as flight on the back of a horse. Johnson turned, one hand on the wheel and the other on the brown varnished coaming, and stood without moving, his eyes on the *Haven* behind.

We all stood. Through the glasses you could see a graze on the *Haven*'s white paintwork where she had been brought too fast one day into the jetty, and the black lettering on either side of her bows, where her name started and ended. She hit our fresh wake and jolted, and the wheel moved itself crossly, correcting. But she was no longer devouring the distance between us.

Spry said, "You've done it, sir. We'll hold her for a little."

"Christ, I hope so," said Trotter. The brown of his face glowed like beechwood under a running varnish of sweat; sweat had checkered Harry's smart colored beach shirt with great patches of gray. Johnson's hair was merely wet at the edges. He didn't say anything. He looked at Spry, and Spry vanished below, his lips pressed together.

To try and restart the engine. Because if *Haven*'s engine was faster than *Dolly*'s, then it was certainly faster than *Dolly*'s top sailing speed under canvas. *We'll hold her for a little* was all Spry had said.

He was away for less than two minutes. He came up shaking his head just as Johnson silently laid down the radio telephone. Johnson said, "Still no joy? Spry, will you check the electrical stuff? I'm getting no response from the R.T."

Harry said, "What?" and the bifocals turned coolly on him.

"The R.T. isn't functioning, and neither are the radar or echo sounder. It may be a simple connection, or it may all be tied up with the engine . . . Yes?"

Spry's head, reappearing, said, "You won't get through, sir. Someone's crossed the leads on the alternator. When you pressed the starter button, you blew every wire on the ship."

No engine. No S O S. No help, unless a ship appeared by a

miracle from the outside, uncaring, luxurious world. Harry said in a high, scratchy voice:

"What *is* this? Big business? Black Power? Politics? What's it got to do with me?"

"Nothing," said Sergeant Trotter harshly. "It's got nothing to do with me either, but I'm not wasting time yapping. Not yet. Not till I know if I'm going to survive. It's all to do with that fellow Edgecombe. Someone's trying to kill him. I suppose they got the *Haven* launched before they found out Edgecombe had gone off back home."

"Did you know that?" said Harry to Johnson.

"Yes," said Johnson. He was looking at the burgee.

"And you allowed him to come here?" said Harry. "Jesus Christ . . . Come fishing, you told us. Come and get your god-dam gizzard fly posted because the boat's been evil-eyed by the Mafia . . ."

Harry wasn't Trotter's ideal officer. Trotter said, "He only made one mistake, didn't he? He came right along with us all . . . Mr. Johnson, what happens if the wind drops?"

A sail rattled. Spry, glancing at Johnson, ducked forward and tightened a sheet. From the blue sky, the sun shone naked as fire. Behind, the white boat had settled insensibly nearer. We were going fast, but *Haven* was slowly catching up on us. Trotter began to repeat, "What happens . . . ?" and Johnson turned his dark glasses from the luff of the mainsail.

I said, "It *is* dropping. Isn't it?"

"Yes," said Johnson. Another sail rattled. We were losing speed. The wind was all we had to propel us. If that failed, we should merely sail slower and slower until we finally sat there, like a piece of cracked driftwood, waiting for that long white boat full of explosives to drive up and hit us.

I said, "What now?"

"What now?" said Johnson, and turned from contemplation of

his sails and the *Haven* to the charts spread afresh on his knees. "We now employ strategy. Listen, my children."

We listened as if he were God: Trotter tense, Harry frowning. They were trusting their lives, they believed, to a vague and unremarkble man with an ill-maintained boat. They obeyed him because there was no alternative. And also, I realized suddenly, because he knew quite well how to make himself obeyed.

We listened, and ran to our places, and Johnson threw the helm hard over to starboard and sent *Dolly* straight for the sandbanks.

You can find some of the best deep-sea fishing in the world in those islands, and soundings between the big groups can reach a thousand fathoms or more. But there are shoals on the west coast of the Berry Islands: a pattern of grass bars and shifting sandbanks which the settlement boats sometimes use, but which charter and freight boats keep clear of. If you draw over four feet, you can't use some of the channels at all.

Dolly drew 5.75 feet, and we were at the lowest point of the tide. We were going to reduce sail and enter the sandbanks, keeping to the thin, winding canals of deep water as shown on the chart. We were going to do it abruptly, and as fast as we could, and we were going to enter a channel whose southern access was guarded by the largest sandbank in the shoal.

If we set the sails right, and if Johnson steered us correctly, we should scrape past that shoal as we tacked into the channel. But *Haven,* radio controlled, wouldn't follow us blindly. A homing beacon drew its partner toward it by the shortest route possible. We should alter course and sail hard to starboard. The signals would change. *Haven* would receive them and transmit the changed course to her rudder. That, we knew, took thirty-five seconds to answer. *Dolly* would be on her way during that time, and to reach her, *Haven* would have to cut corners. And if she cut corners she would land, inescapably, into that sandbank.

They say blue water sailing is easy, compared with inshore

pilotage. I suppose canals are simple compared with sailing on rivers. I'm glad I didn't fully realize what we were doing, taking a boat of *Dolly*'s size into that winding, riverlike channel with a crew of five, of whom two were casual amateurs and one — I myself — was a novice.

Johnson didn't look worried; but then there seemed nothing of his face which wasn't inset with lenses. He had pinned the chart to the bulkhead, a precaution for which I felt a gratitude encroaching on love. Then he started giving directions again, and we freed the sail, turning *Dolly* to port, and then brought her around again almost immediately, hardening up to the wind. I belayed and watched the water change from cerulean to almond to apricot off our right flank. Harry was watching it, too, his face even greener. It was the bank at the entrance: a drifted pile-up of white coral sand so near in that clear water that there might have been inches between its long spine and the surface, or nothing at all. Spry said, "Port a little, sir," from the bowsprit, the jib sheet gripped in his hands; but Johnson smiled and said, "In a moment."

Harry didn't protest, and neither did I. It only needed a glance to the left. We had no sea room there either. The channel had silted. It was the precise width of *Dolly* at present: no less, and no more.

Then *Dolly*'s sides shaved the sand . . . No one spoke. There was a long hiss like compressed steam escaping, and we felt her slow, quicken, and slow. Then Johnson said, "All right. Free her a little," and she eased a fraction into the left, and someone gave a long sigh.

I saw there was green water there now, and green water ahead, a narrow band of it, twisting out of our vision, like a soft, grassy canyon: a fairway between low limestone bluffs. I thought of Denise, and Great Harbour Cay, and all the small, violent events which had so shocked me, set in the everyday world with telephones and traffic and people and police. Here there was nothing at all to rely on but ourselves. I had always been self-sufficient. I had despised indeed all those who were not. But now I wanted my fellow men. I wanted them very badly indeed.

I drew in sheets, and let them out, and watched *Haven*. Since the beginning, she had never gained on us as quickly as now, traveling over deep water with her engine evenly roaring, while we with our maneuvering sail felt our way along that tortuous cut. Behind us the big sandbank showed now as a patch in the watered silk of the passage, with the deeper blue of the channel beside it.

From the top of the cabin, you could see *Haven*'s bow adjusting to reach us across the shoaled stretch of water. She had not yet reached the sandbank, the bunker, the trap in her fairway. A move of ours to the right, and her bows, it seemed, pointed straight for the shallows. A move to the left, and *Haven* swung back a little, safely headed for the deep, seaworthy channel. Johnson glanced at the chart and said, "Damn. There's a stretch to port coming."

Trotter said, "Drop the mizzen? Anchor?" Desperate counsel for desperate measures.

Johnson said, "No. We'd land in a sandbank if we lose much more way."

Harry said, "Would it matter? Why not ram *Dolly* to starboard? Then she'd lead *Haven* straight through the sandbank."

Johnson was steering one-handed from the sidedeck, watching the chart, the sails, and *Haven* behind us. "There *are* risks," he said. "She's nearly got to the channel."

"What risks?" said Harry hoarsely. "You don't want to lose your bloody boat, that's what."

"I don't want to lose my bloody life, that's what," said Johnson. "Free her. We're going to port."

"No, we're not," Harry said. He leaped forward to stop Johnson freeing the mizzen, but not soon enough. Johnson turned the wheel hard to the left and I freed the main and leaped like a hare to winch it in on the starboard: beside me Trotter worked like a fiend. The boom swung, catching Harry neatly behind his tanned ear, and flinging him into the cockpit where he landed on Johnson and pulled him with his weight to the floor. I grabbed the wheel.

Dolly, wavering, turned to port in a few swaying motions, caught the wind, and settled down on her side. I looked aft. *Haven* had got to the channel.

Johnson rose to his feet, followed by Harry, their eyes on the white boat astern. Johnson said, "Keep her there," to me, and got up on top of the cabin; the others all followed. Over our wake the shoals were now hard to distinguish. Green water or biscuit, channel or sandbank, which was she entering?

"Well?" said Johnson.

Trotter had taken two steps up the shrouds. A little above us, shielding his eyes from the sun, he watched and said nothing, and climbed higher and watched again. Harry said, "Well? Has she missed? Has she got into the channel?"

Trotter said, "No. She hasn't missed. She's got to the sandbank."

"Hell," said Johnson with feeling.

Trotter looked down on him. "Yes," he said. "You're right. She's over the sandbank. She's sailing over the sandbank and she hasn't bloody well stuck. That was the risk you took, wasn't it? Why wouldn't you jam *Dolly?* The tide's making too fast and *Haven*'s draft is too shallow. *Haven* can cross them sandbanks. And we can't."

I saw Harry stop breathing. And for the first time I knew, really knew, what it is like to be advised of forthcoming death. Straight as a ruler death was coming toward us: *Haven* was beating toward us over deep water and shallows alike. And idling here, trapped in our imprisoning channel, we had no means now left to avoid her.

Johnson said: "Beltanno, sail straight. Get a bearing and stay on it until I give the word. Spry!"

He was moving aft as he spoke. Trotter said, "What sail do you want, Doctor? Is she pulling the wheel?" I told him, and he and Harry did what they could with the sheets. I watched the burgee and the wheel, and when I could, the racing blur of the white boat behind. You didn't need to look. The engine noise was enough, and the sound of the spray. In fact, it was better not to look, and watch the wheel, moving magically, a fraction this way and that. Trotter said, "Doctor . . . What are they doing?"

For a moment I couldn't see it myself. And then I said, "They've got up a net."

It was a heavy, coarse-meshed nylon affair, of the kind they use in fast catamarans, and bright red in color. I remember thinking how gay and incongruous it looked, lying on Johnson's fine varnish. But then it was all out of key: the blue sky and hot beating sun, the marvelous shades of the water, the long white luxury yacht with her elegant cushions. And the workmanlike boat with its neat, roped cargo, now devouring the short space between us.

Johnson said, raising his voice, "Right. If this doesn't work, I want you to jump. There's not a great deal of hope; we'll be too near the collision. But dive: don't stay on the surface a moment longer than you have to. And keep in deep water. No lifebelts. There'll be plenty of wreckage . . ."

He didn't mention the sharks. He said, *"Now!"* And the red net flew over the stern and into the water, straight in the path of the oncoming *Haven*. He added gently, "Now, Beltanno." And I knew why I had to keep *Dolly* straight.

I was better off than the others, perhaps, because I had *Dolly* to think of. The others had nothing to do but to stare helplessly aft, watching the scarlet net float gently backward, and *Haven* racing closer and closer toward it: toward it and us.

It had seemed a tension past bearing, a moment ago on the sandbank. This time it was happening here, the crisis. If the net didn't float toward *Haven* — if it didn't stop her or slow her or hinder her — death would be upon us in seconds.

She got to the net in a gush of white spray. Harry said, "Oh Christ!" on a gulp, and I could hear Trotter swear. *Haven*'s engine roared undiminished. Johnson's voice said curtly, "Ready about!" and he put the wheel hard down to the left while Spry jumped to the ropes. After a second Trotter went to help him. I didn't see that it mattered. In fact, if we were to jump to starboard, it merely meant that *Haven* would overtake *Dolly* beside us. Then Johnson said, "All right. Get ready to jump," and I guessed what he was doing, and saw by Spry's face that I was right. He was going to unload us and stay there on board, in order to sail *Dolly* clear.

I am used to making decisions. This is one which, thank God, I was saved from completing. Johnson drew breath to call, "Jump," when he saw me coming toward him. He said instead sharply, "Get back, Beltanno," and in that instant, one of *Haven*'s twin screws missed its beat.

Spry turned, and the two other faces showed from the weather rail, bloodless and taut. The engine grunted again.

We watched. We had reached the safe right-hand wall of the channel; Johnson turned the wheel gently and Spry without being told adjusted the sail for midchannel. No one said anything. There was another splutter behind, a moment's slience, and then the rattling sound of *Haven*'s engine resuming on a new and wholly alien tone.

The spray at her bows had quite vanished. The boat was still moving; it was still following us; but her speed was now no more than our own. One of her propellers had taken the net.

One by one we left the side deck, our eyes on *Haven*, and stepped slowly into the cockpit where Johnson stood, his hand on the wheel, his lips under the dark glasses twitching. "Hallo," he said. "And how are *your* emboli doing?"

Surprisingly, it was Trotter who laughed: a cackle of pure amusement which owed nothing to hysteria. "I tell you something," he said. "At least I know me heart's good for a century, and you could shove a ball-point pen clean down me arteries. I may, of course, still go off me poor bleedin' nut."

"Don't boast," said Johnson. "She's swallowed the net, but she may chew it up and discard it. At best she's going at the same speed as we are. The wind may die, or we may be stuck on a sandbank. And talking of sandbanks . . ."

Bad news comes soon enough. I hadn't told him, but of course he had noticed. Where the chart had been were four drawing pins adhering to four scraps of paper. "It was torn off," I said. "When Harry fell into the cockpit. At least, it was gone when I took the wheel. It must have flipped overboard. I've looked," I added.

They looked as well, but the chart wasn't aboard. And while they were looking, Trotter got up in the shrouds and started to call out the soundings.

Perhaps it sounds easy. He didn't know the tricks of these waters: he didn't know what the colors denoted. The person who knew them best was Harry; and Harry, it turned out, had no head for heights. Spry took charge of the sails, with Harry and myself to help him, while high above on the ratlines, Trotter leaned on the top, swaying spar and called out.

To this day, I remember the lesson: a light blue for ten to

fifteen fathoms, said Harry; a light green, four to five fathoms; a pale green one and a half to two fathoms; the pale marine straw of the shoals, a fathom or less. They called that white water, and if we sailed there, we were dead. Watch out, he said, for patches of coral and rock: yellow brown, deep brown, or black. Watch out for coral heads embedded in debris: grass, or sponges, or marine vegetation. Then they are harder to spot. But look for the ring of white sand around the rock or the coral, where the fish swim and wait for their prey and their plankton, and the bed is fanned clear of grass.

Trotter had a clear voice: an enunciation ungainly but perfect through years of instructing obscure foreign militia when to jump through their hoops. He had well-trained responses and an ability to keep his head and his balance on a thin swaying ratline on a slow, tacking ketch. He called out what he could see, and we hauled on ropes and released and belayed them; we ducked as the booms swayed across and the next moment seemed to sway back, guided by Spry and by Johnson and by Harry, interpreting the crazy mosaic of that brilliant seabed into a channel which would bear the passage of *Dolly*.

And all the time the choked whine of *Haven*'s engine sang in our ears, cutting corners — always there, never falling behind. And I knew what Johnson was doing: stealing every inch to port that he could make with the channel: bearing left and always left, trying to win out of the shallows he had entered so desperately and reach the deep water where we had been once before.

Then, with our engine failed and wind dropping, we had been no match for *Haven*. Now, with full sail crammed on her, *Dolly* could draw away from the crippled storeship and run until she found help or harbor. Help, in the form of another ship which could take us on board, or could explode the *Haven* by fire from a safe distance; harbor, only when we were free of our enemy.

But the shoals held us trapped. The channel wound around the sandbars, but whether it was the right channel we had no means of knowing. Sometimes the sand brushed our keel or our sides and we were all silent, wondering if, like a party astray in a maze, we had come up a blind alley and, unable to reverse, must wait there to be caught. Dazed with sun and strain, my hands raw from the ropes, my back aching with something which would soon become total exhaustion, I wondered how the others were faring. The men might be stronger, but I wouldn't give much for Harry's mental endurance and the strain Trotter was undergoing, up there on those swaying shrouds under the glare of the sun. About Spry I knew nothing and he showed nothing of weakness. But then neither did Johnson; and I knew more about Johnson than he had wanted me to know.

And still the sand closed us in. Sometimes ahead Trotter would spy freer water, and we would sail for it, letting the sails fill all they would. But always in the end the channel thickened and narrowed.

In one of these spaces, Johnson called Trotter down, and when I saw him, I knew he shouldn't go up again, although he was convinced he could, and said so all the time he was resting. I gave him a drink and a wet towel and dodged along to attend to the sheets on the foredeck, while Spry climbed the ratlines as lookout. But I knew I hadn't Spry's endurance, or his speed or his grip. In Harry and myself, Johnson had a pretty poor crew. And if Trotter came down with heatstroke . . .

Then Johnson gave Trotter the wheel and ducked forward to where I was crouching. "Doctor MacRannoch," he said.

I said, "He can't . . ."

"I know he can't," said Johnson mildly. "Neither can you, or any of us for very much longer. But listen to Trotter's suggestion. We haven't enough speed for skiing. But if we let out a warp, he thinks he can drop back to *Haven* on it and board her."

I looked at him, but the dark glasses told nothing. I said, "The sharks. He's tired. What if he loses his grip? We couldn't stop. We couldn't pick him up, could we?"

"Not before *Haven* reaches us," Johnson said. Behind us, Harry was complaining. The main basis for it, so far as I could gather, was that if Trotter drowned, or was carelessly mown down by *Haven*, we should not only have lost ground, but be short of one man to sail *Dolly*. Johnson added, "Beltanno, if only three of us are left to run *Dolly*, could you go up that shroud?"

I was glad at least that he knew what was happening to Harry. And there was no avoiding the issue. If only Spry and Johnson were left to tackle *Dolly*, I should have to be pilot. "I don't see why not," I replied.

He nodded, but his attention had left me. Trotter strode by, stripped to his trunks. He spoke, and Johnson put up his hand. Spry had already belayed a long coil of rope near the sternpost. There was a light grappling iron, I saw, at one end.

Johnson brought *Dolly* half up into the wind to let Trotter drop overboard, and for a moment I think we all believed she had lost way for good. Then Trotter's head, shaking off spray, appeared in the water. We saw him lean over, exposing one brown, sinewy shoulder and his two powerful forearms, the broad fists clutching the rope. The wind filled *Dolly*'s sails. She drew away, and Trotter's body, rising, began to cut through the water. His head in the crook of his right arm was turned left cheek upward, drawing air from the vortex caused by the shape of his body resisting the drive of the sea.

He was a magnificent swimmer. We all knew that. We had watched him scores of times towed by *Dolly*'s launch skimming up ramps and leapfrogging barrels on water skis. Broad and small with a body like muscular teak, he ignored his tiredness.

He braced himself, foetuslike in the water, and was drawn through it, his gasping mouth taking the air as Spry, as fast as he dared, paid out the cable.

It disturbed his rhythm, the lengthening cable. The first time, Spry misjudged it and the rope suddenly slackened, slamming Trotter under the water. He rose half-choked, legs threshing to keep him on top and swimming, until *Dolly* drew off and the rope tautened again. After that, Spry kept the warp tight, releasing it little by little, his eyes on *Haven* as much as on the swimmer.

We had lost ground. The white boat was far closer: the gap getting shorter. There was only so much time this maneuver could cost. But Spry didn't lose Trotter again; and Trotter, snatching glance after glance over his shoulder, must have seen *Haven*'s bows getting closer. He was almost upon her.

It was then that I found the wheel in my hands. "Good luck," said Johnson; he grinned briefly, and walked to the rail. He wasn't wearing his glasses. I stared after him, and then my attention was snatched back to Trotter by a shout from Spry and from Harry.

The swimmer was just ahead of the *Haven*. Trotter lifted a hand, raising himself out of the water, and Spry allowed to spin loose all the remaining free cable. We watched the spray settle. Trotter's head came up, cropped in the sunlight, and his hands flashed as he gathered the rope. For ten seconds maybe, he waited: the small tough sergeant-major, his brown shoulders washed by the blue surging sea, watching the approaching white boat with its sheer sides and its empty wheel and its well filled with explosives.

Lifting himself like a seal from the waves, Rodney Trotter drew back the arm with the cable, and threw. The rope hissed through the air, dropping a string of white water; a sparkle of spray left the grapple. We saw the iron hit the coaming of

Haven's white starboard bow, hesitate, and then drop down in-side out of sight.

The rope tightened. As the launch swerved unevenly past him, it drew Trotter swinging out of the sea, hands working, one strong foot already finding a purchase. By sheer momentum he got two-thirds up her sides before *Haven* forced past him, swinging the rope to her stern and unsettling the grip of the grappling iron. The rope came loose and he snatched instead, with both hands at *Haven*'s top side.

He caught it, and with the same movement, vaulted onto her deck like a gymnast.

Johnson stayed only to see Trotter board the *Haven*. Then, just as he was, he dove off *Dolly* and struck out toward the white boat and the sergeant.

Harry and Spry didn't see him. Nor did Trotter, working fast by the square engine casing in *Haven*'s bows. *Haven*'s engine droned on, and the white water sheared at her bows. Above me a sail flapped and Spry called sharply: "Doctor! Take her about!"

I thought: we ought to stop. I should bring her into the wind. But *Haven* wasn't stopping and the gap between us was closing, was shrinking again as it had in those first terrible moments. I brought *Dolly* around, my gaze half on our sails and half on Johnson's head, black in the water. He had been swimming, but as I watched, he leaned back and began to tread water. There was no need to go on. *Haven* was still advancing toward him.

Then, like a pronouncement from God, *Haven*'s engine coughed once, and was silent.

I remember that the channel had narrowed, so that we were forced to sail on. Spry took the wheel and I climbed that swaying ladder of ratlines in the shrouds, but my binoculars were as often on *Haven* behind as conning the sandbanks in front. I saw Trotter rise from stopping the engine, fling over a rope, and let himself overboard to do something efficient, I hoped, to the rudder. I saw Johnson arrive and board *Haven,* using the same rope, as Trotter emerged from the water. We could hear clearly Trotter's shout of surprise, and then the sound of their conversation, carried over the blessed, still waters. Below me, Spry and Harry had their binoculars on them also.

We saw Johnson edge around the well to the rear of the boat and come back after a brief burst of activity. He took a moment as he did so to have a look under the tarpaulin. Then he leaned out to help Trotter clamber aboard for the second time, spoke with him, and scrambling around, settled in front of the helm.

We watched, buffeted by the stillness, as if we had been prepared for an operation, and did not realize even now that the operation was not going to take place. I think that was why, when *Haven*'s engine suddenly started and that deathly roar, the roar we had throttled, came suddenly into rebirth, Harry's nerves burst into screaming disorder. He heard the noise, and he saw those white bows begin again to move, to quicken, to drive along freely and powerfully and with ease begin to overhaul us. He dropped the mainsheet, and ran for the starboard sidedeck, as once he had been told. Then he tried to throw himself over.

Spry and I caught him and manhandled him down to the cockpit, while Johnson throttled *Haven* well down and brought her docilely behind us and then up to and past us as *Dolly,* unattended, drifted herself into the sandbar. Spry had Harry immobilized by that time, and I got out the syringe and the ampoules and immobilized him further. Then we put him into the salon.

Haven warped *Dolly* off that sandbank; then Johnson let her float off behind, sea cocks open, while he and Trotter climbed aboard on the cable. She sank very gently in the clear, clear water among the sponges and the sea grasses and the small colored fish. I don't think any of us felt anything: we carried our own precipitins, for the moment, against fear and danger and even relief. Besides, there was *Dolly* still to look after.

I climbed the shrouds again while Johnson took the wheel rather silently, a towel around his shoulders; and Trotter lay still and dripped on the afterdeck without doing anything at all. He deserved it. No one tried to disturb him, and very soon I saw open water and steered Johnson into it, and was allowed to come down. The sea all around us was midgreen and purple and blue. We were in deep water, and could begin to tack our way home.

I took the wheel in some of the long reaches and Spry and Johnson shared the rest. Once the sails were set on each tack, there was little to do. We took it in turns to go below into the saloon and stretch out on the cushions. Trotter recovered quickly, but Johnson slept for an hour. I left the wheel to go into the owner's cabin to rouse him. Spry had made tea, on my advice, instead of pouring us alcohol, and I knocked and put the cup down by his side.

He grunted and opened his eyes. His hair was a mess, and he hadn't put on his glasses since swimming, but his social adjustments as ever were effortlessly bang on the nail. He said, "I bet it's sweet and weak, and God knows how you blackmailed Spry into producing it, but because I am suffering from fluid deprivation, I'll drink it." He got off the bed, his beach shirt crumpled where he had been lying on it, put on his bifocal glasses, and said: "Sit down, then, and let me look at you."

I sat down. I was no picture. My turban had stayed somehow in place, but my sunsuit was filthy with oil and salt water and sweat, and I had larded Noxema all over the sunburn on my arms and my shoulders and nose. I stared back at Johnson as he stood leaning there drinking his tea; and to my disgust a pricking sensation made itself felt behind my puncta lacrimalia. I con-

234

trolled myself and said stiffly, "We've missed the barbecue, I'm afraid."

"We rather did down the National Morbidity Survey as well," Johnson said. "Didn't we?"

He put down his cup and, twitching a tissue out of its holder, leaned forward and wiped the surplus cream off my nose. Then he sat down beside me in the same suave and damnable silence, and putting up his two hands like a milliner, straightened the turban over my naked crop of tufted black hair. And like a child, a schoolgirl, a nurse under reprimand, I burst into tears — into, I discerned distantly some moments later, the creased bosom of Johnson's beach shirt.

He made no remarks, but merely patted me on the back with one hand and produced a concatenation of tissues with the other until the worst of the outburst was over; and it took a long time. I can't remember ever crying like that. I suppose I had, some time, when I was a child. Eventually I wiped my eyes for the last time and blew my nose for the last time and lifted my head and sat soggily up. "Postoperative reaction," I said in bleary apology.

"Partly. But some post-MacRannoch reaction, I fancy, as well," Johnson said. He got up and unlatching a locker, produced and began to pour two glasses of whiskey. He held one out to me. "To Beltanno Douglas MacRannoch, human being. Don't marry Mr. Tiko," he said.

I took what he gave me and drank it. "Why not?" I said. It was all very surprising, I suppose. Except that I had no emotions left to be surprised with.

"I've done an Eysenck personality inventory on you both," Johnson said, and put his glass on a locker and held it. We were sailing hard, on the port tack. Someone was sober, and working. "You wouldn't suit."

235

"Whom would I suit?" I said impatiently.

Johnson took a long drink and then leaned back and took off his glasses. "In a long life, I've heard that said in many ways, but never grimly," he said. "The answer, of course, is *most people,* however poorly supported by data to date. Most people, provided you let go of James Ulric MacRannoch."

"*Let go* of my father?" I exclaimed.

"That's what I said. You know you're the cause of his asthma?"

Nonsense. I was rather stiff, I recall, in my answer. "My father has been hyposensitized against pollen, house dust, *Aspergillus fumigatus,* the wheat weevil, dandruff, and budgerigars. Without me, he has quite enough to be going along with."

Johnson ignored me. "And he is the cause of your belligerent bachelor doctorhood. He said he wanted a line of baby MacRannochs. But you gave him what you thought he really wanted, didn't you? You turned yourself into a son."

It was a lie. It was none of his business. I would consider it later. I said, "Amateur psychiatry, Mr. Johnson?"

"And avoidance behavior, Doctor MacRannoch," said Johnson.

We stared at one another. My whiskey, somehow, had almost got finished. "He's going to marry the Begum," I said.

"He would have married her years ago," said Johnson uncompromisingly, "if he'd got you off his hands."

"If I don't marry Mr. Tiko . . . I don't want to marry," I said.

"You don't need to marry. All you want are a few nice, meaningful human relationships, like Krishtof Bey. Let me recommend a well-tried and traditional therapy: people."

"People are Harry," I said.

"Well, Christ; you turned *him* off and disposed of the carcass," said Johnson. "And anyway, what's the matter with him? He had his postoperative shock before the operation, that's all. What do you expect? A world peopled with B. Douglas MacRannochs?" He paused. "I suppose you can get it, if you opt out and go for research. We're all the same in ash weight of bones."

I had a splitting headache, but I wasn't going to stand for that kind of nonsense. "Some people," I said, "prefer pure thought to the painful vacuity of ill-considered social exchanges."

I was rather pleased with that. Johnson sat down on the bed. "Now you mention it," he said, "that's why I took off my glasses." And putting his two hands hard on my shoulders, he kissed me.

It was an extremely nice kiss. It didn't go on quite as long as Krishtof Bey's, nor was it unpleasant or torrid. Halfway through he shifted his grip so that the leverage was better; and since he had wiped off my cream, I didn't have to worry what he did with my nose. At the end he drew off and said, "You've been practicing. Can I have afters?"

If I hadn't been scarlet with sunburn I suppose I would have been flushed up to the eyes. "Maybe I have," I said. "But you don't need any. You need an inhibiting agent."

"I don't mind, if she's nice," said Johnson, continuing to gaze into my eyes. He kissed me again, briefly, and then sat grinning maliciously at me and holding my hands.

Believe it or not, I had forgotten that tape recorder on Crab. I even returned the smile, gasping a little. "I thought I should remind you," said Johnson frankly. "Anyway, everyone else seems to have had a ball, barring perhaps Mr. Tiko. What was all that stuff again about painful vacuity?"

"And pure thought," I said.

"And pure thought. For some people, yes, Beltanno."

"But not for me?"

"You haven't had a pure thought since you were born," said Johnson cheerfully. "You're a mixture of horrible complexes, and you know it. But underneath that freeze-dried exterior lies a splendid unprogramed community known as Beltanno B. Loving."

Outside the door, Trotter's voice called from the cockpit, and we heard him go forward, and the rush of Spry's feet. "We're back," said Johnson. "Back from danger; back from isolation; back into the great big world. Are you sorry?"

"Are you?" I said. Until that moment, I had forgotten.

He said, "It's my chosen profession. I'm sorry that this time it seems to have coopted yourself, but don't let it fret you. One more day will see the whole business finished, provided we can keep Harry quiet. Can we keep Harry quiet?"

"Why?" I said. "How? Will you bring the police over? Will they tell you who did all these things?"

Johnson got up. He collected my glass and his own, and putting them both in their slots, relatched the locker and put on his bifocal glasses. They flashed at me under the skylight: familiar, anonymous, unreadable. He said: "No need. I know who did all these things. I've known, actually, for a fairly long time."

Chapter 14

JOHNSON MAY HAVE THOUGHT he had spotted the culprit, but he refused blandly to drop even a hint. It was beneath me to argue. But I wanted to.

The green Daimler convertible was waiting for us when we landed on Crab Island, and we laid Harry in it and made for the barbecue, which was half over, as it had taken us all afternoon to tack south against that misguided wind. Spry had given us something to eat and we had all had more whiskey. Trotter and Johnson quarreled all the way to the house over whether to call the police forthwith or give Edgecombe twenty-four hours to try and deal with it.

I didn't blame Trotter for wanting to broadcast his recent perils to the horrified ears of officialdom. Someone had tried to blow up a boatload of people, including me, and I thought it was time he was found and firmly led away in handcuffs. I can't imagine, therefore, why I argued on Johnson's side.

Not that it made a great deal of difference, since we couldn't say who Johnson was. We arrived, and all we had got Trotter to promise was to give Edgecombe a hearing before informing the London *Times,* the British Minister for Defence and the University of Miami's School of Marine and Atmospheric Sciences. The assumption, of course, was that Sir Bartholomew Edgecombe was still alive; but we couldn't appear to question that either.

All the same, when we drew up at the steps of the castle and Johnson made his way up to the doors with Harry folded over his shoulder, I found it hard to disguise my uneasiness. Behind us, strains of stereo music and laughter came from the beach and the gardens, and there were a lot of flushed-out flamingoes snaking moodily over the pathways and lawns. Then we followed Johnson inside, and the Begum's butler came into the hall, and Johnson said, "Another casualty, I'm afraid, but not a serious one: just a bump on the head. Do you have a bed he could rest on?" And as houseboys appeared and removed Harry, dangling limply from his second injection, Johnson added, "Tell me, how is Sir Bartholomew?"

The Begum's permanent staff were white, discreet, and formidably efficient. "Sir Bartholomew is remarkably well, sir, considering," said the Begum's butler. "He's still in his room resting, but the nurse was quite pleased with him, so she said. I believe he is to come down for dinner." He paused. "I'm quite sure he's awake, sir, if you wish to visit him. Miss Violet has been with him for most of the afternoon."

Miss Violet, I thought, has probably saved his life. But I didn't say so.

She was just leaving as we reached Edgecombe's room. She looked just the same except that she wore a net snood with a bow instead of the floppy white hat. Her make-up was impeccable. She asked us, I remember, how many fish we had caught, and Johnson said we had disposed of it all to a factory ship. Neither of them smiled.

Inside, Edgecombe was looking better, lying in bed with a book beside him and his bandaged arm laid stiffly beside it. Johnson and Trotter found two chairs and sat down talking, and I shut the door and went to perch on the bed. Johnson stopped discussing fish and said: "Bart. We want your advice. After you left, someone made a bonus effort to detonate *Dolly*. We know it's aimed at you; we know the whole thing is classified, but Sergeant Trotter here thinks perfectly rightly that we can't keep this to ourselves any longer. This time, we might all have been killed; next time we may be less lucky." He paused. "Trotter wants to call the police right away. I'm willing to give you twenty-four hours to cover your tracks, or call in your superiors, or whatever you do in your dream world. Then I think really we shall have to take action."

He had stuck, I observed, just the right note of uneasy officiousness. He was, of course, buying time: preventing Trotter and Harry from making the whole business instantly public. I hoped Edgecombe was well enough to appreciate it.

"My God," said Edgecombe blankly. He looked from me to Johnson to Trotter. He said, "I wanted to come back, but Brady was so damned insistent . . ." He broke off and repeated, "My God, I've been lying here thinking, if they haven't come back there can't be anything wrong, because I'm not on board. How did it happen? Hell, how *could* it happen when I wasn't there?"

We managed to raise his temperature a couple of points before we left him, which made me a little arbitrary with Johnson: I put both men out and stayed behind to administer a mild dose of quinalbarbitone. Then I sat beside Edgecombe until he stopped apologizing. Between them, he and Johnson had persuaded Trotter to let them have their precious twenty-four hours, although I didn't see what they were going to do with it. Find out who set off *Haven* maybe, although I thought it unlikely. Wait for another attack on Bart Edgecombe, perhaps? Edgecombe grinned when I suggested it to him.

"I expect so," he said. "But in the nature of a controlled experiment next time, I think. Johnson will tell me. Meanwhile within these four walls I'm all right. No hatches; no hidden doors;

plenty of microphones, a radio transmitter, and an extremely strong lock on the door. You're the one, poor girl, who's had all the danger. I should think you'll look back on all this as the weirdest two weeks of your life." He leaned back drowsily, his hair ruffled, and took my hand as it lay on the coverlet. "Are you falling for Johnson?"

"Good heavens," I said. "What makes you think so?"

"People do," Edgecombe said. "Because he likes to surprise them."

I smiled professionally. "Doctors aren't easily surprised." After a moment I said, "What sort of people?"

"His wife," said Edgecombe gently, "for one."

He was, in many ways, a feminine man. He would have made a good general practitioner. He understood women. He had understood Denise.

Unlike Johnson, who appeared feminine, and wasn't. I said, without much of a pause, "I wish it would finish. He says he knows who it is, but he won't tell."

"I wonder if he does," Edgecombe said.

It hadn't occurred to me that Johnson might have been bluffing. I said, "It was Brady who loaded the *Haven*. And Brady who made sure he escaped before *Dolly* blew up. It was Brady who was there on the golf course when your wife . . ."

I broke off. This wasn't the treatment he needed. But he answered me as I got to my feet. "So your guess would be Brady? But wasn't it risky for him to be on board *Dolly* at all? What if my accident hadn't happened? What if you hadn't insisted on sending me back in the launch?"

"He would have made an excuse, surely," I suggested. "A pain; an urgent appointment. But for Trotter and Johnson, none of us would have survived to check it."

"Then what about Trotter?" said Edgecombe.

"*Trotter?*" I stared at him, I remember. That exhausted,

obstinate, sun-blistered little man in the ratlines, conning us through all the shallows. The steadfast swimmer on the end of a cable, dragging himself onto that live bomb of a boat.

"It was Trotter who caused the death of the waiter, or so Johnson said. At the water tower."

I said, "But for Sergeant Trotter we shouldn't be alive. Any of us."

"Of course," said Edgecombe. "He had to save his own skin. But for all you know, he may have been quite as anxious as Brady to take that launch back from *Dolly*, or to create a chance to leave you all and get back to Crab Island. Maybe Brady spoiled his plan, that was all."

I was silent. It was not as easy as I had imagined.

"Or it might have been Krishtof Bey," said Edgecombe sleepily, "who stayed behind and risked nothing at all. I rather like the idea of Krishtof Bey. That young man is by no means the romantic egoist that he seems." He looked at me and smiled, his eyes heavy. "Poor Beltanno. Surrounded by decent young men, and you daren't choose, do you? In case one of them is a very nasty young man indeed."

"True," I said bitterly. "But I can always sit on my ass and then see what's left over."

I changed, wigged, and looked up the old *Who's Who* in the Begum's dark library on my way out to the barbecue's fading attractions.

JOHNSON JOHNSON it said; and a lot of truncated stuff about expensive education, a Royal Navy career, portrait painting, clubs, a public appointment or two, and addresses in London and Surrey. He was in his late thirties. And ten years ago he had married Judith Cicely Ballantyne, daughter of high court judge the Rt. Hon. Lord Ballantyne, without evident issue.

An unprolific espionage agent.

Krishtof Bey wasn't married. Wallace Brady wasn't in it.

The barbecue table was a large drum of wrought iron and concrete, designed for the Begum by Bjørn Wiinblad, with a hand-painted ceramic top in the green Akbar motif, price, including delivery and fitting, $1500 because I asked.

I had a late steak bespoken by the Begum, who mentioned Bart Edgecombe and my painful sunburn in the same courteous passage, but was more concerned that I should meet the lustier of her other seventy-four guests. Johnson I saw at a beach table surrounded by a knot of glossy admirers: Trotter beside him was busy with three cans of beer and another plateful of steak.

I have never seen so many photographed people together in one place: for one-night stands the Begum evidently invited one-night people. The quality might not be durable, but for a battery life of five or six hours, the sparkle was stunning.

I got between a top male model and an Italian producer and began to glow presently with well-being and sunburn like a small-bore central heating conversion between a pair of quartz iodine spot lamps.

"Why, hullo, Doctor MacRannoch!" said Wallace Brady.

The male model turned full face his glorious profile. He said, "You can't fool me: don't expect me to dig it. A beautiful girl like you can't be a doctor?"

"She is," said Brady. "Ask them at the United Commonwealth Hospital."

"Nonsense," said the producer. "Doctors play golf and wear boned foundations with many suspenders. Even male doctors wear many suspenders. I know. I have been to every doctor in Rome with my feet."

"I have," I said, "an infallible cure of my own for the many who suffer in such silence, such fortitude, with their feet."

"Yes?" said the producer. The male model's magnificent mane bent close to mine.

"You will need pencil and paper," I said.

"I have it. I have it!" said the producer. He slit a reefer in half, smoothed the paper and waited, ball point poised. I dictated.

I left while they were still expressing their abstracted thanks, and correcting their spelling. Wallace Brady said, "Beltanno?"

"Yes?" I said. There were seventy-odd people around me, but I clung to my beach bag with my gun in it.

"Am I mistaken, or was that a prescription for pure sulphuric acid?" said Wallace Brady.

The sun was hot between the beach chairs and the umbrellas: *Dolly*'s launch passed with a man and a girl on monoskis, showing off. The stereo was whisking the Cream and the sea was full of sailfish and dark glasses and brown, naked spines. Brady led me over the beach and up to the Begum's long palmetto-thatched bar, where he put in an order. "It was," I said, "an inert placebo containing the constituents of an excellent itching powder. Why didn't you come back and take me off *Dolly?*"

"Did you want me to?" Brady said. "Edgecombe's all right, you know. The nurse was waiting for us when we stepped on the jetty." He grinned. "And the Lady Violet was a tower of strength." He was wearing swimming trunks and, set in the deeply tanned face, the gray eyes were paler than ever. I said, "It turned out all right, but I would have felt happier. And Sir Bart says he wanted to come back."

"He did," said Wallace Brady without any visible hesitation whatever. "But I put him off it. If you want the real truth, Beltanno, I didn't want you with Edgecombe at all, and to hell with M.I. Five and C.I.A. and all the rest of the guys earning their Civil List pensions. I got knocked out last time for saying so, but that doesn't stop me from saying so again. That Edgecombe business is dangerous. They've no right to get a person like you mixed up in it."

"A beautiful girl like me," I corrected him. The drink order had come. It consisted of a whole pineapple with a couple of straws in it.

"I don't use other people's vapid expressions," said Wallace Brady. He indicated the pineapple. "I got it this way, since you're creeping about like the Great Gatsby's girl friend. You suck that straw and I suck this one, and all we get are each other's diseases. Stick your gun under the table."

I pushed my beach bag in silence under the table, while he carried the pineapple down and set it between us. It was filled with a number of things. Lemon. Vermouth. Angostura. And of course, at least two types of rum. We sucked, with our noses nearly touching, and Wallace Brady stroked my hand under the table.

If he was disconcerted that we had come back alive, he didn't show it: quite the reverse. All it proved was that he was perfectly sure of himself, and that neither the damage on *Dolly* or the radio installations on the *Haven* could possibly be traced back to him. We talked, rather stiltedly, about golf. He didn't ask me to go anywhere with him, and I wouldn't have gone if he had. I had the larger share of the pineapple because I wanted rather suddenly to get away quickly. As my straw bubbled its way to dry dock he raised his head and said, "Beltanno: don't marry Mr. Tiko."

Jesus Christ, Mr. Tiko. I rose to my feet and the Begum, floating gauzily in the distance, turned and registered reception of my anxiety. I bent and received my beach bag from Wallace Brady. I thanked him for that and the punch. "You won't, will you?" he said. "His long game is maybe all right, but his putting is terrible."

I walked off without answering him, and the Begum received me. "You've remembered your dear Japanese gentleman."

I do not enjoy apologizing, but it was through me, after all, that Mr. Tiko had been invited at all. The Begum heard me with a smile and said, "Darling Beltanno, he is charming and I would marry him myself tomorrow were I five feet high and not already supporting the id of James Ulric."

It came to me that the Begum improved on acquaintance. I said, "What happened?" There was no trace of a blood bath.

"Mr. Tiko has been the center of attention," said the Begum. "Do you know what happens if a woman eats too much Yang in the Zen macrobiotic diet?"

"No," I said.

"That's funny," said the Begum, looking thoughtful. "I thought you did."

"But my father?" I said impatiently.

"Hasn't even met him, my dear," said the Begum with a kind of quiet triumph. "The moment he came into the house, I sent Mr. Tiko down to the beach, and the moment he came down to the beach, I sent Mr. Tiko back to the house. You know those Japanese watches with dumped Russian movements?"

"Yes," I said, and waited, but she appeared to believe her remark fully concluded. I said, "Does Mr. Tiko know who we are?"

"Mr. Tiko," said the Begum, "knows that you and your father are resident in my house and that your name is MacRannoch. He has no doubt discovered that numbers of his fellow guests are also named MacRannoch. Whether he has made any deduction from this, I cannot quite say. My own dear late Achmed had the same gift for concealing his systems." She put an arm on my shoulder and said, "While you are here, darling. Has someone tried to kill Sir Bartholomew Edgecombe again? Krishtof wanted to know."

It was too complicated to go into details. "Yes," I said. "But I can't tell you who it was. Johnson is working on it."

There was a little silence. Then, "*Johnson?*" said the Begum slowly, and the blood retreated from my digestive organs, leaving my steak in bleak tête-à-tête with my rum.

I had made a gross error of judgment. In order to provoke the opposition into action, Johnson had let it be known to our limited circle who and what Edgecombe was. He had said nothing of his own share in the present giant slalom event. I had blown his cover.

The Begum's large, made-up eyes grew steadily luminous. She stood struck into stillness, her painted nails still on my shoulder. "Not *two* of them?" she said. "Two espionage agents in one Hurst Volumetric Spore Trap?"

I looked around. There was no one in earshot. "Should I have James desensitized?" asked the Begum with some anxiety.

Even after ten days of this, I still felt at times like a corn weevil in a shredded-wheat packet. I pulled myself together. "I shouldn't have told you. I'm sorry, but you realize that no one is supposed to know that. Promise me, please promise me, you won't tell anyone else."

The Begum's eyes, on closer inspection were not anxious at all. "Only James Ulric?" she suggested.

My God. "Not James Ulric. Especially not James Ulric."

The Begum put her dark glasses on, effectively preventing me from evaluating all her further pronouncements. "You are asking me," she said, "to destroy the spirit of the whole fine relationship between your father and me, built up trust upon trust, through the years of endurance and love?" She slid her grasp down to my elbow and, turning me, walked slowly through waves of Nancy Sinatra back up to the house. "I wouldn't consider it," said the Begum, "unless . . ."

We were nearing the castle. From behind the battlements my father's carrying voice could be heard. "Where's that bloody woman?" he was roaring.

"Unless what?" I prompted. I was gravely anxious. If the Begum informed James Ulric of Johnson's identity, the news would spread like a barium meal. My father's voice yelled, *"Thelma!"*

The Begum's handsome black head cocked to one side. "Perhaps," she said, "we should go in." And discarding both Johnson and blackmail in a single, unreliable smile, she began to sweep her way up the wide castle steps.

My father appeared at the top, heaving. "Thelma," he said. "That bloody Nip! That you invited to your bloody barbecue!"

Mr. Tiko and James Ulric had met.

"Well?" said the Begum Akbar calmly.

"He's finished the jigsaw!" screamed my father. The air filled with spume. Mr. Tiko, appearing deferentially behind his left elbow said, "My humble regrets, Mr. MacRannoch. I understood from your wife that she wished the puzzle completed."

My father, throbbing, gazed from Mr. Tiko to the Begum and back. "That's not my wife!" he shouted.

Mr. Tiko gazed at him impassively. "I beg your pardon," he said.

My father, who looked like Albert Schweitzer this evening, had sudden trouble with his Wurlitzer. Gliding past him, the Begum slid Mr. Tiko and myself from the threshold into the library and waited until James Ulric beat in with a full head of steam. She shut the door. James Ulric pointed a muscular finger at his Japanese guest and said, "You're running after the bitch for her money!"

"I beg your pardon," said Mr. Tiko again. Above his neat beach shirt his face was still courteous, but he was bending his mind to the problem. "The Begum, I understand, is not your wife," said Mr. Tiko. "But Doctor MacRannoch is your daughter?"

My father walked around him. The distance was not far. "You thought all Achmed's bloody rupees were coming to Beltanno," he said. "You thought you were marrying money. I have news for you, my funny, wee, buff Mickey Mouse. If you marry my daughter, you won't get the decimal point in my bank book. I'll spend it all."

"James," said the Begum's voice smoothly.

Beside himself, my father merely swelled and jerked his white quiff at his mistress. "And I'll spend all *her* money as well."

The Begum's thin eyebrows rose. Mr. Tiko said, "Pardon me. I am one of your daughter's most devoted admirers, but — "

The Begum said, "But James. We are not married yet."

"No," said my father. "And neither are they. You'll see. Tell him no money, and he'll be on the next jumbo jet back to the geishas." He paused. "What do you mean, we're not married yet?"

The Begum sat down with grace. "It semed to have a bearing on the conversation," she said. "Further, I have told you I will not become Mrs. MacRannoch until Beltanno is married."

My father gasped. "You want her to marry that Nip?" he said. "And all my grandchildren sweetie-egg color?"

"I didn't say so," said the widow of the late Achmed Akbar, with some coolness.

"I beg your pardon," said Mr. Tiko, but he hadn't a chance. My father broke in, snapping his fingers. "Broody! Who was that man who phoned you, Beltanno? I offered him . . ."

"Wallace Brady," I said. I was surprised I could still speak. "That was Wallace Brady. I told you."

"I offered him . . ." said my father, and got no further, because the door opened and Wallace Brady poked his head around.

"Calling me, someone?" he said.

"Yes," said James Ulric smartly. I opened my mouth. My

father said, "I offered you seventy-five thousand dollars once to marry my daughter."

My all-American golf partner entered the library very carefully and shut the door after him, his eyes sliding over the persons of Mr. Tiko and the Begum, sitting bolt upright in her chair. "Yes," he said. "You sure did. I thought you were pulling my leg."

"I'll double it," said James Ulric briefly.

There was a short silence. Wallace Brady's round pale eyes wandered in my direction. "Don't trouble," I said. "I've got my own plans. Mr. Tiko, I owe you an apology."

Like a canary whose cage has been opened, Mr. Tiko hopped with relief into the sunshine. "Not at all," he said. "I think it is your father who has mistaken my intentions. Long your admirer, I have at no time ventured to aspire to your hand. I say so with personal regret."

I smiled at him. The pineapple of rum had left my mind perfectly clear. I said, "Your intentions were perhaps somewhat in doubt, but mine have been fixed from our first meeting. Mr. Tiko, setting aside all question of money . . . would you consider me as your wife?"

Mr. Tiko's mouth opened. He shut it, looked around the room, and then gave a small bow. "It would be an honor," he said. "I could wish for no higher. But in my country, there is a custom before which all must bow. I could not bind myself without the consent of your venerable parent."

"Right. Wallace?" said James. He hardly let Mr. Tiko finish speaking. He was steaming with triumph and malice.

"Will you marry me, Beltanno?" said Wallace. "For nothing," he added.

"No," I said. I remembered with a pang the moment when he attacked Johnson Johnson in my defense. Then I remembered the *Haven* and felt a little less like a failed premium offer. The Begum said reasonably, "But, Beltanno, you must marry someone."

I saw my father shoot her a look of surprise and gratitude. "Brady. It's settled," he said.

"Or Krishtof Bey," said the Begum. "He'd take you with seventy-five thousand dollars." She stared hard at my father, daring him to visualize sweetie-mouse-colored grandchildren in ballet tights. There was an unfriendly silence.

"Or Krishtof Bey," said my father weakly, after a moment. The Begum sat back with a sigh. I said, "I'm not marrying Krishtof Bey either."

The Begum said sweetly, "You're marrying one of them. Or one of your friends will be sorry."

I had forgotten Johnson Johnson entirely. I stared at her, plumbing her perfidy. Unless I married, said that brittle, mandarin smile, she would betray Johnson Johnson's identity.

I smiled back. "All right," I said. "I choose Mr. Tiko."

"You can't," said my father. "You heard him. I've refused my consent."

"We know why, as well," said the Begum. "You're afraid of his golf handicap."

"You're mad," said my father. "I could beat any one of that tribe from a bus with one hand in my pocket."

"Then play him for Beltanno," said the Begum.

A simple solution conceived by Medusa. You would not think for a moment that any sane person would consider it seriously. You would never dream that, having embraced the principle, Wallace Brady should complain that he too should be allowed to play golf for a wife, and that the Begum, judiciously holding the balance, would decree that Krishtof Bey must also have a share in the match.

Account for it as you might — mispaired chromosomes, pancreatic deficiency, or straightforward mental retardation — you would still barely believe that a group of coherent, mixed adults could agree to meet the next afternoon at the golf course at Great Harbour Cay, and there compete, match play over an eighteen-hole course, for the privilege of marrying Dr. B. Douglas MacRannoch: winner gets the bride, with veto rights over any candidate possessed by James Ulric MacRannoch, provided that he wins more holes than the man to be vetoed.

I think I used a lot of strong language for which I failed to apologize. I know that at first, all my brain could grasp was that I was being asked to mortgage my whole future for Johnson's despicable safety. It further came to me that I risked being linked in holy matrimony with a murderer. Was this why Wallace Brady had asked for my hand? Why Krishtof Bey had expressed a wholly unexpected interest in legal attachments?

On the other hand, it came to me through the sound of my own protestations, Johnson Johnson had undertaken in twenty-four hours to expose Edgecombe's would-be assassin. If he didn't, Sergeant Trotter was going to put the whole thing in the hands of the police, and the Begum could expose whom she wished. If he did, we should know the name of the miscreant by the end of the golf match, and it was quite on the cards that my prospective fiancé, whichever he might be, would be led off the golf course in handcuffs.

I wondered what kind of game Krishtof Bey played.

I said, "All right. I think you're all drunk. But I'll do it."

There was a hazy silence. It came to me that none of us was entirely stone sober, and that further, no one had expected me to agree. James Ulric sat down suddenly. Mr. Tiko bowed, an expression of faint alarm on his face. Wallace Brady was grinning.

The Begum Akbar rose, shook out her long, filmy wrappings, and crossing, laid a hand on Mr. Tiko's bowed shoulders.

"And," she said, "all you did was finish their jigsaw."

*   *

The rest of that evening and the following night are obscured by a deep fuzz of sleep.

A normal reaction to stress, not to mention a crisis of an unprecedented and personal nature. I recall using much these words to describe my weary condition to Johnson, a little later that evening.

I remember his patient rejoinder. "You're tiddly," he said. "Go to bed. You look like an overworked loofah."

That was after I had broken the news of the golf competition. I see now why he thought I was intoxicated. At the time, he showed only mild hysteria and was willing enough to answer my questions.

Once the Begum's guests had all left, Johnson had been busy. Without consulting me or anyone else, he had roused Sir Bartholomew Edgecombe, and helped by Spry, had put him in *Dolly*'s speedboat. Sir Bartholomew was now safely at home on Great Harbour Cay, guarded by his own houseboys and with Spry to supervise for good measure. So that I could relax. Edgecombe was safe.

"Bully for Edgecombe," I said. I cannot excuse the blight which attacks my vocabulary. "But what about us? I suppose that means the murderer is still on Crab Island? Who is it? You said that you knew."

"I do," Johnson said. "But it still can't be proved. Any one of our suspects could have doctored the *Haven* after she was loaded . . . although I've discovered one thing. When she took on the explosives, the job was done by a team from Bullock's

Harbour. A group who naturally knew Pentecost and his brothers."

The deceased waiter from the Bamboo Conch Club. "On Mr. Brady's instructions?" I asked.

"Exactly. But for all we know, Mr. Brady's instructions may have been perfectly innocent. Someone else may have given Pentecost's friends their less legitimate orders. One of them, we suppose, dived and placed *Dolly*'s beacon under her hull."

"And fixed the alternator leads? And put the sugar into the fuel tank?" I said.

Johnson's bifocals were two blank enigmas. "Oh no," he said. "That had to be done by someone aboard."

Letting out Krishtof Bey. Unless Krishtof Bey was working with someone. I said, "Is it possible that two of these people are in league together against Edgecombe?"

"Yes," said Johnson. "It's not only possible, it is certain. The question being, naturally, which two?"

I went to bed almost immediately afterward. Whichever two they were, they had to be brilliant golfers. Otherwise it just wouldn't be my bloody luck.

*   *

I awoke to cloudless skies and a thoughtful breakfast tray, followed rather tentatively by the Begum, who sat erect at the foot of my bed and said: "Everyone is quite well and Sir Bartholomew has had a splendid night I am told. Beltanno dear, I expect you want to call the whole golf match off?"

I said, "If I don't marry, will you really walk out on my father?"

She gazed at me for quite a long time from those painted eyes. At length: "Yes," she said.

"And tell everyone who Johnson is?"

This time the silence was longer. "No," she said.

"That wasn't what you said downstairs yesterday."

"If I had," said the Begum, "you wouldn't have agreed to the match."

"And you wanted me to agree to it? To have my husband picked out by his putting?"

"Yes," said the Begum with disarming simplicity. "I want you and James Ulric to discover that you can't control one another by force any more. Will you do it, Beltanno? Now you've had time to consider?"

"Try," I said heavily, "and keep me away."

*　　　*

The morning dragged. Sergeant Trotter sailed off to Great Harbour Cay to measure the ground for the unspeakable Mac-Rannoch Gathering. Wallace Brady ostensibly went swimming and was actually found at the back of the orchid wood with a driver and a bucket of golf balls. Krishtof Bey posed by the swimming pool for Johnson until I walked past by accident, upon which he jumped to his feet and leaped around me, finishing in a one-footed arabesque with both my hands pinned to his bosom.

When I protested, he assembled himself back in the normal standing position and said, "I am behindhand with my mating proposal. Is there a standard form of wording particular to the MacRannochs, or may I express it in the universal language of the dance?"

"Can you play golf?" I said.

He could. I let him dance around me for a bit, and then went to look for my father.

I found him with a bag of golf balls by the flamingo pond. I went away without speaking, and made sure that the Begum had put his nose filters into his suitcase. I had a feeling he was going to need them.

Then I went to my room with the Chinese vase and the white bearskin carpet, and packed my own suitcase for Great Harbour Cay. My fate was going to be decided there this afternoon, and I wasn't going to miss it.

Chapter 15

My father is a man of firm prejudices, and has driven many a sociologist out of his mind on a golf course. He has a swing like a flail forage harvester which can carry a British ball 260 yards and an American one 3 feet, still teed up on its divot. James Ulric dislikes American balls. James Ulric dislikes hundred-yard tees and large greens with five pin positions. He doesn't like big trees in his way. He doesn't like soft sculpted sand traps, which he likes to call bunkers; or Old Man Par, whom he refers to as Bogey. He doesn't like conspicuous golf wear but neither does he like to be heated, so my father walks around a golf course wearing long, seated shorts, tennis shoes, and a white jockey cap a trifle too large for him. Today, as a concession to Hymen, he had put on a shirt.

We were all nervously jocular, there on the terrace in front of the Great Harbour Cay golf club. Stepping ashore from the restored splendors of *Dolly*, we had enjoyed iced drinks on the club sun deck while Johnson made a necessary trip to see Sir Bartholomew Edgecombe, and Wallace Brady went off to check our golf carts and booking.

James Ulric was grumbling, I remember, because it was later than planned through Johnson's delay in bringing around *Dolly*.

I thought it a little unfair, since after all, he had had to sail her single-handed with Spry gone. Then I realized that James Ulric would have grumbled in just the same way before playing Toulouse Lautrec at lawn tennis. My father likes to be certain of winning.

Wallace Brady on the other hand was thoughtfully silent both before and after his absence, and Krishtof Bey concealed whatever he was feeling by paying shameless compliments to the Begum. Mr. Tiko, whom I had seated as far as possible from my father, discoursed a little distractedly on how to rake a Zen garden. We were all, I think, thankful when the time came to walk down to the terrace with our golf clubs, where Johnson soon joined us.

Sir Bartholomew Edgecombe, we gathered, was still in good health, and his arm was making sound progress. My father cleared his throat. "Trotter tells me you're calling the police in this evening. About time, too. If that man Edgecombe's an Intelligence agent, I'm not surprised the Russians are everywhere."

The Begum Akbar gazed at him severely. "You don't read enough thrillers," said Thelma. "Of course he is being attacked by enemy agents, and he has volunteered to remain so that his colleagues may trap them. The island is probably full of M.I. Five at this moment."

"Planting the bloody palm trees heads down," said my father. "I know the Civil Service. And I say call the police. You know that fellow Harry? I had a talk with him just before coming away. He says you were all nearly killed on *Dolly* yesterday morning."

There is a limit to the length of time even a broker may be anaesthetized. The failure to blow up *Dolly* had been a public act which had forced Johnson's hand no less than the murderer's. There had been five people on board *Dolly*, and not all of them were going, as I had, to make stupid promises of silence. With Harry awake and Trotter restless and the rest of us thoroughly alarmed, the private stalking bit was going to stop, as of this evening. Either Johnson got results or Sir Bartholomew was going to be whipped off to safety and the chances of finding the culprit had vanished forever.

And I didn't see, frankly, how Johnson was going to get results during a golf match with Sir Bartholomew safely under guard in his house. Unless I was wrong, and not all of his suspects were going to take part in the golf match? For example —

"Good afternoon all," said Sergeant Trotter, beaming across the bridge to the terrace. "I heard you were foregathered for a historic occasion. Any room for a little 'un?"

My father's face was a remarkable blend of unnatural courtesy strongly tinctured with blatant hostility.

"Not as a candidate: no, no!" went on Sergeant Trotter, with speed. "A great admirer and all that, but the rover type I am. No. But a cracking good golf game, now: that I should like to see. If nobody has any objection?"

Wallace Brady, Krishtof Bey, and my father were silent. Mr. Tiko bowed. The Begum said, "Not at all. Come along. Johnson and I are going to watch, too. How shall we pair off the golf carts? James, shall I drive for you?"

The carts were standing two by two with their blue and white canopies, freshly out from the feeding grounds. The Begum, peach colored tissue fluttering, took the leading one beside the white-hatted person of my father. Mr. Tiko, bowing, led the way to the next and invited Sergeant Trotter to take the high wheel while he strapped on his golf bag. Johnson, in a creased khaki bush shirt, said to Krishtof Bey, "Come on. They call me the Devil of Brooklyn," and they got into the third. I looked at Wallace Brady.

"Well?" he said. He was looking rather presentable, in a

chalk-striped cream tunic and trousers, which set off his tan. He said, "Can you stand it? I feel it gives me an unfair advantage — to sit beside my incentive."

"I can stand it," I said. Conversation became suddenly full of unnatural pitfalls.

Brady strapped on his golf bag and came to sit beside me on the white passenger seat. He said, "Edgecombe's got you in a hole, hasn't he? I guess since the whole story is going to be bust wide open this evening, this must be Sir Bartholomew's last chance to pull off a capture. And I'd further guess this golf game is no accident. He thinks one of us is trying to kill him still, doesn't he? Trotter, Krishtof, or me?"

"I don't know," I said. The other three carts had set off before us, rolling silently down the smooth slope.

"I think he does," said Brady. I moved my foot slowly onto the right starter pedal, and he laid his hard hand over mine on the steering wheel. "No. Don't go yet. I tell you, I don't believe Sir Bartholomew Edgecombe is lying there in his home, surrounded by a thicket of bodyguards. I'd give even money that before this game is finished, we see him out on the golf course."

"I don't know," I said again, rather dimly. "But I can tell you one thing. It was never like this at North Berwick."

He laughed, and took his hand off the wheel. "No. It sure has its own brand of gamesmanship," Brady said. "And I'm as mixed up over it all as you are. But I wanted to say one thing, Beltanno Douglas MacRannoch. Whoever wins this game, remember I want to marry you. And remember, if you don't want to marry me, you just have to say so."

It was a gallant offer, and I was grateful for it. I thanked him and set the cart in motion, white fringe jogging, down the broad pale path under the palm trees, and up to the bright, fresh-sprayed green of the No. 1 tee.

The first hole at Great Harbour Cay is a goodish par 5, followed by a short par 3 and a nasty par 4. By the time we all reached hole No. 4, all conversation in my wing of the convoy had stopped. Krishtof Bey, when he remembered, was still deploying a few flamboyant gestures for Johnson, but he didn't remember so often. Mr. Tiko's golf cart was silent because Mr. Tiko was not a talkative man. Only in cart No. 1 did disharmony ring to the skies, borne on a threatening gale of inspirational rhonci, as James Ulric consigned American golf to the abyss. Mr. Tiko was winning.

Mr. Tiko was winning because he was, self-evidently, a brilliant player who had no need now to moderate his game to the emotional demands of a Lady Edgecombe. With disbelief, we observed him drive off in his neat navy blue sweater and trousers, knees flexed, shoulders and stance parallel to the exact line of flight. Then his No. 1 would come back like a bird. He would hang there a moment, eyes on the ball, left shoulder tucked neatly under his neat chin. Then the club head would sweep down, *whee-whack*, and the ball disappear.

No. 4 hole was a dog-leg ending just by the commercial plane runway. Mr. Tiko placed himself nicely just over halfway down center fairway, and with his second shot pitched his ball like a peppermint drop exactly onto the green. Wallace Brady, demoralized, landed in the long, pale trap in front of the green and stayed there doing explosive shots with a sand wedge. Krishtof Bey, after an inspired drive, overplayed his approach shot and landed in the other trap at the back of the green, from which he took a chip and two putts to extricate himself.

My father's performance I am ashamed to set down on record. Standing spider knees planted, he took off like a Hawker Harrier at every roar from the airport, and hit fades and banana shots with equal mismanagement. Arrived on the green, he pursued the ball around the pin as if it had black lace underwear and finally sank it at nine. I could hear him shouting as he stumped off to his chariot; he got into it like a man who has just noticed Charlton Heston arrive in the paddock. The Begum leaned over and plugged in his nose filters. Being my father's mistress is not all fast living and glamour. We all moved around to hole No. 5.

I will not pretend that every hole was as abysmal as this. Each of Mr. Tiko's three competitors recovered in some slight degree from the initial shock of appalled recognition. Wallace Brady steadied up to the level I had become acquainted with on Paradise Island. Krishtof Bey was inspired by a different genius and became more fantastic: pitching, cutting, hitting great cracking drives which either landed him in black disaster or, as in hole No. 6, gave him an unheard-of, against-the-wind hole in one.

Coming back to his golf cart and Johnson, he flung his arms around the black hair and bifocals, as I remember, and embraced Johnson warmly on either impassive cheek. "The angels carried it for me," said Krishtof Bey. "I have personally shot an eagle. Will you inform Reuter's, or shall I?"

But Mr. Tiko got a birdie, and was still leading with four holes to two. We left the sea and carried our partners inland with our backs to the wind; past the clutch of Least Grebes in the lake where my father drowned two of his balls and had to be restrained by Sergeant Trotter from following them; past the half-built houses where languid figures sprawled with a tilting hammer, looking down on Mr. Tiko's par 4, and Wallace Brady's breathless long putt to equal it.

My father had found the white golfer's aid and was busy brushing his ball in the warm soapy water and toweling it. When I think of the price, I often feel like doing the same, but in Scotland this is viewed as a weakness. In James Ulric's case, it merely made the ball roll about better, in no special direction. The game labored inexorably on and we labored with it: we four supporters in our blue and white carriages; separating during play; edging down the fairway after our partners; lifting them, exhausted, from one dark nesting place to the next, and silently, from the defeat of one green to the ever-blossoming hope of the following tee.

Anyone betting on Mr. Tiko that day however would have been onto a pretty safe thing. As the afternoon wore on, it became safer and safer; and by the time we reached hole No. 12, the shadows were lying long and blue on the brilliant grass, and it was all too clear that whatever happened, Mr. Tiko had won. I sat in my empty golf cart behind Johnson and Trotter and the Begum and glanced backward at the dark shuttered windows of Sir Bartholomew Edgecombe's house and ahead up the steep, incline to No. 13, where eight days ago his wife Denise had met her death. It was, I suppose, an appropriate spot at which to bury my spinsterhood.

On the green, his three rivals were grouped around Mr. Tiko and my father was arguing. I suppose that Krishtof Bey and Wallace Brady wanted to abandon the game and my father wanted to finish. So far as I could see, it was only of academic interest whether Krishtof or Wallace came second. Neither the police nor my father was going to declare Mr. Tiko's win null. Perhaps my father thought that when it came to the crunch, I would back out myself. If so, he was wrong. Once and for all, James Ulric was going to learn not to interfere in my affairs. James Ulric was going to have a Japanese son-in-law.

Johnson got out of his golf cart and ambled in the direction of my father's white cap. After a moment he left him and came over to me. Behind him the sky was a pale, tender blue, whitening toward the horizon, and the setting sun shone round and red in his bifocals. He said, "Brady and Krishtof Bey have decided to go on. Are you flattered?"

"By an exhibition of the male competitive spirit?" I said bitterly. It was past six o'clock and the light was failing already.

"It's the athletic atmosphere," Johnson said. "Unfortunately, your father also wants to go on. His reasoning is perfectly simple. If he wins five out of the remaining six holes, he will come in second." He paused. "On the other hand, if Krishtof wins the next two holes, your father is out of the reckoning. Would you consider that, in view of his asthmatic history, the Begum should then take him home?"

"That isn't history," I said. "It's a current event. I can hear his F.E.V. rising from here." The roseate glasses did not alter. I got my brain working and said, "You want my father out of here in two holes?"

"Right," said Johnson.

I looked at him, and then at my bag, which lay beside me on the white seat. The Frommer still nestled inside it.

"Right," said Johnson again, though I hadn't spoken. "And I want you and the Begum to go with him."

Wallace Brady was walking toward us. Ahead, Krishtof Bey was sliding into his golf cart, the pink Bulgar blouse luminescent in the coppery sunset. "No, thank you," I said. "I think I'd like to see the game through."

"Beltanno — " said Wallace, and stopped when he saw Johnson.

Johnson removed the frown from his face. "She knows," he said. "Medical advisor to Matsushita electric."

Wallace said, "Beltanno, there are limits to what a nice girl will do just to spite her old man."

"I am going to marry Mr. Tiko," I said. I think I spoke between my teeth.

"Are you surprised?" said Johnson calmly to Brady. "Remember, James Ulric's her father."

Wallace Brady, clearly, was thinking about it. "I'm not surprised," he said at length, gloomily.

"I know," said Johnson. "You thought you were integrating vertically, Brady my boy. But it's lateral thinking nowadays, you know. Broad, lateral thinking. And there are a hell of a lot of MacRannochs once you start looking around you." He clapped my suitor's chalk stripe on the shoulder. "Good luck, cat," said Johnson gravely. "Get out there and slay them."

By the fourteenth hole, my father was out of the game. It took the concerted efforts of the Begum, Johnson, and myself to persuade him to go back to the clubhouse. He maintained that if Mr. Tiko could strap up his clubs and travel around as a spectator, it was no less his duty to supervise his own match. The Begum pointed out that as a competitor it wasn't his duty to supervise anything, and that Johnson, Trotter, and I could more than adequately see that the rules were observed.

In the end, James Ulric disappeared wheezily into the dusk with the Begum, and I felt a pang as I watched the brave blue and white shade travel behind the palmetto on its angular struts. He was too old for golf anyway, and he had to learn it someday. And he had the Begum, for God's sake. My father wasn't marrying a Japanese golfer.

I turned to get back into the cart just as someone beyond the green called, "Hullo there!"

Sergeant Trotter had already entered his cart. The other five of us stood where we were. Then Johnson walked down from the green to the pathway beyond and said, "Hullo?"

From where I stood, I could see the top of a car. Great Harbour Drive, the broad white road marked out along the eastern shore of the island lay, I remembered, between this hole and the beachside green of the next. Reminded of the sea, I listened, and there it was, beyond the enclosing jagged horizon of palmetto scrub and dark bushes, the hissing boom of the translucent green waves, there ahead out of sight. I realized that it had become very quiet. The low buzz of the generators, the whine of machinery, the voices of work gangs had all stopped with the dip of the sun, and there was only the stir of the light wind through the dense, man-high jungle on either side of the fairway and a little whine as it made its way through the beams of the black service hut by the green. Johnson said, without moving further, "Edgecombe? You shouldn't be here. Is Spry there with you?"

His voice, carrying on the trade wind, floated clearly over the fairway. Sergeant Trotter, waiting in the first cart ahead of me, got out and began to walk over the green. Mr. Tiko, after hesitating a moment, returned to his cart and sat down patiently, his small hands on his neat blue knees. Brady and Krishtof stood where they were, Brady with the pin still in his hand. Edgecombe's voice said, "No. I let him off the hook for a bit. Who's winning?"

"It's a Japanese triumph," Johnson said. "Mr. Tiko is champion, and Krishtof and Brady are playing it out for second and third. We'll come and have a victory drink at your house." He paused and said, "Look, pack it in, Bart. There isn't much point in the protective custody bit if you're going to rove about like an unraveled jersey. We shan't be long."

It was convincingly said, but I stood there, cold in the warm evening, and knew it wasn't said for Bart Edgecombe's ears. What was it Brady had already remarked? *I bet even money that we'll see Edgecombe out on this course.* And here he was, on his cue; just as the Begum and my father had been hustled out of the way; just as Johnson had tried to get rid of me as well. For this was their last chance, his and Edgecombe's, to capture their assassin. And this, with Edgecombe in full view of his enemies, was how Johnson had chosen to do it.

I had got to that phase in my thinking just as Johnson said,

". . . shan't be long." I think all of us heard the light rustle of leaves to one side of the path, well beyond Johnson. I know Krishtof looked around. Brady was staring still, frowning, at Johnson. Then a man, a dim silhouette in the bushes, rose to his feet, drew back his right arm, and threw something.

I heard Johnson yell, *"Run!"* and saw the gun appear in his hand as he flung himself on the ground. I did the same. Wallace Brady dropped like a stone, pulling the dancer down with him. Mr. Tiko, beyond in his cart, half rose to his feet. As he did, the world, and Bart Edgecombe's car with it, exploded into a curdling glare of black smoke and fire.

The blast whipped the palmetto toward us, and the four canopies billowed and jerked, fringes twisted. A red star burned from the bushes where Johnson was lying, and then another; the crack of the gun was lost in the rumble and crash of Edgecombe's car dissolving and twisting in flames. From the other side of the fairway, fire answered back. Trotter, running bent and incredibly fast, came halfway across the green and flung himself in the lee of Mr. Tiko's blue cart. Mr. Tiko, his pallid face half-lit by the fire, hesitated a moment and then slid down beside him. Wallace Brady had left the green also, a dark shadow rolling toward me. A moment later he blundered on top of me, his hand, hard on my arms, and dragged me behind his own cart. He said, *"Give me your gun."*

He was breathing hard. I couldn't see Johnson, and Krishtof had vanished. My handbag with the gun in it lay under me. I said crisply, "It's in the cart," and thrust my hand into my bag as I felt him raise himself to look. He glanced down just as I got the Frommer by the barrel and I saw the surprise and anger on his face as he blocked the sky out above me, his hand ready to snatch. From the dark line of palmetto brush opposite came the snap and sparkle of gunfire, and not far from me a gun thudded in reply — Johnson's — and then another. A cultivated voice just behind me said swiftly, "Do you know, I don't think we want you to have a gun, Mr. Brady."

I turned. A very efficient fist connected with Wallace Brady's jaw, and the dark bulk above me suddenly rolled off and vanished. "One down and one more to go," said Sir Bartholomew Edgecombe, smiling. He put my Frommer into my rather limp hand. "It's all right: I wasn't in the car when it exploded. All part of the system to draw their attack."

I heard Johnson call, "Bart!" and Edgecombe smiled reassuringly at me again. One hand was heavily bandaged and he had a very businesslike-looking gun in the other. He said, "Don't worry. We've got them surrounded. Get into the bushes and if one of Pentecost's friends comes across you, shoot to kill. They're paid assassins, this crowd."

Then he had gone. I looked at Brady. The brief dusk was already sinking to darkness. My all-American golfer lay on his back, his cream chalk-striped tunic all crumpled and stained. At the foot of the green, Trotter's cart was still stationary with Mr. Tiko lying beside it, his heels together and his arms over his head. Then I saw Trotter had left it again and was traveling, in that extraordinary professional way, head down away from me and toward the third empty cart.

A moment later and he was in it, crouched down on the floor. For a bit, nothing happened. Then it shook and began to move forward slowly, under a rattle of gunfire. In the black jungle beyond it a man suddenly screamed and someone else gave a yell of triumph. The burning car sent a tongue of flame into the air and in its light I saw Krishtof Bey's pink Bulgar shirt as he leapt to his feet from the bushes, brandishing somebody's rifle, primitive triumph on the brown, hollow face.

Then, like a shimmer of oil, he was out of the rough and into

269

the fourth and last cart, bouncing over the grass after Trotter. Unlike Trotter, Krishtof Bey didn't trouble to lie down on the floor of the cart. Rifle on shoulder, he knelt on the white seat and fired back whenever a dark figure moved on the skyline, warbling a quarter-tone war cry at intervals. From somewhere, I could hear Spry's voice telling him to mind how he went.

There was a lot of noise suddenly. Behind the brush on the other side of the fairway came the coughing roar of a series of engines starting up, and then the sound of creaking demolition as a line of heavy vehicles began to move forward, crushing the cane and wireweed and burgrass, the pockwood and Hercules'-club, the elders, the plantains, the tangle of trefoil and honeysuckle to move up at the back of the gunmen. Behind me, and ahead on the road beside the wreck of the car, I could hear other engines starting and stopping, and a number of voices, among which I thought I could make out both Edgecombe's and Johnson's. The trap around their enemies was being snapped shut at last.

Beside me, Brady groaned and stirred. I rolled into the bushes just as the gunfire at the end of the green suddenly intensified. I thought: They know it's a trap. And they know Edgecombe isn't dead — it's their last effort to kill him.

Krishtof Bey's cart had reached the dark bulk of the hut. I saw him jump out, his rifle gleaming, and blend into the gloom of its walls. Trotter's cart had stopped also, and I saw Trotter was running again, but in the opposite direction, where Edgecombe and Johnson were firing on my side of the green. I thought: He's wiser than Krishtof. In a moment those tractors are going to flush out the gunmen and then they are going to come out in the open here, firing.

Trotter had nearly got to the rough when he stopped. I heard Edgecombe's voice call sharply, "Come on, man!" and guessed Trotter was blocking their fire. Then I saw that Trotter had raised his right hand, and that the gun in it was pointing at Edgecombe.

Trotter aimed, steadied, and fired.

Edgecombe cried, "Oh, my God."

For a moment — for a tenth of a second — it seemed as if everything had stopped: the machinery, the shouting, the firing. Then someone moved clumsily in the bushes where Edgecombe had spoken. Moved, rose, took half a step forward, and then fell to his knees and then on his face at the edge of the grass. I could distinguish the crumpled bush tunic and, as he dropped, the flash of reflected fire in the twin lenses of his bifocals. Then Edgecombe's big frame in turn forced its way out from the coppice, and his tightened voice said: "You've killed him. You bloody traitor, you've killed Johnson instead."

I think I got to my feet. I know that Edgecombe lunged forward, firing, and that in his face I saw the look of a man bent on retribution and death. Trotter fired one shot wildly, ducking, and then turned tail and ran. I saw Edgecombe break cover and follow, across the green to the hut and the car, regardless of his safety in the blazing, flickering light, firing again and again. I saw Trotter stagger and steady himself, and turning, take aim at Edgecombe again; I saw Edgecombe duck and fire and then curse as the revolver clicked, empty.

Behind me Wallace Brady got to his feet, slowly at first. Then with a lurch he began to move, running, toward Edgecombe's exposed back. Unaware of his danger, Edgecombe slowed, intent on reloading. In a moment, Brady would reach him. The Frommer, heavy and hot, was still in my hand. I thumbed off the safety catch, raised it, and took steady aim at my all-American golfing companion.

A hand came down hard on my wrist and another, in the same movement closed my opening mouth. "Not this time, Doctor," said Johnson. "Wallace Brady is mine and the Begum's."

I looked at him, the Frommer dropped from my hand. He released me and regarded me, grinning, and then spread his hand under my arm rather quickly. "Hold on," he said. "I told you about my chilled and rolled underwear. We're bear-leading the baddies, remember? We do six permutations of this, and then someone really gets killed."

My head had cleared, and I didn't need anyone's help to stand up. I moved away from his hand. "It looks to me," I said coldly, "as if you're letting them both escape."

Johnson followed my gaze. Outlined against the glowing car, Trotter appeared for a moment, glanced briefly to left and to right, and then stooping, raced left toward the dunes and the sea. Rifle fire from the lee of the hut followed him, and then the dark figure of Edgecombe ran past, gun in hand once again. Brady, veering at the last moment, had plunged into the scrub on the left and was running diagonally on a course converging with Trotter's.

"They have a car along there," Johnson said. "Driven into a beach path off Great Harbour Drive. We've blocked the drive, and they'll have to go through the seaside fairways to reach it."

He had started running, and I was running beside him. Ahead the fire was illuminating Krishtof Bey's beautiful shirt and his rifle; Spry was standing beside him and a number of other men unknown to me were moving out of the undergrowth. Firing still sounded, but a good way ahead.

"Two of Pentecost's friends have been accounted for," Johnson said. "I think what you heard just now will be the remainder." He had reached the road and crossed it. I saw Spry look around unsurprised, and Krishtof give a jump. Spry put out a hand and stopped him advancing. No one else made a move to accompany us. I trotted after.

The road to the right was blocked by a dark line of cars, and there were men standing about. The dying light from the wreck flickered on a lime-rubble track sweeping up and into the dark on the right; from ahead came the swish of the sea. There was no sound of footsteps. I realized that Trotter had been directed this way, together with those of his friends who survived; that they were being neatly coraled without further shooting; and that the get-away car would be their ultimate pen. Johnson said, "I'm going to the car. There's no need for you to be in on the kill."

I said, "Yes, there is." We were running along the grass edge of the road. On our left, down the fairway, there was no sound at all. It was hard to imagine that there, parallel with us, two men were running for their lives, believing that ahead of them lay a car and escape. I added, under my breath, "Where's Sir Bartholomew?"

Johnson said, "Heading them off. He knows where the car is. They've got a boat, just past the airport. Look. Here we are."

Between shrubs on the left, a dim gritty track led toward the rustling boom of the sea. We were almost upon the dark shadow lying within before I realized it was a fast convertible coupé, drawn backward off the road, its hood down. In the deep shadow to the right of it, men were lying. Johnson spoke to them softly, then took his place on the path just beyond them, drawing me down to lie at his side.

It was almost dark now, and the afterglow had quite gone from the pale, open sky over the sea. The beach lay concealed behind a black frieze of pine trees and coconut palms, their feet in the rough, mixed scrub edging the long sixteenth fairway. The raised green lay beside me, its flag invisible against the dark trees, and into the darkness ran the even turf of the fairway, the two pale bunkers to left and to right dim patches before the invisible plateau of the tee.

All this I could see, barely raising my head beyond the rear wheel of the car. On my left I saw the dark shape of Johnson, and behind him a black sea of scrubland stretching between the beach and the road as far as the eye could distinguish. Far in the distance were the prick lights of the small airport tower. The sea hissed and rumbled and the wind blew lightly southeast, from the airport, and carried all sound away.

The fugitives would arrive from the right, along the long beachside fairways. They would run through the scrub. I wondered whether they would choose the rough ground by the sea, where the waves would drown their footsteps but might also deaden their hearing. Or the low jungle between the fairways and the road, pitted with cuttings and the half-built foundations of villas, good for an ambush or merely a broken ankle for the unwary. Unlike Johnson and myself, they couldn't take the open, straight road. Theirs, creeping, ducking, silently moving from bush to bush and cover to cover, would take so much longer.

There was no sound now but the sea. The last burst of firing had been some time ago, far over by the blockade. The escaping men had thrown off their pursuers, or had been allowed to believe that they had. Johnson had said that Edgecombe was heading them off. If so, there was no sign of him yet. I wondered if he was lying out there, somewhere under the scented black bushes, with his gun trained on the fairway, waiting for the moment when Trotter and Brady broke cover and made their run for the car.

He had believed Johnson was dead; I had seen it in his face. Nor would I forget the passion of rage in which he had leveled his gun and pulled the trigger on the snarling, swerving figure of Trotter, the smoking gun still in his hand. And now, suddenly, the hunter was the hunted. Trotter had no time to seek out and kill Edgecombe now. If he wanted to escape with his life, he had to reach this car and that boat.

Silence. I wondered what Johnson was thinking. And if Judith Cicely Ballantyne was waiting to welcome him home. The men

274

in the lee of the car lay without speaking. The surf buzzed, and a new wave began to echo along its incoming length and broke and buzzed in its turn, leaving another silence, long and indrawn like a breath.

A long, warbling scream burst upon it, undulating over the fairways, throbbing through the dense, grassy distances far on the right. Johnson's hand, reaching suddenly from behind, pulled me hard and quickly away from the end of the car. I rolled and lay still as the cry came again. Then wriggling out of his grasp, I gripped the sides of the car and raised my head over the side panel to look.

Bucking out of the dangerous darkness — erect, gallant, be-fringed, and straight out of Schwartz's side window — came one of the Tamboo Club golf carts, a flutter of pink silk in the driving seat, a full-blooded Islamic war cry emerging from under the canopy. Krishtof Bey was quartering the ground between fairway and road at a high cruising speed, roaring joyous defiance as he did so.

At the same moment, on the other side of the fairway, a second cart jolted out of the darkness and proceeded to scan the rough by the seaside, slowing now and then and picking up speed, but all the time coming steadily nearer. Dimly, as it approached, I glimpsed within it Bartholomew Edgecombe's gray mane of hair. Johnson, kneeling beside me, began to laugh and then had to stifle it. "My God. The beaters," he said under his breath.

He had just spoken when there was a crack from Krishtof Bey's rifle and a man jumped from the palmetto far on our left, stopped, hesitated, and then turned and ran straight toward us, along the broad open fairway. There was a second shot from Krishtof Bey's; then his cart jerked and began jogging toward us. The runner looked around then, and quickened his pace. As he got nearer, the blur of pale hands and face resolved themselves into familiar features.

275

"Trotter," said Johnson in a murmur. His hand was down, signaling us all to be still. No one moved. His other hand was tight on his gun.

Then I saw Johnson's fist relax and realized that Edgecombe had seen what was happening. Swerving out from the bush-covered dunes, he had set the cart over the fairway, edging the dark, running figure between Krishtof and himself. And as Trotter sensed it and looked around, a red flash of gunfire from Edgecombe's cart splintered the darkness.

Trotter didn't fire back. He ran until we could hear the squeak of his footsteps and the sawing sound of his breath. Johnson let him come. He let him run up to the car on the opposite side of which we were all lying. He let him lay hands on the door handle as Edgecombe's golf cart, cutting in front of its fellow, came to a dead halt.

Trotter had already snatched the door handle open when the silence warned him the cart had stopped moving. He let it go and flung himself on the ground, gun in hand, as Edgecombe knelt by the steering wheel and fired at him, again and again.

He missed him. I heard the bullets ring on the side of the car and the rustle as Trotter rolled off and got to his knees. Beside me, Johnson suddenly rose to his feet and stood, madly, in full view behind the low, open car.

Kneeling where he was, Trotter couldn't possibly see him. But Sir Bartholomew Edgecombe did. He half rose from where he was crouching, his eyes on Johnson: a vision, a man from the dead, and for a moment in his amazement, forgot even the gun in his hand.

It was not a mistake that Trotter, the sergeant-major would make. Edgecombe rose before him, the perfect target; and from where I sprawled by the rear of the car I saw Trotter's hand raise the gun.

I still think I could have stopped him. I know that I put all the strength that I had behind the spring that would take me around the car and drag his gun arm away as he fired.

Johnson prevented me. He flung me sideways with a sudden, swift violence that deprived me of breath, and then pinned me there, gasping and helpless, by the rear wheel of the car.

And so Trotter raised his gun unimpeded, and fired; and a black hole sprang like a coin between Edgecombe's eyes before he fell slowly sideways and dead, onto the perfectly mown grass.

Johnson pulled me away from the car just as Trotter vaulted into the seat and turned on the ignition. He looked around as he put her into gear; I think he saw us all behind him. He must have known the road would be ambushed, the boat gone. But he was an obstinate man. He put off the brake and shot forward just as Johnson, aiming deliberately, shot him twice through the head.

The car crossed the road under its own momentum, hit the verge, and turned over twice. It lay several seconds, wheels spinning, before the explosion burst it apart and the fire rosily flickering, revealed us all to each other. We looked rosy, too, in the bright jolly firelight. Tiny Tim and hot chestnuts and Christmas. Flameproof your nightwear. Flameproof your relationships. No one is ever what he seems.

Krishtof Bey jumped down from his golf cart and Wallace Brady, carrying Krishtof's rifle, stepped out from the passenger seat of the same cart and bent over the dead body of Edgecombe. I watched them without understanding and almost without interest. Cars drew up and all the persons who had been waiting inert about us had suddenly become very busy. A water cart arrived and someone began to play hoses on the half-consumed car. I wondered if it was the boy in the red shirt and the fancy straw hat. I could no longer hear the sound of the sea.

A large, closed Buick slid up beside me and Johnson, emerging from a talking cluster of men, took my arm and said, "Get in, Beltanno. Spry will take you to *Dolly* and it won't be long before you're safe on Crab Island with James Ulric and the Begum. I'll be there as soon as I can get away." He looked at me, and then said, "Wait a bit."

He had a flask of whiskey — what else — in his pocket. I watched him pour it and took the cup, remembering the three stiff ones he had poured in Bart Edgecombe's house, and why. I drank it, and he took the cup back. "Good girl. Explanations later," said Johnson. "But you were a magnificent doctor bird. The undoubted backbone or vertebrae column of the whole bloody exercise."

I didn't say anything. I saw Wallace Brady look over, but I didn't want to say anything to him either. I got into the car and sat stiffly in it as Spry drove me away from the noise and the light into the warm, airy darkness. A faint hissing came to my ears: the sea, clouded by the night spray of all the myriads of sprinklers, grooming the greens for the next championship match. Who had won? Mr. Tiko, perhaps. No one else.

It wasn't until the car stopped moving that I realized we were at the quay where *Dolly*'s speedboat was lying. The Begum and James Ulric were already on Crab Island, he said. Mr. Tiko would be there soon, I supposed. And Krishtof and Wallace Brady. Or were they part of the plot too? Were even Johnson and *Dolly* what they seemed? Did anyone know?

Or perhaps they all knew, except me. The backbone of the whole scheme, he had called me. The dupe. The laughing stock, the bartered bride, the cropped dummy, the fall guy.

Spry was holding open the door.

I said, "No. I'm sorry, but I don't want to go to Crab Island. I want to go straight back to Nassau. There must be plenty of planes leaving with all this upheaval. Do you think you could take me instead to the airport?"

I thought he would stall me, or try to make some objection, but he didn't. He took me straight to the airport, and I was in a plane and heading for Nassau inside of an hour.

Even from the air you could see it all: the criss-crossing lights of the cars, and the ruddy, spiraling light and smoke from the dying bonfire of Trotter's wrecked car. Then the little plane heeled around and flew off, leaving Great Harbour Cay and its golf course lying behind on the dark sea.

Chapter 16

I HAD TO WORK a month's notice in the United Commonwealth Hospital, and no one bothered me during that time, although I had two calls from James Ulric asking me if I was all right, and Mr. Tiko rang once to say that he had been called back to New York but wished me to know that he would be happy to accede to whatever plans I wished to make for the future. I thanked him, and said that I would write to him presently. I found I was glad, if surprised, that Johnson hadn't killed him as well. He wrote back that perhaps he would meet me at the MacRannoch Gathering.

Perhaps.

I worked very hard at my job. Perhaps a holiday was what I had needed. Or perhaps it was energy released by the act of resignation. It had pleased my father, even when I informed him that in future I proposed to draw on our joint account. He had never wanted me to work. He had only wanted me to become married. And so I might have, if I had never met Johnson.

I didn't ask him about the outcome on Great Harbour Cay, and there was nothing of moment in the *Nassau Guardian,* only the heading EDGECOMBE RITES MONDAY and a large respectful obituary on Sir Bartholomew, fatally wounded while grappling with an army deserter in his Great Harbour Cay garden. There was a brief recapitulation of Lady Edgecombe's recent tragic demise. I read them both sketchily and stopped thinking about it again.

I took a weekend trip to New York and bought some clothes and went to the theater and had a large Bossa Nova in the interval, which was a mistake, as it made me think of Miami all over again. Next day I wore my dark glasses in hospital, but no one commented adversely.

I had never found the hospital atmosphere so clear and so pleasant as it had been this last month. Perhaps because they knew I was leaving. Perhaps because of my wig? My C.M.O. took me out to lunch and unfolded two risqué jokes and a long account of how he had always wanted to be a veterinary surgeon while I had two Yellowberries without noticeable effect. I was getting used to them. I was getting used to everything except being utilized and being ignored.

My father rang up for the third time and said the Begum wanted to know if she could get married, and I said, "Ask Johnson." He said Johnson had gone away, and what was it to do with him anyway? It was too complicated to explain, so I rang off.

I got home two days later, operating day, to be met by Daffodil at the door, and the smell of pipe smoke curling around from the hallway. A gentleman had stopped in to see me. "A Mr. — "

"I know," I said. "Good evening, Mr. Johnson."

He was standing in my father's sitting room in a crumpled shirt and tie, evidently put on in my honor, and a serious look around the bifocals, saying nothing at all. I uttered a few commonplace bromides while Daffodil closed the door and walked with reluctance away from the keyhole. Johnson said, "I apologize for coming along uninvited, but I knew you wouldn't see me if I telephoned. The Begum tells me I have made an impression midway between Mussolini and a Chubb TDR safe. I am here to adjust my image. You weren't expected to suffer all that without a word of decent explanation."

"I know," I said. "I got the dose without the antidepression pill. It was my own fault for leaving so quickly." I didn't ask him to sit down.

"You were seen," said Johnson gravely, "drinking Yellowberries. But if you don't want to listen, I'm not going to pressure you. The other reason I came was to carry out a commission." He glanced at the wall. "I've been asked to leave you a painting."

I walked two steps in and looked where he nodded. A square artist's canvas, unframed, had been propped between the floor and the wall. Out of it, cheerful and enigmatic, gazed the dark face of Krishtof Bey, his hands clasped below at his knees.

"With the sitter's compliments," Johnson said. "I was also to convey to you Wallace Brady's competitive love, and James Ulric wants to know if you've married that little buff wop yet."

"Nip," I said automatically. I stared from Johnson's bifocals to Krishtof Bey's large painted eyes with their shameless false lashes. There was no doubt at all. He was a fiendishly good painter. I said, "You *are* a bloody Mussolini."

"It's a lie," he said calmly.

"I ought to turn you out. I don't want any more dirt on my hands. I don't want to hear — "

"You do," said Johnson. "You want to know why Wallace Brady isn't in prison and you want to know if Krishtof Bey is married or not."

"He isn't," I said. "I looked him up in *Who's Who*."

There was an attentive movement of the bifocals. "You don't mean the Begum's folio edition?" Johnson said. "You should try an up-to-date one. You've missed half his love life. I don't suppose it said a word about my six children."

"No," I said. "But it mentioned Judith Cicely Ballantyne."

The bifocals remained completely impassive. "The daughter," he said, "of perhaps the most famous Russian spy the world has ever known, Igor Vasily Balinski. She married me on Kremlin orders to extirpate all my secrets, and when the truth came out later, we shot each other. They gave her a Soviet state funeral. Her aim had always been poor."

We stared at one another, on the heels of this farrago. Whatever other precepts I had hurled out of the window, I could still respect privacy. "I'm sorry," I said. "Sit down. What will you drink?"

He remained standing. He said thoughtfully, "Why should you suppose that it had any truth in it?"

Ever since I had met him here in this house, the night he had taken me sailing on *Dolly,* he had been deceiving me. He must have been. Hardly anything he told me during all those subsequent days had been truthful. Why then should I believe that his wife was dead, and that he had loved her? He wanted me to listen, and sympathetically. He had made sure that I would.

I thought about it, standing there with the cap of the Haig bottle unscrewed in my hand. It wasn't hard, once I did think about it. "I believed you," I said, "because I watched you shoot those two men on the golf course."

He said, "I only shot one."

"No," I said. "You took Edgecombe's life. It only happened to be Trotter who fired the bullet that killed him."

Johnson moved. He removed the cap from my fingers and taking up the bottle of whiskey, he set out two glasses and poured. "If you will allow me," he said. The lower lenses perched, two bald Chads, on the edge of his glass as he lifted it, unsmiling, to toast me. He said, "To the Scottish teaching hospitals and all they produce."

I let him drink, and sit down, and put his whiskey on the table beside him before I asked the question I had forbidden myself until now even to think about. "All the time," I said, "from the beginning, that day in the airport — who was trying to kill Sir Bartholomew Edgecombe?"

I thought I was ready for anything. I thought no answer he could give would surprise me. Instead he said, "You've had a month of worry, haven't you, Beltanno? That was what I had been hoping to save you. You see, no one was trying to kill Bartholomew Edgecombe. You were only intended to believe someone was."

"Play acting?" I said helpfully. I wondered if he expected me to believe him this time as well. I said, "The arsenic at the airport? The further dose on the plane? Pentecost's attempt at the Bamboo Conch Club? The attempts to warn me off there and in New York and at Coral Harbour? The attack on me at Miami and the disappearance of your luggage and mine before my notes vanished on Crab Island? Denise's death? The attempt to blow up Edgecombe on *Dolly?* The grenade someone threw at his car here that night? No one was trying to kill Bart Edgecombe, were they?" I said with some forgivable sarcasm. "Except that someone did kill him, and you did nothing at all to prevent him."

"We had an industrious week or two, didn't we?" said Johnson, his eyebrows raised, his glasses filled with mild contemplation. "You and I and the Mighty Leveler, raking together a scratch-and-dent sale. Of course I did nothing to stop Bart Edgecombe's murder that evening. I'd just spent twenty-four hours organizing the whole bloody opera. I couldn't kill Edgecombe myself; the Royal Academy wouldn't be happy. Trotter had to do it."

"He hated both you and Edgecombe," I said slowly. "Trotter's plan misfired at the Bamboo Conch Club, but he made sure you wouldn't catch that waiter, or that if you did, the waiter wouldn't live to confess. He could have caused all the disasters on *Dolly,* expecting to make some excuse to disembark before *Haven* struck her. He saved our lives, but only because he had to save his own. And on the golf course that night, you fell to his bullet."

You've killed him, Edgecombe had shouted at Trotter. *You bloody traitor, you've killed Johnson instead.*

"I dare say you thought so," said Johnson mildly. "It looked like it from every angle but mine. Trotter aimed into the bushes where we both were, but he was actually shooting at Edgecombe. And Edgecombe, who was expecting it, was tough and quick and above all, a splendid opportunist. He ducked when he saw Trotter lift his revolver and turning, took his own sights. When Trotter fired, Edgecombe fired as well. Of course he thought I was dead. He had just shot me himself, as I looked at him, full in the chest."

God bless the drip-dry titanium underwear. I said, "He might have chosen your head."

Johnson said, "I tried not to give him the chance. But it was a risk that had to be taken."

I knew my voice had gone flat. I said, "You expected Sir Bartholomew sometime to turn on you? Your own colleague and agent?"

He smiled a little, nursing his whiskey, but his glasses were bleak as the North Sea in the deepening dusk. He said, "Edgecombe and I were on opposite sides from the moment I landed in Nassau. He was a double agent, Beltanno: a man being paid by and cheating both sides. We suspected it, but his other employers had found out for certain. They offered him his life on one condition only: that in return he delivered them mine."

"He was to kill you?" I said. I could not conceive of it. The big, gray-haired pleasant man lying sick in my own private ward.

"He was to kill me. And because he was anxious that on no account should our people ever suspect him, he made an elaborate plan. The attacks were to appear directed at him. The outside world was to believe them accidental; we should gradually come to perceive that it was a personal grudge. And to make sure that we knew, he picked you, Beltanno."

"Picked me?" I said.

"He had seen you at the hospital, remember? And been impressed by your efficiency. A forthright and independent young woman, who would have her own views about a sudden attack of food poisoning, and would be likely to act on them. He was in New York, Beltanno, because you were going to be in New York; and Trotter was there as his assistant."

"And Wallace Brady?" I asked. I wouldn't have gone so far if he hadn't mentioned him already.

"Wallace Brady," said Johnson with evident enjoyment, "is an innocent bystander who likes building bridges and doesn't think young women are to be trusted with guns in their handbags. He and Krishtof did sterling work in the last lap, driving both Trotter and Edgecombe toward the car and into our hands."

For a moment, it had appeared to make sense. I said snappishly, "But *Trotter* shot *Edgecombe*."

"I should think so," said Johnson. "After all, Edgecombe had just arranged his own accident and got safely off *Dolly* without returning as promised to take Trotter off too. I must confess that even if Edgecombe had wanted to come back on board, I had asked Brady not to allow him. A dependable young man, I thought him. All that stuff with the reverse gears."

I said, "Then you knew already that Edgecombe and Trotter were working together?"

He had known. I closed the screens and switched on the lamps as he gave me, encapsuled in that cool voice, the true events of that series of days which had ended my medical life.

To begin with, Edgecombe's reports were already troubling his masters. Slight omissions, slight inaccuracies had led to Johnson's presence in this part of the world, planned for two months to appear to coincide with an exhibition in Miami: a fortuitous visit which would allow him to call on Edgecombe in passing and judge for himself what was happening.

When news of Edgecombe's illness had reached him, brought by me, he had at once felt uneasy. It was no place of Edgecombe's to appoint an intermediary, however innocent. With the news he had to tell, he himself should have contacted *Dolly* immediately.

But of course, said Johnson, Edgecombe had chosen me with a purpose. I had to authenticate the attack. I was there to prove that he really had been poisoned, and once one realized that, one also realized that my life throughout would be sacrosanct.

The telephoned threat to me he had also found curious, and the odd repetition of words at the nightclub and at Coral Harbour. Where I might have reported my findings direct to the hospital or the police, the threats had led me at least to talk to Sir Bartholomew, and had given him a chance to take me into his confidence. They had also given further proof, which I could later vouch for, that Sir Bartholomew's life was indeed under attack.

But these had only been vague suspicions until the fire at the Bamboo Conch Club. Then the coincidences, said Johnson, became oddly marked. The club had been Lady Edgecombe's choice, on her husband's recommendation. A suitcase of clothes had been stolen, resulting in Johnson's wearing an outfit of Edgecombe's. Whether the ensuing fire resulted in death or in injury, the claim could be made that the attack had been intended for Edgecombe.

"But how odd, I thought," said Johnson pensively, "that the attack had been prepared, and by a resident waiter. What would have happened if Lady Edgecombe had chosen to go to Charley Charley's? It seemed to me that whoever made that choice of club also knew what was likely to happen there. And after the waiter died, I was also prepared to believe that Sergeant Trotter knew more than he should. At that point," went on Johnson's quiet voice, "it seemed quite likely that the assault was intended for me, and that the culprit might be Lady Edgecombe. For example, any man whose family lived on Great Harbour Cay would surely know Sir Bartholomew Edgecombe's family by sight."

I said coldly, "Do I gather that when I was sent to stay at their home on the island, you held Sir Bartholomew Edgecombe and his wife in equal suspicion?"

Johnson was reassuring. "But of course you were perfectly safe. You were always perfectly safe: you were the evidence that Edgecombe had been poisoned; you were to be the evidence that he had been grievously assaulted. Nothing was going to happen to you. But I had begun to realize that if I wanted to pursue my suspicions, I ought to stay apart from both of the Edgecombes until the facts, whatever they were, had become plainer. So I remained on Crab Island while Denise drowned her sorrows in drink, and her husband reached the conclusion that drunk, she could no longer be trusted. That was my cardinal error."

I remembered. Big Daddy. The only time I had seen Johnson drink more than he could easily carry. I said, "Sir Bartholomew killed his own wife?"

If he remembered at all, there was no trace of sentiment in his manner. "I don't suppose she knew everything," Johnson said. "But a little too much. Enough to become nervous about all these mysterious accidents; enough to send her to the bottle for comfort. And when she was drunk, she talked. So she became the victim of another of those accidents aimed at Sir Bartholomew.

"The brooch she lost was his anniversary present. Do you

288

remember how he drew attention to it, and got her to put it into her pocket? Brady remembered it clearly. A moment later, with his arm around her waist, it would have been very easy for him to slip it out and place it just where he wanted. She didn't struggle when she was pushed over the edge. She made no attempt to run away, nor were her footmarks the deep, staggering kind you would expect from someone held against her will, an ether pad over her mouth. She knew who it was. She let him walk her to the edge of the excavation, maybe under the pretext that he had seen her brooch there. He may have embraced her and drugged her while she was in his arms. At any rate, analysis has shown that she was never inside the tarpaulin. It was flung down afterward, on top of the body . . ."

He paused, and added, "The little scene after with Edgecombe, which so drastically lowered my ratings, was one I should apologize for. It was extremely necessary to reassure Edgecombe that I had no doubts at all about him. You helped a lot."

I remembered standing there shaking with anger, my hand on Bart Edgecombe's shoulder. Bart, who had just killed his wife, and Johnson, who suspected it. I had helped everyone, it appeared, but myself.

Johnson was watching. I drew a long, even breath, and dismissed my emotions. Edgecombe, for his own ends, had warned me about Johnson. Edgecombe had told me that he was married, but not that he was a widower. Edgecombe and Johnson, I had to remember, had been trained in the same school . . . "So you didn't suspect Mr. Tiko," I said. "Or Wallace Brady?"

"I suspected everyone," Johnson said, in the same even, conversational voice. "But Lady Edgecombe was a rather large woman and Mr. Tiko is a very small man. Brady was another matter. By the time we got to Crab Island my money was on Trotter for henchman, but I tried the small experiment of the arsenic test papers to see what we would flush. And talking of flushing . . ."

I took the reel of tape he handed me in dignified silence. I tried not to imagine the full score for the Polovtsian Dances thundering through the chaste cabins of *Dolly*. I said frigidly, "At any rate, I'm glad it enabled you to see your way clear to beginning your portrait."

Johnson glanced at the almond-eyed face on the canvas. "I must admit, I deferred it until I was certain I shouldn't have to end it in Pentonville. Brady was in my view also clean from that moment. He couldn't have invented that performance. Not really."

He sat, obviously thinking humorous thoughts about my all-American suitor. I said pointedly, "And did you find the papers you'd lost?"

"In Trotter's room," Johnson said. "An interesting outcome, because they were still intact. Which meant either that Trotter was blackmailing a murderer, or that he had pinched them for Bartholomew Edgecombe in case I destroyed them. In which case they would have been discovered safe and sound on some appropriate occasion in the future. Edgecombe, remember, wanted to prove he'd been poisoned. Then he came back from the funeral, and the arsenic papers disappeared from Trotter's room."

"Into Edgecombe's?" I asked.

"Edgecombe was far too clever for that. No, they vanished. Perhaps he posted them to somewhere in Nassau. We haven't found them yet, but we will. At the time, it was another petered-out trail. Except that their disappearance on the very day Edgecombe returned seemed coincidental. And since Denise was dead, suspicion was now in fact fairly firmly pinned on Sir Bartholomew himself. Given that, as you can see, the *Haven* episode made his guilt and Trotter's complicity very likely indeed. The key point there was that he engineered his own accident to enable him to leave *Dolly* plausibly. As I told you, I got Brady to mess about with the speedboat, and to suggest that they didn't come back for you or for Trotter."

"I wondered," I said, "how you reached the simple decision to allow Violet of New York off the hook, and not me?"

Daffodil, stirred by the prospect of high jinks in the bedrooms, had produced a reasonable supper for two. I recall at this moment attempting to fix Johnson's bifocals with one or both of my eyes, across my daiquiri and chicken with whiskey. He merely went on talking, his lenses bent on dissection.

"Violet of New York," said Johnson, "is a very tough cookie who kept Edgecombe out of mischief, on my orders, for the rest of the day until we arrived. On the other hand, if Bart Edgecombe had your signed arsenic tests, he had no longer quite the same need to worry over your health. I thought you would be safer on *Dolly*."

I laid down my knife and fork. "But you knew that something was going to happen to *Dolly*."

"I know," said Johnson. "But I also thought that, whatever it was, Trotter would halt it."

"So the *Haven*," I said, "was a dreadful surprise."

"I shouldn't like to exaggerate," said Johnson thoughtfully. "Trotter halted it."

"And went back to shore vowing vengeance on Edgecombe for leaving him. Did Edgecombe in fact intend Trotter to die?" I asked. "Or was it simply your happy suggestion through Brady?" I realized now why Johnson had had to dive into the sea; why it was so necessary to police what Trotter was doing on *Haven*.

"I don't know," Johnson said after a moment. "I think he

meant to get rid of Trotter, as in fact he got rid of Pentecost's friends in the outcome by running them into a trap. He talked freely of Trotter's claims as a suspect. I don't think Edgecombe would have risked a lifetime of blackmail from Trotter, when with a little care, Trotter might act as his scapegoat. I suppose he got Trotter to help in the first place because of something he knew of Trotter's past army career. They were uneasy bedfellows. At any rate, the moment when Edgecombe learned that we weren't all dead, and saw Trotter glaring at him across his own bedclothes, must have been one of the worst in his life.

"Because this time, the whole thing had happened in public. No one could pretend a boat loaded with explosives and following a radio signal came there by accident. If we'd all died, it wouldn't have mattered. The story would have involved a runaway boat and an accidental collision. No one need have suspected a thing. But here was a boatload of witnesses, including such a weak vessel as Harry, who was bound to demand that the police be told.

"Trotter made a show of agreeing, and I helped set a deadline of twenty-four hours. To Edgecombe, it would appear that this was all the leeway I thought we could reasonably secure ourselves before the whole thing had to be made public. He would expect me in that time to redouble my efforts to trap his would-be assassin. So far as he was concerned, he would know that he had only twenty-four hours in which to engineer my death once and for all. And now, of course, there was no point in an elaborate faking of accidents. It was an affair of murder. The *Haven* had shown that up clearly. Hence the golf game."

I stopped trying to eat. "What do you mean, hence the golf game? Mr. Tiko finished the jigsaw, that was all. You can't pretend you foresaw . . ." I broke off. "Or do you have the brazen gall to tell me . . ."

"The Begum," said Johnson apologetically, "told me to give her ten minutes."

I stared at him. "The golf game. She engineered it at your suggestion?"

He nodded.

"It took fifteen minutes," I said viciously. "And I nearly said no."

"Well," said Johnson, "I'm glad you didn't. We shipped Edgecombe under sympathetic guard to Great Harbour Cay, where he was out of Trotter's vengeance-bent reach and I, incidentally, was safe out of his — but not before I had planned the great trap and put the details before him. He was most enthusiastic and agreed to cooperate by turning up at the right hole at the right time. We left him plenty of time to get hold of Pentecost's friends or anyone else who took his fancy and arrange to have his empty car shot at or blown up or whatever he pleased.

"Then Spry went along and combed the ground near the fourteenth green until he found the getaway car. He did more. When Trotter arrived at the clubhouse, he told him about it. According to Spry's story, it was merely a good open car which he had found oddly abandoned. But the chances were that Trotter would know about it, and would realize that it was there for a purpose — a useless purpose, as it would have turned out. Edgecombe hadn't told his men that they would be surrounded by police and observers; that this time, in staging an attack on himself, they were to be the victims as well as I.

"At any rate, we got the proof that we wanted. Three of my own private witnesses saw Trotter fire into the bushes between Edgecombe and myself, and saw Edgecombe rise under cover of this fire and, as he thought, successfully kill me. I did a superb Fairbanks fall, and I don't need to tell you the rest. The police hiding there by the getaway car saw nothing but Trotter's last stand, in which he succeeded at last in shooting down Edgecombe, the man who knew too much of his past. They saw Trotter kill Edgecombe and try to escape. They saw me shoot at the car and kill Trotter. Poor, insane Trotter. The case is now closed."

There was a long silence. He was filling his pipe, leaning back on one of my father's Chippendale dining chairs. I realized we had been sitting there a long time, and rising, led the way back to the sitting room.

Gracious living. The hi-fi radio caught my eye and kneeling, I switched it on and, unthinking, moved one or two knobs, while Johnson settled back, prodding tobacco. The soulful inanities of the song called *Yellow Bird* floated around the air conditioning:

> Yellow Bird, up high in banana tree
> Yellow Bird, you sit all alone like me —
> You can fly away
> In the sky away
> You are luckier than me.

I switched it off sharply. I said, still kneeling, "I didn't ask you. You said until Edgecombe had my notes, I was sacrosanct. So why was I hit on the head?"

Johnson, head down, puffed devotedly at his pipe. He took it out of his mouth, looked at it, and inserted it between his teeth finally, as if forced to a distasteful concession. A haze of smoke wandered after "Yellow Bird," unaccompanied by sound. I said, with growing suspicion, "What have I said to cause that kind of gap?"

"You have posed," said Johnson, "a problem in ethics."

"Oh," I said. I allowed myself, slowly and lucidly, to think of Miami, and the dog track, and that unpleasant race through the car lot. I said, "Krishtof Bey doctored my tomato juice. On the Begum's instructions?"

"Right," Johnson said.

"The Begum?" I said, frowning in uneasy thought. The Begum, who had been distinctly troubled by the extent of my injury, the next day at the hospital. Troubled and guilty. Why had they taken my dress, I had asked myself often enough, and yet hadn't assaulted me while I lay there in the parking lot unconscious? How had they known that a call for a doctor would bring out a woman? Why had they stopped to do something so senseless as crop my hair into bristles?

So that the Begum, began an incredible thought, falling into my laboring senses — so that the Begum could bring me a wig and a dress, and so that Johnson . . .

"Pally Loo-loo?" I found myself saying, accusation ringing in every ludicrous syllable.

"A very fine bitch," said Johnson guardedly. His pipe emitted a column of protective black smoke.

"Who never won a race in its life," I said. I could feel my face as stiff as washed unwashable leather. "Whose money was it? The Begum's?"

Johnson said, "I thought you'd got over this hang-up about money. You can't deny we gave your social habits a skin-pop."

"I don't deny it," I said. "The lesson was made all too blindingly clear. Without the wig and the wardrobe I was Dracula. Who was going to look at me twice?"

"No one," Johnson said. "Because the first time around, you sank your teeth in his jugular. We all know James Ulric didn't read Spock. And since James Ulric did all the harm, you may as well let James Ulric's bank account fix it. There are three men hanging about wanting to know if you'll marry them."

Mr. Tiko, Wallace Brady, and Krishtof . . . "*Three* men?" I said, frankly astonished.

"Two men," Johnson corrected himself on the instant. "Krishtof Bey is anxious to live in sin with you, but will marry you if you're going to be fussy."

The mild figure puffed at its pipe stem, and I gave him the same alarmed attention you would give to a circular saw. "The Begum phoned," I said casually, "asking if she ought to get married. I referred her to you."

"She phoned me as well," Johnson said. "I said yes. Beltanno, I told her, will be permanently attached one way or the other by the end of the MacRannoch Gathering. Six P.M. on the thirtieth at Great Harbour Cay, tickets five guineas a whack. Only genuine MacRannochs need apply."

"My God," I said, and I said it with reverence. "What's he doing?"

"Continuous flights," said Johnson, "from Nassau to Great Harbour Cay, where at seven-thirty P.M. the Combined Tattoo and Highland Event will be held by floodlight in a new stadium built at the airport, followed by a State March with pipers to the new MacRannoch residence on Crab Island, where the Grand Banquet will be held. There have been two thousand acceptances."

"Tattoo?" I said flinchingly.

"Supervised by Brigadier Walter McCanna, Sergeant Trotter's superior," Johnson said. "The army felt they had been put on their mettle. Nothing has been lost. Except, I believe, the trained sheepdogs rounding up the flamingoes, excised because of the rabies laws." He grinned. "You really ought to attend. It'll be an occasion unmatched in history. Especially when the two thousand walk over the bridge from Great Harbour Cay to Crab Island."

In my mind's eye, clear as a photograph, sprang a picture of the cold green straits between Castle Rannoch and the mainland of Scotland running deep over the sea-rounded boulders of James Ulric's five spavined bridges, buried with his virility.

"Oh Christ," I said, varying it. "It's got to be stopped."

"You won't stop it," said Johnson with ghoulish cheerfulness. "But I've organized a sort of Dunkirk of small boats around the piers, and we'll save them all if their kilts keep them afloat long enough. They deserve a resident doctor."

I thought of it. I forgot the thirteenth hole and Denise's body, lying in its gully under the tarpaulin. I forgot the burning wreck of the car with Trotter's body lying inside, Johnson's bullet in his head. I forgot about Edgecombe and the insane single-mindedness which had involved us all in his own sordid game. Instead I considered, fascinated, the spectacle of James Ulric MacRannoch and his affianced if elderly bride, greeting two thousand filibegged MacRannochs and arraying before them a Bahamian steel band jumping through flaming hoops.

I thought of Brady. I thought of Krishtof Bey. I thought of a dress I had seen in the window of Bonwit Teller's at Christmas time, set in salt snow and swansdown, with silver lights running down the shop shades. There had been a matching long silver wig.

"I'll think about it," I said. "Are you going?"

"No," he said. "I'm not a MacRannoch."

"Sailing off," I said, "into the sunset?" I said it collectedly. I had had a good deal of practice.

"Sailing off," he said, "to paint a stout Italian princess who runs a shoe business in Naples. Don't think I don't regret it. As jobs go, this one would have sickened a soap boiler. If anyone made the thing bearable, it was B. Douglas MacRannoch. The one person who, through thick and thin, continued to say what she meant."

"I shall miss you," I said. "I think you've been a good teacher."

"I should like to be missed," said Johnson. He kissed my hand on the doorstep, and then my cheek, but not in the manner of *Dolly*. The lesson was over.

I closed the door slowly and went and looked at his picture.

* *

The MacRannoch Gathering, Tattoo, and Highland Event on Great Harbour Cay is of course a matter of history.

I flew there into the sunset with a cloak over my trouser suit of silver lamé and white ostrich feathers, and my long silver wig sparkled in the plane windows. The Begum and James Ulric waited to greet us on a dais covered with MacRannoch tartan and a row of gray potted thistles slumping ear to ear in the still, tropical heat.

The Begum, her hair dyed black and her eye make-up thicker than ever, was wearing a stiff brocade sari with the MacRannoch sash over it. My father in full Highland dress looked like a small wishing well in need of a tidy. His mouth dropped open when he saw me, hitting the amethyst in his jabot with a crack. Then he said, "Beltanno! Well, this is just what we were hoping for. B. Douglas, meet your new stepmother."

The Begum's smile was broad, and gave nothing away except a general sort of satisfaction. "You haven't been hasty?" I asked.

The Begum's smile became broader. "Not while you look like that, darling," she said. "And look who's behind you."

It was Wallace Brady, in a white tuxedo and rosebud, with a smile like a rutting stud oyster. I smiled back. "Hullo," I said. "Where's Mr. Tiko?" There is no point in fostering too great a sense of security.

"He's coming," the Begum said quickly. James Ulric was having his pipe-cleaner hand kneaded by a stonehenge of New Zealand MacRannochs. "There are still quite a few planes to come in. I'll send him along to you. Wallace, will you take her into the stadium?"

We walked off arm in arm, and he was telling me how wonderful I was, and how much he had missed me, which was pleasant. They had laid a tartan-lined walk on the runway, which was almost impassable for crowds of people studded with cairngorms and daggers and milling around discussing their feet. "What have you been doing?" said Wallace Brady. I told him.

The stadium had been contrived from a section of runway flanked by two broad-raked stands hung with tartan. At the far end, the runway disappeared into the maw of a marquee from which, clearly, the performers were to emerge. Flags fluttered above it. I said, "Will they have a fat woman?" and Wallace Brady said, "No, but I hear the clowns are really something."

I began to warm to him once again. I let him lead me to the row of armchairs behind the first garlanded ledge. The Mac-Rannoch's pew, I deduced. I said, "But you're not a Mac-Rannoch?"

"I've got special dispensation," said Wallace Brady, and followed me along the front row of the stand.

A figure in full Highland evening dress rose from the furthest seat, bowed, and said, "And so have I," in a strong Turkish accent.

I stared at Krishtof Bey. He had his false eyelashes on.

Wallace Brady laughed. "Where did you get it?"

The original of Johnson's portrait looked down at his garments with pride. "*La Sylphide*, Act 1. The Lincoln Center forwarded them. Observe the frills at the wrist. The cross-binding of cords on the calves. The crested buttons. The buckles. The sporran."

Wallace Brady gazed at the sporran, which was exceedingly hairy. "For Chrissakes, what's that?"

"The head of a former conductor of the Budapest opera and ballet," Krishtof Bey said. "In the last scene of *Scheherazade* I excised it. He kept regrettable tempi."

I laughed. I suddenly felt very cheerful. I shook hands with the tall, kilted figure of Brigadier McCanna, the tattoo director, and without qualms watched him leave to prepare for his program. He looked nothing like Trotter.

The seats filled up. A message came that Mr. Tiko was at Nassau Airport and hoped to be with us shortly. The sun went down and the floodlights came on in a faintly dismaying eau-de-nil color, coinciding with the distant sound of inflating bagpipes. Preceded by the Pipe Major in a cloud of red-hot fluttering tartan, my father and stepmother marched hand in hand down the runway to a storm of clapping and took their places in the principal armchairs beside us. The minister of St. Andrew's Presbyterian Church, Nassau, rising up unexpectedly beside them, announced a prayer and a psalm into the public address system, catching most of the MacRannoch men undoubtedly on the hop: their women kicked them onto their feet.

During the eighth verse the Begum leaned over to whisper that Mr. Tiko seemed to be having some sort of trouble in Nassau. My father grunted and shaded his error of pitch from a third to a full semitone. Krishtof Bey flinched. I tried to visualize James Ulric's head as a sporran.

The psalm ended; we all sat down; the marquee at the end grew a spotlight and the Massed Pipes and Drums of the 1st Battalion of the Royal Scots, the 2nd Battalion of the Scots Guards and the Federation of Malaya Police marched out in a rhythmic, befurred body. The great MacRannoch Tattoo and Highland Event had got under way.

There are some memories the mind works to preserve, and others which demand to be jettisoned at the earliest convenient moment. I cannot now remember precisely when I noticed that something was wrong: it was certainly after the putting of the 16-pound ball and the flinging of the 56-pound weight, and probably after the combined display of massed limbo dancers and firefighting demonstration by units of the Nassau Brigade (music: *I Don't Want to Set the World on Fire*).

Certainly the matter came to a head during the jeep assembly exercise by two teams of the Royal Electrical and Mechanical Engineers (music: *Pack Up Your Troubles*). Hurrying wheels bisected the runway, with electrical and mechanical engineers running doggedly after them and falling on their medals with great regularity. It looked like a drunk clockmaker's workshop. The moment the first jeep stood, splayed and creaking in a welter of washers, they announced the winners and shoved in the British Legion Boys' Band blowing *Semper Fidelis,* while the Mechanical Engineers and their jeeps were shoveled up off the field. A uniformed lieutenant, politely excusing himself along my row of the stand, turned out to be bearing a message from the tattoo director. The brigadier wanted a doctor.

In my silver lamé and feathers, silently I followed him out.

In the marquee the trouble was glassily obvious. Amid a dishevelment of jeeps sat or lay the giggling members of the two mechanical teams. "Rum?" I said. "They're all that high on rum?"

Brigadier McCanna spoke heavily. "One tot. I can't understand it. It's regulation, back at the Castle. One tot to put heart into them. And see them!"

I saw them. I touched one on the shoulder and he yelped. I rolled his sleeve up and he smiled and lay down on the ground. A thin white bandage, one of Currie's best jobs, encircled his upper left arm. The United Commonwealth Hospital had run short of frigates this month.

I said, "Don't you know what happens if you give a blood donor alcohol?" and Brigadier McCanna, staring at me, said, "My God," with the greatest simplicity. He added, "What can I do?"

"Sort out the sober ones," I said (music: *Reel for My Hame*), "and trust to the ingenuity of your MacRannoch friends."

Nothing short of stereotaxic surgery will ever obliterate the events of the rest of that night. The brigadier, six feet high in cock's feathers, holding up five Italian Bersagliere on his shoulders in the Musical and Physical Training Display. The high jump Wallace Brady competed for in singlet and kilt, and the sixteensome reel Krishtof Bay danced as my partner before racing off to take four different parts in Fighting Men Through the Ages.

The MacRannochs greeted it all with a violent and warming enthusiasm. The applause, the cheers, the encores increased until the program wallowed on to its end, and in the marquee Wallace, Krishtof, and the brigadier met, full of exhausted hilarity, for the Final March Past of Massed Bands and Salute. Pipes tuned, drums thudding and thundering, they would walk past the saluting MacRannoch, and behind would fall in the chief and the two thousand clansmen, to cross to Crab Island and dinner.

Across the bridge. I heard the brigadier preparing his pipers; I heard Krishtof and Wallace shouting with laughter but I wasn't laughing. Five bridges had fallen under the chief of the MacRannochs. No MacRannoch had succeeded in building a bridge between the shore and his castle since the thirteenth, and he had had the help of the fairies. I said to Wallace, "I don't want them to go over the bridge."

He broke off at once and came over. He said, "Look: I know what happened in Scotland. Believe me, it won't happen here."

"No?" I said after a pause. "But you don't know my family. It's a legend."

A man in full piper's uniform fell at my feet, someone took him by the armpits and dragged him away. Wallace Brady said, "I'm going to cross that bridge, and so is your father. We'll break the legend between us. We'll make a new one, Beltanno."

Brigadier McCanna said, "Doctor MacRannoch?"

"Lay him down somewhere cool and let him sleep it off," I said, without turning.

"Doctor MacRannoch," he said again, and I turned at the alarm in his voice. "That was the only damned man among them who could play the solo *The MacRannoch Forever*."

They all looked at me in my silver wig and my silver suit with the white ostrich feathers, and they saw nothing at all. They saw a woman doctor who could play on the bagpipes.

I lifted the pipes. I tucked the bag under my arm and threw the drones over my shoulder and put the blow pipe to my lips and settled my grip on the chanter. I nodded. Then the massed pipes struck up and we marched, Brady and Krishtof on either side, out of the marquee.

My father fell in before us as we passed the main stand. He had the Begum with him and they were both smiling politely because of the roar of applause that had gone up when we three emerged from the tent. James Ulric patted me on the back and muttered something about Mr. Tiko.

I wasn't playing, but the massed pipe band was. "What?" I said. The pipes had switched to *The Bonawe Highlanders*.

"He says the place on your right ought to be occupied by the heir," shouted the Begum. The rest of the two thousand were shuffling into place behind us, but we couldn't hear them and they certainly couldn't hear us. "It's a shame about Mr. Tiko."

I shouted back, "What happened to him?"

Wallace Brady cupped his hands around his mouth and aimed it at my father. "They wouldn't let him in," he yelled, "because he wasn't a MacRannoch."

"Mr. Tiko," I shouted. "We're talking about Mr. Tiko."

"I know," yelled Wallace. "He wasn't a MacRannoch."

I said, "But he said . . ."

"No, he didn't," yelled Wallace. "He just said his name was hard to pronounce. And that he was a doctor as well. It was you who said he was called T. K. MacRannoch."

What with rage and astonishment and confusion, I had almost

nothing to shout with. I croaked, "But his name was on the Paradise Island golf register."

"No, it wasn't," said Krishtof Bey, flicking a strand of silver off his impeccable Lincoln Center filibeg and plush doublet. "I played a round of golf just behind Mr. Tiko. It wasn't his name you saw in the book, it was mine."

The pipers switched to *The Garb of Old Gaul* and got halfway through it quite uninterrupted. I could hear my father's F.E.V.'s revving up. The Begum was smiling, strolling along. I said, "What?"

Krishtof Bey said mildly, "I am T. Krishtof MacRannoch. It is a bizarre name for a ballet dancer. I do not use it."

My father said, in a fixed voice, "The name of my heir after Beltanno is T. K. MacRannoch. A Japanese."

"A Turk," said the Begum dreamily. "James, I ought to have told you. But after Wallace mentioned what Krishtof's real name was, I went over the papers again. The genealogical people didn't mean to mislead you, darling. It was a typing error. T. K. MacRannoch, Turk. Krishtof Bey is the heir to the chieftainship."

"And?" I said thinly. It was another damnable plot. It was a plot between the Begum and Brady. I remembered she had even got James Ulric to agree to my marrying Krishtof. "What about me? What about Mr. Tiko?"

"Mr. Tiko is polite," said the Begum. "He will marry you if you insist, but I believe he would be rather relieved not to have James Ulric for a father-in-law."

"And Krishtof?" I said.

Krishtof was admiring the swing of his kilt. "I? I never interfere," he remarked. "I am interested in love, not in chieftains or marriage."

"I've noticed as much," said James Ulric. His face had brightened. "But I'll not deny you're a treat at the sixteensome. You'll mind, Beltanno, that *The MacRannoch Forever* is due at the bridge?"

His words fell into a wheezing withdrawal of bedlam. The pipes had ceased. The files were opening and halting, displaying before me the dazzle of concrete under a flock of bright, floodlit banners, with the standard of the MacRannochs flying over it all. Ahead, in the darkness, on either side of the white arch before me, I could hear the low chuckle of water, and smell the salt, soft air of the sea. Here was the new bridge. And here was I, at the head of two thousand, to pipe the forty-fifth chief to his castle.

The MacRannoch Forever is not a difficult solo, but there is a knack to it. I had the knack. I settled the bag and put the blow pipe into my mouth and sent up a prayer and drew in all the sea air I could muster between there and the Florida coast. The drones started up, and then the first note, clear and steady; and I launched into my father's own tune as I set foot on his bridge.

I played steadily as I walked over, and behind me I could sense the trample and thud as the MacRannochs flocked after the piping, whether as rats or as children it is not for me, a MacRannoch, to say. I filled my own ears with my music so that no lesser rumble could reach me: no crumbling chasm of concrete; no cracking and sliding of piers.

Beneath my feet the new bridge was solid. Solid to the midway reach of the strait, with the lights twinkling in front and behind. Solid as the far end came nearer, and the lights of the castle shone sharp cut and welcoming there.

I walked on, and James Ulric walked firmly behind me; and when we both stepped onto dry land, he moved forward and, laying his hands on my shoulders, he embraced me for the first time since childhood.

"The curse is broken," he said.

He underestimated his reticuloendothelial system; but success is an excellent doctor. I kissed him back fondly. And through the fronds of his tall chieftain's bonnet, I saw not MacRannoch Castle before me, but a palm tree with a banana bird in it, and beneath it, B. Douglas MacRannoch — mistress to the man on my one hand, or wife to the man on my other; or both.

Thank you, Johnson. Thank you for everything.